Mystery for Christmas

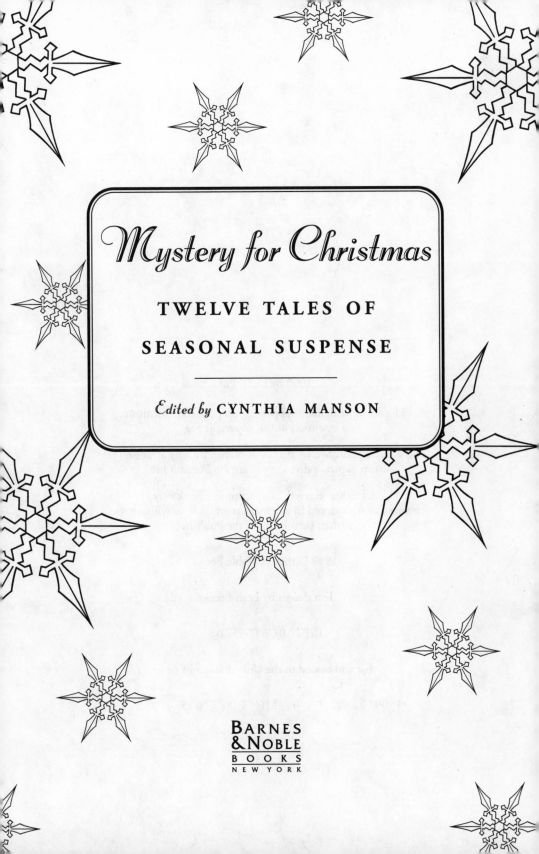

Mystery for Christmas

TWELVE TALES OF
SEASONAL SUSPENSE

Edited by CYNTHIA MANSON

BARNES
&NOBLE
BOOKS
NEW YORK

Copyright © 1990 by Davis Publications, Inc.

The acknowledgments appearing on page 231 constitute
an extension of this copyright page.

This edition published by Barnes & Noble, Inc., by arrangement
with Signet, a division of Penguin Putnam Inc.

1999 Barnes & Noble Books

Text design by Leah Lococo

ISBN 0-7607-1571-8

Printed and bound in the United States of America

99 00 01 02 03 04 MC 9 8 7 6 5 4 3 2 1

QF

9/00
gift

Contents

❦

Introduction

THE STORIES IN THIS COLLECTION ARE FROM THE pages of *Ellery Queen's Mystery Magazine* and *Alfred Hitchcock's Mystery Magazine*. They were chosen primarily because, as the title suggests, each story takes place at Christmas time, but also because they are gift wrapped in entertainment and suspense. What distinguishes this particular anthology from others of this kind is that all the stories are mysteries with a "conscience"—a moral underlies each story, which each author conveys with masterful subtlety. It is this "conscience" which gives these stories their true Christmas spirit.

Our cast of characters is quite a lively bunch ranging from Christmas bears and bright-eyed children to a jaded Manhattan cop and a murderous Mommy to criminals with big hearts. There are new twists to our classic Christmas tales which feature our old-time favorites: Marley's Ghost, Ebenezer Scrooge, Bob Cratchit. And what would Christmas be without Santa Claus?

The time is past, present and future and the settings move from small town U.S.A. to big city streets. More importantly, the message is clear—nothing is as it appears to be because no matter what the nature of the crime, each story contains that special sparkle that we all recognize as the magic of Christmas.

CYNTHIA MANSON

The Christmas Bear

HERBERT RESNICOW

U P THERE, GRANDMA," DEBBIE POINTED, ALL excited, tugging at my skirt, "in the top row. Against the wall. See?" I'm not really her grandma, but at six and a half the idea of a great-grandmother is hard to understand. All her little friends have grandmothers, so she has a grandmother. When she's a little older, I'll tell her the whole story.

The firehouse was crowded this Friday night, not like the usual weekend where the volunteer firemen explain to their wives that they have to polish the old pumper and the second-hand ladder truck. They give the equipment a quick lick-and-a-promise and then sit down to an uninterrupted evening of pinochle. Not that there's all that much to do in Pitman anyway—we're over fifty miles from Pittsburgh, even if anyone could afford to pay city prices for what the big city offers—but still, a man's first thought has to be of his wife and family. Lord knows I've seen too much of the opposite in my own generation and all the pain and trouble it caused, and mine could've given lessons in devotion to this new generation that seems to be interested only in fun. What they call fun.

Still, they weren't all bad. Even Homer Curtis, who was the worst boy of his day, always full of mischief and very disrespectful, didn't turn out all that bad. That was after he got married, of course; not before. He was just voted fire chief and, to give him credit, this whole Rozovski affair was his idea, may God bless him.

Little Petrina Rozovski—she's only four years old and she's always been small for her age—her grandfather was shift foreman over my Jake in the mine while we were courting. We married young in those days because there was no future and you grabbed what happiness you could and that's how I came to be the youngest great-grandmother in the county, only sixty-seven, though that big horsefaced Mildred Ungaric keeps telling everybody I'm over seventy. Poor Petrina has to have a liver transplant, and soon. Real soon. You wouldn't believe what that costs, even if you could find the right liver in the first place. Seventy-five thousand dollars, and it could go to a lot more than that, depending. There isn't that much money in the whole county.

There was talk about going to the government—as if the government's got any way to just give money for things like this or to make somebody give her baby's liver to a poor little girl—or holding a raffle, or something, but none of the ideas was worth a tinker's dam. Then Homer, God bless him, had this inspiration. The volunteer firemen—they do it every year—collect toys for the poor children, which, these days, is half the town, to make sure every child gets *some* present for Christmas. And we all, even if we can't afford it, we all give something. Then one of them dresses up as Santa Claus and they all get on the ladder truck and, on Christmas Eve, they ride through the town giving out the presents. There's a box for everyone, so nobody knows who's getting a present, but the boxes for the families where the father is still working just have a candy bar in them or something like that. And for the littlest kids, they put Santa on top of the ladder and two guys turn the winch and lift him up to the roof as though he's going to go down the chimney and the kids' eyes get all round and everybody feels the way a kid should on Christmas Eve.

We had a town meeting to discuss the matter. "Raffles are no good," Homer declared, "because one person wins and everybody else loses. This year we're going to have an auction where everybody wins. Everybody who can will give a good toy—it can be used, but it's got to be good—in addition to what they give for the poor kids. Then the firemen will auction off those extra toys and the idea of that auction is to pay as *much* as possible instead of as little." That was sort of like the Indian potlatches they used to have around here that my grandfather told me about. Well, you can imagine the opposition to that one. But Homer overrode them all. Skinny as he is, when he stands up and raises his voice—he's the tallest man in town by far—he usually gets his way. Except with his wife, and that's as it should be. "Anyway," he pointed out, "it's a painless way of getting the donations Rozovski needs to get a liver transplant for Petrina."

Shorty Porter, who never backed water for anyone, told Homer, "Your brain ain't getting enough oxygen up there. Even if every family in town bought something for ten dollars on the average, with only twelve hundred families in town, we'd be short at least sixty-three thousand dollars, not to mention what it would cost for Irma Rozovski to stay in a motel near the hospital. And not everybody in town can pay more than what the present he bids on is worth. So you better figure on getting a lot less than twelve thousand, Homer, and what good that'll do, I fail to see." Levi Porter always had a good head for figures. One of these days we ought to make him mayor, if he could take the time off from busting his butt in his little back yard farm which, with his brood, he really can't.

"I never said," Homer replied, "that we were going to raise enough money this way to take care of the operation and everything. The beauty of my plan is . . . I figure we'll raise about four thousand. Right, Shorty?"

"That's about what I figured," Shorty admitted.

"We give the money to Hank and Irma and they take Petrina to New York. They take her to a TV station, to one of those news reporters who are always looking for ways to help people. We have a real problem here, a real emergency, and Petrina, with that sweet little face and her big brown eyes, once she appears on TV, her problems are over. If only ten percent of the people in the U.S. send in one cent each, that's all, just one cent, we'd get two hundred fifty thousand dollars. That would cover everything and leave plenty over to set up an office, right here in Pitman, for a clearing house for livers for all the poor little kids in that fix. And the publicity would remind some poor unfortunate mother that her child—children are dying in accidents every day and nobody knows who or where, healthy children—her child's liver could help save the life of a poor little girl."

Even Shorty had to admit it made sense. "And to top it all," Homer added, "if we do get enough money to set up a liver clearing house, we've brought a job to Pitman, for which I'd like to nominate Irma Rozowski, to make up for what she's gone through. And if it works out that way, maybe even two jobs, so Hank can have some work too." Well, that was the clincher. We all agreed and that's how it came about that I was standing in front of the display of the auction presents in the firehouse on the Friday night before Christmas week while Deborah was tugging and pointing at that funny-looking teddy bear, all excited, like I'd never seen her before.

Deborah's a sad little girl. Not that she doesn't have reason, what with her father running off just before the wedding and leaving Caroline in trouble; I never did like that Wesley Sladen in the first place. The Social Security doesn't give enough to support three on, and nobody around here's about to marry a girl going on twenty-nine with another mouth to feed, and I'm too old to earn much money, so Carrie's working as a waitress at the Highway Rest. But thanks to my Jake, we have a roof over our heads and we always will. My father was against my marrying him. I was born a Horvath, and my father wanted me to marry a nice Hungarian boy, not a damn foreigner, but I was of age and my mother was on my side and Jake and I got married in St. Anselm's and I wore a white gown, and I had a right to, not like it is today.

That was in '41 and before the year was out we were in the war. Jake volunteered and, not knowing I was pregnant, I didn't stop him. He was a good man, made sergeant, always sent every penny home. With me working in the factory, I even put a little away. After Marian was born, the foreman was nice enough to give me work to do at home on my sewing machine, so it was all right. Jake had taken out the full G.I. insurance and, when it happened, we got ten thousand dollars, which was a lot of money in those days. I bought the house, which cost almost two thousand dollars, and put the rest away for the bad times.

My daughter grew up to be a beautiful girl and she married a nice boy, John Brodzowski, but when Caroline was born, complications set in and Marian never made it out of the hospital. I took care of John and the baby for six months until John, who had been drinking, hit a tree going seventy. The police said it was an accident. I knew better but I kept my mouth shut because we needed the insurance.

So here we were, quiet little Deborah pulling at me and pointing at that teddy bear, all excited, and smiling for the first time I can remember. "That's what I want, Grandma," she begged. "He's my bear."

"You have a teddy bear," I told her. "We can't afford another one. I just brought you to the firehouse to look at all the nice things."

"He's not a teddy bear, Grandma, and I love him."

"But he's so funny looking," I objected. And he was, too. Black, sort of, but shining blueish when the light hit the right way, with very long hair. Ears bigger than a teddy bear's, and a longer snout. Not cute at all. Some white hairs at the chin and a big crescent-shaped white patch on his chest. And the eyes, not round little buttons, but slanted oval pieces of purple glass. I couldn't imagine what she saw in him. There was a tag, with #273 on it, around his neck. "Besides," I said, "I've only got eighteen dollars for all the presents, for everything. I'm sure they'll want at least ten dollars for him on account of it's for charity."

She began crying, quietly, not making a fuss; Deborah never did. Even at her age she understood, children do understand, that there were certain things that were not for us, but I could see her heart was broken and I didn't know what to do.

Just then the opening ceremonies started. Young Father Casimir, of St. Anselm's, gave the opening benediction, closing with "It is more blessed to give than to receive." I don't know how well that set with Irma Rozovski and the other poor people there, but he'll learn better when he gets older. Then Homer brought up Irma, with Petrina in her arms looking weaker and yellower than ever, to speak. "I just want to thank you all, all my friends and neighbors, for being so kind and . . ." Then she broke down and couldn't talk at all. Petrina didn't cry, she never cried, just looked sad and hung on to her mother. Then Homer came and led Irma away and said a few words I didn't even listen to. I knew what I had to do and I'd do it. Christmas is for the children, to make the children happy, that's the most important part. The children. I'd just explain to Carrie, when she got home, that I didn't get her anything this year and I didn't want her to get me anything. She'd understand.

I got hold of Homer in a corner and told him, "Look, Homer, for some reason Deborah's set on that teddy bear in the top row. Now all I've got is eighteen dollars, and I don't think you'd get anywhere near that much for it at the auction, but I don't want to take a chance on losing it and break Deborah's heart. I'm willing to give it all to you right now, if you'll sell it to me."

"Gee, I'd like to, Miz Sophie," he said, "but I can't. I have to go according to the rules. And if I did that for you, I'd have to do it for everybody, then with everybody picking their favorites, nobody would bid on anything and we couldn't raise the money for Petrina to go to New York."

"Come on, Homer, this ain't the first time you've broken some rules. Besides, I wouldn't tell anyone; I'd just take it off the shelf after everybody's left and no one would know the difference. It's an ugly looking teddy bear anyway."

"I'm real sorry, Mrs. Slowinski," he said, going all formal on me, "but I can't. Besides, there's no way to get it now. Those shelves, they're just boxes piled up with boards across them. You look at them crooked, and the whole thing'll fall down. There's no way to get to the top row until you've taken off the other rows. That's why the numbers start at the bottom."

"You're a damned fool, Homer, and I'm going to get that bear for Deborah anyway. I'm going to get him for a lot less than eighteen dollars too, so your stubbornness has cost the fund a lot of money and you ought to be ashamed of yourself."

We didn't go back to the firehouse until two days before Christmas Eve, Monday, when Carrie was off. Deborah had insisted on showing the bear to her mother to make sure we knew exactly which bear it was she wanted, but when we got there the bear was gone. Poor Deborah started crying, real loud this time, and even Carrie couldn't quiet her down. I picked her up and told her, swore to her, that I would get that bear back for her, but she just kept on sobbing.

I went right up to Homer to tell him off for selling the bear to somebody else instead of to me but before I could open my mouth, he said, "That wasn't right, Mrs. Slowinski, but as long as it's done, I won't make a fuss. Just give me the eighteen dollars and we'll forget about it."

That was like accusing me of stealing, and Milly Ungaric was standing near and she had that nasty smile on her face, so I knew who had stolen the bear. I ignored what Homer said and asked, "Who was on duty last night?" We don't have a fancy alarm system in Pitman; one of the firemen sleeps in the firehouse near the phone.

"Shorty Porter," Homer said, and I went right off.

I got hold of him on the side. "Levi, did you see anyone come in last night?" I asked. "I mean late."

"Only Miz Mildred," he said. "Just before I went to sleep."

Well, I knew it was her, but that wasn't what I meant. "I mean after you went to sleep. Did any noise wake you up?"

"When I sleep, Miz Sophie, only the phone bell wakes me up."

She must have come back later, the doors are never locked, and taken the bear. She's big enough, but how could she reach it? She couldn't climb over the shelves, everything would be knocked over. And she couldn't reach it from the floor. So how did she do it? Maybe it wasn't her, though I would have liked it to be. I went back to Homer. He was tall enough and had arms like a chimpanzee. "Homer," I said, "I'm going to forget what you said if you'll just do one thing. Stand in front of the toys and reach for the top shelf."

He got red, but he didn't blow. After a minute he said, sort of strangled, "I already thought of that. If I can't reach it by four feet, nobody can. Tell you what; give me seventeen dollars and explain how you did it, and I'll pay the other dollar out of my own pocket."

"You always were a stupid, nasty boy, Homer, and you always will be. Well, if you won't help me, I'll have to find out by myself, start at the beginning and trace who'd want to steal a funny-looking bear like that. Who donated the bear?"

"People just put toys in the boxes near the door. We pick out the ones for the auction and the ones for the Santa Claus boxes. No way of knowing who gave what."

I knew he wouldn't be any help, so I got Carrie and Debbie and went to the one man in town who might help me trace the bear, Mr. Wong. He doesn't have just a grocery, a *credit* grocery, thank God; he carries things you wouldn't even find in Pittsburgh. His kids were all grown, all famous scientists and doctors and professors, but he still stayed here, even after Mrs. Wong died. Mrs. Wong never spoke a word of English, but she understood everything. Used to be, her kids all came here for Chinese New Year—that's about a month after ours—and they'd have a big feast and bring the grandchildren. Funny how Mrs. Wong was able to raise six kids in real hard times, but none of her children has more than two. Now, on Chinese New Year, Mr. Wong closes the store for a week and goes to one of his kids. But he always comes back here.

"Look I have for you," he said, and gave Debbie a little snake on a stick, the kind where you turn it and the snake moves like it's real. She was still sniffling, but she smiled a little. The store was chock full of all kinds of Chinese things; little dragons and fat Buddhas with bobbing heads and candied ginger. I knew I was in the right place.

"Did you ever sell anyone a teddy bear?" I asked. "Not a regular teddy bear, but a black one with big purple eyes."

"No sell," he said. "Give."

"Okay." I had struck gold on the first try. "Who'd you give it to?"

"Nobody. Put in box in firehouse."

"You mean for the auction?"

"Petrina nice girl. Like Debbie. Very sick. Must help."

"But . . ." Dead end. I'd have to find another way to trace the bear so I could find out who'd want to steal it. "All right, where'd you get the teddy bear?"

"Grandmother give me. Before I go U.S. Make good luck. Not teddy bear. Blue bear. From Kansu."

"You mean there's a bear that looks like this?"

"Oh yes. Chinese bear. Moon bear. Very danger. Strong. In Kansu."

"Your grandmother *made* it? For you?"

"Not *make*, make. Grandfather big hunter, kill bear. Moon bear very big good luck. Eat bear, get strong, very good. Have good luck in U.S."

"That bear is real bearskin?"

"Oh yes. Grandmother cut little piece for here," he put his hand under his chin, "and for here," he put his hand on his chest. "Make moon." He moved his hand in the crescent shape the bear had on its chest. "Why call moon bear."

"You had that since you were a little boy?" I was touched. "And you gave it for Petrina? Instead of your own grandchildren?"

"Own grandchildren want sportcar, computer, skateboard, not old Chinese bear."

Well, that was typical of all modern kids, not just Chinese, but it didn't get me any closer to finding out who had stolen the teddy bear, the moon bear. Deborah, though, was listening with wide eyes, no longer crying. But what was worse, that romantic story would make it all the harder on her if I didn't get that bear back. She went up to the counter and asked, "Did it come in?"

"Oh yes." He reached down and put a wooden lazy tongs on top of the counter.

"I got it for you, Grandma," Debbie said, "for your arthritis, so you don't have to bend down. I was going to save it for under the tree, but you looked so sad . . ."

God bless you, Deborah, I said in my heart, that's the answer. I put my fingers in the scissor grip and extended the tongs. They were only about three feet long, not long enough, and they were already beginning to bend under their own weight. No way anyone, not even Mildred Ungaric, could use them to steal the moon bear. Then I knew. For sure. I turned around and there it was, hanging on the top shelf. I turned back to Mr. Wong and said, casually, "What do you call that thing grocers use to get cans from the top shelf? The long stickhandle with the grippers at the end?"

"Don't know. In Chinese I say, 'Get can high shelf.'"

"Doesn't matter. Why did you steal the bear back? Decided to sell it to a museum or something?"

"No. Why I steal? If I want sell, I no give." He was puzzled, not insulted. "Somebody steal moon bear?"

He was right. But so was I. At least I knew *how* it was stolen. You didn't need a "get can high shelf." All the thief needed was a long thing with a hook on the end. Or a noose. Like a broomstick. Or a fishing rod. Anything that would reach from where you were standing to the top of the back row so you could get the bear without knocking over the shelves or the other toys. It had to be Mildred Ungaric; she might be mean, but she wasn't stupid. Any woman had enough long sticks in her kitchen, and enough string and hooks to make a bear-stealer, though she'd look awful funny walking down the street carrying one of those. But it didn't have to be that way. There was something in the firehouse that anyone could use, one of those long poles with the hooks on the end they break your windows with when you have a fire. All you'd have to do is get that hook under the string that held the number tag around the moon bear's neck and do it quietly enough not to wake Levi Porter. Which meant that anyone in town could have stolen the moon bear.

But who would? It would be like stealing from poor little Petrina herself. Mildred was mean, but even she wouldn't do that. Homer was nasty; maybe he accused me to cover up for himself. Mr. Wong might have changed his mind, in spite of what he said; you don't give away a sixty-year-old childhood memory like that without regrets. Levi Porter was in the best position to do it; there was only his word that he slept all through the night and he has eight kids he can hardly feed. Heck, anyone in town could have done it. All I knew was that I didn't.

So who stole the moon bear?

That night I made a special supper for Carrie, and Deborah served. There's nothing a waitress enjoys so much on her time off as being served. I know; there was a time I waitressed myself. After supper, Carrie put Deborah to bed and read to her, watched TV for a while, then got ready to turn in herself. There's really nothing for a young woman to do in Pitman unless she's the kind that runs around with the truckers that stop by, and Carrie wasn't that type. She had made one mistake, trusted one boy, but that could have happened to anybody. And she did what was right and was raising Deborah to be a pride to us all.

I stayed up and sat in my rocker, trying to think of who would steal that bear, but there was no way to find that out. At least it wasn't a kid, a little kid, who had done it; those firemen's poles are heavy. Of course it could have been a teenager, but what would a teenager want with a funny-looking little bear like that? There were plenty of better toys in the lower rows to tempt a teenager, toys that anyone could take in a second with no trouble at all. But none of them had been stolen. No, it wasn't a teenager; I was pretty sure of that.

Finally, I went to sleep. Or to bed, at least. I must have been awake for half the night and didn't come up with anything. But I did know one thing I had to do.

That night being the last night before Christmas Eve, they were going to hold the auction for Petrina in the firehouse. I didn't want to get there too early; no point in making Deborah feel bad seeing all the other presents bought up and knowing she wasn't going to get her moon bear. But I did want her to know it wasn't just idle talk when I promised I'd get her bear back.

Debbie and I waited until the last toy was auctioned off and Porter announced the total. Four thousand, three hundred seventy-two dollars and fifty cents. More than we had expected and more than enough to send the Rozovskis to New York. Then I stood up and said, "I bid eighteen dollars, cash, for the little black bear, Number 273."

Homer looked embarrassed. "Please, Mrs. Slowinski, you know we don't have that bear anymore."

"I just want to make sure, *Mr.* Curtis, that when I find that bear, it's mine. Mine and Deborah's. So you can just add eighteen dollars to your total, *Mr.* Porter, and when that bear turns up, it's mine." Now if anyone was seen with the bear, everybody'd know whose it was. And what's more, if the thief had a guilty conscience, he'd know where to return the bear.

That night I stayed in my rocking chair again, rocking and thinking, thinking and rocking. I was sure I was on the right track. Why would anyone want to take the moon bear? That had to be the way to find the thief; to figure out why anyone would take the bear. But as much as I rocked, much as I thought, I was stuck right there. Finally, after midnight, I gave up. There was no way to figure it out. Maybe if I slept on it . . . Only trouble was, tomorrow was Christmas Eve, and even if I figured out who took the bear, there was no way I could get it back in time to put it under the tree so Debbie would find it when she woke up Christmas morning. For all I knew, the bear was in Pittsburgh by now, or even back in China. Maybe I shouldn't have warned the thief by making such a fuss when I bought the missing bear.

Going to bed didn't help. I lay awake, thinking of everything that had happened, from the time we first stood behind the firetrucks and saw the bear, to the time in Mr. Wong's store when I figured out how the bear had been stolen. Then all of a sudden it was clear. I knew who had stolen the bear. That is I knew *how* it had been stolen and that told me *who* had stolen it which told me how, which . . . What really happened was I knew it all, all at once. Of course, I didn't know *where* the bear was, not exactly, but I'd get to that eventually. One thing I had to remember was not to tell Deborah what I had figured out. Not that I was wrong—I *wasn't* wrong; everything fit too perfectly—but I might not be able to get the bear back. After all, how hard would it be to destroy the bear, to burn it or throw it in the dump, rather than go to jail?

The next morning Deborah woke me. "It's all right, Grandma," she said. "I didn't really want that old moon bear. I really wanted a wetting doll. Or a plain doll. So don't cry." I wasn't aware I was crying, but I guess I was. Whatever else I had done in my life, whatever else Carrie had done, to bring to life, to bring up such a sweet wonderful human being, a girl like this, one to be so proud of, that made up for everything. I only wished Jake could have been here with me to see her. And Wesley Sladen, the fool, to see what he'd missed.

I didn't say anything during breakfast—we always let Carrie sleep late because of her hours but right after we washed up, I dressed Deborah warmly. "We're going for a long walk," I told her. She took my hand and we started out.

I went to the garage where he worked and motioned Levi Porter to come out. He came, wiping his hands on a rag. Without hesitating, I told him what I had to tell him. "You stole the teddy bear. You swiveled the ladder on the ladder truck around, pointing in the right direction, and turned the winch until the ladder extended over the bear. Then you crawled out on the flat ladder and stole the bear. After you put everything back where it was before, you went to sleep."

Well, he didn't bat an eye, just nodded his head. "Yep, that's the way it was," he said, not even saying he was sorry. "I figured you knew something when you bought the missing bear. Nobody throws away eighteen dollars for nothing." Deborah just stared up at him, not understanding how a human being could do such a thing to her. She took my hand for comfort, keeping me between her and Shorty Porter.

"Well, that's *my* bear," I said. "I bought it for Deborah; she had her heart set on it." He wasn't a bit moved. "She loved that bear, Porter. You broke her heart."

"I'm sorry about that, Miz Sophie," he said. "I really didn't want to hurt anybody. I didn't know about Debbie when I stole the bear."

"Well, the least you could do is give it back. If you do, I might consider, just *consider,* not setting the law on you." I didn't really want to put a man with eight children in jail and, up till now, he'd been a pretty good citizen, but I wasn't about to show him that. "So you just go get it, *Mr.* Porter. Right now, and hop to it."

"Okay, Miz Sophie, but it ain't here. We'll have to drive over."

He stuck his head in the shop and told Ed Mahaffey that he had to go someplace, be back soon, and we got in his pickup truck.

I wasn't paying attention to where we were going and when he stopped, my heart stopped too. Petrina was lying on the couch in the living room, clutching the moon bear to her skinny little chest. Irma was just standing there wondering what had brought us. "It's about the teddy bear," Levi Porter apologized. "It belongs to Debbie. I have to take it back."

We went over to the couch. "You see," he explained to me, "on opening night, Petrina fell in love with the bear. I wanted to get it for her, but I didn't have any money left. So I took it, figuring it wasn't really stealing; everything there was for Petrina anyway. If I'd knowed about Debbie, I would've worked out something else, maybe."

He leaned over the couch and gently, very gently, took the moon bear out of Petrina's hands. "I'm sorry, honey," he told the thin little girl, "it's really Debbie's. I'll get you a different bear soon." The sad little girl let the bear slip slowly out of her hands, not resisting, but not really letting go either. She said nothing, so used to hurt, so used to disappointment, so used to having everything slip away from her, but her soft dark eyes filled with tears as Shorty took the bear. I could have sworn that the moon bear's purple glass eyes looked full of pain, too.

Shorty put the bear gently into Debbie's arms and she cradled the bear closely to her. She put her face next to the bear's and kissed him and whispered something to him that I didn't catch, my hearing not being what it used to be. Then she went over to the couch and put the bear back into Petrina's hands. "He likes you better," she said. "He wants to stay with you. He loves you."

We stood there for a moment, all of us, silent. Petrina clutched the bear to her, tightly, lovingly, and almost smiled. Irma started crying and I might've too, a little. Shorty picked Deborah up and kissed her like she was his own. "You're blessed," he said to me. "From heaven."

He drove us home, and on the way back I asked Debbie what she said to the bear. "I was just telling him his name," she said innocently, "and he said it was exactly right."

"What is his name?" I asked.

"Oh, that was *my* name for him, Grandma. Petrina told him *her* name; he has a different name now," and that's all she would say about it.

I invited Shorty in but he couldn't stay; had to get back to the garage. If he took too long—well, there were plenty of good mechanics out of work. He promised he'd get Deborah another gift for Christmas, but he couldn't do it in time for tonight. I told him not to worry; I'd work out something.

When we got home, I got started making cookies with chocolate sprinkles, the kind Deborah likes. She helped me. After a while, when the first batch of cookies was baking, her cheeks powdered with flour and her pretty face turned away, she said, quietly, "It's all right not to get a present for Christmas. As long as you know somebody *wanted* to give it to you and spent all her money to get it."

My heart was so full I couldn't say anything for a while. Then I lifted her onto my lap and hugged her to my heart. "Oh, Debbie my love, you'll understand when you're older, but you've just gotten the best Christmas present of all: the chance to make a little child happy."

I held her away and looked into her wise, innocent eyes and wondered if, maybe, she already understood that.

Christmas Cop

THOMAS LARRY ADCOCK

B Y THE SECOND WEEK OF DECEMBER, WHEN they light up the giant fir tree behind the statue of a golden Prometheus overlooking the ice-skating rink at Rockefeller Center, Christmas in New York has got you by the throat.

Close to five hundred street-corner Santas (temporarily sober and none too happy about it) have been ringing bells since the day after Thanksgiving; the support pillars on Macy's main selling floor have been dolled up like candy canes since Hallowe'en; the tipping season arrives in the person of your apartment-house super, all smiles and open-palmed and suddenly available to fix the leaky pipes you've complained about since July; total strangers insist not only that you have a nice day but that you be of good cheer on top of it; and your Con Ed bill says HAPPY HOLIDAYS at the top of the page in a festive red-and-green dot-matrix.

In addition, New York in December is crawling with boosters, dippers, yokers, smash-and-grabbers, bindlestiffs on the mope, aggressive pross offering special holiday rates to guys cruising around at dusk in station wagons with Jersey plates, pigeon droppers and assorted other bunco artists, purveyors of all manner of dubious gift items, and entrepreneurs of the informal branch of the pharmaceutical trade. My job is to try and prevent at least some of these fine upstanding perpetrators from scoring against at least some of their natural Yuletide prey—the seasonal hordes of out-of-towners, big-ticket shoppers along Fifth Avenue, blue-haired Wednesday matinee ladies, and wide-eyed suburban matrons lined up outside Radio City Music Hall with big, snatchable shoulder bags full of credit cards.

I'm your friendly neighborhood plainclothesman. *Very* plain clothes. The guy in the grungy overcoat and watch cap and jeans and beat-up shoes and a week's growth of black beard shambling along the street carrying something in a brown paper bag—that ubiquitous New York bum you hurry past every day while holding your breath—might be me.

The name is Neil Hockaday, but everybody calls me Hock, my fellow cops and my snitches alike. And that's no pint of muscatel in my paper bag, it's my point-to-point shortwave radio. I work out of a boroughwide outfit called Street Crimes Unit-Manhattan, which is better known as the befitting S.C.U.M. patrol.

For twelve years, I've been a cop, the last three on S.C.U.M. patrol, which is a prestige assignment despite the way we dress on the job. In three years, I've made exactly twice the collars I did in my first nine riding around in precinct squad cars taking calls from sector dispatch. It's all going to add up nicely when I go for my gold shield someday. Meanwhile, I appreciate being able to work pretty much unsupervised, which tells you I'm at least a half honest cop in a city I figure to be about three-quarters crooked.

Sometimes I do a little bellyaching about the department—and who doesn't complain along about halfway through the second cold one after shift?—but mainly I enjoy the work I do. What I like about it most is how I'm always up against the elements of chance and surprise, one way or another.

That's something you can't say about most careers these days. Not even a cop's, really. Believe it or not, you have plenty of tedium if you're a uniform sealed up in a blue-and-white all day, even in

New York. But the way my job plays, I'm out there on the street mostly alone and it's an hour-by-hour proposition: fifty-eight minutes of walking around with my pores open so I don't miss anything and two minutes of surprise.

No matter what, I've got to be ready because surprise comes in several degrees of seriousness. And when it does, it comes out of absolutely nowhere.

On the twenty-fourth of December, I wasn't ready.

To me, it was a day like any other. That was wishful thinking, of course. To a holiday-crazed town, it was Christmas Eve and the big payoff was on deck—everybody out there with kids and wives and roast turkeys and plenty of money was anxious to let the rest of us know how happy they were.

Under the circumstances, it was just as well that I'd pulled duty. I wouldn't have had anyplace to go besides the corner pub, as it happened—or, if I could stand it, the easy chair in front of my old Philco for a day of *Christmas in Connecticut* followed by *Miracle on Thirty-fourth Street* followed by *A Christmas Carol* followed by *March of the Wooden Soldiers* followed by Midnight Mass live from St. Patrick's.

Every year since my divorce five years ago, I'd dropped by my ex-wife's place out in Queens for Christmas Eve. I'd bring champagne, oysters, an expensive gift, and high hopes of spending the night. But this year she'd wrecked my plans. She telephoned around the twentieth to tell me about this new boy friend of hers— some guy who wasn't a cop and whose name sounded like a respiratory disease, Flummong—and how he was taking her out to some rectangular state in the Middle West to meet his parents, who grow wheat. Swell.

So on the twenty-fourth, I got up at the crack of noon and decided that the only thing that mattered was business. Catching bad guys on the final, frantic shopping day—that was the ticket. I reheated some coffee from the day before, then poured some into a mug after I picked out something small, brown, and dead. I also ate a week-old piece of babka and said, "Bah, humbug!" right out loud.

I put on my quilted longjohns and strapped a lightweight .32 automatic Baretta Puma around my left ankle. Then I pulled on a pair of faded grey corduroys with holes in the knees, a black turtleneck sweater with bleach stains to wear over my beige bulletproof vest and my patrolman's badge on a chain, a New York Knicks navy-blue stocking cap with a red ball on top, and Army-surplus boots. The brown paper bag for my PTP I'd saved from the past Sunday when I'd gotten bagels down on Essex Street and shaved last.

I strapped on my shoulder holster and packed away the heavy piece, my .44 Charter Arms Bulldog. Then I topped off my ensemble with an olive-drab officer's greatcoat that had seen lots of action in maybe the Korean War. One of the side pockets was slashed open. Moths and bayonet tips had made holes in other places. I dropped a pair of nickel-plated NYPD bracelets into the good pocket.

By half past the hour, I was in the Bleecker Street subway station near where I live in the East Village. I dropped a quarter into a telephone on the platform and told the desk sergeant at Midtown South to be a good guy and check me off for the one o'clock muster. A panhandler with better clothes than mine and a neatly printed plywood sandwich sign hanging around his shoulders caught my eye. The sign read, TRYING TO RAISE $1,000,000 FOR WINE RESEARCH. I gave him a buck and caught the uptown D train.

When I got out at Broadway and Thirty-fourth Street, the

weather had turned cold and clammy. The sky had a smudgy grey overcast to it. It would be the kind of afternoon when everything in Manhattan looks like a black-and-white snapshot. It wasn't very Christmaslike, which suited me fine.

Across the way, in a triangle of curbed land that breaks up the Broadway and Sixth Avenue traffic flow at the south end of Herald Square, winos stood around in a circle at the foot of a statue of Horace Greeley. Greeley's limed shoulders were mottled by frozen bird dung and one granite arm was forever pointed toward the westward promise. I thought about my ex and the Flummong guy. The winos coughed, their foul breath hanging in frosted lumps of exhaled air, and awaited a ritual opening of a large economy-sized bottle of Thunderbird. The leader broke the seal and poured a few drops on the ground, which is a gesture of respect to mates recently dead or imprisoned. Then he took a healthy swallow and passed it along.

On the other side of the statue, a couple of dozen more guys carrying the stick (living on the street, that is) reclined on benches or were curled up over heating grates. All were in proper position to protect their stash in the event of sleep: money along one side of their hat brims, one hand below as a sort of pillow. The only way they could be robbed was if someone came along and cut off their hands, which has happened.

Crowds of last-minute shoppers jammed the sidewalks everywhere. Those who had to pass the bums (and me) did so quickly, out of fear and disgust, even at this time of goodwill toward men. It's a curious thing how so many comfortable middle-class folks believe vagrants and derelicts are dangerous, especially when you consider that the only people who have caused them any serious harm have been other comfortable middle-class folks with nice suits and offices and lawyers.

Across Broadway, beyond the bottle gang around the stone Greeley, I recognized a mope I'd busted about a year ago for boosting out of a flashy clothes joint on West Fourteenth Street. He was a scared kid of sixteen and lucky I'd gotten to him first. The store goons would have broken his thumbs. He was an Irish kid who went by the street name Whiteboy and he had nobody. We have lots of kids like Whiteboy in New York, and other cities, too. But we don't much want to know about them.

Now he leaned against a Florsheim display window, smoking a cigarette and scoping out the straight crowd around Macy's and Gimbels. Whiteboy, so far as I knew, was a moderately successful small-fry shoplifter, purse snatcher, and pickpocket.

I decided to stay put and watch him watch the swarm of possible marks until he got up enough nerve to move on somebody he figured would give him the biggest return for the smallest risk, like any good businessman. I moved back against a wall and stuck out my hand and asked passers-by for spare change. (This is not exactly regulation, but it guarantees that nobody will look at my face and it happens to be how I cover the monthly alimony check.) A smiling young fellow in a camel topcoat, the sort of guy who might be a Jaycee from some town up in Rockland County, pressed paper on me and whispered, "Bless you, brother." I looked down and saw that he'd given me a circular from the Church of Scientology in the size, color, and shape of a dollar bill.

When I looked up again, Whiteboy was crossing Broadway. He tossed his cigarette into the street and concentrated on the ripe prospect of a mink-draped fat lady on the outside of a small mob shoving its way into Gimbels. She had a black patent-leather purse dangling from a rhinestone-studded strap clutched in her hand. Whiteboy could pluck it from her pudgy fingers so fast and gently she'd be in third-floor housewares before she noticed.

I followed after him when he passed me. Then, sure enough, he made the snatch. I started running down the Broadway bus lane toward him. Whiteboy must have lost his touch because the fat lady turned and pointed at him and hollered "Thief!" She stepped right in front of me and I banged into her and she shrieked at me, "Whyn't you sober up and get a job, you bum you?"

Whiteboy whirled around and looked at me full in the face. He made me. Then he started running, too.

He darted through the thicket of yellow taxicabs, cars, and vans and zigzagged his way toward Greeley's statue. There was nothing I could do but chase him on foot. Taking a shot in such a congestion of traffic and pedestrians would get me up on IAD charges just as sure as if I'd stolen the fat lady's purse myself.

Then a funny thing happened.

Just as I closed in on Whiteboy, all those bums lying around on the little curbed triangle suddenly got up and blocked me as neatly as a line of zone defensemen for the Jets. Eight or ten big, groggy guys fell all over me and I lost Whiteboy.

I couldn't have been more frustrated. A second collar on a guy like Whiteboy would have put him away for two years' hard time, minimum. Not to mention how it would get me a nice commendation letter for my personal file. But in this business, you can't spend too much time crying over a job that didn't come off. So I headed east on Thirty-second toward Fifth Avenue.

At mid-block, I stopped to help a young woman in a raggedy coat with four bulging shopping bags and three shivering kids. She set the bags on the damp sidewalk and rubbed her bare hands as I neared her. Two girls and a boy, the oldest maybe seven, huddled around her. "How much farther?" one of the girls asked.

I didn't hear an answer. I walked up and asked the woman, "Where you headed, lady?" She looked away, embarrassed because of the tears in her eyes. She was small and slender, with light-brown skin and black hair pulled straight back from her face and held with a rubber band. A gust of dry wind knifed through the air.

"Could you help me?" she finally asked. "I'm just going up to the hotel at the corner. These bags are cutting my hands."

She meant the Martinique. It's a big dark hulk of a hotel, possibly grand back in the days when Herald Square was nearly glamorous. Now it's peeling and forbidding and full of people who have lost their way for a lot of different reasons—most of them women and children. When welfare families can't pay the rent anymore and haven't anyplace to go, the city puts them up "temporarily" at the Martinique. It's a stupid deal even by New York's high standards of senselessness. The daily hotel rate amounts to a monthly tab of about two grand for one room and an illegal hotplate, which is maybe ten times the rent on the apartment the family just lost.

"What's your name?" I asked her.

She didn't hesitate, but there was a shyness to her voice. "Frances. What's yours?"

"Hock." I picked up her bags, two in each hand. "Hurry up, it's going to snow," I said. The bags were full of children's clothes, a plastic radio, some storybooks, and canned food. I hoped they wouldn't break from the sidewalk dampness.

Frances and her kids followed me and I suppose we looked like a line of shabby ducks walking along. A teenage girl in one of those second-hand men's tweed overcoats you'd never find at the Goodwill took our picture with a Nikon equipped with a telephoto lens.

I led the way into the hotel and set the bags down at the admitting desk. Frances's three kids ran off to join a bunch of other kids who were watching a couple of old coots with no teeth struggling with a skinny spruce tree at the entry of what used to be the dining room. Now it was dusty and had no tables, just a few graffiti-covered vending machines.

Frances grabbed my arm when I tried to leave her. "It's not much, I know that. But maybe you can use it all the same." She let me go, then put out a hand like she wanted to shake. I slipped off my glove and took hold of her small, bone-chilled fingers. She passed me two dimes. "Thanks, and happy Christmas."

She looked awfully brave and awfully heartsick, too. Most down-and-outers look like that, but people who eat regularly and know where their next dollar will likely come from make the mistake of thinking they're stupid and confused, or maybe shiftless or crazy.

I tried to refuse the tip, but she wouldn't have any of that. Her eyes misted up again. So I went back out to the street, where it was starting to snow.

The few hours I had left until the evening darkness were not productive. Which is not to say there wasn't enough business for me. Anyone who thinks crooks are nabbed sooner or later by us sharp-witted, hard-working cops probably also thinks there's a tooth fairy. Police files everywhere bulge with unfinished business. That's because cops are pretty much like everybody else in a world that's not especially efficient. Some days we're inattentive or lazy or hung-over—or in my case on Christmas Eve, preoccupied with the thought that loneliness is all it's cracked up to be.

For about an hour after leaving Frances and the kids at the Martinique, I tailed a mope with a big canvas laundry sack, which is the ideal equipment when you're hauling off valuables from a place where nobody happens to be home. I was practically to the Hudson River before I realized the perp had made me a long time back and was just having fun giving me a walk-around on a raw, snowy day. Perps can be cocky like that sometimes. Even though I was ninety-nine percent sure he had a set of lock picks on him, I didn't have probable cause for a frisk.

I also wasted a couple of hours shadowing a guy in a very uptown cashmere coat and silk muffler. He had a set of California teeth and perfect sandy-blond hair. Most people in New York would figure him for a nice simple TV anchorman or maybe a *GQ* model. I had him pegged for a shoulder-bag bus dipper, which is a minor criminal art that can be learned by anyone who isn't moronic or crippled in a single afternoon. Most of its practitioners seem to be guys who are too handsome. All you have to do is hang around people waiting for buses or getting off buses, quietly reach into their bags, and pick out wallets.

I read this one pretty easily when I noticed how he passed up a half empty Madison Avenue bus opposite B. Altman's in favor of the next one, which was overloaded with chattering Lenox Hill matrons who would never in a thousand years think such a nice young man with nice hair and a dimple in his chin and so well dressed was a thief.

Back and forth I went with this character, clear up to Fifty-ninth Street, then by foot over to Fifth Avenue and back down into the low Forties. When I finally showed him my tin and spread him against the base of one of the cement lions outside the New York Public Library to pat him down, I only found cash on him. This dipper was brighter than he looked. Somewhere along the line, he'd ditched the wallets and pocketed only the bills and I never once saw the slide. I felt fairly brainless right about then and the crowd of onlookers that cheered when I let him go didn't help me any.

So I hid out in the Burger King at Fifth and Thirty-eighth for my dinner hour. There aren't too many places that could be more depressing for a holiday meal. The lighting was so oppressively even that I felt I was inside an ice cube. There was a plastic Christmas tree with plastic ornaments chained to a wall so nobody could steal it, with dummy gifts beneath it. The gifts were strung together with vinyl cord and likewise chained to the wall. I happened to be the only customer in the place, so a kid with a bad complexion and a broom decided to sweep up around my table.

To square my pad for the night, I figured I had to make some sort of bust, even a Mickey Mouse. So after my festive meal (Whopper, fries, Sprite, and a toasted thing with something hot and gummy inside it), I walked down to Thirty-third Street and collared a working girl in a white fake-fox stole, fishnet hose, and a red leather skirt. She was all alone on stroll, a freelance, and looked like she could use a hot meal and a nice dry cell. So I took her through the drill. The paperwork burned up everything but the last thirty minutes of my tour.

When I left the station house on West Thirty-fifth, the snow had become wet and heavy and most of midtown Manhattan was lost in a quiet white haze. I heard the occasional swish of a car going through a pothole puddle. Plumes of steam hissed here and there, like geysers from the subterranean. Everybody seemed to have vanished and the lights of the city had gone off, save for the gauzy red-and-green beacon at the top of the Empire State Building. It was rounding toward nine o'clock and it was Christmas Eve and New York seemed settled down for a long winter's nap.

There was just one thing wrong with the picture. And that was the sight of Whiteboy. I spotted him on Broadway again, lumbering down the mostly blackened, empty street with a big bag on his back like he was St. Nicholas himself.

I stayed out of sight and tailed him slowly back a few blocks to where I'd lost him in the first place, to the statue of Greeley. I had a clear view of him as he set down his bag on a bench and talked to the same bunch of grey, shapeless winos who'd cut me off at the chase. Just as before, they passed a bottle. Only this time Whiteboy gave it to them. After everyone had a nice jolt, they talked quickly for a couple of minutes, like they had someplace important to go.

I hung back in the darkness under some scaffolding. Snow fell between the cracks of planks above me and piled on my shoulders as I stood there trying to figure out their act. It didn't take me long.

When they started moving from the statue over to Thirty-second Street, every one of them with a bag slung over his shoulder, I hung back a little. But my crisis of conscience didn't last long. I followed Whiteboy and his unlikely crew of elves—and wasn't much surprised to find the blond shoulder-bag dipper with the cashmere coat when we got to where we were all going. Which was the Martinique. By now, the spindly little spruce I'd felt sorry for that afternoon was full of bright lights and tinsel and had a star on top. The same old coots I'd seen when I helped Frances and her kids there were standing around playing with about a hundred more hungry-looking kids.

Whiteboy and his helpers went up to the tree and plopped down all the bags. The kids crowded around them. They were quiet about it, though. These were kids who didn't have much experience with Norman Rockwell Christmases, so they didn't know it was an occasion to whoop it up.

Frances saw me standing in the dimly lit doorway. I must have been a sight, covered in snow and tired from walking my post most of eight hours. "Hock!" she called merrily.

And then Whiteboy spun around like he had before and his jaw dropped open. He and the pretty guy stepped away from the crowd of kids and mothers and the few broken-down men and walked quickly over to me. The kids looked like they expected all along that their party would be busted up. Frances knew she'd done something very wrong hailing me like she had, but how could she know I was a cop?

"We're having a little Christmas party here, Hock. Anything illegal about that?" Whiteboy was a cool one. He'd grown tougher and smarter in a year and talked to me like we'd just had a lovely chat the other day. We'd have to make some sort of deal, Whiteboy and me, and we both knew it.

"Who's your partner?" I asked him. I looked at the pretty guy in cashmere who wasn't saying anything just yet.

"Call him Slick."

"I like it," I said. "Where'd you and Slick get all the stuff in the bags?"

"Everything's bought and paid for, Hock. You got nothing to worry about."

"When you're cute, you're irritating, Whiteboy. You know I can't turn around on this empty-handed."

Then Slick spoke up. "What you got on us, anyways? I've just about had my fill of police harassment today, Officer. I was cooperative earlier, but I don't intend to cooperate a second time."

I ignored him and addressed Whiteboy. "Tell your friend Slick how we all appreciate discretion and good manners on both sides of the game."

Whiteboy smiled and Slick's face grew a little red.

"Let's just say for the sake of conversation," Whiteboy suggested, "that Slick and me came by a whole lot of money some way or other we're unwilling to disclose since that would tend to incriminate us. And then let's say we used that money to buy a whole lot of stuff for those kids back of us. And let's say we got cash receipts for everything in the bags. Where's that leave us, Officer Hockaday?"

"It leaves you with one leg up, temporarily. Which can be a very uncomfortable way of standing. Let's just say that I'm likely to be hard on your butts from now on."

"Well, that's about right. Just the way I see it." He lit a cigarette, a Dunhill. Then he turned back a cuff and looked at his wristwatch, the kind of piece that cost him plenty of either nerve or money. Whiteboy was moving up well for himself.

"You're off duty now, aren't you, Hock? And wouldn't you be just about out of overtime allowance for the year?"

"Whiteboy, you better start giving me something besides lip. That is, unless you want forty-eight hours up at Riker's on suspicion. You better believe there isn't a judge in this whole city on straight time or overtime or any kind of time tonight or tomorrow to take any bail application from you."

Whiteboy smiled again. "Yeah, well, I figure the least I owe you is to help you see this thing my way. Think of it like a special tax, you know? Around this time of year, I figure the folks who can spare something ought to be taxed. So maybe that's what happened, see? Just taxation."

"Same scam as the one Robin Hood ran?"

"Yeah, something like that. Only Slick and me ain't about to start living out of town in some forest."

"You owe me something more, Whiteboy."

"What?"

"From now on, you and Slick are my two newest snitches. And I'll be expecting regular news."

There is such a thing as honor among thieves. This is every bit as true as the honor among Congressmen you read about in the newspapers all the time. But when enlightened self-interest rears its ugly head, it's also true that rules of gallantry are off.

"Okay, Hock, why not?" Whiteboy shook my hand. Slick did, too, and when he smiled his chin dimple spread flat. Then the three of us went over to the Christmas tree and everybody there seemed relieved.

We started pulling merchandise out of the bags and handing things over to disbelieving kids and their parents. Everything was the best that money could buy, too. Slick's taste in things was top-drawer. And just like Whiteboy said, there were sales slips for it all, which meant that this would be a time when nobody could take anything away from these people.

I came across a pair of ladies' black leather gloves from Lord & Taylor, with grey rabbit-fur lining. These I put aside until all the kids had something, then I gave them to Frances before I went home for the night. She kissed me on the cheek and wished me a happy Christmas again.

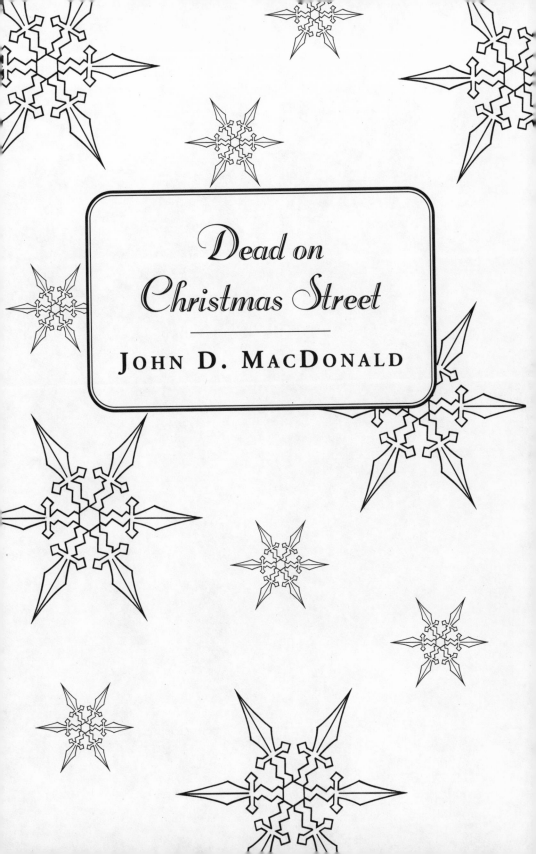

Dead on Christmas Street

John D. MacDonald

THE POLICE IN THE FIRST PROWL CAR ON THE scene got out a tarpaulin. A traffic policeman threw it over the body and herded the crowd back. They moved uneasily in the gray slush. Some of them looked up from time to time.

In the newspaper picture the window would be marked with a bold X. A dotted line would descend from the X to the spot where the covered body now lay. Some of the spectators, laden with tinsel- and evergreen-decorated packages, turned away, suppressing a nameless guilt.

But the curious stayed on. Across the street, in the window of a department store, a vast mechanical Santa rocked back and forth, slapping a mechanical hand against a padded thigh, roaring forever, "Whaw haw ho ho ho. Whaw haw ho ho ho." The slapping hand had worn the red plush from the padded thigh.

The ambulance arrived, with a brisk intern to make out the DOA. Sawdust was shoveled onto the sidewalk, then pushed off into the sewer drain. Wet snow fell into the city. And there was nothing else to see. The corner Santa, a leathery man with a pinched, blue nose, began to ring his hand bell again.

Daniel Fowler, one of the young Assistant District Attorneys, was at his desk when the call came through from Lieutenant Shinn of the Detective Squad. "Dan? This is Gil. You heard about the Garrity girl yet?"

For a moment the name meant nothing, and then suddenly he remembered: Loreen Garrity was the witness in the Sheridan City Loan Company case. She had made positive identification of two of the three kids who had tried to pull that holdup, and the case was on the calendar for February. Provided the kids didn't confess before it came up, Dan was going to prosecute. He had the Garrity girl's statement, and her promise to appear.

"What about her, Gil?" he asked.

"She took a high dive out of her office window—about an hour ago. Seventeen stories, and right into the Christmas rush. How come she didn't land on somebody, we'll never know. Connie Wyant is handling it. He remembered she figured in the loan-company deal, and he told me. Look, Dan. She was a big girl, and she tried hard not to go out that window. She was shoved. That's how come Connie has it. Nice Christmas present for him."

"Nice Christmas present for the lads who pushed over the loan company, too," Dan said grimly. "Without her there's no case. Tell Connie that. It ought to give him the right line."

Dan Fowler set aside the brief he was working on and walked down the hall. The District Attorney's secretary was at her desk. "Boss busy, Jane?"

She was a small girl with wide, gray eyes, a mass of dark hair, a soft mouth. She raised one eyebrow and looked at him speculatively. "I could be bribed, you know."

He looked around with exaggerated caution, went around her desk on tiptoe, bent and kissed her upraised lips. He smiled down at her. "People are beginning to talk," he whispered, not getting it as light as he meant it to be.

She tilted her head to one side, frowned, and said, "What is it, Dan?"

He sat on the corner of her desk and took her hands in his, and he told her about the big, dark-haired, swaggering woman who had gone out the window. He knew Jane would want to know. He had regretted bringing Jane in on the case, but he had had the unhappy hunch that Garrity might sell out, if the offer was high enough. And so he had enlisted Jane, depending on her intuition. He had taken the two of them to lunch, and had invented an excuse to duck out and leave them alone.

Afterward, Jane had said, "I guess I don't really like her, Dan. She was suspicious of me, of course, and she's a terribly vital sort of person. But I would say that she'll be willing to testify. And I don't think she'll sell out."

Now as he told her about the girl, he saw the sudden tears of sympathy in her gray eyes. "Oh, Dan! How dreadful! You'd better tell the boss right away. That Vince Servius must have hired somebody to do it."

"Easy, lady," he said softly.

He touched her dark hair with his fingertips, smiled at her, and crossed to the door of the inner office, opened it and went in.

Jim Heglon, the District Attorney, was a narrow-faced man with glasses that had heavy frames. He had a professional look, a dry wit, and a driving energy.

"Every time I see you, Dan, I have to conceal my annoyance," Heglon said. "You're going to cart away the best secretary I ever had."

"Maybe I'll keep her working for a while. Keep her out of trouble."

"Excellent! And speaking of trouble—"

"Does it show, Jim?" Dan sat on the arm of a heavy leather chair which faced Heglon's desk. "I do have some. Remember the Sheridan City Loan case?"

"Vaguely. Give me an outline."

"October. Five o'clock one afternoon, just as the loan office was closing. Three punks tried to knock it over. Two of them, Castrella and Kelly, are eighteen. The leader, Johnny Servius, is nineteen. Johnny is Vince Servius's kid brother.

"They went into the loan company wearing masks and waving guns. The manager had more guts than sense. He was loading the safe. He saw them and slammed the door and spun the knob. They beat on him, but he convinced them it was a time lock, which it wasn't. They took fifteen dollars out of his pants, and four dollars from the girl behind the counter and took off.

"Right across the hall is the office of an accountant named Thomas Kistner. He'd already left. His secretary, Loreen Garrity, was closing up the office. She had the door open a crack. She saw the three kids come out of the loan company, taking their masks off. Fortunately, they didn't see her.

"She went to headquarters and looked at the gallery, and picked out Servius and Castrella. They were picked up. Kelly was with them, so they took him in, too. In the lineup the Garrity girl made a positive identification of Servius and Castrella again. The manager thought he could recognize Kelly's voice.

"Bail was set high, because we expected Vince Servius would get them out. Much to everybody's surprise, he's left them in there. The only thing he did was line up George Terrafierro to defend them, which makes it tough from our point of view, but not too tough—if we could put the Garrity girl on the stand. She was the type to make a good witness. Very positive sort of girl."

"Was? Past tense?"

"This afternoon she was pushed out the window of the office where she works. Seventeen stories above the sidewalk. Gil Shinn tells me that Connie Wyant has it definitely tagged as homicide."

"If Connie says it is, then it is. What would conviction have meant to the three lads?"

"Servius had one previous conviction—car theft; Castrella had one conviction for assault with a deadly weapon. Kelly is clean, Jim."

Heglon frowned. "Odd, isn't it? In this state, armed robbery has a mandatory sentence of seven to fifteen years for a first offense in that category. With the weight Vince can swing, his kid brother would do about five years. Murder seems a little extreme as a way of avoiding a five-year sentence."

"Perhaps, Jim, the answer is in the relationship between Vince and the kid. There's quite a difference in ages. Vince must be nearly forty. He was in the big time early enough to give Johnny all the breaks. The kid has been thrown out of three good schools I know of. According to Vince, Johnny can do no wrong. Maybe that's why he left those three in jail awaiting trial—to keep them in the clear on this killing."

"It could be, Dan," Heglon said. "Go ahead with your investigation. And let me know."

Dan Fowler found out at the desk that Lieutenant Connie Wyant and Sergeant Levandowski were in the Interrogation Room. Dan sat down and waited.

After a few moments Connie waddled through the doorway and came over to him. He had bulging blue eyes and a dull expression.

Dan stood up, towering over the squat lieutenant. "Well, what's the picture, Connie?"

"No case against the kids, Gil says. Me, I wish it was just some-body thought it would be nice to jump out a window. But she grabbed the casing so hard, she broke her fingernails down to the quick.

"Marks you can see, in oak as hard as iron. Banged her head on the sill and left black hair on the rough edge of the casing. Lab matched it up. And one shoe up there, under the radiator. The ra-diator sits right in front of the window. Come listen to Kistner."

Dan followed him back to the Interrogation Room. Thomas Kistner sat at one side of the long table. A cigar lay dead on the glass ashtray near his elbow. As they opened the door, he glanced up quickly. He was a big, bloated man with an unhealthy grayish complexion and an important manner.

He said, "I was just telling the sergeant the tribulations of an accountant."

"We all got troubles," Connie said. "This is Mr. Fowler from the D.A.'s office, Kistner."

Mr. Kistner got up laboriously. "Happy to meet you, sir," he said. "Sorry that it has to be such an unpleasant occasion, however."

Connie sat down heavily. "Kistner, I want you to go through your story again. If it makes it easier, tell it to Mr. Fowler instead of me. He hasn't heard it before."

"I'll do anything in my power to help, Lieutenant," Kistner said firmly. He turned toward Dan. "I am out of my office a great deal. I do accounting on a contract basis for thirty-three small re-tail establishments. I visit them frequently.

"When Loreen came in this morning, she seemed nervous. I asked her what the trouble was, and she said that she felt quite sure somebody had been following her for the past week.

"She described him to me. Slim, middle height, pearl-gray felt hat, tan raglan topcoat, swarthy complexion. I told her that because she was the witness in a trial coming up, she should maybe report it to the police and ask for protection. She said she didn't like the idea of yelling for help. She was a very—ah—independent sort of girl."

"I got that impression," Dan said.

"I went out then and didn't think anything more about what she'd said. I spent most of the morning at Finch Pharmacy, on the north side. I had a sandwich there and then drove back to the office, later than usual. Nearly two.

"I came up to the seventeenth floor. Going down the corridor, I pass the Men's Room before I get to my office. I unlocked the door with my key and went in. I was in there maybe three minutes.

"I came out and a man brushes by me in the corridor. He had his collar up, and was pulling down on his hatbrim and walking fast. At the moment, you understand, it meant nothing to me.

"I went into the office. The window was wide open, and the snow was blowing in. No Loreen. I couldn't figure it. I thought she'd gone to the Ladies' Room and had left the window open for some crazy reason. I started to shut it, and then I heard all the screaming down in the street.

"I leaned out. I saw her, right under me, sprawled on the sidewalk. I recognized the cocoa-colored suit. A new suit, I think. I stood in a state of shock, I guess, and then suddenly I remembered about the man following her, and I remembered the man in the hall—he had a gray hat and a tan topcoat, and I had the impression he was swarthy-faced.

"The first thing I did was call the police, naturally. While they were on the way, I called my wife. It just about broke her up. We were both fond of Loreen."

The big man smiled sadly. "And it seems to me I've been telling the story over and over again ever since. Oh, I don't mind, you understand. But it's a dreadful thing. The way I see it, when a person witnesses a crime, they ought to be given police protection until the trial is all over."

"We don't have that many cops," Connie said glumly. "How big was the man you saw in the corridor?"

"Medium size. A little on the thin side."

"How old?"

"I don't know. Twenty-five, forty-five. I couldn't see his face, and you understand I wasn't looking closely."

Connie turned toward Dan. "Nothing from the elevator boys about this guy. He probably took the stairs. The lobby is too busy for anybody to notice him coming through by way of the fire door. Did the Garrity girl ever lock herself in the office, Kistner?"

"I never knew of her doing that, Lieutenant."

Connie said, "Okay, so the guy could breeze in and clip her one. Then, from the way the rug was pulled up, he lugged her across to the window. She came to as he was trying to work her out the window, and she put up a battle. People in the office three stories underneath say she was screaming as she went by."

"How about the offices across the way?" Dan asked.

"It's a wide street, Dan, and they couldn't see through the snow. It started snowing hard about fifteen minutes before she was pushed out the window. I think the killer waited for that snow. It gave him a curtain to hide behind."

"Any chance that she marked the killer, Connie?" Dan asked.

"Doubt it. From the marks of her fingernails, he lifted her up and slid her feet out first, so her back was to him. She grabbed the sill on each side. Her head hit the window sash. All he had to do was hold her shoulders, and bang her in the small of the back with his knee. Once her fanny slid off the sill, she couldn't hold on with her hands any longer. And from the looks of the doorknobs, he wore gloves."

Dan turned to Kistner. "What was her home situation? I tried to question her. She was pretty evasive."

Kistner shrugged. "Big family. She didn't get along with them. Seven girls, I think, and she was next to oldest. She moved out when she got her first job. She lived alone in a one-room apartment on Leeds Avenue, near the bridge."

"You know of any boy friend?" Connie asked.

"Nobody special. She used to go out a lot, but nobody special."

Connie rapped his knuckles on the edge of the table. "You ever make a pass at her, Kistner?"

The room was silent. Kistner stared at his dead cigar. "I don't want to lie to you, but I don't want any trouble at home, either. I got a boy in the Army, and I got a girl in her last year of high. But you work in a small office alone with a girl like Loreen, and it can get you.

"About six months ago I had to go to the state Capital on a tax thing. I asked her to come along. She did. It was a damn fool thing to do. And it—didn't work out so good. We agreed to forget it ever happened.

"We were awkward around the office for a couple of weeks, and then I guess we sort of forgot. She was a good worker, and I was paying her well, so it was to both our advantages to be practical and not get emotional. I didn't have to tell you men this, but, like I said, I don't see any point in lying to the police. Hell, you might have found out some way, and that might make it look like I killed her or something."

"Thanks for leveling," Connie said expressionlessly. "We'll call you if we need you."

Kistner ceremoniously shook hands all around and left with obvious relief.

As soon as the door shut behind him, Connie said, "I'll buy it. A long time ago I learned you can't jail a guy for being a jerk. Funny how many honest people I meet I don't like at all, and how many thieves make good guys to knock over a beer with. How's your girl?"

Dan looked at his watch. "Dressing for dinner, and I should be, too," he said. "How are the steaks out at the Cat and Fiddle?"

Connie half closed his eyes. After a time he sighed. "Okay. That might be a good way to go at the guy. Phone me and give me the reaction if he does talk. If not, don't bother."

Jane was in holiday mood until Dan told her where they were headed. She said tartly, "I admit freely that I am a working girl. But do I get overtime for this?"

Dan said slowly, carefully, "Darling, you better understand, if you don't already, that there's one part of me I can't change. I can't shut the office door and forget the cases piled up in there. I have a nasty habit of carrying them around with me. So we go someplace else and I try like blazes to be gay, or we go to the Cat and Fiddle and get something off my mind."

She moved closer to him. "Dull old work horse," she said.

"Guilty."

"All right, now I'll confess," Jane said. "I was going to suggest we go out there later. I just got sore when you beat me to the draw."

He laughed, and at the next stop light he kissed her hurriedly.

The Cat and Fiddle was eight miles beyond the city line. At last Dan saw the green-and-blue neon sign, and he turned into the asphalt parking area. There were about forty other cars there.

They went from the check room into the low-ceilinged bar and lounge. The only sign of Christmas was a small silver tree on the bar; a tiny blue spot was focused on it.

They sat at the bar and ordered drinks. Several other couples were at the tables, talking in low voices. A pianist played softly in the dining room.

Dan took out a business card and wrote on it: *Only if you happen to have an opinion.*

He called the nearest bartender over. "Would you please see that Vince gets this?"

The man glanced at the name. "I'll see if Mr. Servius is in." He said something to the other bartender and left through a paneled door at the rear of the bar. He was back in less than a minute, smiling politely.

"Please go up the stair. Mr. Servius is in his office—the second door on the right."

"I'll wait here, Dan," Jane said.

"If you are Miss Raymer, Mr. Servius would like to have you join him, too," the bartender said.

Jane looked at Dan. He nodded and she slid off the stool.

As they went up the stairs, Jane said, "I seem to be known here."

"Notorious female. I suspect he wants a witness."

Vincent Servius was standing at a small corner bar mixing himself a drink when they entered. He turned and smiled. "Fowler, Miss Raymer. Nice of you to stop by. Can I mix you something?"

Dan refused politely, and they sat down.

Vince was a compact man with cropped, prematurely white hair, a sunlamp tan, and beautifully cut clothes. He had not been directly concerned with violence in many years. In that time he had eliminated most of the traces of the hoodlum.

The over-all impression he gave was that of the up-and-coming clubman. Golf lessons, voice lessons, plastic surgery, and a good tailor—these had all helped; but nothing had been able to destroy a certain aura of alertness, ruthlessness. He was a man you would never joke with. He had made his own laws, and he carried the awareness of his own ultimate authority around with him, as unmistakable as a loaded gun.

Vince went over to the fieldstone fireplace, drink in hand, and turned, resting his elbow on the mantel.

"Very clever, Fowler. 'Only if you happen to have an opinion.' I have an opinion. The kid is no good. That's my opinion. He's a cheap punk. I didn't admit that to myself until he tried to put the hook on that loan company. He was working for me at the time. I was trying to break him in here—buying foods.

"But now I'm through, Fowler. You can tell Jim Heglon that for me. Terrafierro will back it up. Ask him what I told him. I said, 'Defend the kid. Get him off if you can, and no hard feelings if you can't. If you get him off, I'm having him run out of town, out of the state. I don't want him around.' I told George that.

"Now there's this Garrity thing. It looks like I went out on a limb for the kid. Going out on limbs was yesterday, Fowler. Not today and not tomorrow. I was a sucker long enough."

He took out a crisp handkerchief and mopped his forehead. "I go right up in the air," he said. "I talk too loud."

"You can see how Heglon is thinking," Dan said quietly. "And the police, too."

"That's the hell of it. I swear I had nothing to do with it." He half smiled. "It would have helped if I'd had a tape recorder up here last month when the Garrity girl came to see what she could sell me."

Dan leaned forward. "She came here?"

"With bells on. Nothing coy about that kid. Pay off, Mr. Servius, and I'll change my identification of your brother."

"What part of last month?"

"Let me think. The tenth it was. Monday the tenth."

Jane said softly, "That's why I got the impression she wouldn't sell out, Dan. I had lunch with her later that same week. She had tried to and couldn't."

Vince took a sip of his drink. "She started with big money and worked her way down. I let her go ahead. Finally, after I'd had my laughs, I told her even one dollar was too much. I told her I wanted the kid sent up.

"She blew her top. For a couple of minutes I thought I might have to clip her to shut her up. But after a couple of drinks she quieted down. That gave me a chance to find out something that had been bothering me. It seemed too pat, kind of."

"What do you mean, Servius?" Dan asked.

"The set up was too neat, the way the door *happened* to be open a crack, and the way she *happened* to be working late, and the way she *happened* to see the kids come out.

"I couldn't get her to admit anything at first, because she was making a little play for me, but when I convinced her I wasn't having any, she let me in on what really happened. She was hanging around waiting for the manager of that loan outfit to quit work.

"They had a system. She'd wait in the accountant's office with the light out, watching his door. Then, when the manager left, she'd wait about five minutes and leave herself. That would give him time to get his car out of the parking lot. He'd pick her up at the corner. She said he was the super-cautious, married type. They just dated once in a while. I wasn't having any of that. Too rough for me, Fowler."

There was a long silence. Dan asked, "How about friends of your brother, Servius, or friends of Kelly and Castrella?"

Vince walked over and sat down, facing them. "One—Johnny didn't have a friend who'd bring a bucket of water if he was on fire. And two—I sent the word out."

"What does that mean?"

"I like things quiet in this end of the state. I didn't want anyone helping those three punks. Everybody got the word. So who would do anything? Now both of you please tell Heglon exactly what I said. Tell him to check with Terrafierro. Tell him to have the cops check their pigeons. Ask the kid himself. I paid him a little visit. Now, if you don't mind, I've got another appointment."

They had finished their steaks before Dan was able to get any line on Connie Wyant. On the third telephone call he was given a message. Lieutenant Wyant was waiting for Mr. Fowler at 311 Leeds Street, Apartment 6A, and would Mr. Fowler please bring Miss Raymer with him.

They drove back to the city. A department car was parked in front of the building. Sergeant Levandowski was half asleep behind the wheel. "Go right in. Ground floor in the back. 6A."

Connie greeted them gravely and listened without question to Dan's report of the conversation with Vince Servius. After Dan had finished, Connie nodded casually, as though it was of little importance, and said, "Miss Raymer, I'm not so good at this, so I thought maybe you could help. There's the Garrity girl's closet. Go through it and give me an estimate on the cost."

Jane went to the open closet. She began to examine the clothes. "Hey!" she exclaimed.

"What do you think?" Connie asked.

"If this suit cost a nickel under two hundred, I'll eat it. And look at this coat. Four hundred, anyway." She bent over and picked up a shoe. "For ages I've dreamed of owning a pair of these. Thirty-seven fifty, at least."

"Care to make an estimate on the total?" Connie asked her.

"Gosh, thousands. I don't know. There are nine dresses in there that must have cost at least a hundred apiece. Do you have to have it accurate?"

"That's close enough, thanks." He took a small blue bankbook out of his pocket and flipped it to Dan. Dan caught it and looked inside. Loreen Garrity had more than $1100 on hand. There had been large deposits and large withdrawals—nothing small.

Connie said, "I've been to see her family. They're good people. They didn't want to talk mean about the dead, so it took a little time. But I found out our Loreen was one for the angles—a chiseler—no conscience and less morals. A rough, tough cookie to get tied up with.

"From there, I went to see the Kistners. Every time the old lady would try to answer a question, Kistner'd jump in with all four feet. I finally had to have Levandowski take him downtown just to get him out of the way. Then the old lady talked.

"She had a lot to say about how lousy business is. How they're scrimping and scraping along, and how the girl couldn't have a new formal for the Christmas dance tomorrow night at the high school gym.

"Then I called up an accountant friend after I left her. I asked him how Kistner had been doing. He cussed out Kistner and said he'd been doing fine; in fact, he had stolen some nice retail accounts out from under the other boys in the same racket. So I came over here and it looked like this was where the profit was going. So I waited for you so I could make sure."

"What can you do about it?" Dan demanded, anger in his voice, anger at the big puffy man who hadn't wanted to lie to the police.

"I've been thinking. It's eleven o'clock. He's been sitting down there sweating. I've got to get my Christmas shopping done tomorrow, and the only way I'll ever get around to it is to break him fast."

Jane had been listening, wide-eyed. "They always forget some little thing, don't they?" she asked. "Or there is something they don't know about. Like a clock that is five minutes slow, or something. I mean, in the stories . . ." Her voice trailed off uncertainly.

"Give her a badge, Connie," Dan said with amusement.

Connie rubbed his chin. "I might do that, Dan. I just might do that. Miss Raymer, you got a strong stomach? If so, maybe you get to watch your idea in operation."

It was nearly midnight, and Connie had left Dan and Jane alone in a small office at headquarters for nearly a half hour. He opened the door and stuck his head in. "Come on, people. Just don't say a word."

They went to the Interrogation Room. Kistner jumped up the moment they came in. Levandowski sat at the long table, looking bored.

Kistner said heatedly, "As you know, Lieutenant, I was perfectly willing to cooperate. But you are being high-handed. I demand to know why I was brought down here. I want to know why I can't phone a lawyer. You are exceeding your authority, and I—"

"Siddown!" Connie roared with all the power of his lungs.

Kistner's mouth worked silently. He sat down, shocked by the unexpected roar. A tired young man slouched in, sat at the table, flipped open a notebook, and placed three sharp pencils within easy reach.

Connie motioned Dan and Jane over toward chairs in a shadowed corner of the room. They sat side by side, and Jane held Dan's wrist, her nails sharp against his skin.

"Kistner, tell us again about how you came back to the office," Connie said.

Kistner replied in a tone of excruciating patience, as though talking to children, "I parked my car in my parking space in the lot behind the building. I used the back way into the lobby. I went up—"

"You went to the cigar counter."

"So I did! I had forgotten that. I went to the cigar counter. I bought three cigars and chatted with Barney. Then I took an elevator up."

"And talked to the elevator boy."

"I usually do. Is there a law?"

"No law, Kistner. Go on."

"And then I opened the Men's Room door with my key, and I was in there maybe three minutes. And then when I came out, the man I described brushed by me. I went to the office and found the window open. I was shutting it when I heard—"

"All this was at two o'clock, give or take a couple of minutes?"

"That's right, Lieutenant." Talking had restored Kistner's self-assurance.

Connie nodded to Levandowski. The sergeant got up lazily, walked to the door, and opened it. A burly, diffident young man came in. He wore khaki pants and a leather jacket.

"Sit down," Connie said casually. "What's your name?"

"Paul Hilbert, officer."

The tired young man was taking notes.

"What's your occupation?"

"I'm a plumber, officer. Central Plumbing, Incorporated."

"Did you get a call today from the Associated Bank Building?"

"Well, I didn't get the call, but I was sent out on the job. I talked to the super, and he sent me up to the seventeenth floor. Sink drain clogged in the Men's Room."

"What time did you get there?"

"That's on my report, officer. Quarter after one."

"How long did it take you to finish the job?"

"About three o'clock."

"Did you leave the Men's Room at any time during that period?"

"No, I didn't."

"I suppose people tried to come in there?"

"Three or four. But I had all the water connections turned off, so I told them to go down to sixteen. The super had the door unlocked down there."

"Did you get a look at everybody who came in?"

"Sure, officer."

"You said three or four. Is one of them at this table?"

The shy young man looked around. He shook his head. "No, sir."

"Thanks, Hilbert. Wait outside. We'll want you to sign the statement when it's typed up."

Hilbert's footsteps sounded loud as he walked to the door. Everyone was watching Kistner. His face was still, and he seemed to be looking into a remote and alien future, as cold as the back of the moon.

Kistner said in a husky, barely audible voice, "A bad break. A stupid thing. Ten seconds it would have taken me to look in there. I had to establish the time. I talked to Barney. And to the elevator boy. They'd know when she fell. But I had to be someplace else. Not in the office.

"You don't know how it was. She kept wanting more money. She wouldn't have anything to do with me, except when there was money. And I didn't have any more, finally.

"I guess I was crazy. I started to milk the accounts. That wasn't hard; the clients trust me. Take a little here and a little there. She found out. She wanted more and more. And that gave her a new angle. Give me more, or I'll tell.

"I thought it over. I kept thinking about her being a witness. All I had to do was make it look like she was killed to keep her from testifying. I don't care what you do to me. Now it's over, and I feel glad."

He gave Connie a long, wondering look. "Is that crazy? To feel glad it's over? Do other people feel that way?"

Connie asked Dan and Jane to wait in the small office. He came in ten minutes later; he looked tired. The plumber came in with him.

Connie said, "Me, I hate this business. I'm after him, and I bust him, and then I start bleeding for him. What the hell? Anyway, you get your badge, Miss Raymer."

"But wouldn't you have found out about the plumber anyway?" Jane asked.

Connie grinned ruefully at her. He jerked a thumb toward the plumber. "Meet Patrolman Hilbert. Doesn't know a pipe wrench from a faucet. We just took the chance that Kistner was too eager to toss the girl out the window—so eager he didn't make a quick check of the Men's Room. If he had, he could have laughed us under the table. As it is, I can get my Christmas shopping done tomorrow. Or is it today?"

Dan and Jane left headquarters. They walked down the street, arm in arm. There was holly, and a big tree in front of the courthouse, and a car went by with a lot of people in it singing about We Three Kings of Orient Are. Kistner was a stain, fading slowly.

They walked until it was entirely Christmas Eve, and they were entirely alone in the snow that began to fall again, making tiny perfect stars of lace that lingered in her dark hair.

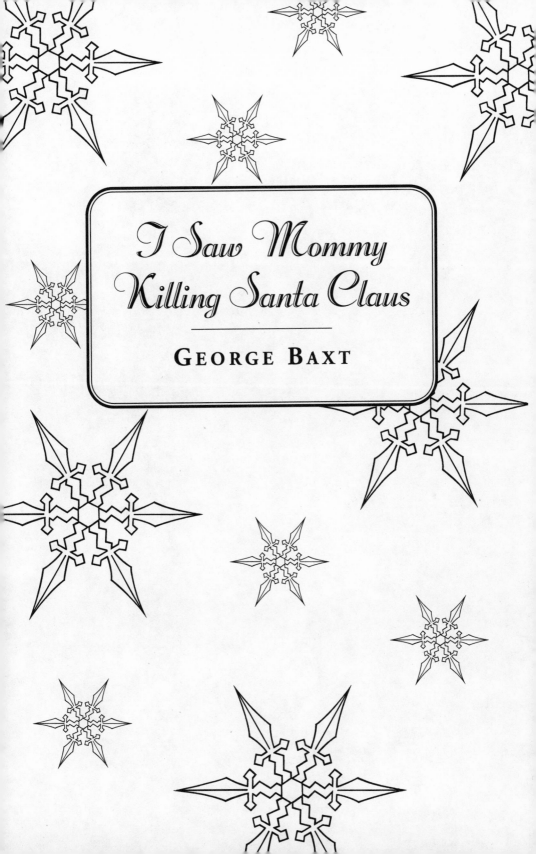

I Saw Mommy Killing Santa Claus

GEORGE BAXT

WE BURIED MY MOTHER YESTERDAY, SO I feel free to tell the truth. She lived to be ninety-three because, like the sainted, loyal son I chose to be, I didn't blab to the cops. I'm Oscar Leigh and my mother was Desiree Leigh. That's right—Desiree Leigh, inventor of the Desiree face cream that promised eternal youth to the young and rejuvenation to the aged. It was one of the great con games in the cosmetics industry. I suppose once this is published, it'll be the end of the Desiree cosmetics empire, but frankly, my dears, I don't give a damn. Desiree Cosmetics was bought by a Japanese combine four years ago, and my share (more than two billion) is safely salted away. I suppose I inherit Mom's billions, too, but what in heaven's name will I do with it all? Count it, I guess.

Desiree Leigh wasn't her real name. She was born Daisy Ray Letch, and who could go through life with a surname like Letch? For the past fourteen years she's been entertaining Alzheimer's and that was when I began to take an interest in her past. She was always very mysterious about her origins and equally arcane about the identity of my father. She said he was killed in North Africa back in 1943 and that his name was Clarence Kolb. I spent a lot of money tracing Clarence, until one night, in bed watching an old movie, the closing credits rolled and one of the character actors was named Clarence Kolb. I mentioned this to Mother the next morning at breakfast, but she said it was a coincidence and she and my father used to laugh about it.

She had no photos of my father, which I thought was strange. When they married a few months before the war, they settled in Brooklyn, in Coney Island. Surely they must have had their picture taken in one of the Coney Island fun galleries? But no, insisted Mother, they avoided the boardwalk and the amusement parks— they were too poor for such frivolities. How did Father make his living? He was a milkman, she said—his route was in Sheepshead Bay. She said he worked for the Borden Company. Well, let me tell you this; there is no record of a Clarence Kolb ever having been employed by the Borden Milk Company. It cost an ugly penny tracking that down.

Did Mom work, too, perhaps? "Oh, yes," she told me one night in Cannes where our yacht was berthed for a few days, "I worked right up until the day before you were born."

"What did you do?" We were on deck playing honeymoon bridge in the blazing sunlight so Mom could keep an eye on the first mate, with whom she was either having an affair or planning to have one.

"I worked in a laboratory." She said it so matter of factly while collecting a trick she shouldn't have collected that I didn't believe her. "You don't believe me." (She not only conned, stole, and lied, she was a mind-reader.)

"Sure I believe you." I sounded as convincing as an East Berlin commissar assuring would-be emigrés they'd have their visas to freedom before sundown.*

---

*Ed. note: A joyful note to anachronism—shortly after this story was written.

"It was a privately owned laboratory," she said, sneaking a look at the first mate, who was sneaking a look at the second mate. "It was a couple of blocks from our apartment."

"What kind of a laboratory was it?" I asked, mindful that the second mate was sneaking a look at me.

"It was owned by a man named Desmond Tester. He fooled around with all kinds of formulas."

"Some sort of mad scientist?"

She chuckled as she cheated another trick in her favor. "I guess he *was* kind of mad in a way. He had a very brilliant mind. I learned a great deal from him."

"Is that where you originated the Desiree creams and lotions?"

"The seed was planted there."

"How long were you with this—"

"Desmond Tester. Let me see now. Your daddy went into the Army in February of '42. I didn't know I was pregnant then or he'd never have gone. On the other hand, I suppose if I *had* known, I would have kept it to myself so your dad could go and prove he was a hero and not just a common everyday milkman."

"I don't see anything wrong in delivering milk."

"There's nothing heroic about it, either. Where was I?"

"Taking my king of hearts, which you shouldn't be."

She ignored me and favored the first mate with a seductive smile, and I blushed when the second mate winked at me. "Anyway, I took time off to give birth to you and then I went right back to work for Professor Tester. A nice lady in the neighborhood looked after you. Let me think, what was her name? Oh, yes—Blanche Yurka."

"Isn't that the name of the actress who played Ma Barker in a gangster movie we saw on the late show?"

"I don't know, isn't it? That's my ten of clubs you're taking," she said sharply.

"I've captured it fair and square with the queen of clubs," I told her. "How come you never married again?"

"I guess I was too busy being a career woman. I was assisting Professor Tester in marketing some of his creams and lotions by then. I had such a hard time cracking the department stores."

"When did you come up with your own formulas?"

"That was after the professor met with his unfortunate death."

Unfortunate, indeed. I saw her kill him.

It was Christmas of 1950—in fact, it was Christmas Day. Mom was preparing to roast a turkey at the professor's house—our apartment was much too small for entertaining—and I remember almost everyone who was there. It was mostly kids from the neighborhood, the unfortunate ones whose families couldn't afford a proper Christmas dinner. There must have been about ten of them. Mother and the professor were the only adults, although Mom still insists there was a woman there named Laurette with whom the professor was having an affair. Mom says this woman was jealous of her because she thought Mom and the professor were having a little ding-dong of their own. (I've always suspected my mother of doing quite a bit of dinging and donging in the neighborhood when she couldn't meet a grocery bill or a butcher bill or satisfy the landlord or Mr. Kumbog, who owned the liquor store.)

Mom says it was Laurette who shot the professor in the heart and ran away (and was never heard of again, need I tell you?)—but I'm getting ahead of myself. It happened like this: Mom was in the kitchen stuffing the turkey when Professor Tester appeared in the doorway dressed in the Santa Claus suit. He had stuffed his stomach but still looked no more like Santa Claus than Monty Woolley did in *Life Begins at Eight-Thirty.*

"Daisy Ray, I have to talk to you," he said.

"Just let me finish stuffing this turkey and get it in the oven," she told him. "I'd like to feed the kids by around five o'clock when I'm sure they'll be tired of playing Post Office and Spin the Bottle and Doctor." I remember her asking me, "Sonny, have you been playing Doctor?"

"As often as I can," I replied with a smirk. And I still do. Now I'm a specialist.

"Daisy Ray, come with me to the laboratory," Tester insisted.

"Oh, really, Desmond," Mother said, "I don't understand your tone of voice."

"There are a lot of things going on around here that are hard to understand," the professor said ominously. "Daisy Ray!" He sounded uncannily like Captain Bligh summoning Mr. Christian.

I caught a very strange and very scary look on my mother's face. And then she did something I now realize should have made the professor realize that something unexpected and undesirable was about to befall him. She picked up her handbag, which was hanging by its strap on the back of a chair, and followed him out of the room. "Sonny, you stay here." Her voice sounded as though it was coming from that echo chamber I heard on the spooky radio show, *The Witch's Tale.*

"Yes, Mama."

I watched her follow Professor Tester out of the kitchen. I was frightened. I was terribly frightened. I had a premonition that something awful was going to happen, so I disobeyed her orders and tiptoed after them.

The laboratory was in the basement. I waited in the hall until I heard them reach the bottom of the stairs and head for the main testing room, then I tiptoed downstairs, praying the stairs wouldn't squeak and betray me. But I had nothing to worry about. They were having a shouting match that would have drowned out the exploding of an atom bomb.

The door to the testing room was slightly ajar and I could hear everything.

"What have you done with the formula?" he raged.

"I don't know what you're talking about." Mama was quite cool, subtly underplaying him. It was one of those rare occasions when I almost admired her.

"You damn well know what I'm talking about, you thief!"

"How dare you!" What a display of indignation—had she heard it, Norma Shearer would have died of envy.

"You stole the formula for my rejuvenating cream! You've formed a partnership with the Sibonay Group in Mexico!"

"You're hallucinating. You've been taking too many of your own drugs."

"I've got a friend at Sibonay—he's told me everything! I'm going to put you behind bars unless you give me back my formula!"

Although I didn't doubt for one moment that my mother had betrayed him, I still had to put my hand over my mouth to stifle a laugh. I mean, have you ever seen Santa Claus blowing his top? It's a scream in red and white.

"Don't you touch me! Don't you lay a hand on me!" Mother's handbag was open and she was fumbling for something in it. He slapped her hard across the face. Then I heard the *pop* and the professor was clutching at his chest. Through his fingers little streams of blood began to form. Mom was holding a tiny pearl-handled pistol in her hand, the kind Kay Francis used to carry around in a beaded bag. My God, I remember saying to myself, I just saw Mommy killing Santa Claus.

I turned tail and ran. I bolted up the stairs and into the front of the house, where the other kids who couldn't possibly have heard what had gone on in the basement were busy choosing up sides for a game called Kill the Hostess. I joined in and there wasn't a peep out of Mom for at least half an hour.

I began to wonder if maybe I had been hallucinating, if maybe I hadn't seen Mom slay the professor. I left the other kids and—out of curiosity and I suppose a little anxiety—I went to the kitchen.

You've got to hand it to Mom (you might as well, she'd take it anyway): the turkey was in the oven, roasting away. She had prepared the salad. Vegetables were simmering, timed to be ready when the turkey was finished roasting. She was topping a sweet-potato pie with little round marshmallows. She looked up when I came in and asked, "Enjoying yourself, Sonny?"

I couldn't resist asking her. "When is Santa Claus coming with his bag of presents for us?"

"Good Lord, when indeed! Now, where could Santa be, do you suppose?"

Dead as a doornail in the testing room, I should have responded, but instead I said, "Shucks, Mom, it beats me."

She thought for a moment and then said brightly, "I'll bet he's downstairs working on a new formula. Go down and tell him it's time he put in his appearance."

Can you top that? Sending her son into the basement to discover the body of the man she'd just assassinated?

Well, I dutifully discovered the body and started yelling my head off, deciding that was the wisest course under the circumstances.

Mom and the kids came running. When they saw the body, the kids began shrieking, me shrieking the loudest so that maybe Mom would be proud of me, and Mom hurried and phoned the police.

What ensued after the police arrived was sheer genius on my mother's part. I don't remember the detective's name—by now he must be in that Big Squadroom in the Sky—but I'm sure if he was ever given an I.Q. test he must have ended up owing them about fifty points. Mom was saying hysterically, "Oh, my God, to think there was a murderer in the house while I was in the kitchen preparing our Christmas dinner and the children were in the parlor playing guessing games!" She carried the monologue for about ten minutes until the medical examiner came into the kitchen to tell the detective the professor had been done in by a bullet to the heart.

"Any sign of the weapon?" asked the detective.

"It's not *my* job to look for one," replied the examiner testily.

So others were dispatched to look for a weapon. Knowing Mom, it wouldn't be in her handbag, but where, I wondered, could she have stashed it? I stopped in mid-wonder when I heard her say, "It might have been Laurette."

"Who's she?" asked the detective.

Mom folded her hands, managing to look virtuous and sound scornful. "She was the professor's girl friend, if you know what I mean. He broke it off with her last week and she wasn't about to let him off so easy. She's been phoning and making threats, and this morning he told me she might be coming around to give him his Christmas present." She added darkly, "That Christmas present was called—*death!*"

"Did you see her here today?" the detective asked. Mom said she hadn't. He asked us all if we'd seen a strange lady come into the house. I was tempted to tell him the only strange lady I saw come into the house was my mother, but I thought of that formula and how wealthy we'd become and I became a truly loving son.

"She could have come in by the cellar door," I volunteered.

It was the first time I saw my mother look at me with love and admiration. "It's on the other side of the house, and with all the noise we were making—"

"And I had the radio on in the kitchen, listening to the *Make Believe Ballroom*," was the fuel Mother added to the fire I had ignited. The arson was successful. The police finally left—without finding the weapon—taking the body with them, and Mom proceeded with Christmas dinner as though killing a man was an everyday occurrence.

The dinner was delicious, although some of us kids noted the turkey had a slightly strange taste to it.

"Turkey can be gamey," Mama trilled—and within the next six months she was on her way to becoming one of the most powerful names in the cosmetics industry.

I remained a bachelor. I worked alongside Mother and her associates and watched as, one by one over the years, she got rid of all of them. She destroyed the Sibonay people in Mexico by proving falsely and at great cost, that they were the front for a dope-running operation. She thought it would be fun if I could become a mayor of New York City, but a psychic told me to forget about it and go into junk bonds—which I did and suffered staggering losses. (The psychic died a mysterious death, which she obviously hadn't foretold herself.)

Year after year, Christmas after Christmas, I was sorely tempted to tell Mama I saw her kill Santa Claus. Year after year, Christmas after Christmas, I was aching to know where she had hidden the weapon.

And then I found out. It was Christmas Day fourteen years ago.

The doctors, after numerous tests, had assured me that Mom was showing signs of Alzheimer's. Such as when applying lipstick, she ended up covering her chin with rouge. And wearing three dresses at the same time. And filing her shoes and accessories in the deep freeze. It was sad, really, even for a murderess who deserved no mercy. Yet she insisted on cooking the Christmas dinner herself that year.

"It's going to be just like that Christmas Day when we had that wonderful dinner with the neighborhood kiddies," she said. "And Professor Tester dressed up as Santa Claus and brought in that big bag of games and toys. And he gave me the wonderful gift of the exclusive rights to the formula for the Desiree Rejuvenating Lotion."

There were twenty for dinner and, believe it or not, Mother cooked it impeccably. The servants were a bit nervous, but the guests were too drunk to notice. Then, while eating the turkey, Mother asked me across the table, "Does the turkey taste the same way it did way back when, Sonny?"

And then I remembered how the turkey had tasted that day forty years ago when Mama had said something about turkey sometimes tasting gamey. I looked at her and, ill or not, there was mockery in her eyes. It was then that I said to her, not knowing if she would understand what I meant: "Mama, I saw what you did."

There was a small smile on her face. Slowly her head began to bob up and down. "I had a feeling you did," she said. "But you haven't answered me. Does the turkey taste the same way it did then?"

I spoke the truth. "No, Mama, it doesn't. It's very good."

She was laughing like a madwoman. Everyone at the table

looked embarrassed and there was nowhere for me to hide. "Is this a private joke between you and your mother?" the man at my right asked me. But I couldn't answer. Because my mother had reached across the table and shoved her hand into the turkey's cavity, obscenely pulling out gobs of stuffing and flinging it at me.

"Don't you know why the turkey tasted strange? Can't you guess why, Sonny? Can't you guess what I hid in the stuffing so those dam fool cops wouldn't find it? Can't you guess, Sonny? Can't you?"

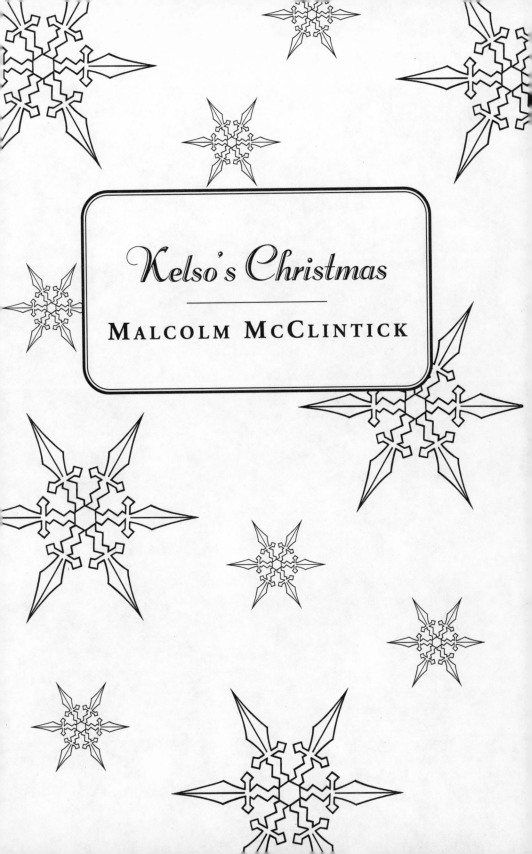

Kelso's Christmas

MALCOLM McCLINTICK

SOMEONE HAD MURDERED A SANTA CLAUS.

The body, rotund and clad in the traditional red suit, lay in a corner behind the gift wrap section, in the basement, hidden from the view of passing customers by a counter and stacks of cardboard boxes. He still wore his long white beard and mustache, but the hat had come off and lay a foot from his head, revealing black hair with a bald spot on top.

George Kelso looked down at the body, then at Detective Sergeant Meyer. It was ten A.M., three days before Christmas, in one of the larger downtown department stores.

"Okay," Meyer said, "let's get this area cleared so the lab boys can get to work." He sounded tired. Kelso understood that it wasn't fatigue, but depression. Every year at Christmas Meyer, a small dark Jewish man, became depressed and usually withdrawn. It was no good talking to him about it, it was something Meyer had to live with and work out for himself, at least until he became willing to confide in his associates at the police department.

"I was supposed to go shopping this afternoon with Susan," Kelso said to nobody in particular. "I suppose that's out of the question now."

"I suppose it is," Meyer replied. "All right, Kelso, why don't you take the offices upstairs and I'll check with the clerks. The other guys are talking to customers to see if anybody noticed anything unusual."

"I'll go talk to the business staff," Kelso agreed. When Meyer was in his Christmas funk, it was best to agree with whatever he said. The store's music system was playing "Winter Wonderland" over the noise and confusion of shoppers, and a few feet away, a little boy was screaming and trying to kick his mother, who looked flustered.

Kelso headed for the elevators.

Kelso himself became somewhat depressed at Christmas, but not for the same reasons as Meyer. For one thing, he found himself constantly thrown in with relatives at this time of year, and none of them especially liked him. Being unable to understand what had possessed him to seek a career as a police detective, they tended to regard him with suspicion and hostility. One of his more enlightened uncles had once referred to Kelso behind his back (but within easy hearing distance) as "that fascist," and a younger niece had often called him a pig. He had been forbidden to bring his gun to the various family dinners, though it was the last thing he would have brought, and whenever he entered a room everyone stopped talking and stared as if, he thought, expecting him to make an arrest.

For another, Christmas jarred his nerves. He had been brought up in a deeply religious family and the season had been the highlight of his year. It had seemed magical, with its aura of good cheer, its feeling of universal peace. Then he'd grown into adulthood to find all of that shattered by the reality of global conflict, mass murders, tough cynicism, and his own rapidly fading belief in anything magical. Ultimately, he'd come to view Christmas as an elaborate hoax perpetrated on a gullible public by department store managers, advertising executives, and toy manufacturers.

And now someone had killed Santa Claus.

But the dead man wasn't really Santa Claus. Kelso rode up to the eighth floor executive offices, going over the victim's particulars in his mind. Arnold Wundt, fifty-five, in charge of accounting, divorced, wife and kids on the west coast, quiet and bookish, non-drinker, nonsmoker, rarely dated, few friends. Who would want to kill such a man? Someone had wanted to.

Someone, at about nine thirty that morning, according to the coroner's man, had cornered Arnold Wundt behind the gift wrapping counter and shoved a long thin knife directly into his plump body, angling it upward from just below his ribs and penetrating his heart, killing him almost instantly. That someone had left the knife in the bloodstained corpse and was now back at work, or shopping for presents, or on a plane bound for the Bahamas. It was anybody's guess.

"May I help you, sir?"

Kelso had entered the manager's outer office and stood looking down at a receptionist's desk, suddenly realizing where he was, as if he'd awakened abruptly from a dream. He found his unlit pipe in one hand, his overcoat in the other.

"Sergeant Kelso," he said. "Police department. I wonder if I could talk to Mr. Anderson?"

"Oh, is it about the murder?" The girl was under twenty-five, blonde, cheerful, blue-eyed, slightly plump. She was the kind of healthy, well-fed girl who'd have been a cheerleader at some midwestern university. Ohio State, Kelso thought. Or Purdue.

"Yes, ma'am," he said, noticing a gold band on her ring finger.

A big, healthy smile. "Just a minute, sergeant." She got up and went through a door behind her desk, returned almost immediately with another smile. "Go right in. Mr. Anderson's out right now, but his assistant, Mr. Briggs, will help you."

"Thanks."

Mr. Briggs was short, probably five seven or so, heavy, with oversized glasses that greatly magnified his round, staring eyes, making him look like some sort of surprised bug. His wide lips were fixed in a permanent smile. A surprised, happy bug. He held a large sandwich, trying to stuff oversized bites of it into his wide mouth. There were reddish stains on the sleeves of his white shirt, and a piece of lettuce on his pants leg.

"Stupid cafeteria," he said around a mouthful, and dabbed with a napkin at his sleeve. "They always get too much ketchup on these things. I must've told them a hundred times." He swallowed, finally, and glared. "Can't finish it. Too messy." He wrapped the remains in a paper napkin and dropped it into a wastebasket, then held out a small pale hand. "Glad to meet you, Sergeant Kelsy."

"Kelso," he corrected, and sighed.

"Right. Kelso. Glad to meet you. Been shopping, sergeant? We've got some terrific deals on suits." The bug cast a critical eye at Kelso's battered corduroy suit. "Fix you right up. No? Well, I guess it's business, isn't it? Terrible about poor Wundt."

"I'd like to ask you a few questions, Mr. Briggs." Kelso took out his notebook and ballpoint, putting away his pipe and dropping his overcoat onto a chair. "Could you tell me—"

"Listen, sergeant." The bug's manner became suddenly confidential. He hurried across the office to the door, seemed to make certain it was tightly closed, and scurried back behind the polished desk. "I'd better tell you something. I don't know how much it's got to do with poor Wundt, but you'd better know about it. Sergeant—" Briggs glanced left and right in a comic imitation of some movie character about to reveal The Big Secret "—someone in this store's been embezzling money."

The words alone were normal enough; Kelso had encountered numerous embezzlers. It was the exaggerated way in which Briggs had spoken the words—his pop-eyed stare, his stage whisper, his air of a little kid confiding something about men from Mars to his best friend.

"Embezzling?" Kelso scribbled in his notebook. Fortunately Briggs couldn't see it, because Kelso had written: "Comic book character."

"Embezzling, sergeant. Somebody's been skimming money right off the top. It amounts to over a hundred thousand to date. And not only that, I think I know who it was."

Kelso allowed a theatrical pause before asking, "Who?"

Briggs leaned closer, looking immensely satisfied with himself, and whispered loudly: "Arnold Wundt."

"Wundt?" Kelso frowned, not even pretending surprise.

"Right. Listen, sergeant. Wundt was an accountant, and a good one. He was, in fact, in charge of accounting. But as the assistant manager, and I've got a degree in accounting myself—" he cleared his throat loudly "—I'm not only qualified but also duty-bound to check Wundt's work. And I caught him at it, sergeant. Now, if you ask me, someone else caught him at it, too. Someone who maybe tried to blackmail him and then, when he couldn't bleed him any more, got rid of him."

Kelso nodded slowly, as if considering what Briggs had said.

The little bug was a waste of time. It was too hot in the office and he was hungry for lunch.

"You don't happen to know where Mr. Anderson is, do you?" he asked, trying to sound polite.

"I think he was going to meet with Wundt about something," Briggs said, smiling his bugsmile. "I haven't seen him since about nine thirty, when he left to go downstairs. Come to think of it, he said he was on his way to gift wrap. Yes, I'm certain. Gift wrap. About nine thirty." Briggs seemed to emphasize the last words, and gave Kelso a meaningful look.

Suddenly Kelso realized what Briggs reminded him of. Not a bug at all, but a toy he'd gotten one year for Christmas, a rubber or plastic likeness of Froggy the Gremlin, pop eyes, leering smile. Briggs was Froggy the Gremlin with oversized glasses. And probably about as bright.

"I appreciate your help," Kelso told him, trying not to sound sarcastic. "Well, have a nice day."

"Merry Christmas, sergeant," said Froggy. "A *very* merry Christmas."

Kelso winced and left the office. The blonde cheerleader beamed at him and said, "Merry Christmas, sergeant."

"Same to you," he replied, as though returning an insult, and hurried for the elevators.

"I wasn't able to find out a damn thing," Detective Sergeant Meyer said. "As far as anybody knows, Wundt reported to his office in accounting this morning at nine sharp, as usual. He works alone. Nobody saw him or noticed him again till the gift wrap girl found his body behind her counter at a quarter to ten, when she was coming back from the ladies' room." The small detective shrugged. "That's it. Nobody saw anything, nobody knows anything. Everybody liked Wundt, but not very well. Nobody disliked him. He was a nothing, a zero."

"He was a Santa Claus," said Kelso.

They sat in the store's cafeteria, the noon crowd chattering and munching around them. Meyer glared at his meatloaf and said:

"Yeah, he was a Santa Claus. Why can't people make meatloaf anymore? My grandmother used to make delicious meatloaf. This stuff is still red in the center. Don't they cook it?"

"I thought you only ate kosher."

"Nuts. I eat anything. Jewish food happens to taste better, but that doesn't mean I can't eat what I want. I'm enlightened."

"Ah." Kelso nodded. "I wonder if Arnold Wundt's playing Santa had anything to do with his murder."

"He was scheduled to fill in for the regular Santa this morning," Meyer said. "The store's been having Santa in a booth for the kids every morning at ten and every afternoon at two and five, each shopping day till Christmas. What a zoo. I'm glad I don't have kids. All my friends with kids are raising schizophrenics. All of them have split personalities—half Jewish, half Christian. I tell you, it's hell having a kid in this country if you're a Jew at Christmas."

"Schizophrenic doesn't mean split personality," Kelso pointed out. "I've taken some psych courses. It means—"

"Forget what it means." Meyer stabbed at his meatloaf.

Over the hubbub drifted the faint sounds of "Sleigh Ride." At a nearby table two little girls sang "Jingle Bells," egged on by their overweight mother, who seemed to think her mission was to entertain the other shoppers with her offspring and their whining voices.

"Who was supposed to have been Santa this morning?" Kelso asked.

"Huh? Oh, you mean whose place did Wundt take?" Meyer thought for a moment. "The assistant manager. Guy named Briggs."

"Froggy the Gremlin," Kelso murmured.

"What?"

"Nothing. So Briggs was supposed to have been Santa Claus."

"I'm taking this meatloaf back. It's inedible. You'd think with all their peace on earth and good will they could cook a piece of meatloaf enough to make it edible." Meyer got up and carried his plate through the milling crowd to the food line, and returned a few minutes later with the same plate, scowling.

"What happened?" Kelso asked.

"They told me to eat it," he said. "They told me I ordered meatloaf and I got meatloaf. They told me Merry Christmas."

"Greetings of the season," Kelso told him.

Meyer muttered something under his breath. The two little girls sang "Deck the Halls" at the top of their lungs.

Meyer became convinced that the murderer was the gift wrap girl, a tall brunette named Claudia Collins. She stood several inches taller than Meyer, something which, Kelso knew, infuriated him; she was sullen, even while wrapping customers' gifts, which infuriated everybody; and she was the only employee who would admit to having been in or near the gift wrap area at or about the time of the murder, nine thirty that morning.

"I'm going to question her some more," Meyer announced as he and Kelso left the cafeteria. "I'm not letting some dumb broad spoil my holiday. If she stabbed that accountant, I'll get it out of her."

"By the way," Kelso said, resisting the urge to light his pipe. "When I talked to Briggs this morning, he accused Arnold Wundt of embezzling over a hundred thousand dollars from the store."

Meyer shot him a dark look. "You're kidding. How would Briggs know that?"

"He says he's got an accounting degree, and checked Wundt's work."

"Huh." Meyer's wheels turned. They stopped turning. "Claudia Collins probably found out about Wundt's embezzling. She probably tried to extort some money from him. He pulled a knife on her, and she managed to stab him with it. Well, I'm going to find her. You check around the store. Keep your eyes and ears open, and let me know if you hear anything else."

"Have a good time," Kelso said.

Meyer nodded solemnly, as though it had been a serious wish. "I will."

They parted. Kelso watched the detective shove his way into the crowd until it engulfed him; then someone grabbed his arm.

"George!"

He turned. Susan Overstreet's wide brown eyes smiled at him. She was running one hand through wavy blonde hair and using the other to hold a shopping bag crammed with packages.

"Hi."

"Isn't this hectic? I've already got five of the things on my list. Listen, go with me to the children's department, up on three, so we can find something for Peggy and Timmy. Then—"

"Hold on a minute, Susan. I can't—"

"Did you find that aftershave for your uncle? There's a sale in men's stuff. By the way, tonight we've got the eggnog party at my Aunt Eleanor's house, and she says—"

"Susan!"

"Huh? What is it?"

"I can't go shopping with you. Haven't you heard about the murder?"

"Murder! What murder?"

"One of the employees, the head of accounting. They found him this morning, stabbed, in a Santa Claus suit. I'm on duty till further notice."

"But you had the afternoon off."

"I know. But now I don't."

"Well, darn."

A tall gray-haired man in an expensive suit and tie stepped out of the crowd. "Sergeant Kelso?"

"Yes, sir?"

"I'm James Anderson, the store manager." He offered a firm hand. "Sorry I missed you this morning."

"Glad to meet you, Mr. Anderson." He glanced at Susan. "This woman's been following me around the store, but I don't think she's done anything illegal. Did you pay for those items, miss?"

Susan smiled sweetly. "This man seems to think he's a policeman, Mr. Anderson, but I've seen him following other women around the store. I think he may be dangerous. Excuse me."

Kelso smiled blandly at the manager's quizzical look. "Just a little joke, Mr. Anderson. Uh, could we talk in your office?"

"Certainly."

They took the elevator up to eight, passed the cheerleader, and entered the office where Kelso had interviewed Briggs. Anderson sat down behind the polished desk and folded his hands. "Have you come up with anything, sergeant?" He looked grave.

Kelso started to answer, then hesitated. The office door was slightly ajar. By moving a little to his left he could just see the toes of someone's shoes.

"We haven't come up with anything officially," he said.

Anderson looked interested. "But, unofficially?"

"Unofficially, Mr. Anderson, I believe we know who murdered Arnold Wundt." Kelso took out his pipe and some matches. There was an ashtray on the manager's desk. "At least, I believe *I* know who murdered him. He was to have played Santa Claus this morning, right?"

"No, I believe that would have been Mr. Briggs."

"But apparently Wundt took his place for some reason."

"Oh. Right. I remember now. Briggs had a meeting to attend. But who was it, sergeant? Who killed Wundt, and why?"

Kelso got his pipe going and puffed at it a couple of times. "I've sent some of my men over to Headquarters to get an accountant for me. When they get back, the accountant will check some things, and then I'll make an arrest. I really don't want to name names till the accountant gets here."

"I see."

The door opened and Briggs stepped into the office, eyes popping behind his thick lenses. "Mr. Anderson—oh, excuse me, I didn't know you were with someone. Oh, hello, Sergeant Kelso."

Kelso nodded. His pipe went out.

"What is it, Briggs?"

"It's about Santa Claus this afternoon, Mr. Anderson. The customers are really upset about missing him this morning, and it's one thirty now. They're already lining up for the two P.M. Santa."

"Can't you do it, Briggs?" Anderson's tone was sharp.

"No, sir. I'm afraid not. That is, I'd very much like not to. It's occurred to me that it might be dangerous."

"What?"

"I mean, sir—suppose the killer knew I was to play Santa at ten this morning. Suppose the killer found Santa behind the gift wrap counter. Everybody looks alike in that outfit, with the pillow and whiskers and all. The killer would have assumed it was me, and stabbed him. But by now he probably knows it was the wrong person."

"Is that possible, Sergeant Kelso? Could the murderer have been after Briggs here, instead of Wundt?"

"It's possible," Kelso said, trying hard to suppress laughter. He was imagining a cold-blooded killer stalking Froggy the Gremlin.

"Well, who are we going to get? We've got to have someone."

"I've played Santa at the police Christmas party a few times," Kelso said. "I could do it."

Anderson stared, then slowly nodded. Briggs smiled his face-breaking smile, his pop eyes dancing with delight behind his glasses.

"It's not exactly in the line of duty for a police officer," Anderson said. "But we could certainly use you."

"I'd be glad to help out. I tend to put on a few pounds over the holidays." Kelso patted his stomach. "I won't even need much of a pillow."

"Good." The manager stood up, all business. "Briggs, get Sergeant Kelso a Santa suit and show him the booth. Thank you, sergeant. I won't forget this."

Kelso let himself be led away by the assistant manager. When they were out in the hall he said:

"Excuse me, is the Santa Claus outfit at the booth?"

Briggs nodded. "Yes, down on the main floor."

"I'll meet you there," Kelso said. "I've got to go to the men's room."

Briggs nodded, beaming, and Kelso hurried down the hall.

The killer stood in line, waiting for Santa. With his left hand he held the hand of a little boy whom he'd talked into standing in line with him, a third grader named Kevin whose mother worked in Credit and Layaway. The killer had paid Kevin five dollars and told him he wanted to talk to Santa but, as an adult, was embarrassed to go without a child. Kevin had taken the money and agreed to help.

In front of the killer and Kevin stood a fat woman whose two small girls had just finished singing "Rudolph the Red-nosed Reindeer" in strident voices and were starting "Silent Night," encouraged by their mother. Ahead of them an attractive black woman waited her turn, whispering to a frightened little boy. Just inside a white cardboard fence surrounding a cardboard sleigh and eight cardboard reindeer, a jolly Santa sat on a red chair, holding a small girl on his knee while the girl's mother, presumably, looked on. There was so much noise in the store, with all the talking and laughter and music and the whining of the fat lady's daughters, that the killer couldn't make out what was being said by the jolly Santa and the small girl, but it didn't matter to him.

The killer's other hand was inside his suitcoat pocket, gripping the handle of a small automatic pistol, fully loaded. He smiled as if thoroughly enjoying himself and nodded once in a while at little Kevin, who kept chattering something about a Star Wars toy. He wanted to tell little Kevin that he was an obnoxious brat, but he kept smiling and pretended to be having a good time.

The killer's name was Briggs.

For over a year he'd been embezzling money from the department store, but last week that fool, Arnold Wundt, had caught him at it. Wundt had threatened to go to the police unless Briggs replaced every cent he'd taken. He'd had to kill him, of course.

And now this detective, this Kelso, seemed to have gotten wise to him. An accountant was coming. Kelso would manage to link the embezzlement to Wundt's murder. Briggs couldn't let that happen.

He hadn't planned to kill Wundt in the Santa suit; it had just happened that way. But now the cops, except Kelso, were looking for a Santa Claus connection. He'd kill Kelso in the Santa suit and add to the confusion.

His fingers tightened on the automatic as the attractive black woman stepped forward and boosted her little boy onto Santa's knee.

"Ho ho ho," said the jolly Santa in a strangely rasping voice, but Briggs wasn't fooled by the disguise.

Next in line were the two singing brats; then it would be the killer's turn.

Briggs watched little Kevin step up to the red-painted chair.

"Ho ho ho," rasped the voice.

He had to admit that the disguise was good—with the full white beard and drooping mustache, the red hat pulled low over the forehead, steel-rimmed spectacles on the nose, and the padding in the suit, the character bore little resemblance to Sergeant Kelso. But Briggs knew it was.

He stepped forward, drew the automatic from his pocket, and held it close to his chest, aimed at the Santa suit. The gun was between his body and Santa's, invisible to the waiting shoppers.

"That's enough, Kevin," Briggs said, smiling. "Get down now, and let me have my turn."

Kevin nodded, slid down, and walked away.

The eyes behind the spectacles widened slightly.

"I don't want to shoot you," Briggs said, smiling. "But I will. Believe me, I will. Take a break now. I'll tell them Santa has to take a break." He jabbed with the gun.

Santa stood up. Briggs hid the gun and turned to face the crowd.

"Ladies and gentlemen, old Santa has to take a short break, but he'll be right back." He turned. "Get moving, Kelso. We're going to the basement. If you do what I say, maybe you've got a chance."

He would kill him in the basement. No one would hear the shot over this bedlam. They walked through the crowd.

"Keep walking," he said.

It was taking too long. He couldn't shoot Kelso here in the middle of the main floor. If they didn't get to the basement before something happened, he'd have to turn and run from the store. He felt confused. The plan no longer seemed nearly as workable as when he'd first thought of it. Kelso is the only one who's sure, Briggs had thought. Get rid of Kelso and everything will be all right. But now it occurred to him that some of those women and children might remember him, remember that he'd gone off with Santa. He'd have to kill Kelso, if he could, and leave town immediately with what money he had. His chances were limited. He was sweating.

It was too late to turn back now. He'd made his move.

Briggs held one of Santa's arms, steering him around a corner and along a narrow corridor that led to a basement stairway, aiming the gun with his other hand. Briggs was short; for some reason Kelso seemed shorter than he had earlier. Just as his face went hot with the realization that something was wrong, a hand came from nowhere and gripped his wrist painfully, twisting it so that he dropped the pistol. Powerful hands grabbed him and shoved him hard against the wall of the corridor.

"You're under arrest," said George Kelso. Kelso stood in the middle of the hall in his corduroy suit, flanked by three uniformed cops with drawn revolvers. "The charges are embezzlement and murder."

Briggs stared. "Kelso! Then who the hell . . ."

The Santa person pulled the beard and mustache away and removed the hat. Briggs saw a smiling, attractive girl with blonde hair and brown eyes.

"Are you all right, Susan?" Kelso asked.

"Ho ho ho," said the girl.

Kelso, Meyer, and Susan Overstreet sat at a table in the store's cafeteria. "Silver Bells" played from the speakers, and shoppers at neighboring tables laughed and rustled their packages.

"Look at this meatloaf," said Meyer, poking at it with his fork. "Now they've practically burned it."

"Actually, mine's not too bad." Kelso took a bite. "I was starving."

"So how did you make the switch with Susan?" Meyer asked.

"I went to the men's room," Kelso said. "When I was sure nobody else was in there, I let Susan in and we put the Santa outfit on her."

"Incredible," Meyer shook his head. "You're lucky nobody walked in on you."

"I was leaning against the door."

"Sergeant Meyer?" Susan smiled at the detective. "Would you like to come over to my aunt's house tonight for some eggnog? If you wouldn't be uncomfortable. I mean, we won't sing any carols or anything, and Aunt Eleanor doesn't have a tree this year, just a few lights in the window."

"Trees are too expensive for people on fixed incomes," Kelso said, trying not to sound angry.

"So, will you come? We'd like to have you."

Meyer put down his fork and cleared his throat. "Nobody's ever invited me to have eggnog before," he said quietly. "Tell your aunt I'd like to come." He stood up. "I can't eat this stuff. I'll leave you two alone." He started away, then added: "Take the rest of the afternoon off, Kelso."

"Gee, thanks." Kelso glanced at his watch. "All forty-three minutes, huh?"

"Well," Susan said, eyeing him closely, "are you going to tell me how you knew?"

"Knew what?"

"Don't do that. How you knew it was Briggs."

"Oh." He shrugged. "Briggs made a couple of mistakes. He tried to convince me that Anderson, the store manager, had gone down to gift wrap at nine thirty. He kept emphasizing nine thirty. But why? I was the first one to question him, and only the other cops knew about the coroner's estimate of nine thirty as the time of the stabbing. But the murderer would have known. That was one thing."

"Hmm. What else?"

"He was too eager to tell me about the embezzlement, and to blame it on Arnold Wundt. If he'd been so certain, why hadn't he exposed Wundt himself, earlier? So I wondered if maybe Briggs was the embezzler, and not Wundt. Maybe Wundt had found him out, and Briggs had killed him to keep him quiet." Kelso shrugged. "Turns out I was right."

Susan blinked and folded her arms across her chest. "That's it? That's all? I put on a Santa suit and risked my life for nine thirty and some talk about an embezzlement?"

"Well, there was one other thing . . ."

"Tell me."

"Well, when I visited Briggs in Anderson's office, he was eating a sandwich of some kind. He kept dabbing at his shirtsleeve and complaining about how the cafeteria always put too much ketchup on the bread. But after I left him in the hall, I went back to the office and found his sandwich in the trash. There wasn't any ketchup on it." Kelso paused. "That stuff on his sleeve was blood."

"Yuk."

"Incidentally, can't your aunt really afford a tree this year?"

"It'd be tough. She buys a lot of presents. You're coming tonight, aren't you? Do you think Meyer will come?"

"Sergeant Kelso—" A tall, well-dressed man hurried up to their table. It was Anderson, the store manager, looking breathless. "Finally found you."

"Don't tell me something else has happened," Kelso said.

"We're supposed to have another Santa session in fifteen minutes, sergeant. With Wundt dead and Briggs in custody, there's nobody to do it. So I was wondering . . ."

It wasn't fair, he thought. He was almost off duty. He was tired. He wanted to go home and relax. He needed a bath, and he was sick to death of the chatter of mothers and children, the tinny music, the announcements of sales in this or that department.

Susan had done it once. She'd looked cute in the padded red suit and whiskers. He turned a pleading glance in her direction, trying to look desperate. She smiled, but slowly shook her head no.

"What do you say, sergeant? Will you help out? Please?"

It wasn't fair. He sighed heavily in resignation. He nodded.

"Good man," said Anderson.

"That's the Christmas spirit," Susan said.

Kelso scowled.

Kelso met Meyer at the door. Outside it was snowing. "Come in. You're late."

"I could leave," said Meyer testily.

"Nonsense. Susan's aunt wants to meet you, and there's still plenty of eggnog. You're letting in the snow."

Meyer came in dragging a small, well-shaped tree and a paper bag.

"What's this?" Kelso asked suspiciously.

"Some sort of festive plant." Meyer frowned. "Silly lights and ornaments to hang on it. Somebody killed a tree so you people could celebrate."

Kelso was moved. He stood for a moment, feeling a little of the old magic.

"Happy holidays, Meyer," he said.

Meyer nodded. "Merry Christmas, Kelso."

There was much cheer in the house that night.

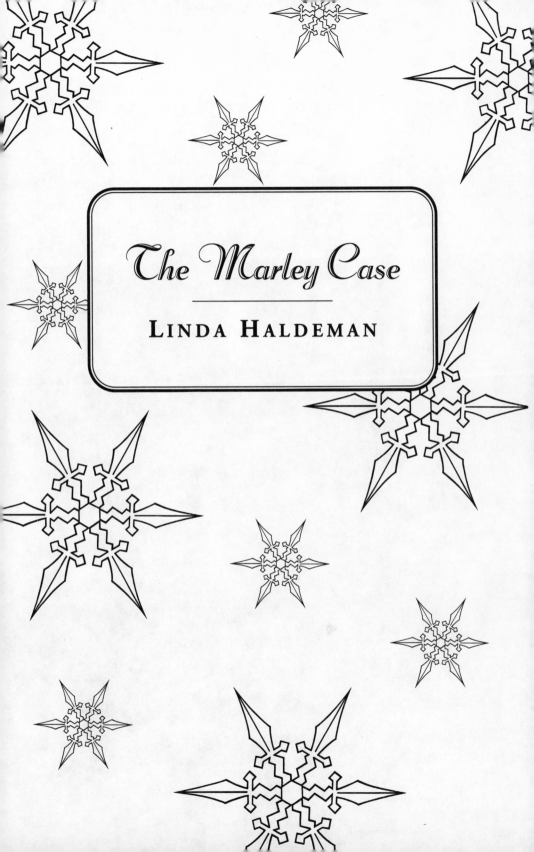

The Marley Case

LINDA HALDEMAN

W E DO CHRISTMAS RIGHT AT OUR HOUSE— the holly and the ivy and the manger and the tree. Stockings all hung and an ever full wassail bowl for thirsty carollers. I use the pronoun "we" editorially, for all this holiday jollity comes your way with the compliments of Joyce and the kids. I'm not much of a celebrator myself, and even in my youth avoided when possible all those cherished tribal rituals.

Some people don't. Joyce, for instance. For years I didn't understand. I thought it was just for the children, all the decking of halls and jingling of bells and harking of herald angels. But as the children grew up, the merry mayhem diminished not at all, and I still find myself in my middle years surrounded by a trio of oversized moppets bandaging boxes in miles of red satin ribbon and spreading tinsel all over everything.

A week before this Christmas just past, I was force fed a certain minimal dose of spirit when I was carted to the church youth club's annual dramatization of *A Christmas Carol*. This, I must admit, is one of the less objectionable parts of the customary Saturnalia. It's not the Royal Shakespeare Company, to be sure, but it certainly is an improvement on the pageants of my childhood, where at least one angel fainted every year and the wise men always forgot their lines. As in everything else seasonal, the family had a considerable stake in this production. Stephanie, in a billowy gauze gown that reminded me painfully of a Sunday School angel's robe, was the Ghost of Christmas Past.

"Long past?" the boy who played Scrooge asked warily.

"No, your past," Steffy replied in a thin, æthereal voice that actually made me, her father, shiver. I have at times envisioned Steffy as a basketball coach or a carnival barker, but certainly not as an actress, and not with that voice. Remarkable.

Mark played, of course, Tiny Tim. He's small for his age and is able to project a deceptive air of cherubic innocence.

"God bless us every one," he intoned with the falsetto intensity of a child evangelist. It was a performance that melted poor sentimental old Scrooge's heart. It hardened mine, not just because I could not fully separate Mark smiling sweetly onstage from Mark raising hell at the dinner table, but because I always suspect virtuous children.

We stopped at Mister Donut on the way home. Steffy, no longer ghostly, had a double chocolate doughnut and a cup of hot chocolate. I could almost see the acne pop out. Mark, choosing, it seems, to remain for a while in character, selected something gooey called "angel filled."

"It's remarkable," said Joyce, "how a great piece like that doesn't date. But then the Christmas spirit doesn't date, either."

"Bah!" I said. "Humbug!"

"Oh, Daddy," Steffy sighed as only an adolescent daughter can.

"You know," I went on, "I've often wondered about one thing. Just as it says: 'Marley was dead: to begin with. There is no doubt whatever about that.'" (I was proud to quote with such perfect accuracy, for the kids were obviously impressed. And how often can a man of my age and shortcomings impress his kids?) "Okay. Marley was dead. But what did he die of?"

"I don't know, probably a stroke or a heart attack," said Joyce. "After all, he was a classic type A personality."

"Have you considered the possibility of foul play?"

There. I had caught their attention, dropped a curdling dollop of vinegar into their emotional eggnog of peace and goodwill. What fun.

"Oh, I get it," Mark exclaimed in an astounding show of insight, for him. "He could have been murdered."

"Now who would do that?" Joyce laughed.

"Look for a motive."

"Scrooge himself would be a prime suspect," said Steffy. She's quick-witted for a ghost and a sophomore, and she shares my love of detective fiction. "He had a motive. Money. He inherited Marley's half of the business, right?"

"Too obvious," I said. "The obvious suspect is never the real culprit."

"Anyhow," Mark chimed in, "if Scrooge had done him in, why would Marley have come back from the dead to save him? I bet it was good old Tiny Tim, bashed the old skinflint's brains out with his crutch for not paying his father a decent wage."

"Impossible," Steffy snickered. "How old do you think Tiny Tim was, midget? He probably wasn't even born when Marley died. 'Mr. Marley has been dead these seven years,' Scrooge says. Bob Cratchit might not even have worked for Scrooge and Marley then. Faced you, hosehead!"

Occasionally, not often, mind you, but every now and then, your children make you proud.

We celebrate Christmas early now that the children are older, one tradition that I like, for it gets the worst of it out of the way and permits the household to settle back more quickly into the blessed monotony of the midwinter doldrums. It all starts on Christmas Eve, with an extensive carolling tour of the neighborhood, ending up at St. Nicholas (no less) Parish Church in time for Midnight Mass. I don't attend, especially at Christmas, for of all tinsel, liturgical tinsel is the most incongruous.

I was feeling particularly Scroogish about the whole business this year, so I took my dinner, a slapdash hoagie on an undersized bun (fast before feast, I suppose), sought refuge in the den, and did not show my face until the merry revellers were ready to leave. Then I sent them off with a resounding, "Bah! Humbug!" which was greeted with much untoward merriment.

"Oh, Daddy," said Stephanie.

"Don't get into the brandy," Joyce warned.

I waved to them from the doorway, then went back inside the house and watched them from the living room window until they had turned a corner and could no longer see the house. Then I turned off the string of colored lights that outlined our front porch, pulled the plug on the Christmas tree, and got into the brandy. Not terribly, for brandy gives a vicious hangover, just enough to make me mellow. Once I was sufficiently mellow, I turned out all the other lights and went to bed.

That was a mistake. Sometimes brandy works, and sometimes it backfires. I don't know that it really was the brandy's fault. The house was so empty, so silent. For the last month I had longed and prayed for silence and solitude, but now that I had it in abundance I found it a hollow and empty state.

And then there was the moon, which had the bad taste to be full on a cloudless cold night. It was a silver-white moon, shining down unshaded on a silver-white earth. Too much, much too much, as if the entire universe had been hung with tinsel. And the light wouldn't stay outside where it belonged; the damned washed-out white light slithered in around gaps in the lined drapes and crawled across the bed to sit glaring on my eyelids and murder sleep. I lay under that light brooding, I don't know why, on the fate of one Jacob Marley, dead nearly a century and a half.

Finally giving up the struggle, I crept out from under the electric blanket, shrugged on my slippers and went downstairs. The moonlight followed me, illuminating the stairs and the wide entrance hall. The living room curtains were sheer and generously invited all the moonlight in the vicinity inside, as to a silver-white open house. The Christmas tree stood before the large bay window looking tacky as only an unlighted Christmas tree can. The trees outside, undecorated even by their own natural foliage, silhouetted by the overpowering moonlight, appeared like black spectres, skeletal, ominous. I turned quickly about, went into my study across the hall, closed the door, drew the drapes, and turned on the comfortably warm yellow reading lamp.

The third shelf of the bookcase that lined one wall held a handsome leather bound set of the complete works of Dickens, an inheritance from my grandfather that I had not bothered for years. I took out the volume titled *Christmas Stories* and settled back in my recliner, opened it, and read aloud softly into the moonlight.

"'Marley was dead: to begin with. There is no doubt whatever about that.'"

"Amen say I to that," declared a voice deep as the Pit, yet thin as a breath. I jumped up with a cry, dropping the book. In front of me stood the ghost of Jacob Marley, exactly as Dickens had described it, a tall stocky man in waistcoat and boots dragging along with him a large wrought iron chain to which ledgers, keys, padlocks, purses, and the like were attached every few links, like charms on a bracelet. He was so transparent that I could read through him the titles of my grandfather's set of Dickens on the bookshelf behind him.

"What the hell?" I cried, realizing as the words left my mouth how absurdly unDickensian they sounded. The apparition did not crack a smile, prevented perhaps by a strip of white cloth bound around its head from jaw to balding crown.

"Marley, sir," he said. "Jacob Marley."

He offered his transparent hand, and I automatically held my own out to shake, then drew back.

"With all due respect, Mr. Marley," I said, my voice admittedly a little tremulous, "this is very absurd. What do you want with me, anyway? God knows, I keep Christmas. Look at that damned tree out there. It must have a pound of tinsel on it. Do you know that I actually sing along at the elementary Christmas program sing-along? That's keeping Christmas with a vengeance."

"Keep Christmas in your own way, and let me keep it in mine," the Ghost said illogically.

"By scaring the living daylights out of innocent people in the middle of the night?"

The Ghost sighed. "I am doomed to wander through the world trying to do the good I failed to do in life."

"What possible good could you do me?"

"I would lay you," replied the Ghost.

I said, "Good God," and sat down quickly. My chair of its own will flew back into the reclining position, pitching me back with a jarring thump. I closed my eyes and tried to bring order to my gyrating thoughts. It was possible, of course, that all this time I was safe and asleep under the warmth of the electric blanket and the influence of a slight overdose of brandy, dreaming. Or my subconscious had finally won the battle for my mind, and I was

hallucinating in the den, enthroned like some mad king on my recliner, where I couldn't do anyone much harm. But, being a ratio-
nal person, even in the worst extremity, I expect my hallucinations
to be consistent and make sense.

"I think you have that wrong, Jacob," I said very quietly, wondering if it might be wiser to attempt to wake myself rather than
waste intellectual energy reasoning with a trick of the right brain.
On the other hand, I was a little afraid I would find that I was not
asleep at all. "As you are the ghost, I ought to be laying you."

"If you could, I should be most grateful," Marley's Ghost said
courteously. "For you see, though you are in the flesh and I in the
spirit, we share a common affliction. We do not find rest in the
night."

"Well, if someone would turn the moon down, I might be able
to get some sleep."

"You walk the night only when the moon is full?" the Ghost
asked. "I do not think so."

"Well, a little darkness might help. I don't know why the hell I
can't sleep. If the story runs true, you can't rest because you were a
miserable, stingy bastard in life, and now you have to go around
scaring other miserable, stingy bastards into playing Santa Claus. If
that's what you're after here, you certainly picked the wrong house."

"I came here because you thought of me," said Marley's Ghost.
"It is the thought of me that keeps you awake. You have asked a
question that has never been asked before, not even by he who created me. To lay you is an easy matter; we must simply find the answer to your question."

I looked at the shade in astonishment. "Surely you know what
you died of?"

He shook his head. "I exist only to the degree in which I have
been thought about. He who created me did not think about the

manner of my death; therefore the manner of my death did not exist, at least not until you inquired into it."

"I wasn't all that interested," I grumbled. "I was just making conversation."

"If you were just making conversation, how is it that you do not sleep?"

"Damned if I know."

The Ghost shuddered, causing his chain to roll thuddingly along the carpeting. "My dear sir, I beseech you. Avoid that expression. As it stands you have aroused my curiosity, and since for whatever reason we have both been deprived of our repose this Christmas Eve, we might amusingly and perhaps profitably pass the time exploring the mystery, eh?"

I shrugged. "Why don't you go on without me? I think I'm going to mosey on back to bed."

I got up and started to move past him, but his transparent hand caught my forearm in a remarkably strong grip.

"Come now, my dear fellow, don't be hasty. I cannot travel alone, incorporeal as I am, and a very minor ghost at that. I must justify any journey that I make like some otherworldly civil servant, and you could be my justification. Besides I was a man of business and had not the imagination to solve mysteries. You could be of much assistance."

"And what do I get out of it?"

"Unless I am much mistaken, my dear sir," said Marley's Ghost, "you are not the sort of fellow who sleeps well on an empty belly or an unanswered question. What I offer you is a rare opportunity to travel through time, to observe the world as it was and will never be again. You have in your secret heart longed to be a detective and solve some great mystery; here is your chance, perhaps your only chance, to fulfill that wish. Corporeal life, believe me, is woefully short. There is much time on this side to regret lost opportunities."

I walked slowly back to the recliner and sat down.

"You probably died of a heart attack or a stroke or—or food poisoning."

"You do not see it that way," said Marley's Ghost, "so that is not the way it will be."

"What do you mean by that?"

"I mean, my dear sir, that you are the author."

He picked up the tooled leather volume from the floor where I had dropped it and handed it to me. I pushed the chair into the reclining position and began to read aloud. The Ghost, leaning on the back of the chair, looked over my shoulder at his own likeness in a reproduction of the original engraving.

"'Marley was dead: to begin with. There is no doubt whatever about that. The register of his burial was signed by the clergyman, the undertaker, and the chief mourner. Scrooge signed it, and Scrooge's name was good. . . .'"

A reclining chair is not the best place for reading; it is too comfortable. I have often dropped into a doze even while reading some remarkable thriller, so it is not so awfully strange that I did so now. I was startled into wakefulness by the resonant striking of the hour, twelve. That did not seem so awfully strange either, until it occurred to me that we do not have a clock that strikes the hour.

I sat up quickly, jerking the chair upright. The moonlight, it appeared, had taken over my den, touching everything in it with a silver glow of tinsel. And directly in front of me, in the place where old Marley had first appeared, stood my daughter Stephanie, in the billowy Christmas angel gown, her light brown hair caught in a circlet of holly, a mysterious half smile on her lips. The tinsel moonlight reflected off her in such a way that she appeared to glow.

I struggled to regain my equilibrium.

"Back from Mass already, hon?"

"I am the Ghost of Christmas Past," she said in that voice of wind-rattled icicles that made me shudder.

"My past?" I decided to play along.

"No. Long past. Come, my time is short."

"As is your stature."

I fully expected the usual, "Oh, Daddy," but got instead an outstretched hand and a calm but firm order.

"Rise! and walk with me!"

"No thanks, hon . . ." I started to say, but then saw that the beckoning hand was transparent and slightly iridescent. I shrank back against the Naugahyde upholstery of the chair, my cold, but quite opaque, hands firmly gripping the armrests. "M-must I?"

The apparition, so like yet so unlike my daughter, shook its shining head solemnly, and little sparkles of tinsel floated in the air around it.

"You are under no compulsion and may decline, without retribution, to accompany me. Though it is strange that you would do so, as you are one of the fortunate ones who is spared the painful journey into your own past. What you are being offered is an opportunity offered to few, to visit a past that is not your own, simply for the satisfaction of your curiosity."

"Really? No strings attached? No moral?"

The Spirit's slight smile broadened just a trifle. "Few journeys are made in what you call the 'real world' without something being learned. You will be shown things; what you do with them is your business. The opportunity will not arise again. Come with me now, or close the book forever."

I am a man incapable of passing an open door without peering into the room, so this challenge left me no choice but to accept it. I grasped the Spirit's hand, surprised to find that it felt like solid flesh. Its grip was, indeed, very strong, pulling me up abruptly from my chair and leading me through the den and across the hall to the silver-bathed living room. I can well remember Steffy in the flesh dragging me from the comfort of the den with this same eagerness to see the decorated tree. I saw it now, shining in the moonlight, and it seemed larger, fuller, more brilliant and, goodness knows, gaudier, than it had before.

"Where are you taking me?" I asked as we hastened toward the bay window.

"London, December 24, 1836." It spoke in the tone and manner of the narrative voice that so often opens cheaply made historical or science fiction films. The date, seven years prior to the publication of *A Christmas Carol,* reminded me all of a sudden of the purpose of my journey.

"Wait, where's old Marley?"

"Right with you, my dear sir."

And there he was indeed, peering over my left shoulder, bandage and all; apparently he had been there, unnoticed, the whole time. Now he grasped my left hand, and together the three of us passed through the bay window's leaded panes. I felt the solid glass brush past me like the strips of a beaded curtain.

I had closed my eyes as I approached the window and did not open them at first when I felt the cold outside air. For one thing the air itself felt different, damp and chilly rather than sharp and crisp. And all about me was a confusion of noise and smells. So many smells: coal fires smoking, gas fumes, old fish, beer, sewage, sweat, and then rising above all this the sweet, pungent odor of mince pie. I stood for a moment in wonder, my head raised like that of a hound downwind of a herd of deer, just sniffing. Then I had the strange, vaguely unpleasant, sensation of someone passing through me, as if I were a beaded curtain, and I opened my eyes.

I knew at once where I was, for I had been there before, in the City of London late on a winter afternoon, at a busy intersection just east of those three brooding stone edifices that form the hub around which the ancient city spins: the Bank of England, the Mansion House, and the Royal Exchange. I marvelled at how similar the scene was to the one I had enjoyed in my student days, watching schools of office workers crowding down the old streets through the early twilight into underground and railway stations. And yet, as I recovered from the shock of finding myself in that well remembered spot, I saw it all as very familiar yet marvelously strange.

Leadenhall, that was the name of the street, between two churches, St. Michael Cornhill to the west, its stolid, rectangular, pinnacled tower standing out above everything, and to the east St. Andrew Undershaft, the site, it is said, in older times of a gigantic maypole. It is the churches, the ubiquitous churches, that give the City of London its illusion of timelessness. The London I now stood in was older, dirtier, noisier, and even more charming than the one I had known.

I am a city person, revelling in the urban rush and clutter and racket. But this was almost too much city for even me, noisy beyond belief, with the clatter of donkey carts and hackneys and great lumbering omnibuses over the stone paving, the shouts of peddlers urging their wares on the passerby, and the intermittent clanging of bells. I counted the chimes of the hour coming from St. Michael's tower with some surprise. It was only three o'clock, yet it was dark enough for the gas lamps to be lighted. The air was thick with an oppressive dark green smog that penetrated everywhere but softened the roughness of the street life as if wrapping it in gray-green chiffon.

I was finding it difficult to see, a problem the natural inhabitants of the place seemed to have overcome, and blundered into a young woman who materialized suddenly out of the fog, hurrying along the street, a dark knit shawl wrapped around her striped silk gown, a wide-brimmed bonnet shielding her face. I got a look at it, though, a pretty, childlike, bright-eyed face set with a grimness that seemed contrary to its nature. I attempted to excuse myself, but realized, when the stack of petticoats rustled right through my astonished leg, that apologies were not just unnecessary, they were downright useless.

I fell in step beside her, curious about where she might be going and why she was so nervous. Invisibility, by the way, is a very useful attribute to have in a crowded city street, especially when trying to keep up with someone who is in a great hurry and doesn't even know you're there. I was enjoying myself thoroughly, drinking in the wonderful grimy aliveness of the city, feeling the rush and the gaiety, observing with delight the sideshow of strange and colorful characters free in their anonymity. I took pleasure now and then as I hurried through (literally) the crowds in playing childish "invisible man" games, swinging unseen from a lamppost and passing right through the polished brass "can" of a baked potato vendor stationed on the pavement in the shelter of Whittington Avenue as it leads into the old Leadenhall Market. I must have caused a bit of a breeze, for the coals in the iron firepot suspended beneath the large, showy receptacle shot up in a sudden surge of orange flame and died down. Then I remembered Marley and the superstition that flames rise in the presence of ghosts.

"Sorry about that," I said over my shoulder but saw only the

Ghost of Christmas Past helping the hot potato man get the con-
flagration under control before his primitive steam table blew up.
Marley had hurried on ahead through the confusion of the great
poultry market.

"Where are you going?" I shouted over the racket of hundreds
of chickens, turkeys, geese, ducks, and, for all I know, dodos and
emus, bewailing their fate in the overcrowded condemned cells of
the market, a Dickensian slum for poultry if ever there was one. A
group of three or four very dirty, ragged boys hoarsely chanting
some tuneless carol passed through me, surrounding the potato
vendor in an effort to take advantage of the generosity of his clients
and the warmth of his fire.

"My chambers," Marley panted, pointing vaguely toward the
street ahead of us. "I lived there, and still do, in a way of speaking,
in the wine cellars."

"Nice work if you can get it," I murmured.

I followed the Ghost down a narrow byway along the back wall
of a great stone house, relieved to be free of the feathered bedlam of
the poultry market. We came out on a street of large, impressive
buildings only slightly less congested than the thoroughfare, and
Marley's Ghost, apparently oblivious to the chill drizzle of sleet that
was beginning to fall from the gunmetal gray sky, and the black city
mud splashed up from the street by passing hooves and bare metal
wheels, jaywalked joyously across toward a narrow courtyard almost hidden between two buildings. I hesitated a moment before
following him into that nineteenth century rush hour, for I still did
not quite trust my bodiless condition.

A light touch on my arm caused me to turn. The Ghost of
Christmas Past, disguised as my daughter Stephanie, pointed
northward along the side of the great stone house.

"East India House. Torn down in 1862. You ought to have a look at the front portico facing Leadenhall Street. You will have seen something no person living has seen."

That sort of exclusiveness holds little appeal for me. I was much more interested in exploring Marley's wine cellars, but something else facing Leadenhall Street did catch my interest. A nervous young woman in a striped silk dress and a dark shawl and bonnet had just crossed the thoroughfare and was turning north by the soot-stained gothic church of St. Andrew Undershaft.

"Hey, Marley! Up this way!" I shouted. "I want to see where that girl's going."

He followed me with an obedience I have yet to inspire in the living.

"May I presume to ask why we are stalking this particular person?" he asked when he had caught up.

"I don't know, really. It's just a hunch. Good detectives always follow hunches."

Crossing Leadenhall at that hour was dangerous and indeed all but impossible for ordinary mortals, but we floated easily through hansom cabs and hackney coaches, piemen and holly decorated donkey carts. We followed the girl northward past aging mansions and half timbered Elizabethan relics into an area of small shops with living quarters above them.

"Where are we?" I asked Marley.

"Simmery Axe."

St. Mary Axe, I translated. English place names are marvelous and their pronunciation even more marvelous. I couldn't say at first how I happened to know this particular pronunciation, but a song began to run through my head as I trotted up the pavement in pursuit of my hunch.

"Oh! my name is John Wellington Wells,
     I'm a dealer in magic and spells,
          In blessings and curses
          And ever-filled purses,
     In prophecies, witches and knells."

Gilbert and Sullivan, wasn't it? I used to know all the words to most of the patter songs when I was younger and could sing after a fashion. The clatter of the horses and the rhythmic clanging of a muffin man's bell formed an accompaniment, and I sang aloud, safe in the realization that no mortal ear could hear me. Marley, however, regarded me with some pain.

"If you want a proud foe to 'make tracks'—
     If you'd melt a rich uncle in wax—
          You've but to look in
          On our resident Djinn,
     Number seventy Simmery Axe!"

Good Lord. I stopped abruptly in front of one of the small shabby shops, for the girl in the bonnet had stopped and was looking uncertainly at it. The stone front was black, as was the door. The bowed windows—meant, I suppose, to display wares—were so soot begrimed as to appear black as well. The uncertain flicker of candles inside the shop only helped to obscure the view. I looked up. Over door and window in polished brass letters was the name of the shop, with the number 70 set like quotation marks at each end.

70 J. W. WELLS & CO.,
SORCERERS 70

I started to laugh. The whole thing was so preposterous. I was not used to having such literary dreams. But this was stuff I knew about, and I couldn't let a gaffe like that pass.

"I'm sorry," I said to Christmas Past, who still floated on my right. "You just can't do that."

"I beg your pardon?" said the courteous Spirit.

"Anachronism. Blatant, baldfaced anachronism. Gilbert wrote *The Sorcerer* in 1877. This is supposed to be the London of 1836. Gilbert was born in 1836! Now, how do you explain that away?"

"Elementary," said the Ghost. "It's an old established family firm. The present proprietor is Gilbert's sorcerer's grandfather."

"That's ridiculous. How could the company exist before its author invented it? You can't do that, even in fiction."

"You can do anything in fiction as long as you're consistent," the Ghost explained with a great show of patience. "And once something, a place, a character, is conceived, it acquires an existence of its own—a past, a present, and a future."

I laughed. "What a cop-out. Are you trying to tell me there's no difference between flesh-and-blood historical reality and—and the figment of somebody's imagination?"

"My dear sir," the Spirit replied, "we are all figments of Somebody's imagination."

That's what you get for arguing with a ghost.

I returned to my hunch.

The girl, after taking another quick, frightened look about her, entered the shop, activating a tinkly little bell. I followed, passing through the door after she had closed it, just for the thrill of doing it that way while I could. After all, I'm going to have to open doors for the rest of my life.

The inside of the shop was as dark as the outside, and the soot-saturated fog seemed to have passed through the closed door and filled every crevice. What little I could see through this miasma looked like a combination of old fashioned hardware store and the sort of cheap magic tricks emporium found on seaside boardwalks between the penny arcade and the bingo parlor. A small, round, bald man wearing a blue herringbone checked waistcoat over a pink shirt looked up from behind a low wooden counter where he sat playing solitaire with a set of ancient tarot cards by the light of a close-trimmed oil lamp. A meagre coal fire provided the only other light.

"And what may I do for you, madam?" he asked the girl in a carefully smoothed down cockney accent. His face was pink, his smile somewhat cherubic; his voice was oily and self-deprecating, a pudgy Uriah Heep.

The girl's hand, when she removed it from her fur muff, was trembling, and her voice was thin and strained with tension.

"I—I've come for the—uh—the effigy."

The proprietor raised his spectacles to the top of his head and looked carefully into her face for perhaps half a minute.

"Ah, yes," he said slowly. "Mr. Scrooge."

He spun around to face a cluttered shelf on the wall behind his desk, although I have no idea how he did it, since the chair did not swivel.

"Ah, here we are. Mr. Scrooge."

He took down a cylindrical package wrapped in newspaper like an order of chips and handed it to her. She took it gingerly and stared at it a moment.

"Oh, dear. How dreadful. I don't know how I could do this."

J. W. Wells smiled slightly. "The first time is always the hardest."

"Oh, dear," the girl cried in agitation. "I certainly shan't be doing this again. It's not for me, you know. I never could do such a thing for my own gain. It's for Fred, poor dear Fred. He hasn't a far-thing, and it's so dreadfully unfair."

"And if dear Fred 'asn't a farthing, he can't marry you, eh?"

The girl lowered her head. "He hasn't asked me yet."

"He 'asn't? Bless my soul." The little shopkeeper chuckled, catching the girl's hand in a quick, gentle, but firm movement. "Come now, let's see what we 'ave here." He took the package from her hand and spread the palm out under the lamp, raising the wick just a trifle. "Now this is very nice, don't you see? Such a lovely long life line. I see marriage, but not so soon. No matter, it's a very fine hand: happiness, many children, prosperity in due time. Be pa-tient, say the Stars, your time will come."

He released her hand and placed the package back into it.

"A Christmas gift for poor, dear Fred. That'll come to five quid, madam, and a bob for the reading. For you. Regular clients I charge 'arf a crown."

"Oh." She fumbled in her muff and pulled out a small purse from which she carefully counted out coins.

"You're sure this is Mr. Scrooge?" she asked, staring at the little package. "Do you know Mr. Scrooge?"

The chuckle was less cherubic, more malevolent. "Know Mr. Scrooge? My dear lady, there's not a chap within the sound of Bow bells that don't know Mr. Scrooge, more's the pity. His chambers being just over the way, I'm privileged betimes to share the street with 'im. 'Mr. Scrooge?' says I and tips me hat. 'Umph,' says he, if he says anything at all. Not a kindly man, our Mr. Scrooge." He leaned over the counter familiarly. "It's a favor we're doing this old town, you and me."

The girl shuddered and drew back. "For Fred," she whispered. "Just for Fred. What do I do with it?"

"Set it in the fire, madam, saying these words . . ." He drew her face close to his and whispered a series of phrases in her ear which I, though I leaned close, could not make out. "You've got that now? Good. Wouldn't you care to have a look at it? It's a marvelous likeness, I must say."

"Oh no. I couldn't bear it. I'd rather not know what he looked—looks like."

She secreted the package in her muff and ran from the shop, the bell on the door tinkling in her wake.

"Thank you very much, and a Merry Christmas to you," the shopkeeper called. "And a Merry Christmas to Fred, the lucky fellow."

I passed through the closed door just as the great bell of St. Andrew Undershaft boomed the hour of four. The sky was dark, what sky could be seen, but the street was bright with torches and gaslights. Marley materialized beside me.

"Who is this Fred?" he asked.

"Scrooge's nephew."

"Oh yes, that dreadfully jolly young fellow who came around to the counting house every Christmas Eve, spreading cheer, like marzipan, all over everything. Scrooge assumed he was after his money. But I don't recognize her. Who is she, and what's she up to?"

"She's Scrooge's niece-in-law to be, I think. And, if I'm not mistaken, she's attempting to melt a rich uncle in wax, so to speak. Come on."

I pushed through the crowd, for I was losing my hunch. Suddenly there was a diversion on the southwest corner of Leadenhall Street, in front of the brashly neoclassic facade of East India House. Two slightly drunken porters had collided and were now settling the question of right-of-way with bare fists. The nearby market emptied into the street to join the melee. I passed through the center of the mob, having caught sight of a dark bonnet disappearing down Whittington Avenue. Then I saw her standing in front of the brass baked potato can temporarily left untended. She looked around, white-faced, then quickly threw her package onto the glowing coals of the firepot and fled westward.

By the time I reached the vessel the paper had burst into yellow flame and shrivelled to a blackened crust, and the wax effigy itself was starting to melt. It was a rather horrid sight, as recognizable human features began to run together. Recognizable indeed, for it was a good likeness, a perfect likeness of Jacob Marley.

"Hey!" I called to the girl's rapidly retreating back, forgetting my ghostly state. "You hexed the wrong man!"

The effigy was beginning to melt rapidly, and I put my hand into the pot, attempting to retrieve it. A firm, transparent grip on my wrist prevented me.

"You are free to observe only," said the Ghost of Christmas Past, "not to intervene. The past cannot be altered, even in fiction."

So we stood, three ill-matched spectres in the sooty darkness as snow began to fall lightly over the scene, watching the effigy slowly dissolve and run in rivulets of molten wax around and between the hot coals.

"I don't understand," said Marley's Ghost.

"It's a form of black magic," I explained. "A wax image of the victim is slowly melted with appropriate curses or whatever."

"That bright-eyed, dimpled, fresh-faced child involved in such dark deeds? I find that difficult to comprehend."

"She was driven to it by necessity, I think."

"Oh?" Marley's Ghost was puzzled. "Not by me, surely."

"No. By your partner. She wants to marry Fred, you see, as in time she will and make him very happy. And I suppose in time she will also secretly be glad that her attempt at witchcraft failed. It wasn't her fault, of course, that it did, or the sorcerer's either. Apparently he mistook you for Scrooge. I gather you sometimes answered to the name of Scrooge, as it is written of him: 'Sometimes people . . . called Scrooge Scrooge and sometimes Marley, but he answered to both names: it was all the same to him.'"

Marley's Ghost nodded solemnly, his jaws clacking together under the white bandage.

"We were like that, as it were one person in two bodies. It was also a device for keeping clients guessing. If an unwanted solicitor asked for Mr. Marley, he would be out for the day. I would be Mr. Scrooge. It was something of a game, I venture."

"A game that cost you your life."

Just at that moment Marley's Ghost gave a gasp and backed into the baked potato can, pointing at something with a trembling finger. Following his gesture I saw Marley himself, in the flesh, a solid identical twin of my companion of the evening in all aspects except the bandage, stumbling eastward, somewhat unsteady on his feet, as though the curse had already begun to take effect. He tripped on a loose paving stone and fell through me, catching himself on the large round handle of the can. He leaned on it an instant to get his balance and inadvertently looked down into the glowing coals of the fire pot. The effigy had melted from the back of the head forward and the face now spread over the coals like a projected relief map. I tried to shield Marley from the sight, but of course he saw through me, as many do. With a cry the poor fellow staggered back, holding his chest, took three steps forward, and fell. We three stood there, helpless in our insubstantiality, and watched a crowd gather around the stricken man, make a corridor for a doctor to come through, and then close up again around him, and after a while six strong men, like premature pallbearers, carried the dying man down the street to his chambers. For though some of the bystanders weren't certain whether this was Mr. Scrooge or

Mr. Marley, all knew that he was one of those gentlemen and that his home was above the wine cellars and offices in the old dark house in the courtyard off Lime Street.

Chimes sounded again from the tower of St. Andrew's Church. It must be six, I reasoned. The great bell tolled once and fell silent. I waited, straining in the sudden oppressive silence for the bell to go on. But it did not. All was darkness and stillness around me, and I was alone. Where was I now? In Scrooge's dark chambers above the wine cellars and holiday vacant offices? He could not have been more alone than I was. I sat back, for wherever I was, I was sitting, and wished fervently for companionship, longed to hear the ominous clank of chains, to see some otherworldly luminosity break through the terrible blackness. Then I knew what was Scrooge's curse, and Marley's, to be alone and lonely on Christmas.

In the distance I heard voices, faint but growing stronger. The voices surely of an angel choir sent to redeem my hardened soul. I welcomed it as it drew near.

"God rest ye merry, gentlemen,
Let nothing you dismay.
Remember Christ our Savior
Was born on Christmas Day
To save us all from Satan's pow'r
When we were gone astray.
O tidings of comfort and joy!
Comfort and joy! O tidings of comfort and joy!"

With a rush of comfort and joy I realized that I was in my recliner in the den and the angelic choir was Joyce and the kids coming home from Midnight Mass, strewing vocal tinsel through the dark world as they came.

I stumbled to my feet, groping for a light switch. I must turn the decorations on again before they got back. I had suddenly lost all desire to be mistaken for Scrooge. I felt along the wall, falling into bookcases and knocking over bric-a-brac. The singing was coming closer.

"Glad tidings we bring
To you and your kin—
Glad tidings of Christmas
And a Happy New Year!"

My hand was on the knob, and I pulled the door open. Light, brilliant, festive, many-colored, twinkling, clashing, gaudy Christmas light filled the living room and glowed from the porch. The lights had come on, how or why I did not know, but I thanked the Ghost of Christmas Present, who surely must have been.

The front door burst open, and there were my wife and children, bright and glowing in the light of the outdoor decorations. And I was glad to se them.

Standing like a young orator on the hall carpet, shaking off snow like tinsel, Mark spread out his arms and crowed.

"God bless us every one!"

"Amen say I to that," I answered, turning back to the den just long enough to pick up and carefully close the book that lay on the floor still open to the picture of Marley's Ghost, before I joined the family around the misplaced, overburdened tree in the living room.

"Shall I light the candles?" Joyce asked.

"No, no," I said. "Don't do that.

"There's light enough already, light enough."

And I kissed her quickly, under the mistletoe.

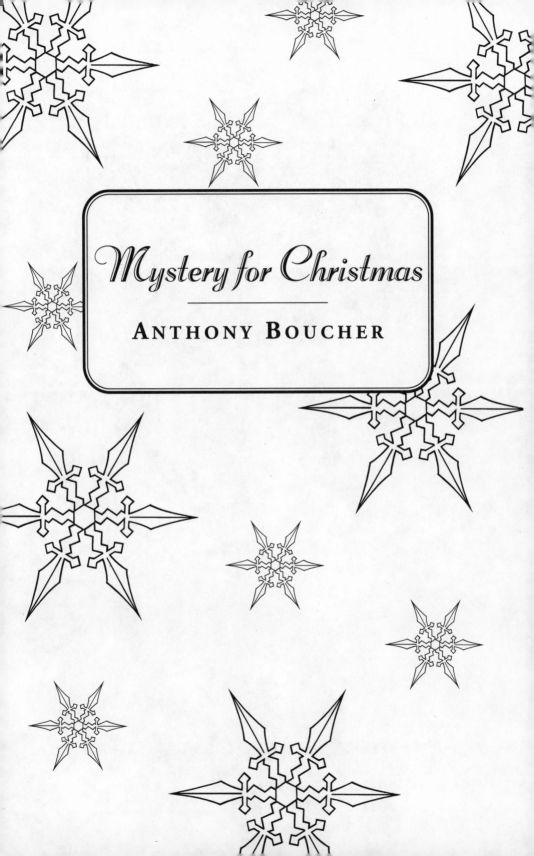

Mystery for Christmas

ANTHONY BOUCHER

THAT WAS WHY THE BENSON JEWEL ROBBERY WAS solved—because Aram Melekian was too much for Mr. Quilter's temper.

His almost invisible eyebrows soared, and the scalp of his close-cropped head twitched angrily. "Damme!" said Mr. Quilter, and in that mild and archaic oath there was more compressed fury than in paragraphs of uncensored profanity. "So you, sir, are the untrammeled creative artist, and I am a drudging, hampering hack!"

Aram Melekian tilted his hat a trifle more jauntily. "That's the size of it, brother. And if you hamper this untrammeled opus any more, Metropolis Pictures is going to be suing its youngest genius for breach of contract."

Mr. Quilter rose to his full lean height. "I've seen them come and go," he announced; "and there hasn't been a one of them, sir, who failed to learn something from me. What is so creative about pouring out the full vigor of your young life? The creative task is mine, molding that vigor, shaping it to some end."

"Go play with your blue pencil," Melekian suggested. "I've got a dream coming on."

"Because I have never produced anything myself, you young men jeer at me. You never see that your successful screen plays are more my effort than your inspiration." Mr. Quilter's thin frame was aquiver.

"Then what do you need us for?"

"What—Damme, sir, what indeed? Ha!" said Mr. Quilter loudly. "I'll show you. I'll pick the first man off the street that has life and a story in him. What more do you contribute? And through me he'll turn out a job that will sell. If I do this, sir, then will you consent to the revisions I've asked of you?"

"Go lay an egg," said Aram Melekian. "And I've no doubt you will."

Mr. Quilter stalked out of the studio with high dreams. He saw the horny-handed son of toil out of whom he had coaxed a masterpiece signing a contract with F.X. He saw a discomfited Armenian genius in the background busily devouring his own words. He saw himself freed of his own sense of frustration, proving at last that his was the significant part of writing.

He felt a bumping shock and the squealing of brakes. The next thing he saw was the asphalt paving.

Mr. Quilter rose to his feet undecided whether to curse the driver for knocking him down or bless him for stopping so miraculously short of danger. The young man in the brown suit was so disarmingly concerned that the latter choice was inevitable.

"I'm awfully sorry," the young man blurted. "Are you hurt? It's this bad wing of mine, I guess." His left arm was in a sling.

"Nothing at all, sir. My fault. I was preoccupied . . ."

They stood awkwardly for a moment, each striving for a phrase that was not mere politeness. Then they both spoke at once.

"You came out of that studio," the young man said. "Do you" (his tone was awed) "do you *work* there?"

And Mr. Quilter had spotted a sheaf of eight and a half by eleven paper protruding from the young man's pocket. "Are you a writer, sir? Is that a manuscript?"

The young man shuffled and came near blushing. "Naw. I'm not a writer. I'm a policeman. But I'm going to be a writer. This is a story I was trying to tell about what happened to me— But are you a writer? In *there?*"

Mr. Quilter's eyes were aglow under their invisible brows. "I, sir," he announced proudly, "am what makes writers tick. Are you interested?"

He was also, he might have added, what makes *detectives* tick. But he did not know that yet.

The Christmas trees were lighting up in front yards and in windows as Officer Tom Smith turned his rickety Model A onto the side street where Mr. Quilter lived. Hollywood is full of these quiet streets, where ordinary people live and move and have their being, and are happy or unhappy as chance wills, but both in a normal and unspectacular way. This is really Hollywood—the Hollywood that patronizes the twenty-cent fourth-run houses and crowds the stores on the Boulevard on Dollar Day.

To Mr. Quilter, saturated at the studio with the other Hollywood, this was always a relief. Kids were playing ball in the evening sun, radios were tuning in to Amos and Andy, and from the small houses came either the smell of cooking or the clatter of dishwashing.

And the Christmas trees, he knew, had been decorated not for the benefit of the photographers from the fan magazines, but because the children liked them and they looked warm and friendly from the street.

"Gosh, Mr. Quilter," Tom Smith was saying, "this is sure a swell break for me. You know, I'm a good copper. But to be honest I don't know as I'm very bright. And that's why I want to write, because maybe that way I can train myself to be and then I won't be a plain patrolman all my life. And besides, this writing, it kind of itches-like inside you."

"*Cacoëthes scribendi,*" observed Mr. Quilter, not unkindly. "You see, sir, you have hit, in your fumbling way, on one of the classic expressions for your condition."

"Now that's what I mean. You know what I mean even when I don't say it. Between us, Mr. Quilter . . ."

Mr. Quilter, his long thin legs outdistancing even the policeman's, led the way into his bungalow and on down the hall to a room which at first glance contained nothing but thousands of books. Mr. Quilter waved at them. "Here, sir, is assembled every helpful fact that mortal need know. But I cannot breathe life into these dry bones. Books are not written from books. But I can provide bones, and correctly articulated, for the life which you, sir— But here is a chair. And a reading lamp. Now, sir, let me hear your story."

Tom Smith shifted uncomfortably on the chair. "The trouble is," he confessed, "it hasn't got an ending."

Mr. Quilter beamed. "When I have heard it, I shall demonstrate to you, sir, the one ending it inevitably must have."

"I sure hope you will, because it's got to have and I promised her it would have and— You know Beverly Benson?"

"Why, yes. I entered the industry at the beginning of talkies. She was still somewhat in evidence. But why . . . ?"

"I was only a kid when she made *Sable Sin* and *Orchids at Breakfast* and all the rest, and I thought she was something pretty marvelous. There was a girl in our high school was supposed to look like her, and I used to think, 'Gee, if I could ever see the real Beverly Benson!' And last night I did."

"Hm. And this story, sir, is the result?"

"Yeah. And this too." He smiled wryly and indicated his wounded arm. "But I better read you the story." He cleared his throat loudly. *"The Red and Green Mystery,"* he declaimed. "By Arden Van Arden."

"A pseudonym, sir?"

"Well, I sort of thought . . . Tom Smith—that doesn't sound like a writer."

"Arden Van Arden, sir, doesn't sound like anything. But go on."

And Officer Tom Smith began his narrative:

The Red and Green Mystery
BY ARDEN VAN ARDEN

It was a screwy party for the police to bust in on. Not that it was a raid or anything like that. God knows I've run into some bughouse parties that way, but I'm assigned to the jewelry squad now under Lieutenant Michaels, and when this call came in he took three other guys and me and we shot out to the big house in Laurel Canyon.

I wasn't paying much attention to where we were going and I wouldn't have known the place anyway, but I knew *her,* all right. She was standing in the doorway waiting for us. For just a minute it stumped me who she was, but then I knew. It was the eyes mostly. She'd changed a lot since *Sable Sin,* but you still couldn't miss the Beverly Benson eyes. The rest of her had got older (not older exactly either—you might maybe say richer) but the eyes were still the same. She had red hair. They didn't have technicolor when she was in pictures and I hadn't even known what color her hair was. It struck me funny seeing her like that—the way I'd been nuts about her when I was a kid and not even knowing what color her hair was.

She had on a funny dress—a little-girl kind of thing with a short skirt with flounces, I guess you call them. It looked familiar, but I couldn't make it. Not until I saw the mask that was lying in the hall, and then I knew. She was dressed like Minnie Mouse. It turned out later they all were—not like Minnie Mouse, but like all the characters in the cartoons. It was that kind of a party—a Disney Christmas party. There were studio drawings all over the walls, and there were little figures of extinct animals and winged ponies holding the lights on the Christmas tree.

She came right to the point. I could see Michaels liked that; some of these women throw a big act and it's an hour before you know what's been stolen. "It's my emeralds and rubies," she said. "They're gone. There are some other pieces missing too, but I don't so much care about them. The emeralds and the rubies are the important thing. You've got to find them."

"Necklaces?" Michaels asked.

"A necklace."

"Of emeralds *and* rubies?" Michaels knows his jewelry. His old man is in the business and tried to bring him up in it, but he joined the force. He knows a thing or two just the same, and his left eyebrow does tricks when he hears or sees something that isn't kosher. It was doing tricks now.

"I know that may sound strange, Lieutenant, but this is no time for discussing the esthetics of jewelry. It struck me once that it would be exciting to have red and green in one necklace, and I had it made. They're perfectly cut and matched, and it could never be duplicated."

Michaels didn't look happy. "You could drape it on a Christmas tree," he said. But Beverly Benson's Christmas tree was a cold white with the little animals holding blue lights.

Those Benson eyes were generally lovely and melting. Now they flashed. "Lieutenant, I summoned you to find my jewelry, not to criticize my taste. If I wanted a cultural opinion, I should hardly consult the police."

"You could do worse," Michaels said. "Now tell us all about it."

She took us into the library. The other men Michaels sent off to guard the exits, even if there wasn't much chance of the thief still sticking around. The Lieutenant told me once, when we were off duty, "Tom," he said, "you're the most useful man in my detail. Some of the others can think, and some of them can act; but there's not a damned one of them can just stand there and look so much like the Law." He's a little guy himself and kind of on the smooth and dapper side; so he keeps me with him to back him up, just standing there.

There wasn't much to what she told us. Just that she was giving this Disney Christmas party, like I said, and it was going along fine. Then late in the evening, when almost everybody had gone home, they got to talking about jewelry. She didn't know who started the talk that way, but there they were. And she told them about the emeralds and rubies.

"Then Fig—Philip Newton, you know—the photographer who does all those marvelous sand dunes and magnolia blossoms and things—" (her voice went all sort of tender when she mentioned him, and I could see Michaels taking it all in) "Fig said he didn't believe it. He felt the same way you do, Lieutenant, and I'm sure I can't see why. 'It's unworthy of you, darling,' he said. So I laughed and tried to tell him they were really beautiful—for they are, you know—and when he went on scoffing I said, 'All right, then, I'll show you.' So I went into the little dressing room where I keep my jewel box, and they weren't there. And that's all I know."

Then Michaels settled down to questions. When had she last seen the necklace? Was the lock forced? Had there been any prowlers around? What else was missing? And suchlike.

Beverly Benson answered impatiently, like she expected us to just go out there like that and grab the thief and say, "Here you are, lady." She had shown the necklace to another guest early in the party—he'd gone home long ago, but she gave us the name and address to check. No, the lock hadn't been forced. They hadn't seen anything suspicious, either. There were some small things missing, too—a couple of diamond rings, a star sapphire pendant, a pair of pearl earrings—but those didn't worry her so much. It was the emerald and ruby necklace that she wanted.

That left eyebrow went to work while Michaels thought about what she'd said. "If the lock wasn't forced, that lets out a chance prowler. It was somebody who knew you, who'd had a chance to lift your key or take an impression of it. Where'd you keep it?"

"The key? In my handbag usually. Tonight it was in a box on my dressing table."

Michaels sort of groaned. "And women wonder why jewels get stolen! Smith, get Ferguson and have him go over the box for prints. In the meantime, Miss Benson, give me a list of all your guests tonight. We'll take up the servants later. I'm warning you now it's a ten-to-one chance you'll ever see your Christmas tree ornament again unless a fence sings; but we'll do what we can. Then I'll deliver my famous little lecture on safes, and we'll pray for the future."

When I'd seen Ferguson, I waited for Michaels in the room where the guests were. There were only five left, and I didn't know who they were yet. They'd all taken off their masks; but they still had on their cartoon costumes. It felt screwy to sit there among them and think: This is serious, this is a felony, and look at those bright funny costumes.

Donald Duck was sitting by himself, with one hand resting on his long-billed mask while the other made steady grabs for the cigarette box beside him. His face looked familiar; I thought maybe I'd seen him in bits.

Three of them sat in a group: Mickey Mouse, Snow White, and Dopey. Snow White looked about fourteen at first, and it took you a while to realize she was a woman and a swell one at that. She was a little brunette, slender and cool-looking—a simple real kind of person that didn't seem to belong in a Hollywood crowd. Mickey Mouse was a hefty blond guy about as tall as I am and built like a tackle that could hold any line; but his face didn't go with his body. It was shrewd-like, and what they call sensitive. Dopey looked just that—a nice guy and not too bright.

Then over in another corner was a Little Pig. I don't know do they have names, but this was the one that wears a sailor suit and plays the fiddle. He had bushy hair sticking out from under the sailor cap and long skillful-looking hands stretched in front of him. The fiddle was beside him, but he didn't touch it. He was passed out—dead to the world, close as I could judge.

He and Donald were silent, but the group of three talked a little.

"I guess it didn't work," Dopey said.

"You couldn't help that, Harvey." Snow White's voice was just like I expected—not like Snow White's in the picture, but deep and smooth, like a stream that's running in the shade with moss on its banks. "Even an agent can't cast people."

"You're a swell guy, Madison," Mickey Mouse said. "You tried, and thanks. But if it's no go, hell, it's just no go. It's up to her."

"Miss Benson is surely more valuable to your career." The running stream was ice cold.

Now maybe I haven't got anything else that'd make me a good detective, but I do have curiosity, and here's where I saw a way to satisfy it. I spoke to all of them and I said, "I'd better take down some information while we're waiting for the Lieutenant." I started on Donald Duck. "Name?"

"Daniel Wappingham." The voice was English. I could tell that much. I don't have such a good ear for stuff like that, but I thought maybe it wasn't the best English.

"Occupation?"

"Actor."

And I took down the address and the rest of it. Then I turned to the drunk and shook him. He woke up part way but he didn't hear what I was saying. He just threw his head back and said loudly, "Waltzes! Ha!" and went under again. His voice was guttural—some kind of German, I guessed. I let it go at that and went over to the three.

Dopey's name was Harvey Madison; occupation, actor's representative—tenpercenter to you. Mickey Mouse was Philip Newton; occupation, photographer. (That was the guy Beverly Benson mentioned, the one she sounded thataway about.) And Snow White was Jane Newton.

"Any relation?" I asked.

"Yes and no," she said, so soft I could hardly hear her.

"Mrs. Newton," Mickey Mouse stated, "was once my wife." And the silence was so strong you could taste it.

I got it then. The two of them sitting there, remembering all the little things of their life together, being close to each other and yet somehow held apart. And on Christmas, too, when you remember things. There was still something between them even if they didn't admit it themselves. But Beverly Benson seemed to have a piece of the man, and where did Dopey fit in?

It sort of worried me. They looked like swell people—people that belonged together. But it was my job to worry about the necklace and not about people's troubles. I was glad Michaels came in just then.

He was being polite at the moment, explaining to Beverly Benson how Ferguson hadn't got anywhere with the prints and how the jewels were probably miles away by now. "But we'll do what we can," he said. "We'll talk to these people and find out what's possible. I doubt, however, if you'll ever see that necklace again. It was insured, of course, Miss Benson?"

"Of course. So were the other things, and with them I don't mind. But this necklace I couldn't conceivably duplicate, Lieutenant."

Just then Michael's eye lit on Donald Duck, and the eyebrow did tricks worth putting in a cartoon. "We'll take you one by one," he said. "You with the tail-feathers, we'll start with you. Come along, Smith."

Donald Duck grabbed a fresh cigarette, thought a minute, then reached out again for a handful. He whistled off key and followed us into the library.

"I gave all the material to your stooge here, Lieutenant," he began. "Name, Wappingham. Occupation, actor. Address—"

Michaels was getting so polite it had me bothered. "You won't mind, sir," he purred, "if I suggest a few corrections in your statement?"

Donald looked worried. "Don't you think I know my own name?"

"Possibly. But would you mind if I altered the statement to read: Name, Alfred Higgins. Occupation, jewel thief—conceivably reformed?"

The Duck wasn't so bad hit as you might have thought. He let out a pretty fair laugh and said, "So the fat's in the fire at last. But I'm glad you concede the possibility of my having reformed."

"The possibility, yes." Michaels underlined the word. "You admit you're Higgins?"

"Why not? You can't blame me for not telling you right off; it wouldn't look good when somebody had just been up to my old tricks. But now that you know— And by the way, Lieutenant, just how do you know?"

"Some bright boy at Scotland Yard spotted you in an American picture. Sent your description and record out to us just in case you ever took up your career again."

"Considerate of him, wasn't it?"

But Michaels wasn't in a mood for bright chatter any longer. We got down to work. We stripped that duck costume off the actor and left him shivering while we went over it inch by inch. He didn't like it much.

At last Michaels let him get dressed again. "You came in your car?"

"Yes."

"You're going home in a taxi. We could hold you on suspicion, but I'd sooner play it this way."

"Now I understand," Donald said, "what they mean by the high-handed American police procedure." And he went back into the other room with us.

All the same that was a smart move of Michaels'. It meant that Wappingham-Higgins-Duck would either have to give up all hope of the jewels (he certainly didn't have them on him) or lead us straight to them, because of course I knew a tail would follow that taxi and camp on his doorstep all next week if need be.

Donald Duck said goodnight to his hostess and nodded to the other guests. Then he picked up his mask.

"Just a minute," Michaels said. "Let's have a look at that."

"At this?" he asked innocent-like and backed toward the French window. Then he was standing there with an automatic in his hand. It was little but damned nasty-looking. I never thought what a good holster that long bill would make.

"Stay where you are, gentlemen," he said calmly. "I'm leaving undisturbed, *if* you don't mind."

The room was frozen still. Beverly Benson and Snow White let out little gasps of terror. The drunk was still dead to the world. The other two men looked at us and did nothing. It was Donald's round.

Or would've been if I hadn't played football in high school. It was a crazy chance, but I took it. I was the closest to him, only his eyes were on Michaels. It was a good flying tackle and it brought him to the ground in a heap consisting mostly of me. The mask smashed as we rolled over on it and I saw bright glitters pouring out.

Ferguson and O'Hara were there by now. One of them picked up his gun and the other snapped on the handcuffs. I got to my feet and turned to Michaels and Beverly Benson. They began to say things both at once about what a swell thing I'd done and then I keeled over.

When I came to I was on a couch in a little dark room. I learned later it was the dressing room where the necklace had been stolen. Somebody was bathing my arm and sobbing.

I sort of half sat up and said, "Where am I?" I always thought it was just in stories people said that, but it was the first thing popped into my mind.

"You're all right," a cool voice told me. "It's only a flesh wound."

"And I didn't feel a thing. . . . You mean he winged me?"

"I guess that's what you call it. When I told the Lieutenant I was a nurse he said I could fix you up and they wouldn't need the ambulance. You're all right now." Her voice was shaky in the dark, but I knew it was Snow White.

"Well, anyways, that broke the case pretty quick."

"But it didn't." And she explained: Donald had been up to his old tricks, all right; but what he had hidden in his bill was the diamonds and the sapphire and the pearl earrings, only no emerald and ruby necklace. Beverly Benson was wild, and Michaels and our men were combing the house from top to bottom to see where he'd stashed it.

"There," she said. She finished the story and the bandaging at the same time. "Can you stand up all right now?"

I was still kind of punchy. Nothing else could excuse me for what I said next. But she was so sweet and tender and good I wanted to say something nice, so like a dumb jerk I up and said, "You'd make some man a grand wife."

That was what got her. She just went to pieces—dissolved, you might say. I'm not used to tears on the shoulder of my uniform, but what could I do? I didn't try to say anything—just patted her back and let her talk. And I learned all about it.

How she'd married Philip Newton back in '29 when he was a promising young architect and she was an heiress just out of finishing school. How the fortune she was heiress to went fooey like all the others and her father took the quick way out. How the architect business went all to hell with no building going on and just when things were worst she had a baby. And then how Philip started drinking, and finally— Well, anyways, there it was.

They'd both pulled themselves together now. She was making enough as a nurse to keep the kid (she was too proud to take alimony), and Philip was doing fine in this arty photographic line he'd taken up. A Newton photograph was The Thing to Have in the smart Hollywood set. But they couldn't come together again, not while he was such a success. If she went to him, he'd think she was begging; if he came to her, she'd think he was being noble. And Beverly Benson had set her cap for him.

Then this agent Harvey Madison (that's Dopey), who had known them both when, decided to try and fix things. He brought Snow White to this party; neither of them knew the other would be here. And it was a party and it was Christmas, and some of their happiest memories were Christmases together. I guess that's pretty much true of everybody. So she felt everything all over again, only—

"You don't know what it's done for me to tell you this. Please don't feel hurt; but in that uniform and everything you don't seem quite like a person. I can talk and feel free. And this has been hurting me all night and I had to say it."

I wanted to take the two of them and knock their heads together; only first off I had to find that emerald and ruby necklace. It isn't my job to heal broken hearts. I was feeling O.K. now, so we went back to the others.

Only they weren't there. There wasn't anybody in the room but only the drunk. I guessed where Mickey and Dopey were: stripped and being searched.

"Who's that?" I asked Snow White.

She looked at the Little Pig. "Poor fellow. He's been going through torture tonight too. That's Bela Strauss."

"Bella's a woman's name."

"He's part Hungarian." (I guess that might explain anything.)

"He comes from Vienna. They brought him out here to write music for pictures because his name is Strauss. But he's a very serious composer—you know, like . . ." and she said some tongue twisters that didn't mean anything to me. "They think because his name is Strauss he can write all sorts of pretty dance tunes, and they won't let him write anything else. It's made him all twisted and unhappy, and he drinks too much."

"I can see that." I walked over and shook him. The sailor cap fell off. He stirred and looked up at me. I think it was the uniform that got him. He sat up sharp and said something in I guess German. Then he thought around awhile and found some words in English.

"Why are you here? Why the po-lice?" It came out in little one-syllable lumps, like he had to hunt hard for each sound.

I told him. I tried to make it simple, but that wasn't easy. Snow White knew a little German, so she helped.

"Ach!" he sighed. "And I through it all slept!"

"That's one word for it," I said.

"But this thief of jewels—him I have seen."

It was a sweet job to get it out of him, but it boiled down to this: Where he passed out was on that same couch where they took me—right in the dressing room. He came to once when he heard somebody in there, and he saw the person take something out of a box. Something red and green.

"Who was it?"

"The face, you understand, I do not see it. But the costume, yes. I see that clear. It was Mikki Maus." It sounded funny to hear something as American as Mickey Mouse in an accent like that.

It took Snow White a couple of seconds to realize who wore the Mickey Mouse outfit. Then she said "Philip" and fainted.

* * *

Officer Tom Smith laid down his manuscript. "That's all, Mr. Quilter."

"All, sir?"

"When Michaels came in, I told him. He figured Newton must've got away with the necklace and then the English crook made his try later and got the other stuff. They didn't find the necklace anywhere; but he must've pulled a fast one and stashed it away some place. With direct evidence like that, what can you do? They're holding him."

"And you chose, sir, not to end your story on that note of finality?"

"I couldn't, Mr. Quilter. I . . . I like that girl who was Snow White. I want to see the two of them together again and I'd sooner he was innocent. And besides, when we were leaving, Beverly Benson caught me alone. She said, 'I can't talk to your Lieutenant. He is *not* sympathetic. But you . . .'" Tom Smith almost blushed. "So she went on about how certain she was that Newton was innocent and begged me to help her prove it. So I promised."

"Hm," said Mr. Quilter. "Your problem, sir, is simple. You have good human values there in your story. Now we must round them out properly. And the solution is simple. We have two women in love with the hero, one highly sympathetic and the other less so; for the spectacle of a *passée* actress pursuing a new celebrity is not a pleasant one. This less sympathetic woman, to please the audience, must redeem herself with a gesture of self-immolation to secure the hero's happiness with the heroine. Therefore, sir, let her confess to the robbery."

"Confess to the . . . But Mr. Quilter, that makes a different story out of it. I'm trying to write as close as I can to what happened. And I promised—"

"Damme, sir, it's obvious. She did steal the necklace herself. She hasn't worked for years. She must need money. You mentioned insurance. The necklace was probably pawned long ago, and now she is trying to collect."

"But that won't work. It really was stolen. Somebody saw it earlier in the evening, and the search didn't locate it. And believe me, that squad knows how to search."

"Fiddle-faddle, sir." Mr. Quilter's close-cropped scalp was beginning to twitch. "What was seen must have been a paste imitation. She could dissolve that readily in acid and dispose of it down the plumbing. And Wappingham's presence makes her plot doubly sure; she knew him for what he was, and invited him as a scapegoat."

Tom Smith squirmed. "I'd almost think you were right, Mr. Quilter. Only Bela Strauss did see Newton take the necklace."

Mr. Quilter laughed. "If that is all that perturbs you . . ." He rose to his feet. "Come with me, sir. One of my neighbors is a Viennese writer now acting as a reader in German for Metropolis. He is also new in this country; his cultural background is identical with Strauss's. Come. But first we must step down to the corner drugstore and purchase what I believe is termed a comic book."

Mr. Quilter, his eyes agleam, hardly apologized for their intrusion into the home of the Viennese writer. He simply pointed at a picture in the comic book and demanded, "Tell me, sir. What character is that?"

The bemused Viennese smiled. "Why, that is Mikki Maus."

Mr. Quilter's finger rested on a pert little drawing of Minnie.

Philip Newton sat in the cold jail cell, but he was oblivious of the cold. He was holding his wife's hands through the bars and she was saying, "I could come to you now, dear, where I couldn't before.

Then you might have thought it was just because you were successful, but now I can tell you how much I love you and need you—need you even when you're in disgrace. . . ."

They were kissing through the bars when Michaels came with the good news. "She's admitted it, all right. It was just the way Smith reconstructed it. She'd destroyed the paste replica and was trying to use us to pull off an insurance frame. She cracked when we had Strauss point out a picture of what he called 'Mikki Maus.' So you're free again, Newton. How's that for a Christmas present?"

"I've got a better one, officer. We're getting married again."

"You wouldn't need a new wedding ring, would you?" Michaels asked with filial devotion. "Michaels, Fifth between Spring and Broadway—fine stock."

Mr. Quilter laid down the final draft of Tom Smith's story, complete now with ending, and fixed the officer with a reproachful gaze. "You omitted, sir, the explanation of why such a misunderstanding should arise."

Tom Smith shifted uncomfortably. "I'm afraid, Mr. Quilter, I couldn't remember all that straight."

"It is simple. The noun *Maus* in German is of feminine gender. Therefore a *Mikki Maus* is a female. The male, naturally, is a *Mikki Mäserich.* I recall a delightful Viennese song of some seasons ago, which we once employed as background music, wherein the singer declares that he and his beloved will be forever paired, *'wie die Mikki Mikki Mikki Mikki Mikki Maus und der Mikki Mäserich.'*"

"Gosh," said Tom Smith. "You know a lot of things."

Mr. Quilter allowed himself to beam. "Between us, sir, there should be little that we do not know."

"We sure make a swell team as a detective."

The beam faded. "As a detective? Damme, sir, do you think I

cared about your robbery? I simply explained the inevitable de-nouement to this story."

"But she didn't confess and make a gesture. Michaels had to prove it on her."

"All the better, sir. That makes her mysterious and deep. A Bette Davis role. I think we will first try for a magazine sale on this. Studios are more impressed by matter already in print. Then I shall show it to F.X., and we shall watch the squirmings of that genius Aram Melekian."

Tom Smith looked out the window, frowning. They made a team, all right; but which way? He still itched to write, but the promotion Michaels had promised him sounded good, too. Were he and this strange lean old man a team for writing or for detection?

The friendly red and green lights of the neighborhood Christmas trees seemed an equally good omen either way.

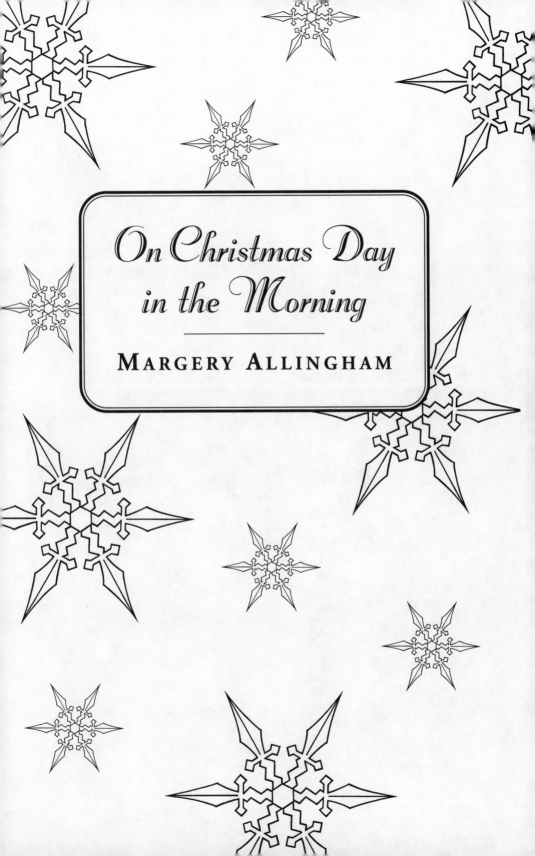

On Christmas Day
in the Morning

MARGERY ALLINGHAM

S IR LEO PERSUIVANT, THE CHIEF CONSTABLE, HAD been sitting in his comfortable study after a magnificent lunch and talking shyly of the sadness of Christmas while his guest, Mr. Albert Campion, most favored of his large house party, had been laughing at him gently.

It was true, the younger man had admitted, his pale eyes sleepy behind his horn-rimmed spectacles, that, however good the organization, the festival was never quite the same after one was middle-aged, but then only dear old Leo would expect it to be, and meanwhile, what a truly remarkable bird that had been!

But at that point the Superintendent had arrived with his grim little story and everything had seemed quite spoiled.

At the moment their visitor sat in a highbacked chair, against a paneled wall festooned with holly and tinsel, his round black eyes hard and preoccupied under his short gray hair. Superintendent Bussy was one of those lean and urgent countrymen who never quite lose their fondness for a genuine wonder. Despite years of experience and disillusion, the thing that simply can't have happened and yet indubitably *has* happened, retains a place in their cosmos. He was holding forth about one now. It had already ruined his Christmas and had kept a great many other people out in the sleet all day; but nothing would induce him to leave it alone even for five minutes. The turkey sandwiches, which Sir Leo had insisted on ordering for him, were disappearing without him noticing them and the glass of scotch and soda stood untasted.

"You can see I had to come at once," he was saying for the third time. "I had to. I don't see what happened and that's a fact. It's a sort of miracle. Besides," he eyed them angrily, "fancy killing a poor old *postman* on Christmas morning! That's inhuman, isn't it? Unnatural."

Sir Leo nodded his white head. "Horrible," he agreed. "Now, let me get this clear. The man appears to have been run down at the Benham-Ashby crossroads . . ."

Bussy took a handful of cigarettes from the box at his side and arranged them in a cross on the table.

"Look," he said. "Here is the Ashby road with a slight bend in it, and here, running at right angles slap through the curve, is the Benham road. As you know as well as I do, Sir Leo, they're both good wide main thoroughfares, as roads go in these parts. This morning the Benham postman, old Fred Noakes, a bachelor thank God and a good chap, came along the Benham road loaded down with Christmas mail."

"On a bicycle?" asked Campion.

"Naturally. On a bicycle. He called at the last farm before the crossroads and left just about 10 o'clock. We know that because he had a cup of tea there. Then his way led him over the crossing and on towards Benham proper."

He paused and looked up from his cigarettes.

"There was very little traffic early today, terrible weather all the time, and quite a bit of activity later; so we've got no skid marks to help us. Well, to resume: no one seems to have seen old Noakes, poor chap, until close on half an hour later. Then the Benham constable, who lives some 300 yards from the crossing and on the Benham road, came out of his house and walked down to his gate to see if the mail had come. He saw the postman at once, lying in the middle of the road across his machine. He was dead then."

"You suggest he'd been trying to carry on, do you?" put in Sir Leo.

"Yes. He was walking, pushing the bike, and had dropped in his tracks. There was a depressed fracture in the side of his skull where something—say, a car mirror—had struck him. I've got the doctor's report. I'll show you that later. Meanwhile there's something else."

Bussy's finger turned to his other line of cigarettes.

"Also, just about 10, there were a couple of fellows walking here on the *Ashby* road, just before the bend. They report that they were almost run down by a wildly driven car which came up behind them. It missed them and careered off out of their sight round the bend towards the crossing. But a few minutes later, half a mile farther on, on the other side of the crossroads, a police car met and succeeded in stopping the same car. There was a row and the driver, getting the wind up suddenly, started up again, skidded and smashed the car into the nearest telephone pole. The car turned out to be stolen and there were four half-full bottles of gin in the back. The two occupants were both fighting drunk and are now detained."

Mr. Campion took off his spectacles and blinked at the speaker.

"You suggest that there was a connection, do you?—that the postman and the gin drinkers met at the crossroads? Any signs on the car?"

Bussy shrugged his shoulders. "Our chaps are at work on that now," he said. "The second smash has complicated things a bit, but last time I 'phoned they were hopeful."

"But my dear fellow!" Sir Leo was puzzled. "If you can get ex-pert evidence of a collision between the car and the postman, your worries are over. That is, of course, if the medical evidence permits the theory that the unfortunate fellow picked himself up and struggled the 300 yards towards the constable's house."

Bussy hesitated.

"There's the trouble," he admitted. "If that were all we'd be sitting pretty, but it's not and I'll tell you why. In that 300 yards of Benham road, between the crossing and the spot where old Fred died, there is a stile which leads to a footpath. Down the footpath, the best part of a quarter of a mile over very rough going, there is one small cottage, and at that cottage letters were delivered this morning. The doctor says Noakes might have staggered the 300 yards up the road leaning on his bike, but he puts his foot down and says the other journey, over the stile and so on, would have been absolutely impossible. I've talked to the doctor. He's the best man in the world on the job and we won't shake him on that."

"All of which would argue," observed Mr. Campion brightly, "that the postman was hit by a car *after* he came back from the cottage—between the stile and the constable's house."

"That's what the constable thought." Bussy's black eyes were snapping. "As soon as he'd telephoned for help he slipped down to the cottage to see if Noakes had actually called there. When he found he had, he searched the road. He was mystified though because both he and his missus had been at their window for an hour watching for the mail and they hadn't seen a vehicle of any sort go by either way. If a car did hit the postman where he fell, it must have turned and gone back afterwards."

Leo frowned at him. "What about the other witnesses? Did they see any second car?"

"No." Bussy was getting to the heart of the matter and his face shone with honest wonder. "I made sure of that. Everybody sticks to it that there was no other car or cart about and a good job too, they say, considering the way the smashed-up car was being driven. As I see it, it's a proper mystery, a kind of not very nice miracle, and those two beauties are going to get away with murder on the strength of it. Whatever our fellows find on the car they'll never get past the doctor's testimony."

Mr. Campion got up sadly. The sleet was beating on the windows, and from inside the house came the more cheerful sound of tea cups. He nodded to Sir Leo.

"I fear we shall have to see that footpath before it gets too dark. In this weather, conditions may have changed by tomorrow."

Sir Leo sighed. "'On Christmas day in the morning!'" he quoted bitterly. "Perhaps you're right."

They stopped their dreary journey at the Benham police station to pick up the constable. He proved to be a pleasant youngster with a face like one of the angel choir and boots like a fairy tale, but he had liked the postman and was anxious to serve as their guide.

They inspected the crossroads and the bend and the spot where the car had come to grief. By the time they reached the stile, the world was gray and freezing, and all trace of Christmas had vanished, leaving only the hopeless winter it had been invented to refute.

Mr. Campion negotiated the stile and Sir Leo followed him with some difficulty. It was an awkward climb, and the path below was narrow and slippery. It wound out into the mist before them, apparently without end.

The procession slid and scrambled on in silence for what seemed a mile, only to encounter a second stile and a plank bridge over a stream, followed by a brief area of what appeared to be simple bog. As he struggled out of it, Bussy pushed back his dripping hat and gazed at the constable.

"You're not having a game with us, I suppose?" he inquired.

"No, sir." The boy was all blush. "The little house is just here. You can't make it out because it's a bit low. There it is, sir. There."

He pointed to a hump in the near distance which they had all taken to be a haystack. Gradually it emerged as the roof of a hovel which squatted with its back towards them in the wet waste.

"Good Heavens!" Sir Leo regarded its desolation with dismay. "Does anybody really live there?"

"Oh, yes, sir. An old widow lady. Mrs. Fyson's the name."

"Alone?" He was aghast. "How old?"

"I don't rightly know, sir. Quite old. Over 75, must be."

Sir Leo stopped in his tracks and a silence fell on the company. The scene was so forlorn, so unutterably quiet in its loneliness, that the world might have died.

It was Campion who broke the spell.

"Definitely no walk for a dying man," he said firmly. "Doctor's evidence completely convincing, don't you think? Now that we're here, perhaps we should drop in and see the householder."

Sir Leo shivered. "We can't *all* get in," he objected. "Perhaps the Superintendent . . ."

"No. You and I will go." Campion was obstinate. "Is that all right with you, Super?"

Bussy waved them on. "If you have to dig for us we shall be just about here," he said cheerfully. "I'm over my ankles now. What a place! Does anybody ever come here *except* the postman, Constable?"

Campion took Sir Leo's arm and led him firmly round to the front of the cottage. There was a yellow light in the single window on the ground floor and, as they slid up a narrow brick path to the very small door, Sir Leo hung back. His repugnance was as apparent as the cold.

"I hate this," he muttered. "Go on. Knock if you must."

Mr. Campion obeyed, stooping so that his head might miss the lintel. There was a movement inside, and at once the door was opened wide, so that he was startled by the rush of warmth from within.

A little old woman stood before him, peering up without astonishment. He was principally aware of bright eyes.

"Oh, dear," she said unexpectedly, and her voice was friendly. "You *are* damp. Come in." And then, looking past him at the skulking Sir Leo. "Two of you! Well, isn't that nice. Mind your poor heads."

The visit became a social occasion before they were well in the room. Her complete lack of surprise, coupled with the extreme lowness of the ceiling, gave her an advantage from which the interview never entirely recovered.

From the first she did her best to put them at ease.

"You'll have to sit down at once," she said, laughing as she waved them to two little chairs one on either side of the small black stove. "Most people have to. I'm all right, you see, because I'm not tall. This is my chair here. You must undo that," she went on touching Sir Leo's coat. "Otherwise you may take cold when you go out. It is so very chilly, isn't it? But so seasonable and that's always nice."

Afterwards it was Mr. Campion's belief that neither he nor Sir Leo had a word to say for themselves for the first five minutes. They were certainly seated and looking round the one downstairs room which the house contained before anything approaching a conversation took place.

It was not a sordid room, yet the walls were unpapered, the furniture old without being in any way antique, and the place could hardly have been called neat. But at the moment it was festive. There was holly over the two pictures and on the mantle above the stove, and a crowd of bright Christmas cards.

Their hostess sat between them, near the table. It was set for a small tea party and the oil lamp with the red and white frosted glass shade, which stood in the center of it, shed a comfortable light on her serene face.

She was a short, plump old person whose white hair was brushed tightly to her little round head. Her clothes were all knitted and of an assortment of colors, and with them she wore, most unsuitably, a maltese-silk lace collarette and a heavy gold chain. It was only when they noticed she was blushing that they realized she was shy.

"Oh," she exclaimed at last, making a move which put their dumbness to shame. "I quite forgot to say it before. A Merry Christmas to you! Isn't it wonderful how it keeps coming round? Very quickly, I'm afraid, but it is so nice when it does. It's such a *happy* time, isn't it?"

Sir Leo pulled himself together with an effort which was practically visible.

"I must apologize," he began. "This is an imposition on such a day. I . . ." But she smiled and silenced him again.

"Not at all," she said. "Oh, not at all. Visitors are a great treat. Not everybody braves my footpath in the winter."

"But some people do, of course?" ventured Mr. Campion.

"Of course." She shot him her shy smile. "Certainly every week. They send down from the village every week and only this morning a young man, the policeman to be exact, came all the way over the fields to wish me the compliments of the season and to know if I'd got my post!"

"And you had!" Sir Leo glanced at the array of Christmas cards with relief. He was a kindly, sentimental, family man, with a horror of loneliness.

She nodded at the brave collection with deep affection.

"It's lovely to see them all up there again, it's one of the real joys of Christmas, isn't it? Messages from people you love and who love you and all so *pretty*, too."

"Did you come down bright and early to meet the postman?" Sir Leo's question was disarmingly innocent, but she looked ashamed and dropped her eyes.

"I wasn't up! Wasn't it dreadful? I was late this morning. In fact, I was only just picking the letters off the mat there when the policeman called. He helped me gather them, the nice boy. There were such a lot. I lay lazily in bed this morning thinking of them instead of moving."

"Still, you heard them come." Sir Leo was very satisfied. "And you knew they were there."

"Oh, yes." She sounded content. "I knew they were there. May I offer you a cup of tea? I'm waiting for my party . . . just a woman and her dear little boy; they won't be long. In fact, when I heard your knock I thought they were here already."

Sir Leo excused them, but not with any undue haste. He appeared to be enjoying himself. Meanwhile, Mr. Campion, who had risen to inspect the display on the mantle shelf more closely, helped her to move the kettle so that it should not boil too soon.

The Christmas cards were splendid. There were nearly 30 of them in all, and the envelopes which had contained them were packed in a neat bundle and tucked behind the clock, to add even more color to the whole.

In design, they were mostly conventional. There were wreaths and firesides, saints and angels, with a secondary line of gardens in unseasonable bloom and Scotch terriers in tam-o'-shanter caps.

One magnificent card was entirely in ivorine, with a cutout disclosing a coach and horses surrounded by roses and forget-me-nots. The written messages were all warm and personal, all breathing affection and friendliness and the out-spoken joy of the season:

The very best to you, Darling, from all at The Limes.

To dear Auntie from Little Phil.

Love and Memories. Edith and Ted.

There is no wish like the old wish. Warm regards, George.

For dearest Mother.

Cheerio. Lots of love. Just off. Writing. Take care of yourself. Sonny.

For dear little Agnes with love from us all.

Mr. Campion stood before them for a long time but at length he turned away. He had to stoop to avoid the beam and yet he towered over the old woman who stood looking up at him.

Something had happened. It had suddenly become very still in the house. The gentle hissing of the kettle sounded unnaturally loud. The recollection of its lonely remoteness returned to chill the cosy room.

The old lady had lost her smile and there was wariness in her eyes.

"Tell me." Campion spoke very gently. "What do you do? Do you put them all down there on the mat in their envelopes before you go to bed on Christmas Eve?"

While the point of his question and the enormity of it was dawning upon Sir Leo, there was silence. It was breathless and unbearable until old Mrs. Fyson pierced it with a laugh of genuine naughtiness.

"Well," she said, "it does make it more fun!" She glanced back at Sir Leo whose handsome face was growing steadily more and more scarlet.

"Then . . . ?" He was having difficulty with his voice. "Then the postman did *not* call this morning, ma'am?"

She stood looking at him placidly, the flicker of the smile still playing round her mouth.

"The postman never calls here except when he brings something from the Government," she said pleasantly. "Everybody gets letters from the Government nowadays, don't they? But he doesn't call here with *personal* letters because, you see, I'm the last of us." She paused and frowned very faintly. It rippled like a shadow over the smoothness of her quiet, careless brow. "There's been so many wars," she said sadly.

"But, dear lady . . ." Sir Leo was completely overcome. There were tears in his eyes and his voice failed him.

She patted his arm to comfort him.

"My dear man," she said kindly. "Don't be distressed. It's not sad. It's Christmas. We all loved Christmas. They sent me their love at Christmas and you see *I've still got it.* At Christmas I remember them and they remember me . . . wherever they are." Her eyes strayed to the ivorine card with the coach on it. "I do sometimes wonder about poor George," she remarked seriously. "He was my husband's elder brother and he really did have quite a shocking life. But he once sent me that remarkable card and I kept it with the others. After all, we ought to be charitable, oughtn't we? At Christmas time . . ."

As the four men plodded back through the fields, Bussy was jubilant.

"That's done the trick," he said. "Cleared up the mystery and made it all plain sailing. We'll get those two crooks for doing in poor old Noakes. A real bit of luck that Mr. Campion was here," he added generously, as he squelched on through the mud. "The old girl was just cheering herself up and you fell for it, eh, Constable? Oh, don't worry, my boy. There's no harm done, and it's a thing that might have deceived anybody. Just let it be a lesson to you. I know how it happened. You didn't want to worry the old thing with the tale of a death on Christmas morning, so you took the sight of the Christmas cards as evidence and didn't go into it. As it turned out, you were wrong. That's life."

He thrust the young man on ahead of him and came over to Mr. Campion.

"What beats me is how you cottoned to it," he confided. "What gave you the idea?"

"I merely read it, I'm afraid." Mr. Campion sounded apologetic. "All the envelopes were there, sticking out from behind the clock. The top one had a ha'penny stamp on it, so I looked at the postmark. It was 1914."

Bussy laughed. "Given to you," he chuckled. "Still, I bet you had a job to believe your eyes."

"Ah." Mr. Campion's voice was thoughtful in the dusk. "That, Super, that was the really difficult bit."

Sir Leo, who had been striding in silence, was the last to climb up onto the road. He glanced anxiously towards the village for a moment or so, and presently touched Campion on the shoulder.

"Look there."

A woman was hurrying towards them and at her side, earnest and expectant, trotted a small, plump child. They scurried past and as they paused by the stile, and the woman lifted the boy onto the footpath, Sir Leo expelled a long sighing breath.

"So there was a party," he said simply. "Thank God for that. Do you know, Campion, all the way back here I've been wonderin'."

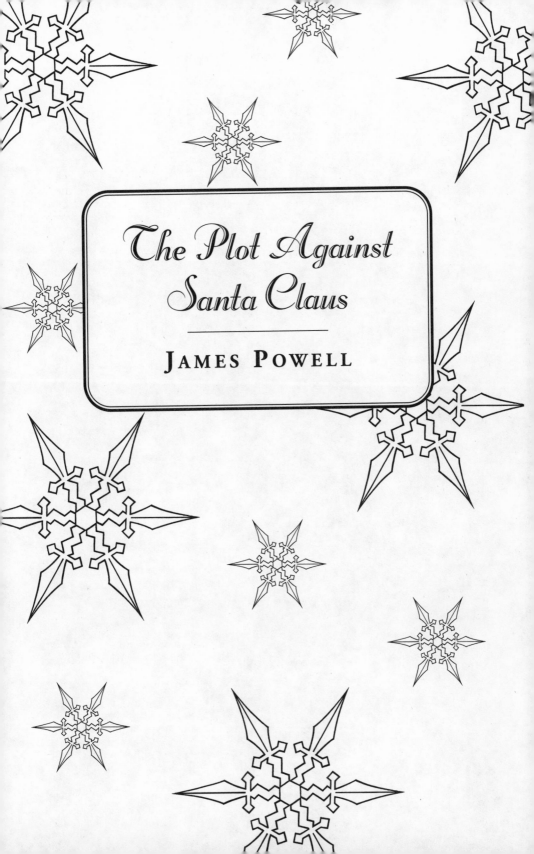

The Plot Against Santa Claus

JAMES POWELL

ORY BIGTOES, SANTA'S SECURITY CHIEF, WAS tall for an elf, measuring almost seven inches from the curly tips of his shoes to the top of his fedora. But he had to stride to keep abreast of Garth Hardnoggin, the quick little Director General of the Toyworks, as they hurried, beards streaming back over their shoulders, through the racket and bustle of Shop Number 5, one of the many vaulted caverns honeycombing the undiscovered island beneath the Polar icecap.

Director General Hardnoggin wasn't pleased. He slapped his megaphone, the symbol of his office (for as a member of the Board he spoke directly to Santa Claus), against his thigh. "A bomb in the Board Room on Christmas Eve!" he muttered with angry disbelief.

"I'll admit that Security doesn't look good," said Bigtoes.

Hardnoggin gave a snort and stopped at a construction site for Dick and Jane Doll dollhouses. Elf carpenters and painters were hard at work, pipes in their jaws and beards tucked into their belts. A foreman darted over to show Hardnoggin the wallpaper samples for the dining room.

"See this unit, Bigtoes?" said Hardnoggin. "Split-level ranch type. Wall-to-wall carpeting. Breakfast nook. Your choice of Early American or French Provincial furnishings. They said I couldn't build it for the price. But I did. And how did I do it?"

"Cardboard," said a passing elf, an old carpenter with a plank over his shoulder.

"And what's wrong with cardboard? Good substantial cardboard for the interior walls!" shouted the Director General striding off again. "Let them bellyache, Bigtoes. I'm not out to win any popularity contests. But I do my job. Let's see you do yours. Find Dirk Crouchback and find him fast."

At the automotive section the new Lazaretto sports cars ($\frac{1}{32}$ scale) were coming off the assembly line. Hardnoggin stopped to slam one of the car doors. "You left out the *kachunk*," he told an elf engineer in white cover-alls.

"Nobody gets a tin door to go *kachunk*," said the engineer.

"Detroit does. So can we," said Hardnoggin, moving on. "You think I don't miss the good old days, Bigtoes?" he said. "I was a spinner. And a damn good one. Nobody made a top that could spin as long and smooth as Garth Hardnoggin's."

"I was a jacksmith myself," said Bigtoes. Satisfying work, building each jack-in-the-box from the ground up, carpentering the box, rigging the spring mechanism, making the funny head, spreading each careful coat of paint.

"How many could you make in a week?" asked Director General Hardnoggin.

"Three, with overtime," said Security Chief Bigtoes.

Hardnoggin nodded. "And how many children had empty stockings on Christmas morning because we couldn't handcraft enough stuff to go around? That's where your Genghis Khans, your Hitlers, and your Stalins come from, Bigtoes—children who through no fault of their own didn't get any toys for Christmas. So Santa had to make a policy decision: quality or quantity? He opted for quantity."

Crouchback, at that time one of Santa's right-hand elves, had blamed the decision on Hardnoggin's sinister influence. By way of protest he had placed a bomb in the new plastic machine. The explosion had coated three elves with a thick layer of plastic which had to be chipped off with hammers and chisels. Of course they lost their beards. Santa, who was particularly sensitive about beards, sentenced Crouchback to two years in the cooler, as the elves called it. This meant he was assigned to a refrigerator (one in Ottawa, Canada, as it happened) with the responsibility of turning the light on and off as the door was opened or closed.

But after a month Crouchback had failed to answer the daily roll call which Security made by means of a two-way intercom system. He had fled the refrigerator and become a renegade elf. Then suddenly, three years later, Crouchback had reappeared at the North Pole, a shadowy fugitive figure, editor of a clandestine newspaper, *The Midnight Elf,* which made violent attacks on Director General Hardnoggin and his policies. More recently, Crouchback had become the leader of SHAFT—Santa's Helpers Against Flimsy Toys—an organization of dissident groups including the Anti-Plastic League, the Sons and Daughters of the Good Old Days, the Ban the Toy-Bomb people and the Hippie Elves for Peace . . .

"Santa opted for quantity," repeated Hardnoggin. "And I carried out his decision. Just between the two of us it hasn't always been easy." Hardnoggin waved his megaphone at the Pacification and Rehabilitation section where thousands of toy bacteriological warfare kits (JiffyPox) were being converted to civilian use (The Freckle Machine). After years of pondering Santa had finally ordered a halt to war-toy production. His decision was considered a victory for SHAFT and a defeat for Hardnoggin.

"Unilateral disarmament is a mistake, Bigtoes," said Hardnoggin grimly as they passed through a door marked *Santa's Executive Helpers Only* and into the carpeted world of the front office. "Mark my words, right now the tanks and planes are rolling off the assembly lines at Acme Toy and into the department stores." (Acme Toy, the international consortium of toymakers, was the elves' greatest bugbear.) "So the rich kids will have war toys, while the poor kids won't even have a popgun. That's not democratic."

Bigtoes stopped at a door marked *Security*. Hardnoggin strode on without slackening his pace. "Sticks-and-stones session at five o'clock," he said over his shoulder. "Don't be late. And do your job. Find Crouchback!"

Dejected, Bigtoes slumped down at his desk, receiving a sympathetic smile from Charity Nosegay, his little blonde blue-eyed secretary. Charity was a recent acquisition and Bigtoes had intended to make a play for her once the Sticks-and-Stones paperwork was out of the way. (Security had to prepare a report for Santa on each alleged naughty boy and girl.) Now that play would have to wait.

Bigtoes sighed. Security looked bad. Bigtoes had even been warned. The night before, a battered and broken elf had crawled into his office, gasped, "He's going to kill Santa," and died. It was Darby Shortribs who had once been a brilliant doll designer. But then one day he had decided that if war toys encouraged little boys to become soldiers when they grew up, then dolls encouraged little girls to become mothers, contributing to overpopulation. So Shortribs had joined SHAFT and risen to membership on its Central Committee.

The trail of Shortribs' blood had led to the Quality Control lab and the Endurance Machine which simulated the brutal punishment, the bashing, crushing, and kicking that a toy receives at the hands of a four-year-old (or two two-year-olds). A hell of a way for an elf to die!

After Shortribs' warning, Bigtoes had alerted his Security elves and sent a flying squad after Crouchback. But the SHAFT leader had disappeared. The next morning a bomb had exploded in the Board Room.

On the top of Bigtoes' desk were the remains of that bomb. Small enough to fit into an elf's briefcase, it had been placed under the Board Room table, just at Santa's feet. If Owen Brassbottom, Santa's Traffic Manager, hadn't chosen just that moment to usher the jolly old man into the Map Room to pinpoint the spot where, with the permission and blessing of the Strategic Air Command, Santa's sleigh and reindeer were to penetrate the DEW Line, there wouldn't have been much left of Santa from the waist down. Seconds before the bomb went off, Director General Hardnoggin had been called from the room to take a private phone call. Fergus Bandylegs, Vice-President of Santa Enterprises, Inc., had just gone down to the other end of the table to discuss something with Tom Thumbskin, Santa's Creative Head, and escaped the blast. But Thumbskin had to be sent to the hospital with a concussion when his chair—the elves sat on high chairs with ladders up the side like those used by lifeguards—was knocked over backward by the explosion.

All this was important, for the room had been searched before the meeting and found safe. So the bomb must have been brought in by a member of the Board. It certainly hadn't been Traffic Manager Brassbottom who had saved Santa, and probably not Thumbskin. That left Director General Hardnoggin and Vice-President Bandylegs . . .

"Any luck checking out that personal phone call Hardnoggin received just before the bomb went off?" asked Bigtoes.

Charity shook her golden locks. "The switchboard operator fainted right after she took the call. She's still out cold."

Leaving the Toyworks, Bigtoes walked quickly down a corridor lined with expensive boutiques and fashionable restaurants. On one wall of Mademoiselle Fanny's Salon of Haute Couture some SHAFT elf had written: *Santa, Si! Hardnoggin, No!* On one wall of the Hotel St. Nicholas some Hardnoggin backer had written: *Support Your Local Director General!* Bigtoes was no philosopher and the social unrest that was racking the North Pole confused him. Once, in disguise, he had attended a SHAFT rally in The Underwood, that vast and forbidding cavern of phosphorescent stinkhorn and hanging roots. Gathered beneath an immense picture of Santa were hippie elves with their beards tied in outlandish knots, matron-lady elves in sensible shoes, tweedy elves and green-collar elves.

Crouchback himself had made a surprise appearance, coming out of hiding to deliver his now famous "Plastic Lives!" speech. "Hardnoggin says plastic is inanimate. But I say that plastic lives! Plastic infects all it touches and spreads like crab grass in the innocent souls of little children. Plastic toys make plastic girls and boys!" Crouchback drew himself up to his full six inches. "I say: quality—quality now!" The crowd roared his words back at him. The meeting closed with all the elves joining hands and singing "We Shall Overcome." It had been a moving experience . . .

As he expected, Bigtoes found Bandylegs at the Hotel St. Nicholas bar, staring morosely down into a thimble-mug of ale. Fergus Bandylegs was a dapper, fast-talking elf with a chestnut beard which he scented with lavender. As Vice-President of Santa Enterprises, Inc., he was in charge of financing the entire Toyworks operation by arranging for Santa to appear in advertising campaigns, by collecting royalties on the use of the jolly old man's name, and by leasing Santa suits to department stores.

Bandylegs ordered a drink for the Security Chief. Their friendship went back to Rory Bigtoes' jacksmith days when Bandylegs had been a master sledwright. "These are topsy-turvy times, Rory," said Bandylegs. "First there's that bomb and now Santa's turned down the Jolly Roger cigarette account. For years now they've had this ad campaign showing Santa slipping a carton of Jolly Rogers into Christmas stockings. But not anymore. 'Smoking may be hazardous to your health,' says Santa."

"Santa knows best," said Bigtoes.

"Granted," said Bandylegs. "But counting television residuals, that's a cool two million sugar plums thrown out the window." (At the current rate of exchange there are 4.27 sugar plums to the U.S. dollar.) "Hardnoggin's already on my back to make up the loss. Nothing must interfere with his grand plan for automating the Toyworks. So it's off to Madison Avenue again. Sure I'll stay at the Plaza and eat at the Chambord, but I'll still get homesick."

The Vice-President smiled sadly. "Do you know what I used to do? There's this guy who stands outside Grand Central Station selling those little mechanical men you wind up and they march around. I used to march around with them. It made me feel better somehow. But now they remind me of Hardnoggin. He's a machine, Rory, and he wants to make all of us into machines."

"What about the bomb?" asked Bigtoes.

Bandylegs shrugged. "Acme Toy, I suppose."

Bigtoes shook his head. Acme Toy hadn't slipped an elf spy into the North Pole for months. "What about Crouchback?"

"No," said Bandylegs firmly. "I'll level with you, Rory. I had a get-together with Crouchback just last week. He wanted to get my thoughts on the quality-versus-quantity question and on the future of the Toyworks. Maybe I'm wrong, but I got the impression that a top-level shake-up is in the works with Crouchback slated to become the new Director General. In any event I found him a very perceptive and understanding elf."

Bandylegs smiled and went on. "Darby Shortribs was there,

prattling on against dolls. As I left, Crouchback shook my hand and whispered, 'Every movement needs its lunatic fringe, Bandylegs. Shortribs is ours.'" Bandylegs lowered his voice. "I'm tired of the grown-up ratrace, Rory. I want to get back to the sled shed and make Blue Streaks and High Flyers again. I'll never get there with Hardnoggin and his modern ideas at the helm."

Bigtoes pulled at his beard. It was common knowledge that Crouchback had an elf spy on the Board. The reports on the meetings in *The Midnight Elf* were just too complete. Was it his friend Bandylegs? But would Bandylegs try to kill Santa?

That brought Bigtoes back to Hardnoggin again. But cautiously. As Security Chief, Bigtoes had to be objective. Yet he yearned to prove Hardnoggin the villain. This, as he knew, was because of the beautiful Carlotta Peachfuzz, beloved by children all around the world. As the voice of the Peachy Pippin Doll, Carlotta was the most envied female at the North Pole, next to Mrs. Santa. Girl elves followed her glamorous exploits in the press. Male elves had Peachy Pippin Dolls propped beside their beds so they could fall asleep with Carlotta's sultry voice saying: "Hello, I'm your talking Peachy Pippin Doll. I love you. I love you. I love you . . ."

But once it had just been Rory and Carlotta, Carlotta and Rory—until the day Bigtoes had introduced her to Hardnoggin. "You have a beautiful voice, Miss Peachfuzz," the Director General had said. "Have you ever considered being in the talkies?" So Carlotta had dropped Bigtoes for Hardnoggin and risen to stardom in the talking-doll industry. But her liaison with Director General Hardnoggin had become so notorious that a dutiful Santa—with Mrs. Santa present—had had to read the riot act about executive hanky-panky. Hardnoggin had broken off the relationship. Disgruntled, Carlotta had become active with SHAFT, only to leave after a violent argument with Shortribs over his anti-doll position.

Today Bigtoes couldn't care less about Carlotta. But he still had that old score to settle with the Director General.

Leaving the fashionable section behind, Bigtoes turned down Apple Alley, a residential corridor of modest, old-fashioned houses with thatched roofs and carved beams. Here the mushrooms were in full bloom—the stropharia, inocybe, and chanterelle—dotting the corridor with indigo, vermilion, and many yellows. Elf householders were out troweling in their gardens. Elf wives gossiped over hedges of gypsy pholiota. Somewhere an old elf was singing one of the ancient work songs, accompanying himself on a concertina. Until Director General Hardnoggin discovered that it slowed down production, the elves had always sung while they worked, beating out the time with their hammers; now the foremen passed out song sheets and led them in song twice a day. But it wasn't the same thing.

Elf gardeners looked up, took their pipes from their mouths, and watched Bigtoes pass. They regarded all front-office people with suspicion—even this big elf with the candy-strip rosette of the Order of Santa, First Class, in his buttonhole.

Bigtoes had won the decoration many years ago when he was a young Security elf, still wet behind his pointed ears. Somehow on that fateful day, Billy Roy Scoggins, President of Acme Toy, had found the secret entrance to the North Pole and appeared suddenly in parka and snowshoes, demanding to see Santa Claus. Santa arrived, jolly and smiling, surrounded by Bigtoes and the other Security elves. Scoggins announced he had a proposition "from one hard-headed businessman to another."

Pointing out the foolishness of competition, the intruder had offered Santa a king's ransom to come in with Acme Toy. "Ho, ho, ho," boomed Santa with jovial firmness, "that isn't Santa's way."

Scoggins—perhaps it was the "ho, ho, ho" that did it—turned purple and threw a punch that floored the jolly old man. Security sprang into action.

Four elves had died as Scoggins flayed at them, a snowshoe in one hand and a rolled up copy of *The Wall Street Journal* in the other. But Bigtoes had crawled up the outside of Scoggins' pantleg. It had taken him twelve karate chops to break the intruder's kneecap and send him crashing to the ground like a stricken tree. To this day the President of Acme Toy walks with a cane and curses Rory Bigtoes whenever it rains.

As Bigtoes passed a tavern—The Bowling Green, with a huge horse mushroom shading the door—someone inside banged down a thimble-mug and shouted the famous elf toast: "My Santa, right or wrong! May he always be right, but right or wrong, my Santa!" Bigtoes sighed. Life should be so simple for elves. They all loved Santa—what did it matter that he used blueing when he washed his beard, or liked to sleep late, or hit the martinis a bit too hard—and they all wanted to do what was best for good little girls and boys. But here the agreement ended. Here the split between Hardnoggin and Crouchback—between the Establishment and the revolutionary—took over.

Beyond the tavern was a crossroads, the left corridor leading to the immense storage areas for completed toys, the right corridor to The Underwood. Bigtoes continued straight and was soon entering that intersection of corridors called Pumpkin Corners, the North Pole's bohemian quarter. Here, until his disappearance, the SHAFT leader Crouchback had lived with relative impunity, protected by the inhabitants. For this was SHAFT country. A special edition of *The Midnight Elf* was already on the streets denying that SHAFT was involved in the assassination attempt on Santa. A love-bead vendor, his beard tied in a sheepshank, had *Hardnoggin*

Is a Dwarf written across the side of his pushcart. *Make love, not plastic* declared the wall of The Electric Carrot, a popular discotheque and hippie hangout.

The Electric Carrot was crowded with elves dancing the latest craze, the Scallywag. Until recently, dancing hadn't been popular with elves. They kept stepping on their beards. The hippie knots effectively eliminated that stumbling block.

Buck Withers, leader of the Hippie Elves for Peace, was sitting in a corner wearing a *Santa Is Love* button. Bigtoes had once dropped a first-offense drug charge against Withers and three other elves caught nibbling on morning-glory seeds. "Where's Crouchback, Buck?" said Bigtoes.

"Like who's asking?" said Withers. "The head of Hardnoggin's Gestapo?"

"A friend," said Bigtoes.

"Friend, like when the news broke about Shortribs, he says 'I'm next, Buck.' Better fled than dead, and he split for parts unknown."

"It looks bad, Buck."

"Listen, friend," said Withers, "SHAFT's the wave of the future. Like Santa's already come over to our side on the disarmament thing. What do we need with bombs? That's a bad scene, friend. Violence isn't SHAFT's bag."

As Bigtoes left The Electric Carrot a voice said, "I wonder, my dear sir, if you could help an unfortunate elf." Bigtoes turned to find a tattered derelict in a filthy button-down shirt and greasy gray-flannel suit. His beard was matted with twigs and straw.

"Hello, Baldwin," said Bigtoes. Baldwin Redpate had once been the head of Santa's Shipping Department. Then came the Slugger Nolan Official Baseball Mitt Scandal. The mitt had been a big item one year, much requested in letters to Santa. Through some gigantic snafu in Shipping, thousands of inflatable rubber ducks had been sent out instead. For months afterward, Santa received letters from indignant little boys, and though each one cut him like a knife he never reproached Redpate. But Redpate knew he had failed Santa. He brooded, had attacks of silent crying, and finally took to drink, falling so much under the spell of bee wine that Hardnoggin had to insist he resign.

"Rory, you're just the elf I'm looking for," said Redpate. "Have you ever seen an elf skulking? Well, I have."

Bigtoes was interested. Elves were straight-forward creatures. They didn't skulk.

"Last night I woke up in a cold sweat and saw strange things, Rory," said Redpate. "Comings and goings, lights, skulking." Large tears rolled down Redpate's cheeks. "You see, I get these nightmares, Rory. Thousands of inflatable rubber ducks come marching across my body and their eyes are Santa's eyes when someone's let him down." He leaned toward Bigtoes confidentially. "I may be a washout. Occasionally I may even drink too much. But I don't skulk!" Redpate began to cry again.

His tears looked endless. Bigtoes was due at the Sticks-and-Stones session. He slipped Redpate ten sugar plums. "Got to go, Baldwin."

Redpate dabbed at the tears with the dusty end of his beard. "When you see Santa, ask him to think kindly of old Baldy Redpate," he sniffed and headed straight for The Good Gray Goose, the tavern across the street—making a beeline for the bee wine, as the elves would say. But then he turned. "Strange goings-on," he called. "Storeroom Number 14, Unit 24, Row 58. Skulking."

"Hardnoggin's phone call was from Carlotta Peachfuzz," said Charity, looking lovelier than ever. "The switchboard operator is a big

Carlotta fan. She fainted when she recognized her voice. The thrill was just too much."

Interesting. In spite of Santa's orders, were Carlotta and Hardnoggin back together on the sly? If so, had they conspired on the bomb attempt? Or had it really been Carlotta's voice? Carlotta Peachfuzz impersonations were a dime a dozen.

"Get me the switchboard operator," said Bigtoes and returned to stuffing Sticks-and-Stones reports into his briefcase.

"No luck," said Charity, putting down the phone. "She just took another call and fainted again."

Vice-President Bandylegs looked quite pleased with himself and threw Bigtoes a wink. "Don't be surprised when I cut out of Sticks-and-Stones early, Rory," he smiled. "An affair of the heart. All of a sudden the old Bandylegs charm has come through again." He nodded down the hall at Hardnoggin, waiting impatiently at the Projection Room door. "When the cat's away, the mice will play."

The Projection Room was built like a movie theater. "Come over here beside Santa, Rory, my boy," boomed the jolly old man. So Bigtoes scrambled up into a tiny seat hooked over the back of the seat on Santa's left. On Bigtoes' left sat Traffic Manager Brassbottom, Vice-President Bandylegs, and Director General Hardnoggin. In this way Mrs. Santa, at the portable bar against the wall, could send Santa's martinis to him down an assembly line of elves.

Confident that no one would dare to try anything with Santa's Security Chief present, Bigtoes listened to the Traffic Manager, a red-lipped elf with a straw-colored beard, talk enthusiastically about the television coverage planned for Santa's trip. This year, live and in color via satellite, the North Pole would see Santa's arrival at each stop on his journey. Santa's first martini was passed from

Hardnoggin to Bandylegs to Brassbottom to Bigtoes. The Security Chief grasped the stem of the glass in both hands and, avoiding the heady gin fumes as best he could, passed it to Santa.

"All right," said Santa, taking his first sip, "let's roll 'em, starting with the worst."

The lights dimmed. A film appeared on the screen. "Waldo Rogers, age five," said Bigtoes. "Mistreatment of pets, eight demerits." (The film showed a smirking little boy pulling a cat's tail.) "Not coming when he's called, ten demerits." (The film showed Waldo's mother at the screen door, shouting.) "Also, as an indication of his general bad behavior, he gets his mother to buy Sugar Gizmos but he won't eat them. He just wants the boxtops." (The camera panned a pantry shelf crowded with opened Sugar Gizmo boxes.) The elves clucked disapprovingly.

"Waldo Rogers certainly isn't Santa's idea of a nice little boy," said Santa. "What do you think, Mother?" Mrs. Santa agreed.

"Sticks-and-stones then?" asked Hardnoggin hopefully.

But the jolly old man hesitated. "Santa always likes to check the list twice before deciding," he said.

Hardnoggin groaned. Santa was always bollixing up his production schedules by going easy on bad little girls and boys.

A new film began. "Next on the list," said Bigtoes, "is Nancy Ruth Ashley, age four and a half . . ."

Two hours and seven martinis later, Santa's jolly laughter and Mrs. Santa's jolly laughter and Mrs. Santa's giggles filled the room. "She's a little dickens, that one," chuckled Santa as they watched a six-year-old fill her father's custom-made shoes with molasses, "but Santa will find a little something for her." Hardnoggin groaned. That was the end of the list and so far no one had been given sticks-and-stones. They rolled the film on Waldo Rogers again. "Santa understands some cats like having their tails pulled," chuckled

Santa as he drained his glass. "And what the heck are Sugar Gizmos?"

Bandylegs, who had just excused himself from the meeting, paused on his way up the aisle. "They're a delicious blend of toasted oats and corn," he shouted, "with an energy-packed coating of sparkling sugar. As a matter of fact, Santa, the Gizmo people are thinking of featuring you in their new advertising campaign. It would be a great selling point if I could say that Santa had given a little boy sticks-and-stones because he wouldn't eat his Sugar Gizmos."

"Here now, Fergy," said the jolly old man, "you know that isn't Santa's way."

Bandylegs left, muttering to himself.

"Santa," protested Hardnoggin as the jolly old man passed his glass down the line for a refill, "let's be realistic. If we can't draw the line at Waldo Rogers, where can we?"

Santa reflected for a moment. "Suppose Santa let you make the decision, Garth, my boy. What would little Waldo Rogers find in his stocking on Christmas morning?"

Hardnoggin hesitated. Then he said, "Sticks-and-stones."

Santa looked disappointed. "So be it," he said.

The lights dimmed again as they continued their review of the list. Santa's eighth martini came down the line from elf to elf. As Bigtoes passed it to Santa, the fumes caught him—the smell of gin and something else. Bitter almonds. He struck the glass from Santa's hand.

Silent and dimly lit, Storeroom Number 14 seemed an immense, dull suburb of split-level, ranch-type Dick and Jane Doll dollhouses. Bigtoes stepped into the papier-mâché shrubbery fronting Unit 24, Row 58 as an elf watchman on a bicycle pedaled by singing "Colossal Carlotta," a current hit song. Bigtoes hoped he hadn't made a mistake by refraining from picking Hardnoggin up.

Bandylegs had left before the cyanide was put in the glass. Mrs. Santa, of course, was above suspicion. So that left Director General Hardnoggin and Traffic Manager Brassbottom. But why would Brassbottom first save Santa from the bomb only to poison him later? So that left Hardnoggin. Bigtoes had been eager to act on this logic, perhaps too eager. He wanted no one to say that Santa's Security Chief had let personal feelings color his judgment. Bigtoes would be fair.

Hardnoggin had insisted that Crouchback was the villain. All right, he would bring Crouchback in for questioning. After all, Santa was now safe, napping under a heavy guard in preparation for his all-night trip. Hardnoggin—if *he* was the villain—could do him no harm for the present.

As Bigtoes crept up the fabric lawn on all fours, the front door of the dollhouse opened and a shadowy figure came down the walk. It paused at the street, looked this way and that, then disappeared into the darkness. Redpate had been right about the skulking. But it wasn't Crouchback—Bigtoes was sure of that.

The Security Chief climbed in through a dining-room window. In the living room were three elves, one on the couch, one in an easy chair, and, behind the bar, Dirk Crouchback, a distinguished-looking elf with a salt-and-pepper beard and graying temples. The leader of SHAFT poured himself a drink and turned. "Welcome to my little ménage-à-trois, Rory Bigtoes," he said with a surprised smile. The two other elves turned out to be Dick and Jane dolls.

"I'm taking you in, Crouchback," said the Security Chief.

The revolutionary came out from behind the bar pushing a .55mm. howitzer (⅟₃₂ scale) with his foot. "I'm sorry about this," he said. "As you know we are opposed to the use of violence. But I'd rather not fall into Hardnoggin's hands just now. Sit over there by Jane." Bigtoes obeyed. At that short range the howitzer's plastic shell could be fatal to an elf.

Crouchback sat down on the arm of Dick's easy chair. "Yes," he said, "Hardnoggin's days are numbered. But as the incidents of last night and today illustrate, the Old Order dies hard. I'd rather not be one of its victims."

Crouchback paused and took a drink. "Look at this room, Bigtoes. This is Hardnoggin's world. Wall-to-wall carpeting. Breakfast nooks. Cheap materials. Shoddy workmanship." He picked up an end table and dropped it on the floor. Two of the legs broke. "Plastic," said Crouchback contemptuously, flinging the table through the plastic television set. "It's the whole middle-class, bourgeois, suburban scene." Crouchback put the heel of his hand on Dick's jaw and pushed the doll over. "Is this vapid plastic nonentity the kind of grownup we want little boys and girls to become?"

"No," said Bigtoes. "But what's your alternative?"

"Close down the Toyworks for a few years," said Crouchback earnestly. "Relearn our ancient heritage of handcrafted toys. We owe it to millions of little boys and girls as yet unborn!"

"All very idealistic," said Bigtoes, "but—"

"Practical, Bigtoes. And down to earth," said the SHAFT leader, tapping his head. "The plan's all here."

"But what about Acme Toy?" protested Bigtoes. "The rich kids would still get presents and the poor kids wouldn't."

Crouchback smiled. "I can't go into the details now. But my plan includes the elimination of Acme Toy."

"Suppose you could," said Bigtoes. "We still couldn't handcraft enough toys to keep pace with the population explosion."

"Not at first," said Crouchback. "But suppose population

growth was not allowed to exceed our rate of toy production?" He tapped his head again.

"But good grief," said Bigtoes, "closing down the Toyworks means millions of children with empty stockings on Christmas. Who could be that cruel?"

"Cruel?" exclaimed Crouchback. "Bigtoes, do you know how a grownup cooks a live lobster? Some drop it into boiling water. But others say, 'How cruel!' They drop it in cold water and then bring the water to a boil slowly. No, Bigtoes, we have to bite the bullet. Granted there'll be no Christmas toys for a few years. But we'd fill children's stockings with literature explaining what's going on and with discussion-group outlines so they can get together and talk up the importance of sacrificing their Christmas toys today so the children of the future can have quality handcrafted toys. They'll understand."

Before Bigtoes could protest again, Crouchback got to his feet. "Now that I've given you some food for thought I have to go," he said. "That closet should hold you until I make my escape."

Bigtoes was in the closet for more than an hour. The door proved stronger than he had expected. Then he remembered Hardnoggin's cardboard interior walls and karate-chopped his way through the back of the closet and out into the kitchen.

Security headquarters was a flurry of excitement as Bigtoes strode in the door. "They just caught Hardnoggin trying to put a bomb on Santa's sleigh," said Charity, her voice shaking.

Bigtoes passed through to the Interrogation Room where Hardnoggin, gray and haggard, sat with his wrists between his knees. The Security elves hadn't handled him gently. One eye was swollen, his beard was in disarray, and there was a dent in his megaphone. "It was a Christmas present for that little beast, Waldo Rogers," shouted Hardnoggin.

"A bomb?" said Bigtoes.

"It was supposed to be a little fire engine," shouted the Director General, "with a bell that goes clang-clang!" Hardnoggin struggled to control himself. "I just couldn't be responsible for that little monster finding nothing in his stocking but sticks-and-stones. But a busy man hasn't time for last-minute shopping. I got a—a friend to pick something out for me."

"Who?" said Bigtoes.

Hardnoggin hung his head. "I demand to be taken to Santa Claus," he said. But Santa, under guard, had already left his apartment for the formal departure ceremony.

Bigtoes ordered Hardnoggin detained and hurried to meet Santa at the elevator. He would have enjoyed shouting up at the jolly old man that Hardnoggin was the culprit. But of course that just didn't hold water. Hardnoggin was too smart to believe he could just walk up and put a bomb on Santa's sleigh. Or—now that Bigtoes thought about it—to finger himself so obviously by waiting until Bandylegs had left the Sticks-and-Stones session before poisoning Santa's glass.

The villain now seemed to be the beautiful and glamorous Carlotta Peachfuzz. Here's the way it figured: Carlotta phones Hardnoggin just before the bomb goes off in the Board Room, thus making him a prime suspect; Carlotta makes a rendezvous with Bandylegs that causes him to leave Sticks-and-Stones, thus again making Hardnoggin Suspect Number One; then when Bigtoes fails to pick up the Director General, Carlotta talks him into giving little Waldo Rogers a present that turns out to be a bomb. Her object? To frame Hardnoggin for the murder or attempted murder of Santa. Her elf spy? Traffic Manager Brassbottom. It all worked out—or seemed to . . .

Bigtoes met Santa at the elevator surrounded by a dozen Security elves. The jolly old eyes were bloodshot, his smile slightly strained. "Easy does it, Billy," said Santa to Billy Brisket, the Security elf at the elevator controls. "Santa's a bit hungover."

Bigtoes moved to the rear of the elevator. So it was Brassbottom who had planted the bomb and then deliberately taken Santa out of the room. So it was Brassbottom who had poisoned the martini with cyanide, knowing that Bigtoes would detect the smell. And it was Carlotta who had gift-wrapped the bomb. All to frame Hardnoggin. And yet . . . Bigtoes sighed at his own confusion. And yet a dying Shortribs had said that someone was going to kill Santa.

As the elevator eased up into the interior of the Polar icecap, Bigtoes focused his mind on Shortribs. Suppose the dead elf had stumbled on your well-laid plan to kill Santa. Suppose you botched Shortribs' murder and therefore knew that Security had been alerted. What would you do? Stage three fake attempts on Santa's life to provide Security with a culprit, hoping to get Security to drop its guard? Possibly. But the bomb in the Board Room could have killed Santa. Why not just do it that way?

The elevator reached the surface and the first floor of the Control Tower building which was ingeniously camouflaged as an icy crag. But suppose, thought Bigtoes, it was important that you kill Santa in a certain way—say, with half the North Pole looking on?

More Security elves were waiting when the elevator doors opened. Bigtoes moved quickly among them, urging the utmost vigilance. Then Santa and his party stepped out onto the frozen runway to be greeted by thousands of cheering elves. Hippie elves from Pumpkin Corners, green-collar elves from the Toyworks, young elves and old had all gathered there to wish the jolly old man godspeed.

Santa's smile broadened and he waved to the crowd. Then everybody stood at attention and doffed their hats as the massed bands of the Mushroom Fanciers Association, Wade Snoot conducting, broke into "Santa Claus Is Coming to Town." When the music reached its stirring conclusion, Santa, escorted by a flying wedge of Security elves, made his way through the exuberant crowd and toward his sleigh.

Bigtoes' eyes kept darting everywhere, searching for a happy face that might mask a homicidal intent. His heart almost stopped when Santa paused to accept a bouquet from an elf child who stuttered through a tribute in verse to the jolly old man. It almost stopped again when Santa leaned over the Security cordon to speak to some elf in the crowd. A pat on the head from Santa and even Roger Chinwhiskers, leader of the Sons and Daughters of the Good Old Days, grinned and admitted that perhaps the world wasn't going to hell in a handbasket. A kind word from Santa and Baldwin Redpate tearfully announced—as he did every year at that time—that he was off the bee wine for good.

After what seemed an eternity to Bigtoes, they reached the sleigh. Santa got on board, gave one last wave to the crowd, and called to his eight tiny reindeer, one by one, by name. The reindeer leaned against the harness and the sleigh, with Security elves trotting alongside, and slid forward on the ice. Then four of the reindeer were airborne. Then the other four. At last the sleigh itself left the ground. Santa gained altitude, circled the runway once, and was gone. But they heard him exclaim, ere he drove out of sight: "Happy Christmas to all and to all a good night!"

The crowd dispersed quickly. Only Bigtoes remained on the windswept runway. He walked back and forth, head down, kicking at the snow. Santa's departure had gone off without a hitch. Had the

Security Chief been wrong about the frame-up? Had Hardnoggin been trying to kill Santa after all? Bigtoes went over the three attempts again. The bomb in the Board Room. The poison. The bomb on the sleigh.

Suddenly Bigtoes broke into a run.

He had remembered Brassbottom's pretext for taking Santa into the Map Room.

Taking the steps three at a time, Bigtoes burst into the Control Room. Crouchback was standing over the remains of the radio equipment with a monkey wrench in his hand. "Too late, Bigtoes," he said triumphantly. "Santa's as good as dead."

Bigtoes grabbed the phone and ordered the operator to put through an emergency call to the Strategic Air Command in Denver, Colorado. But the telephone cable had been cut. "Baby Polar bears like to teethe on it," said the operator.

Santa Claus was doomed. There was no way to call him back or to warn the Americans.

Crouchback smiled. "In eleven minutes Santa will pass over the DEW Line. But at the wrong place, thanks to Traffic Manager Brassbottom. The American ground-to-air missiles will make short work of him."

"But why?" demanded Bigtoes.

"Nothing destroys a dissident movement like a modest success or two," said Crouchback. "Ever since Santa came out for unilateral disarmament, I've felt SHAFT coming apart in my hands. So I had to act. I've nothing against Santa personally, bourgeois sentimentalist that he is. But his death will be a great step forward in our task of forming better children for a better world. What do you think will happen when Santa is shot down by American missiles?"

Bigtoes shaded his eyes. His voice was thick with emotion.

"Every good little boy and girl in the world will be up in arms. A Children's Crusade against the United States."

"And with the Americans disposed of, what nation will become the dominant force in the world?" said Crouchback.

"So that's it—you're a Marxist-Leninist elf!" shouted Bigtoes.

"No!" said Crouchback sharply. "But I'll use the Russians to achieve a better world. Who else could eliminate Acme Toy? Who else could limit world population to our rate of toy production? And they have agreed to that in writing, Bigtoes. Oh, I know the Russians are grownups too and just as corrupt as the rest of the grownups. But once the kids have had the plastic flushed out of their systems and are back on quality handcrafted toys, I, Dirk Crouchback, the New Santa Claus, with the beautiful and beloved Carlotta Peachfuzz at my side as the New Mrs. Santa, will handle the Russians."

"What about Brassbottom?" asked Bigtoes contemptuously.

"Brassbottom will be Assistant New Santa," said Crouchback quickly, annoyed at the interruption. "Yes," he continued, "the New Santa Claus will speak to the children of the world and tell them one thing: Don't trust anyone over thirty inches tall. And that will be the dawning of a new era full of happy laughing children, where grownups will be irrelevant and just wither away!"

"You're mad, Crouchback. I'm taking you in," said Bigtoes.

"I'll offer no resistance," said Crouchback. "But five minutes after Santa fails to appear at his first pit stop, a special edition of *The Midnight Elf* will hit the streets announcing that he has been the victim of a conspiracy between Hardnoggin and the CIA. The same mob of angry elves that breaks into Security headquarters to tear Hardnoggin limb from limb will also free Dirk Crouchback and proclaim him their new leader. I've laid the groundwork well.

A knowing smile here, an innuendo there, and now many elves inside SHAFT and out believe that on his return Santa intended to make me Director General."

Crouchback smiled. "Ironically enough, I'd never have learned to be so devious if you Security people hadn't fouled up your own plans and assigned me to a refrigerator in the Russian Embassy in Ottawa. Ever since they found a CIA listening device in their smoked sturgeon, the Russians had been keeping a sharp eye open. They nabbed me almost at once and flew me to Moscow in a diplomatic pouch. When they thought they had me brainwashed, they trained me in deviousness and other grownup revolutionary techniques. They thought they could use me, Bigtoes. But Dirk Crouchback is going to use them!"

Bigtoes wasn't listening. Crouchback had just given him an idea—one chance in a thousand of saving Santa. He dived for the phone.

"We're in luck," said Charity, handing Bigtoes a file. "His name is Colin Tanglefoot, a stuffer in the Teddy Bear Section. Sentenced to a year in the cooler for setting another stuffer's beard on fire. Assigned to a refrigerator in the DEW Line station at Moose Landing. Sparks has got him on the intercom."

Bigtoes took the microphone. "Tanglefoot, this is Bigtoes," he said.

"Big deal," said a grumpy voice with a head cold.

"Listen, Tanglefoot," said Bigtoes, "in less than seven minutes Santa will be flying right over where you are. Warn the grownups not to shoot him down."

"Tough," said Tanglefoot petulantly. "You know, old Santa gave yours truly a pretty raw deal."

"Six minutes, Tanglefoot."

"Listen," said Tanglefoot. "Old Valentine Woody is ho-ho-ho-ing around with that 'jollier than thou' attitude of his, see? So as a joke I tamp my pipe with the tip of his beard. It went up like a Christmas tree."

"Tanglefoot—"

"Yours truly threw the bucket of water that saved his life," said Tanglefoot. "I should have got a medal."

"You'll get your medal!" shouted Bigtoes. "Just save Santa."

Tanglefoot sneezed four times. "Okay," he said at last. "Do or die for Santa. I know the guy on duty—Myron Smith. He's always in here raiding the cold cuts. But he's not the kind that would believe a six-inch elf with a head cold."

"Let me talk to him then," said Bigtoes. "But move—you've got only four minutes."

Tanglefoot signed off. Would the tiny elf win his race against the clock and avoid the fate of most elves who revealed themselves to grownups—being flattened with the first object that came to hand? And if he did, what would Bigtoes say to Smith? Grownups—suspicious, short of imagination, afraid—grownups were difficult enough to reason with under ideal circumstances. But what could you say to a grownup with his head stuck in a refrigerator?

An enormous squawk came out of the intercom, toppling Sparks over backward in his chair. "Hello there, Myron," said Bigtoes as calmly as he could. "My name is Rory Bigtoes. I'm one of Santa's little helpers."

Silence. The hostile silence of a grownup thinking. "Yeah? Yeah?" said Smith at last. "How do I know this isn't some Commie trick? You bug our icebox, you plant a little pinko squirt to feed me some garbage about Santa coming over and then, whammo, you slip the big one by us, nuclear warhead and all, winging its way into Heartland, U.S.A."

"Myron," pleaded Bigtoes. "We're talking about Santa Claus, the one who always brought you and the other good little boys and girls toys at Christmas."

"What's he done for me lately?" said Smith unpleasantly. "And hey! I wrote him once asking for a Slugger Nolan Official Baseball Mitt. Do you know what I got?"

"An inflatable rubber duck," said Bigtoes quickly.

Silence. The profound silence of a thunderstruck grownup. Smith's voice had an amazed belief in it. "Yeah," he said. "Yeah."

Pit Stop Number One. A December cornfield in Iowa blazing with landing lights. As thousands of elfin eyes watched on their television screens, crews of elves in cover-alls changed the runners on Santa's sleigh, packed fresh toys aboard, and chipped the ice from the reindeer antlers. The camera panned to one side where Santa stood out of the wind, sipping on a hot buttered rum. As the camera dollied in on him, the jolly old man, his beard and eyebrows caked with frost, his cheeks as red as apples, broke into a ho-ho-ho and raised his glass in a toast.

Sitting before the television at Security headquarters, a smiling Director General Hardnoggin raised his thimble-mug of ale. "My Santa, right or wrong," he said.

Security Chief Bigtoes raised his glass. He wanted to think of a new toast. Crouchback was under guard and Carlotta and Brassbottom had fled to the Underwood. But he wanted to remind the Director General that SHAFT and the desire for something better still remained. Was automation the answer? Would machines finally free the elves to handcraft toys again? Bigtoes didn't know. He did know that times were changing. They would never be the same. He raised his glass, but the right words escaped him and he missed his turn.

Charity Nosegay raised her glass. "Yes, Virginia," she said, using the popular abbreviation for another elf toast; "yes, Virginia, there is a Santa Claus."

Hardnoggin turned and looked at her with a smile. "You have a beautiful voice, Miss Nosegay," he said. "Have you ever considered being in the talkies?"

Santa Claus Beat

REX STOUT

CHRISTMAS EVE," ART HIPPLE WAS THINKING TO himself, "would be a good time for the murder."

The thought was both timely and characteristic. It was 3 o'clock in the afternoon of December 24, and though the murder would have got an eager welcome from Art Hipple any day at all, his disdainful attitude toward the prolonged hurly-burly of Christmas sentiment and shopping made that the best possible date for it. He did not actually turn up his nose at Christmas, for that would have been un-American; but as a New York cop not yet out of his twenties who had recently been made a precinct dick and had hung his uniform in the back of the closet of his furnished room, it had to be made clear, especially to himself, that he was good and tough. A cynical slant on Christmas was therefore imperative.

His hope of running across a murder had begun back in the days when his assignment had been tagging illegally parked cars, and was merely practical and professional. His biggest ambition was promotion to Homicide, and the shortest cut would have been discovery of a corpse, followed by swift, brilliant, solo detection and capture of the culprit. It had not gone so far as becoming an obsession; as he strode down the sidewalk this December afternoon he was not sniffing for the scent of blood at each dingy entrance he passed; but when he reached the number he had been given and turned to enter, his hand darted inside his jacket to touch his gun.

None of the three people he found in the cluttered and smelly little room one flight up seemed to need shooting. Art identified himself and wrote down their names. The man at the battered old desk, who was twice Art's age and badly needed a shave, was Emil Duross, proprietor of the business conducted in that room—Duross Specialties, a mail-order concern dealing in gimcrack jewelry. The younger man, small, dark and neat, seated on a chair squeezed in between the desk and shelves stacked with cardboard boxes, was II. E. Koenig, adjuster, according to a card he had proffered, for the Apex Insurance Company. The girl, who had pale watery eyes and a stringy neck, stood backed up to a pile of cartons the height of her shoulder. She had on a dark brown felt hat and a lighter brown woolen coat that had lost a button. Her name was Helen Lauro, and it could have been not rheum in her eyes but the remains of tears.

Because Art Hipple was thorough it took him twenty minutes to get the story to his own satisfaction. Then he returned his notebook to his pocket, looked at Duross, at Koenig, and last at the girl. He wanted to tell her to wipe her eyes, but what if she didn't have a handkerchief?

He spoke to Duross. "Stop me if I'm wrong," he said. "You bought the ring a week ago to give to your wife for Christmas and paid sixty-two dollars for it. You put it there in a desk drawer after showing it to Miss Lauro. Why did you show it to Miss Lauro?"

Duross turned his palms up. "Just a natural thing. She works for me, she's a woman, and it's a beautiful ring."

"Okay. Today you work with her—filling orders, addressing packages, and putting postage on. You send her to the post office with a bag of the packages. Why didn't she take all of them?"

"She did."

"Then what are those?" Art pointed to a pile of little boxes, addressed and stamped, on the end of a table.

"Orders that came in the afternoon mail. I did them while she was gone to the post office."

Art nodded. "And also while she was gone you looked in the drawer to get the ring to take home for Christmas, and it wasn't there. You know it was there this morning because Miss Lauro asked if she could look at it again, and you showed it to her and let her put it on her finger, and then you put it back in the drawer. But this afternoon it was gone, and you couldn't have taken it yourself because you haven't left this room. Miss Lauro went out and got sandwiches for your lunch. So you decided she took the ring, and you phoned the insurance company, and Mr. Koenig came and advised you to call the police, and—"

"Only his stock is insured," Koenig put in. "The ring was not a stock item and is not covered."

"Just a legality," Duross declared scornfully. "Insurance companies can't hide behind legalities. It hurts their reputation."

Koenig smiled politely but noncommittally.

Art turned to the girl. "Why don't you sit down?" he asked her. "There's a chair we men are not using."

"I will never sit down in this room again," she declared in a thin tight voice.

"Okay." Art scowled at her. She was certainly not comely. "If you did take the ring you might—"

"I didn't!"

"Very well. But if you did you might as well tell me where it is because you won't ever dare to wear it or sell it."

"Of course I wouldn't. I knew I wouldn't. That's why I didn't take it."

"Oh? You thought of taking it?"

"Of course I did. It was a beautiful ring." She stopped to swallow. "Maybe my life isn't much, but what it is, I'd give it for a ring like that, and a girl like me, I could live a hundred years and never have one. Of course I thought of taking it—but I knew I couldn't ever wear it."

"You see?" Duross appealed to the law. "She's foxy, that girl. She's slick."

Art downed an impulse to cut it short, get out, return to the station house, and write a report. Nobody here deserved anything, not even justice—especially not justice. Writing a brief report was all it rated, and all, ninety-nine times out of a hundred, it would have got. But instead of breaking it off, Art sat and thought it over through a long silence, with the three pairs of eyes on him. Finally he spoke to Duross:

"Get me the orders that came in the afternoon mail."

Duross was startled. "Why?"

"I want to check them with that pile of boxes you addressed and stamped."

Duross shook his head. "I don't need a cop to check my orders and shipments. Is this a gag?"

"No. Get me the orders."

"I will not!"

"Then I'll have to open all the boxes." Art arose and headed for the table. Duross bounced up and got in front of him and they were chest to chest.

"You don't touch those boxes," Duross told him. "You got no search warrant. You don't touch anything!"

"That's just another legality." Art backed off a foot to avoid contact. "And since I guessed right, what's a little legality? I'm going to open the boxes here and now, but I'll count ten first to give you a chance to pick it out and hand it to me and save both of us a lot of bother. One, two, three—"

"I'll phone the station house!"

"Go ahead. Four, five, six, seven, eight, nine . . ."

Art stopped at nine because Duross had moved to the table and was fingering the boxes. As he drew away with one in his hand Art demanded, "Gimme." Duross hesitated but passed the box over, and after a glance at the address Art ripped the tape off, opened the flap of the box, took out a wad of tissue paper, and then a ring box. From that he removed a ring, yellow gold, with a large greenish stone. Helen Lauro made a noise in her throat. Koenig let out a grunt, evidently meant for applause. Duross made a grab, not for the ring but for the box on which he had put an address, and missed.

"It stuck out as plain as your nose," Art told him, "but of course my going for the boxes was just a good guess. Did you pay sixty-two bucks for this?"

Duross's lips parted, but no words came. Apparently he had none. He nodded, not vigorously.

Art turned to the girl. "Look, Miss Lauro. You say you're through here. You ought to have something to remember it by. You could make some trouble for Mr. Duross for the dirty trick he tried to play on you, and if you lay off I expect he'd like to show his appreciation by giving you this ring. Wouldn't you, Mr. Duross?"

Duross managed to get it out. "Sure I would."

"Shall I give it to her for you?"

"Sure." Duross's jaw worked. "Go ahead."

Art held out the ring and the girl took it, but not looking at it because she was gazing incredulously at him. It was a gaze so intense as to disconcert him, and he covered up by turning to Duross and proffering the box with an address on it.

"Here," he said, "you can have this. Next time you cook up a plan for getting credit with your wife for buying her a ring, and collecting from the insurance company for its cost, and sending the ring to a girl friend—all in one neat little operation—don't do it. And don't forget you gave Miss Lauro that ring before witnesses."

Duross gulped and nodded.

Koenig spoke. "Your name is not Hipple, officer, it's Santa Claus. You have given her the ring she would have given her life for, you have given him an out on a charge of attempted fraud, and you have given me a crossoff on a claim. That's the ticket! That's the old yuletide spirit! Merry Christmas!"

"Nuts," Art said contemptuously, and turned and marched from the room, down the stairs, and out to the sidewalk. As he headed in the direction of the station house he decided that he would tone it down a little in his report. Getting a name for being tough was okay, but not too damn tough. That insurance guy sure was dumb, calling him Santa Claus—him, Art Hipple, feeling as he did about Christmas.

Which reminded him, Christmas Eve would be a swell time for the murder.

Whatever Became of Ebenezer Scrooge?

TOM TOLNAY

SO EBENEZER SCROOGE, THAT SQUEEZING, WRENCH-
ing, grasping, scraping, clutching, covetous old sinner
was led into the past, the present, and the future by three
apparitions on Christmas Eve, and the horrors that he witnessed,
which were his own life and death, convinced him that he'd better
repent or else. Not merely in word, but in deed, for his fears of
moral retribution were profound. Next morning, while still in his
nightcap, he rewarded a boy handsomely to run to the poulterer's
and have a turkey the size of Tiny Tim sent to the humble home of
the Cratchit family. After consuming a bowl of gruel and a cup of
tea with more relish than such feeble fare justified, he brushed the
coal dust from his cuffs and went off on a cold, clear Christmas
Day to join his nephew Fred and family at their holiday feast.
Scrooge delighted the children with gifts in his hard-as-flint fists
and astonished the grown-ups with a steady smile on his bloodless
face. He tasted of the spiced wassail and joined in the carols in bold
voice and bounced their son and daughter upon his knee. It was
like old times, with the kind of merriment he had enjoyed so
unashamedly at Fezziwig's establishment. (Those were the days
when he was a mere apprentice with Dick Wilkins, good old Dick
Wilkins, who had been very attached to him—long before
Ebenezer's soul had been twisted into an ugly thing by the con-
nivances of commerce.) Later that night, when the cheer had sim-
mered down, and the fire had withdrawn its flames, and a slab of

clouds had blocked out the stars, and a cold mist was pressing against the windows, Ebenezer Scrooge, with a wave of his hand, alighted from the glowing doorway of his nephew's home and headed into the gloom of nineteenth century London. It was that sort of penetrating gloom which of times follows hard on the heels of a frolicsome occasion, the way the brightest and most pleasant of rooms becomes dank and dreary when plunged into the bitter darkness of a winter's night. It was the gloom of death itself.

Ebenezer stepped cautiously through the slippery skin of snow that had settled upon the cobblestones, for he was mortal and, as he had reminded the Ghost of Christmas Past, liable to fall. It was feet-stamping cold, and his breath crystallized with each exhalation. The bleakness was so concentrated it seemed to muffle the sputtering gas lamps along his route, but it did not extinguish the gladness in Scrooge's heart, which radiated on the fuel of his recent salvation. So altered was his attitude that as he walked in the direction of his chambers, he kept an expectant eye out for a carriage to carry him forth. Not since he'd been young and wasteful had he hired a carriage; on this particular evening, however, he felt a strong desire to be accompanied by the happy clacking of hoofs and to impress the cabman with a generosity befitting the season. Scrooge spotted a few such conveyances, shiny through the frozen mists, one of them with holly wound in the spokes of its great wheels. But each was loaded with people and packages and the sounds of mirth, hurrying on toward yet another festivity in celebration of the birth of Christ. By the time he came upon a carriage that was free—a young couple was laughing as they stepped down from the sturdy black vehicle, its springs jouncing from the quick loss of weight—Scrooge had already covered three-quarters of the distance to his rooms. And though the air was as harsh as a rasp, he decided to complete his journey by foot. It seemed more trouble to get in and out of the carriage than the short trip warranted. Besides, a long walk on Christmas night was good for the heart and satisfying to the soul, and a man of business in his time of life had to be attentive to both.

The windows of the low brick houses were gleaming with candles and oil lamps, and the scent of baked breads and sweetmeats wafted over the streets. A few men and women wrapped in green and red scarves bobbed past him on the narrow walk. "Merry Christmas!" said they, raising their hats or saluting, though he did not recognize any of them. Scrooge fingered the brim of his tall hat and smiled as best he could, his cracked face aching from having crowded thirty years of smiling into a single day. What the ghosts had demonstrated to him the previous evening appeared to be decidedly true: There was joy, perhaps even a certain profit, to be collected from being pleasant, from being charitable to others.

Not everyone on that particular London street, on that particular Christmas night, was unknown to Ebenezer Scrooge. Hurrying along on the opposite walk was one Jonathan Wurdlewart, who had business with the firm of Scrooge & Marley. Indeed, his loan was due that very night. And when Wurdlewart spotted a gray-faced old man in a tall black hat moving slowly but with a distinct delight in his step, greeting people as they passed, the debtor ducked into an alley and stared out from the shadows. "It can't be," Wurdlewart muttered, rubbing his tired eyes, "it just can't be." After the old man had passed, and the debtor saw that it was indeed Scrooge himself, he cursed him under his breath as a hypocrite as well as a usurer. For a long while Wurdlewart remained in the shadows, as if pondering what course of action to take. At last he began moving in the direction Scrooge had gone.

Scrooge turned off the broad street and down a narrow byway, and before long this brought him into the district of warehouses and factories and countinghouses, not far from where he had inhabited a suite of rooms as cheerless as the London morgue. Those who had a choice did not wish to live amidst the clank of machinery and the clink of coins, to hear the cries of children when they were struck for lack of productivity. Scrooge resided here to be closer to his commercial interests at all times and because rents were far cheaper. (The rest of the rooms in the lowering pile of stone in which he resided were let out as offices.) Others lived out their time nearby because there was nowhere else for them to go. On this singular night of the year the workers were huddled in their drafty, wretched dwellings, many without coal for their fires; some had no more than boiled potatoes for their tables, the skins of which were served as a side dish to introduce variety to their meals. Their windows were mostly dark. In this district the streets were solitary, and the doorways were cut into black relief, and loose windows rattled in their frames, and the debris of manufacture flapped in the gutters, and the alleys were as grim as the grave. Considering all this, it is little wonder that Scrooge was gradually overtaken by a feeling that someone was following him, and he turned around quickly, but saw no one. It is little wonder the smile fell away from his face and he began to think about time: In a few days yet another year in his paltry allotment of years would be gone, and he would not be another hour richer.

As he came upon his countinghouse, with the weathered sign nailed above the door—Scrooge & Marley—the old man spotted something that made him feel as if a headstone had toppled over into his soul. Across the street from his place of business there was a single lamp burning in the window of Pennerpinch, Ltd. So Gladnought Pennerpinch, Ebenezer's long-time and despised competitor, was working on Christmas night, trying to grab an advantage over Scrooge & Marley! Ebenezer stood as dead-still as a door-nail on the crusty walk, regretting passionately having given Cratchit the day off. At year's end we should both have been going over the accounts so as not to fall behind, he thought, so as not to permit that scoundrel Pennerpinch to steal the bread from my mouth! And he clenched his bony fist and shook it at the smoke-blackened brick establishment across the way.

Just then the figure of Pennerpinch, as slick and rigid as an icicle, passed by the window carrying a large ledger, his shadow looming behind him. It was clear to Scrooge that his nemesis was going to do his accounts long into the night. "It's not fair!" Scrooge moaned, and he shivered from standing still too long in the cold. Though he yearned to be home and to free his feet from the tight boots, rather than allow his competitor to expand on the advantage already gained, he turned up the stairs of his countinghouse. Scrooge slid his hand inside his coat, yanked the ring of numerous keys from his vest pocket, and unlocked one, two, three bolts. Just as he reached out to grip the knob, however, he saw a facial configuration on the iron knocker and quickly withdrew his hand. "Not again!" he declared. Looking more closely, Scrooge realized it was an illusion created by a coating of frost. "Humbug!" Entering and closing the door behind him hastily, he proceeded to relock each of the three devices.

The stale dampness made the office feel colder than the night streets. He passed from Cratchit's outer cell into the larger space, moving to his desk in the dimness the way a blind man feels his way through familiar surroundings. Turning his chair so he could keep an eye on Pennerpinch out the window, he sat down. It was too cold to remove his heavy coat, but unlike Cratchit, Scrooge could work without burning his coal as if it were rubbish. After rubbing his hands together briskly to acquire some free warmth, he struck a match into flame and lit the lamp, bringing the chamber into view. The big desk looked overworked, and dusty wooden shelves were stacked with yellowed ledgers, each representing a year of commerce. The iron stove was as cold and black as its owner's heart. At last Scrooge felt some small glimmer of satisfaction, for he knew that sooner or later Pennerpinch would notice the light coming from Scrooge & Marley.

In the flickering paleness, Scrooge opened the ledger stamped 1843 and began to slide his finger down the long list of debtors. This was how he started every business day, for it comforted him to know that he was owed so much. A quick addition of the receivables alarmed him, however. Cratchit had shortchanged him by nine pence. "The sneaking scoundrel!" he declared out loud, for being alone so much had taught him to speak to himself. Again he added up the figures, this time with more care, and the amount totaled up as it should have. To be absolutely certain, he added them yet again, and again the balance appeared to be correct. "You don't know how close you came to losing your position, Cratchit," he said to the empty outer cell. Scrooge moved the tin cash box off the blotter, unlocked the center drawer, and pulled out a sheath of crisp white collection notes. Flipping through them, he slipped out one in particular. In accordance with their agreement, Scrooge & Marley would take possession of Jonathan Wurdlewart's house and shop if the debt were not paid *in full* by twelve o'clock midnight, Christmas, 1843. Wurdlewart had not wanted to put up his home as collateral, but Scrooge had insisted, and the baker was so convinced the shop would bring him a quick return that he agreed. Alas, the interest was so high he couldn't keep up with the payments, and now his time was almost gone. Ebenezer Scrooge checked the clock against the bare wall: eleven forty-six. "In fourteen minutes," he said, "it will all be mine." The glittering eyes of his nephew's children and the joyful chime of the city's bells were no more than dreams of what seemed like a long lost past.

As Scrooge calculated the value of the neat cottage and the busy shop, there was a knocking in the outer chamber. Afraid it might be Wurdlewart, come to pay off the loan, Scrooge quickly blew out the lamp. After all, the countinghouse was shut for Christmas Day so how could he accept a payment? In the dreary darkness he sat, cold in his bones, peeking out the shutter. A gaslight flickered on the street, but the steps of his establishment were set in, making it impossible to see who was at the door. The knocking sounded again, and growing edgy, Scrooge arose quietly and crept into the outer cell. If Wurdlewart had the money in hand, he would be forced to settle the account and would not be able to claim the house and shop. Faced with the possibility of such a loss, Scrooge felt miserable.

At the door he heard the sound again, but it seemed to be coming not from the knocker but above the door. Scrooge determined that Pennerpinch had seen his light and gotten angry, and was out there tampering with his sign! Quickly he began freeing the three locks, and in a few moments swung open the door and cried out, "What d'ya think you're doing?" To his surprise there was no one there, or so he thought at first. Through the thick, frozen mist there did seem to be someone, or something, drifting toward him, and as the shape drew closer he saw that it was his deceased partner, Jacob Marley, dragging his long and heavy chain after him.

"Jacob! You assured me I would not be visited again, that I would be saved."

Marley gurgled. "Already you have forgotten your promise, Ebenezer."

"Well, now, Jacob, I must say I had a pleasant time of it today. But Christmas is finished now, and it is time to get back to business."

"The spirit of Christmas must be honored by every man through the long calendar of the year."

"But don't you see that light in Pennerpinch's window? He is working on Christmas night to gain an advantage over your former partner—I *cannot* allow that."

"Pennerpinch is forging his own chain, link by link, just as I did. Just as you are doing."

"Pennerpinch is making a fortune!"

Marley wailed, and Scrooge begged him to calm down.

"This is your last opportunity for salvation," Marley murmured. "Your last forever and anon."

"I'll be hanged before I hand everything I've worked for over to that wretch!"

"I am sorry for you, Ebenezer," Marley hissed, and the hollow voice, along with the wispy substance that was his body, instantly melted like smoke. The chains, too, had evaporated.

The sudden disappearance of his old partner made Scrooge feel apprehensive. "Marley? Where are you? Speak comfort to me, Jacob."

There was no reply, only the sound of wind gasping in the alley. Now Scrooge spotted a greenish glow sifting out of the mist—rather like the shape of that gruesome, shrouded figure of the Ghost of Christmas Yet to Come. Scrooge backed inside and slammed the door shut, but before he could secure any of the locks, the spirit stood before him, pointing his finger of bone at his chest. Terrified, Scrooge fled into the back office and grabbed hold of Marley's knobbed cane, which he kept in the corner as a warning to charity seekers. Raising the cane as if ready to strike, he waited for the apparition, but there was no movement or sound in the outer cell, and after what seemed a long time, weary, he dropped onto his seat and set the cane across the blotter in front of him. "Humbug!" he snarled.

Reluctant to give anyone or anything a better view of him, and to save oil, Scrooge did not relight the lamp. He simply waited for something to happen. The shadows held their places, however, and feeling less ill at ease, Scrooge proceeded to watch the large black hands of the clock, faintly discernible in the band of gaslight from outside. In three minutes he would acquire the Wurdlewart properties, and the next day would put them on the market for triple their value. All remained quiet and still in the dismal office, while every tick of the clock seemed to be making him richer. At the exact moment of twelve o'clock midnight, Scrooge heard not the stroke of the hour but the clink of a chain—just a breath after the icy iron links yanked brutally tight about his heart.

Bob Cratchit discovered Ebenezer Scrooge the next morning, slumped back against his chair, and exclaimed, "Oh, my God!" After recovering from the shock, the short, skinny clerk pulled a coarse cap over his brittle hair and went to notify the police. Within the hour an officer arrived at the countinghouse, buttoned up in a heavy blue coat and blue vested suit. Cratchit showed him in. Inspector Ignatius Grabbe was a narrow-shouldered man with a wide red mustache and tiny, black, suspicious eyes. As the inspector snooped and sniffed around the chamber and cell for several minutes, the clerk, still shaken, watched in silence, his eyes avoiding the heap of humanity at the desk.

Grabbe, who was rather vain when it came to his powers of deduction, noted out loud that the stiffness of the deceased's skin indicated he had been dead for some hours. "It would appear," the inspector theorized, "that your employer had stopped by his office last night to pick up something important he had forgotten."

"What could he have forgotten, sir?" Cratchit asked, knowing that his master had possessed a powerful memory.

"Well, it could be almost anything," Inspector Grabbe hedged, eyeing the cane in the corner. "How dependent was he on that stick?"

"Oh, that belonged to his partner, Jacob Marley, who is long dead," Cratchit said with a quaver in his throat.

"I see," Grabbe grumbled. "Well, then, perhaps it was for some vital business papers."

"On Christmas night? I should think not."

Annoyed at being foiled, the inspector declared irascibly: "Certainly the deceased did not intend to stop for very long, for he hadn't removed his coat and the ashes in the stove are *quite* cold."

Cratchit refrained from mentioning that Scrooge hated to burn his coal.

Having finally silenced the clerk, Grabbe proceeded with his investigation. He lifted the rusty lid of a small square box on the desk, leafed through a ledger, opened a drawer, flipped through a stack of bills. Then he noticed that the daily calendar was turned to December 26, and that there were no appointments listed. "Hmmm."

Cratchit's eyebrows rose, but his lips remained shut.

Now the inspector looked closely at the latch on the window, which had rusted solid from years of non-use. "Have you keys of your own to these rooms?"

"No one but his own self was permitted to possess keys."

"How did you gain entry this morning, Mr. Cratchit?"

"Upon my arrival the door was unbolted."

Inspector Grabbe looked at Cratchit sadly. "Did you and your employer have . . . harmonious relations?"

Surprised by the directness of the question, the clerk stammered, "Why only yesterday Mr. Scrooge sent a giant turkey to my home for Christmas dinner."

"Would that be the one that had been filling out the window of the poulterer's on the next street?"

"The very bird," Cratchit conceded.

A low whistle emitted from the inspector's lips, and he suddenly did a right-face turn on his heel and moved beside the slumped form of Ebenezer Scrooge, looking over the deceased's head, neck, face. Apparently dissatisfied with his findings, he began reviewing the objects on the desk again. At last he stopped, and put one finger of thought under his chin. The chamber was dense with silence for a few moments.

"Is anything wrong?" Cratchit asked guardedly.

"Not precisely, Mr. Cratchit, but I do find it odd that the cash box is empty."

"Mr. Scrooge would never leave cash in the office. Never."

The conviction with which this statement was delivered did not go unnoticed, and the inspector, taking a deep breath of frustration, suddenly felt compelled to make some display of conclusiveness. "It would appear," he proposed grandly, "it would appear the gentleman known as Ebenezer Scrooge returned to his office to look up his appointment calendar for the following day, suffered an internal malfunction, and expired in his chair."

"Poor, poor Mr. Scrooge," said Cratchit.

Because the clerk had not seemed terribly impressed with the mental process that had led to his deduction, the inspector added, "Of course, there is the lamp to consider."

"The lamp?"

"Either the oil should have all burned out," observed the inspector, "or it should have been lit." At this moment he whipped out the burnt match. "Voilà!"

His eyes widening at this new evidence, Cratchit said, "Is it possible a draft had blown it out, sir?"

"Anything is possible," Grabbe admitted, raising one sharp eyebrow doubtfully.

The inspector did an abrupt left-face turn on his heel, and resumed nosing about the premises. But it was clear to Cratchit, who stood hard by in modest silence, that no new evidence was being uncovered. At long last two men wearing white gloves and white faces arrived at Scrooge & Marley. Without a word they loaded the remains of Ebenezer Scrooge onto a wooden plank and carried their leaden cargo, with some unsteadiness, down the front steps. Here the body was dumped into a wooden box supported by four iron wheels with wooden spokes. Along the street the men pushed their earthly burden, as the curious drew closer to learn which of their number had been called to account for his life. The coarse gray shroud flapped grimly in the smoky breeze, and with a distinct smear of disappointment in his tight face, Inspector Ignatius Grabbe joined in the solemn procession.

At the doorway of the countinghouse stood Cratchit, head slightly bowed, in respect. But something caught his eye. Across the way, the pale visage of Gladnought Pennerpinch had appeared in a window, watching the proceedings intensely; and even at that distance, or so it seemed to Cratchit, there was an expression of pleasure discernible upon the wizened face of Scrooge's fiercest competitor.

For all the inspector's deductions, Bob Cratchit had his own theory. When he'd arrived at the countinghouse, as he'd revealed to the police, the door had been left unlocked. What he did not mention was that this was *extremely* unlike his master. Moreover, Scrooge's hand was clenched tightly about Jacob Marley's cane, and lying on the blotter was the collection note on the Jonathan Wurdlewart account. This debt, Cratchit knew, was due on Christmas night; this debt would ruin a man and his family. And most telling of all was the smudge of rust that Cratchit had noticed across the old sinner's chest, as if he'd been struck by a blunt metal object. Cratchit quickly came to some conclusions, and then he did something strange: The clerk unpried Mr. Scrooge's fingers from the cane and stood it in the corner, and placed the Wurdlewart bill in the stove and set it afire. He mixed the new ashes with the old, and left the door of the office ajar a few minutes to clear the scent of smoke. Finally he brushed away the rust on Scrooge's coat. Only then did Cratchit go to the police. But he never mentioned these clues to them, nor to anyone else—not even to Mrs. Cratchit. After the coroner had reviewed the corpse at the London morgue, and following a period of customary bureaucratic procrastination, the incident went down in police records as "Death by natural causes." When this news reached Cratchit, the humble clerk thought: You're not so smart as you think, Inspector Grabbe.

Upon the death of Jacob Marley seven years hence, the countinghouse of Scrooge & Marley had passed into the hands of Ebenezer Scrooge, although he'd never gotten around to painting over Marley's name on the sign. Now that Scrooge was gone, these assets, considerably greater by 1844, became the lawful property of the only blood survivor the authorities could locate. However, Scrooge's nephew Fred had no talents or interests in this direction, nor any wish to benefit from the misery of others. Not long after his uncle had been laid out and returned to his Maker, the young man visited the bare, chilly abode of Mr. Bob Cratchit and his family. The children were frail and seemed frightened, and one of them, he noticed, leaned on a crutch. Little Mrs. Cratchit, too poor to offer a cup of tea to their guest, said not a word as she sat woodenly on the rough-hewn chair in a black dress washed so often it had turned gray.

The tall young gentleman, holding the brim of his hat with both hands, straight away asked Cratchit: "Would you kindly consider managing Scrooge & Marley on behalf of my family?"

Expressing great surprise—partly because he *was* surprised, and partly because it was good manners—Cratchit said gratefully, nay, heartily: "It would be an honor and a pleasure." That evening everyone in the Cratchit family received an extra spoonful of turkey bone soup.

The first action Bob Cratchit took as manager of Scrooge & Marley was to light a good fire in the office and to heap on the coal. His second action was to write a letter to Jonathan Wurdlewart in which he offered an extension of time and a much more equitable interest rate. Three days later Wurdlewart, looking lean and bewildered, showed up at the countinghouse and inquired cautiously of Cratchit: "Have I understood the terms of your letter correctly?"

"I should think you have."

At which reply Wurdlewart grabbed Cratchit's hand and nearly shook his arm out of its socket. "Thank you so much, kind sir, from me and my family. Thank you so very, very much."

Grinning happily, Cratchit replied: "You're most welcome, I'm sure."

By the following Christmas the baker was free and clear of his debt, and his shop began to prosper. During that period Bob Cratchit and Jonathan Wurdlewart became friends, and several times their families dined together. But not a word about the evidence, or about Cratchit's suspicion, passed between them. Nor did Wurdlewart mention that he had followed Scrooge back to his countinghouse that fateful Christmas night with the idea of appealing to him for more time. After standing out in the dreadful cold awhile, however, Wurdlewart saw through the mist someone who looked thin and short as Cratchit approach and enter the establishment of Scrooge & Marley. But Wurdlewart lost his courage, and so he had wandered back home to seek the comfort of his family. It was only after he heard about Scrooge's death at his desk that he remembered how the old man had viciously belittled Cratchit in front of several people, and Cratchit's fists had clenched in humiliation. So Wurdlewart came to some conclusions of his own, but he never mentioned what he saw that Christmas night—except to his wife, in whom he confided all things.

One autumn evening, when the Cratchits were visiting the Wurdlewarts, Mrs. Wurdlewart, a robust lady famed for her hot toddies, stirred up a great bowl of spirits and kept ladling it into the men's cups. Soon the two husbands were red in the face and sentimental in the heart. Expressing the need for some air, they stepped out onto the moonlit cobblestones and took a walk. In a burst of protective feeling for his friend, Cratchit said to Wurdlewart: "You can be sure of one thing, Jonathan, no matter how long I live, I shall never breathe a word of what I know to another living soul."

Wurdlewart stopped and turned unsteadily toward his friend. "Strange," he said, "I was about to say very much the same thing to you, Bob."

At this time they each revealed their suspicions to one another.

"As God is my witness," said Wurdlewart, "though the thought had passed through my head in a weak moment, I never brought harm to Scrooge. It's not in my nature."

"May God strike me dead if I had anything to do with Mr. Scrooge's demise," declared Cratchit. "It never once entered my mind."

In a flash the two friends knew that the other was speaking the truth. Cratchit realized that the rust he had removed from Scrooge's coat was very likely a marking the old man had acquired when brushing against the rusted lid of the cash box, and Wurdlewart realized that what he had seen that night was probably a configuration of mist, not of man. In the glare of the moon both of their minds continued to wander a few moments: Cratchit thought about Pennerpinch, and Wurdlewart thought about yet another of Scrooge's debtors whom he had heard threaten the usurer in his office. But in a short time both men dismissed these possibilities as highly improbable, and their minds converged on one idea. At virtually the same moment the two friends had concluded that God, in His infinite wisdom, to satisfy His everlasting desire for justice, and by way of one of His innumerable spiritual agents of mercy, had struck down the old miser.

"God is just," said Cratchit, thinking that Inspector Grabbe had been correct about Scrooge's death after all.

"God is good," said Wurdlewart, thinking that his wife had been correct about Cratchit's innocence after all.

With an arm around each other's shoulder, and much more refreshed, the friends swaggered back toward the house to rejoin the festivities.

POSTSCRIPT

Under Bob Cratchit's hard-earned experience and thrifty management the establishment of Scrooge & Marley flourished, and within a few years he was able to move his wife and five children out of the mercantile district into a modest yet handsome house (with three fireplaces) far from the sounds of manufacture. Now when the Wurdlewarts appeared at their home, Mrs. Cratchit served crumpets as well as fancy tea, and she became quite a bit more talkative, especially along these lines: "Bob, I'll be needing a new dress to replace this old rag." Tiny Tim, who did not die as foreshadowed by the last of the ghostly triumvirate, grew stronger every day and, finally, threw away his crutch altogether. At the same time he was growing smarter. One day he joined the firm as his father's apprentice. The lad learned quickly, helping to ease the workload on his father considerably. It was not long before Tim was earning a regular wage, and he began expanding the company's services. In time, the Cratchits were able to buy out Scrooge's nephew, who was pleased to be finished with such business entirely. The following week a new sign appeared over the door of the countinghouse—Cratchit & Son—and Tim, who was no longer so tiny, became shrewder and, with every pound won in commerce, hungrier for more and more profit. And so, as Big Tim observed the following Christmas, "God bless us with another client!"

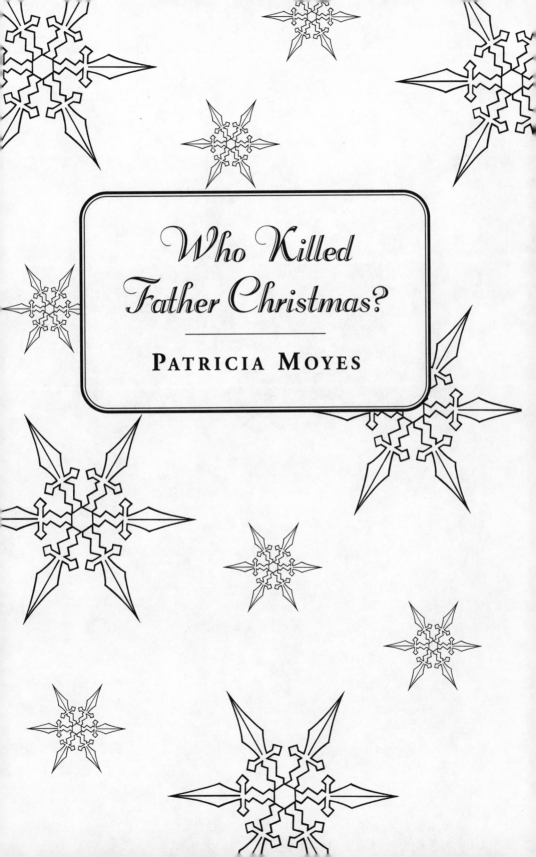

Who Killed Father Christmas?

PATRICIA MOYES

GOOD MORNING, MR. BORROWDALE. NIPPY OUT, isn't it? You're in early, I see." Little Miss MacArthur spoke with her usual brisk brightness, which failed to conceal both envy and dislike. She was unpacking a consignment of stout Teddy bears in the stockroom behind the toy department at Barnum and Thrums, the London store. "Smart as ever, Mr. Borrowdale," she added, jealously.

I laid down my curly-brimmed bowler hat and cane and took off my British warm overcoat. I don't mind admitting that I do take pains to dress as well as I can, and for some reason it seems to infuriate the Miss MacArthurs of the world.

She prattled on. "Nice looking, these Teddies, don't you think? Very reasonable, too. Made in Hong Kong, that'll be why. I think I'll take one for my sister's youngest."

The toy department at Barnum's has little to recommend it to anyone over the age of twelve, and normally it is tranquil and little populated. However, at Christmastime it briefly becomes the bustling heart of the great shop, and also provides useful vacation jobs for chaps like me who wish to earn some money during the weeks before the university term begins in January. Gone, I fear, are the days when undergraduates were the gilded youth of England. We all have to work our passages these days, and sometimes it means selling toys.

One advantage of the job is that employees—even temporaries

like me—are allowed to buy goods at a considerable discount, which helps with the Christmas gift problem. As a matter of fact, I had already decided to buy a Teddy bear for one of my nephews, and I mentioned as much.

"Well, you'd better take it right away," remarked Miss MacArthur, "because I heard Mr. Harrington say he was taking two, and I think Disaster has her eye on one." Disaster was the unfortunate but inevitable nickname of Miss Aster, who had been with the store for thirty-one years but still made mistakes with her stockbook. I felt sorry for the old girl. I had overheard a conversation between Mr. Harrington, the department manager, and Mr. Andrews, the deputy store manager, and so I knew—but Disaster didn't—that she would be getting the sack as soon as the Christmas rush was over.

Meanwhile, Miss MacArthur was arranging the bears on a shelf. They sat there in grinning rows, brown and woolly, with boot-button eyes and red ribbons round their necks.

It was then that Father Christmas came in. He'd been in the cloakroom changing into his costume—white beard, red nose, and all. His name was Bert Denman. He was a cheery soul who got on well with the kids, and he'd had the Father Christmas job at Barnum's each of the three years I'd been selling there. Now he was carrying his sack, which he filled every morning from the cheap items in the stockroom. A visit to Father Christmas cost 50 pence, so naturally the gift that was fished out of the sack couldn't be worth more than 20 pence. However, to my surprise, he went straight over to the row of Teddy bears and picked one off the shelf. For some reason, he chose the only one with a blue instead of a red ribbon.

Miss MacArthur was on to him in an instant. "What d'you

think you're doing, Mr. Denman? Those Teddies aren't in your line at all—much too dear. One pound ninety, they are."

Father Christmas did not answer, and suddenly I realized that it was not Bert Denman under the red robe. "Wait a minute," I said. "Who are you? You're not our Father Christmas."

He turned to face me, the Teddy bear in his hand. "That's all right," he said. "Charlie Burrows is my name. I live in the same lodging house with Bert Denman. He was taken poorly last night, and I'm standing in for him."

"*Well,*" said Miss MacArthur. "How very odd. Does Mr. Harrington know?"

"Of course he does," said Father Christmas.

As if on cue, Mr. Harrington himself came hurrying into the stockroom. He always hurried everywhere, preceded by his small black mustache. He said, "Ah, there you are, Burrows. Fill up your sack, and I'll explain the job to you. Denman told you about the Teddy bear, did he?"

"Yes, Mr. Harrington."

"Father Christmas can't give away an expensive bear like that, Mr. Harrington," Miss MacArthur objected.

"Now, now, Miss MacArthur, it's all arranged," said Harrington fussily. "A customer came in yesterday and made a special request that Father Christmas should give his small daughter a Teddy bear this morning. I knew this consignment was due on the shelves, so I promised him one. It's been paid for. The important thing, Burrows, is to remember the child's name. It's . . . er . . . I have it written down somewhere."

"Annabel Whitworth," said Father Christmas. "Four years old, fair hair, will be brought in by her mother."

"I see that Denman briefed you well," said Mr. Harrington,

with an icy smile. "Well, now, I'll collect two bears for myself—one for my son and one for my neighbor's boy—and then I'll show you the booth."

Miss Aster arrived just then. She and Miss MacArthur finished uncrating the bears and took one out to put on display next to a female doll that, among other endearing traits, actually wet its diaper. Mr. Harrington led our surrogate Father Christmas to his small canvas booth, and the rest of us busied and braced ourselves for the moment when the great glass doors opened and the floodtide was let in. The toy department of a big store on December 23 is no place for weaklings.

It is curious that even such an apparently random stream of humanity as Christmas shoppers displays a pattern of behavior. The earliest arrivals in the toy department are office workers on their way to their jobs. The actual toddlers, bent on an interview with Father Christmas, do not appear until their mothers have had time to wash up breakfast, have a bit of a go around the house, and catch the bus from Kensington or the tube from Uxbridge.

On that particular morning it was just twenty-eight minutes past ten when I saw Disaster, who was sitting in a decorated cash desk labeled "The Elfin Grove," take 50 pence from the first parent to usher her child into Santa's booth. For about two minutes the mother waited, chatting quietly with Disaster. Then a loudly wailing infant emerged from the booth.

The mother snatched her up, and—with that sixth sense that mothers everywhere seem to develop—interpreted the incoherent screams. "She says that Father Christmas won't talk to her. She says he's asleep."

It was clearly an emergency, even if a minor one, and Disaster was already showing signs of panic. I excused myself from my customer—a middle-aged gentleman who was playing with an electric

train set—and went over to see what I could do. By then, the
mother was indignant.

"Fifty pence and the old man sound asleep and drunk as like as
not, and at half-past ten in the morning. Disgraceful, I call it. And
here's poor little Poppy what had been looking forward to—"

I rushed into Father Christmas's booth. The man who called
himself Charlie Burrows was slumped forward in his chair, looking
for all the world as if he were asleep; but when I shook him, his
head lolled horribly, and it was obvious that he was more than
sleeping. The red robe concealed the blood until it made my hand
sticky. Father Christmas had been stabbed in the back, and he was
certainly dead.

I acted as fast as I could. First of all, I told Disaster to put up
the CLOSED sign outside Santa's booth. Then I smoothed down
Poppy's mother by leading her to a counter where I told her she
could select any toy up to one pound and have it free. Under pretext of keeping records, I got her name and address. Finally I cornered Mr. Harrington in his office and told him the news.

I thought he was going to faint. "Dead? Murdered? Are you
sure, Mr. Borrowdale?"

"Quite sure, I'm afraid. You'd better telephone the police, Mr.
Harrington."

"The police! In Barnum's! What a terrible thing! I'll telephone
the deputy store manager first and *then* the police."

As a matter of fact, the police were surprisingly quick and dis-
creet. A plainclothes detective superintendent and his sergeant, a
photographer, and the police doctor arrived, not in a posse, but as
individuals, unnoticed among the crowd. They assembled in the
booth, where the deputy manager—Mr. Andrews—and Mr. Harrington and I were waiting for them.

The superintendent introduced himself—his name was Armitage—and inspected the body with an expression of cold fury on his face that I couldn't quite understand, although the reason became clear later. He said very little. After some tedious formalities Armitage indicated that the body might be removed.

"What's the least conspicuous way to do it?" he asked.

"You can take him out through the back of the booth," I said. "The canvas overlaps right behind Santa's chair. The door to the staff quarters and the stockroom is just opposite, and from there you can take the service lift to the goods entrance in the mews."

The doctor and the photographer between them carried off their grim burden on a collapsible stretcher, and Superintendent Armitage began asking questions about the arrangements in the Father Christmas booth. I did the explaining, since Mr. Harrington seemed to be verging on hysteria.

Customers paid their 50 pence to Disaster in the Elfin Grove, and then the child—usually alone—was propelled through the door of the booth and into the presence of Father Christmas, who sat in his canvas-backed director's chair on a small dais facing the entrance, with his sack of toys beside him. The child climbed onto his knee, whispered its Christmas wishes, and was rewarded with a few friendly words and a small gift from Santa's sack.

What was not obvious to the clientele was the back entrance to the booth, which enabled Father Christmas to slip in and out unobserved. He usually had his coffee break at about 11:15, unless there was a very heavy rush of business. Disaster would pick a moment when custom seemed slow, put up the CLOSED notice, and inform Bert that he could take a few minutes off. When he returned, he pressed a button by his chair that rang a buzzer in the cashier's booth. Down would come the notice, and Santa was in business again.

Before Superintendent Armitage could comment on my remarks, Mr. Harrington broke into a sort of despairing wail. "It must have been one of the customers!" he cried.

"I don't think so, sir," said Armitage. "This is an inside job. He was stabbed in the back with a long thin blade of some sort. The murderer must have opened the back flap and stabbed him clean through the canvas back of his chair. That must have been someone who knew the exact arrangements. The murderer then used the back way to enter the booth—"

"I don't see how you can say that!" Harrington's voice was rising dangerously. "If the man was stabbed from outside, what makes you think anybody came into the booth?"

"I'll explain that in a minute, sir."

Ignoring Armitage, Harrington went on. "In any case, he wasn't our regular Father Christmas! None of us had ever seen him before. Why on earth would anybody kill a man that nobody knew?"

Armitage and the deputy manager exchanged glances. Then Armitage said, "*I* knew him, sir. Very well. Charlie Burrows was one of our finest plainclothes narcotics officers."

Mr. Harrington had gone green. "You mean—he was a policeman?"

"Exactly, sir. I'd better explain. A little time ago we got a tipoff from an informer that an important consignment of high-grade heroin was to be smuggled in from Hong Kong in a consignment of Christmas toys. Teddy bears, in fact. The drug was to be in the Barnum and Thrums carton, hidden inside a particular Teddy bear, which would be distinguished by having a blue ribbon around its neck instead of a red one."

"Surely," I said, "you couldn't get what you call an important consignment inside one Teddy bear, even a big one."

Armitage sighed. "Shows you aren't familiar with the drug scene, sir," he said. "Why, half a pound of pure high-grade heroin is worth a fortune on the streets."

With a show of bluster Harrington said, "If you knew this, Superintendent, why didn't you simply intercept the consignment and confiscate the drug? Look at the trouble that's been—"

Armitage interrupted him. "If you'd just hear me out, sir. What I've told you was the sum total of our information. We didn't know who in Barnum's was going to pick up the heroin, or how or where it was to be disposed of. We're more interested in getting the people—the pushers—than confiscating the cargo. So I had a word with Mr. Andrews here, and he kindly agreed to let Charlie take on the Father Christmas job. And Charlie set a little trap. Unfortunately, he paid for it with his life." There was an awkward silence.

He went on. "Mr. Andrews told us that the consignment had arrived and was to be unpacked today. We know that staff get first pick, as it were, at new stock, and we were naturally interested to see who would select the bear with the blue ribbon. It was Charlie's own idea to concoct a story about a special present for a little girl—"

"You mean, that wasn't true?" Harrington was outraged. "But I spoke to the customer myself!"

"Yes, sir. That's to say, you spoke to another of our people, who was posing as the little girl's father."

"You're very thorough," Harrington said.

"Yes, sir. Thank you, sir. Well, as I was saying, Charlie made a point of selecting the bear with the blue ribbon and taking it off in his sack. He knew that whoever was picking up the drop would have to come and get it—or try to. You see, if we'd just allowed one of the staff to select it, that person could simply have said that it was pure coincidence—blue was such a pretty color. Difficult to prove criminal knowledge. You understand?"

Nobody said anything. With quite a sense of dramatic effect Armitage reached down into Santa's sack and pulled out a Teddy bear. It had a blue ribbon round its neck.

In a voice tense with strain Mr. Andrews said, "So the murderer didn't get away with the heroin. I thought you said—"

Superintendent Armitage produced a knife from his pocket. "We'll see," he said. "With your permission, I'm going to open this bear."

"Of course."

The knife ripped through the nobbly brown fabric, and a lot of stuffing fell out. Nothing else. Armitage made a good job of it. By the time he had finished, the bear was in shreds: and nothing had emerged from its interior except kapok.

Armitage surveyed the wreckage with a sort of bleak satisfaction. Suddenly brisk, he said, "Now. Which staff members took bears from the stockroom this morning?"

"I did," I said at once.

"Anybody else?"

There was a silence. I said, "I believe you took two, didn't you, Mr. Harrington?"

"I . . . em . . . yes, now that you mention it."

"Miss MacArthur took one," I said. "It was she who unpacked the carton. She said that Dis—Miss Aster—was going to take one."

"I see." Armitage was making notes. "I presume you each signed for your purchases, and that the bears are now with your things in the staff cloakroom." Without waiting for an answer he turned to me. "How many of these people saw Burrows select the bear with the blue ribbon?"

"All of us," I said. "Isn't that so, Mr. Harrington?"

Harrington just nodded. He looked sick.

"Well, then," said Armitage, "I shall have to inspect all the bears that you people removed from the stockroom."

There was an element of black humor in the parade of the Teddies, with their inane grins and knowing, beady eyes: but as one after the other was dismembered, nothing more sensational was revealed than a growing pile of kapok. The next step was to check the stockbook numbers—and sure enough, one bear was missing.

It was actually Armitage's Sergeant who found it. It had been ripped open and shoved behind a pile of boxes in the stockroom in a hasty attempt at concealment. There was no ribbon round its neck, and it was constructed very differently from the others. The kapok merely served as a thin layer of stuffing between the fabric skin and a spherical womb of pink plastic in the toy's center. This plastic had been cut open and was empty. It was abundantly clear what it must have contained.

"Well," said the Superintendent, "it's obvious what happened. The murderer stabbed Burrows, slipped into the booth, and substituted an innocent Teddy bear for the loaded one, at the same time changing the neck ribbon. But he—or she—didn't dare try walking out of the store with the bear, not after a murder. So, before Charlie's body was found, the murderer dismembered the bear, took out the heroin, and hid it." He sighed again. "I'm afraid this means a body search. I'll call the Yard for a police matron for the ladies."

It was all highly undignified and tedious, and poor old Disaster nearly had a seizure, despite the fact that the police matron seemed a thoroughly nice and kind woman. When it was all over, however, and our persons and clothing had been practically turned inside out, still nothing had been found. The four of us were required to wait in the staff restroom while exhaustive searches were made for both the heroin and the weapon.

Disaster was in tears, Miss MacArthur was loudly indignant and threatened to sue the police for false arrest, and Mr. Harrington developed what he called a nervous stomach, on account, he said, of the way the toy department was being left understaffed and unsupervised on one of the busiest days of the year.

At long last Superintendent Armitage came in. He said, "Nothing. Abso-bloody-lutely nothing. Well, I can't keep you people here indefinitely. I suggest you all go out and get yourselves some lunch." He sounded very tired and cross and almost human.

With considerable relief we prepared to leave the staffroom. Only Mr. Harrington announced that he felt too ill to eat anything, and that he would remain in the department. The Misses MacArthur and Aster left together. I put on my coat and took the escalator down to the ground floor, among the burdened, chattering crowd.

I was out in the brisk air of the street when I heard Armitage's voice behind me.

"Just one moment, if you please, Mr. Borrowdale."

I turned. "Yes, Superintendent. Can I help you?"

"You're up at the university, aren't you, sir? Just taken a temporary job at Barnum's for the vacation?"

"That's right."

"Do quite a bit of fencing, don't you?"

He had my cane out of my hand before I knew what was happening. The sergeant, an extraordinarily tough and unattractive character, showed surprising dexterity and speed in getting an arm grip on me. Armitage had unscrewed the top of the cane, and was whistling in a quiet, appreciative manner. "Very nice. Very nice little sword stick. Something like a stilletto. I don't suppose Charlie felt a thing."

"Now, look here," I said. "You can't make insinuations like that. Just because I'm known as a bit of a dandy, and carry a sword stick, that's no reason—"

"A dandy, eh?" said Armitage thoughtfully. He looked me up and down in a curious manner, as if he thought something was missing.

It was at that moment that Miss MacArthur suddenly appeared round the corner of the building.

"Oh, Mr. Borrowdale, look what I found! Lying down in the mews by the goods entrance! It must have fallen out of the staffroom window! Lucky I've got sharp eyes—it was behind a rubbish bin, I might easily have missed it!" And she handed me my bowler hat.

That is to say, she would have done if Armitage hadn't intercepted it. It didn't take him more than five seconds to find the packages of white powder hidden between the hard shell of the hat and the oiled-silk lining.

Armitage said, "So you were going to peddle this stuff to young men and women at the university, were you? Charming, I must say. Now you can come back to the Yard and tell us all about your employers—if you want a chance at saving your own neck, that is."

Miss MacArthur was goggling at me. "Oh, Mr. Borrowdale!" she squeaked. "Have I gone and done something wrong?"

I never did like Miss MacArthur.

Acknowledgments

Grateful acknowledgment is made to the following for their permission to reprint their copyrighted material:

"Christmas Cop" by Thomas Larry Adcock, copyright © 1986 by Davis Publications, Inc., reprinted by permission of the author.

"On Christmas Day in the Morning" by Margery Allingham, copyright 1952 by P. and M. Youngman Carter Ltd., reprinted by permission of the Estate.

"I Saw Mommy Killing Santa Claus" by George Baxt, copyright © 1990 by Davis Publications, Inc., reprinted by permission of the author.

"Mystery for Christmas" by Anthony Boucher, copyright © 1942 by Anthony Boucher, reprinted by permission of Curtis Brown Ltd.

"The Marley Case" by Linda Haldeman, copyright © 1982 by Davis Publications, Inc., reprinted by permission of Cherry Weiner Literary Agency.

"Dead on Christmas Street" by John D. MacDonald, copyright © Dorothy P. MacDonald Trust reprinted by permission of Diskant Associates.

"Kelso's Christmas" by Malcolm McClintick, copyright © 1984 by Davis Publications, Inc., reprinted by permission of the author.

"Who Killed Father Christmas?" by Patricia Moyes, copyright © 1980 by Laura W. Haywood & Isaac Asimov, first appeared in *WHO DONE IT?*, reprinted by permission of Curtis Brown Ltd.

"The Plot Against Santa Claus" by James Powell, copyright © 1970 by James Powell, reprinted by permission of Scott Meredith Literary Agency, Inc.

"The Christmas Bear" by Herbert Resnicow, copyright © 1989 by Davis Publications, Inc., reprinted by permission of the author.

"Santa Claus Beat" by Rex Stout, copyright © 1953 by Rex Stout, reprinted by permission of the Estate.

"Whatever Became of Ebenezer Scrooge?" by Tom Tolnay, copyright © 1988 by Davis Publications, Inc., reprinted by permission of the author. All stories previously appeared in *Alfred Hitchcock's Mystery Magazine* or *Ellery Queen's Mystery Magazine,* published by Davis Publications, Inc.

Editor's Acknowledgments

I WANT TO THANK THE FOLLOWING PEOPLE WHO made a significant contribution to this book: Eleanor Sullivan, Cathleen Jordan, Christian Dorbandt, Tracey French and Russell Atwood.

OᵒoₒoᵒOₒ

OᵒoₒoᵒOₒ

OᵒoₒoᵒOₒ

bending toward a reprise of the national anthem, it could tip that way with the slightest nudge, but their voices flower into something softer, sweeter, a rain of sugared rose petals batting the ears

> *Can*
>   *you*
>   *take*
>   *me*
>   *there*
>   *tooooooh-*
>   *niiiiiiiiiiight*

On the far sideline a stage has been concocted, a spangly three-tiered affair with a jigsaw backdrop of multicolored panels that seems to strive for a modernist stained-glass look. A dance troupe is freeze-framed on the various tiers, guys in shimmery white sweat suits and jumbo bling, women in tight slacks or cutoffs and artfully mangled Cowboys jerseys, ripped, cropped, sleeveless, no two alike. To Billy's right Lodis seems to be gagging on his snot. Destiny's Child reprises the *take me there* refrain, then the drums sound off and that's their cue, the entire formation steps out. The cameramen start backpedaling, going on faith. Up ahead the drum line peels left and right, clearing a route to the stage. Later, watching the performance on YouTube, Billy will start to piece together the enormous scale of it, at least five marching bands cycling on and off the field, the frantic sex-show choreography happening onstage, flag girls and drill squads from one end zone to the other, Rotcees, Bravos, Drill grunts, Destiny's Child. The proverbial cast of thousands. Someone

will describe it as a production worthy of a Broadway musical, and though Billy has never set foot in New York, much less seen a musical of any kind, that will sound about right, but while it's happening he's just trying to hang on. A baton twirler skips by in a blur of skin and spinning chrome. High school drill teams in one-piece leotards are doing a shoop-shoop sort of booty-bump routine, they are training to be strippers apparently. Drum lines wheel alongside the soldier column, flying squads of flag girls zigzag across the route and Destiny's Child powers through it all with a back-leaning hip-heavy sashay strut that doesn't look quite possible from where Billy is, as if some mystical combination of diva mojo and StairMastered thighs keeps them upright when mere mortals would fall flat on their ass. Up ahead troupes of dancers flank the stage, guys in floppy shirts and pants, caps to the back, girls in silver sports bras and royal-blue tights. Already there's so much for the mind to absorb and then the disco lights get going, rows of blue and white strobes between the stage tiers, more strobes trimming the steel-pipe frame and everything flashing all at once, electro-visual spaz-pulse and epileptic overload, retinal scarring, frontal lobes blown to caterpillar fuzz—

This is yr brain on meth! Lodis is flinching, his poor head keeps swagging to the side, then the explosions start and they all flinch, *boom boom boom boom,* lum rounds are shooting off from somewhere backstage, smokers that explode with the arid crackle of cluster bombs scattering over a wheat field. A howl commences deep in Lodis's throat. "It's cool," Billy murmurs, "it's cool, it's cool, *it's just fireworks.*" Lodis starts laughing, gasping for breath. On Billy's other side Crack is looking clammy and grim. If there was ever a prime-time trigger for PTSD you couldn't do much better than this, but lucky for Norm, the crowd, America, the forty-million-plus TV viewing audience, Bravos can deal, oh yes! Pupils dilated, pulse and blood pressure through the roof, limbs trembling with stress-reflex cortisol rush, but it's cool, it's good, their shit's down tight, no Vietnam-vet crackups for Bravo squad! You can march these boys

straight into sound-and-light-show hell and Bravos can deal, but, damn, isn't it rude to put them through it.

The formation moves on eight-to-five step with the beat, *boody-Boom boody-Boom boody-bood-bood-BOOM,* snare drums make a fella damn proud to be a soldier. It's not a joke, Billy realizes. They spent too much money and went to too much effort for halftime to be intentionally ridiculous, which isn't to say that big expensive things can't be dumb. The *Titanic* was dumb. Enron was dumb. Hitler invading Russia, dumb. *Boom-diddy boom-diddy boom-buddah-dit-BOOM,* so go the Prairie View drums, thunder's wind chimes. Lodis knocks into Billy, steadies. "Sorry, Biyee." At the north hash mark all soldiers will about-face and march south while Destiny's Child proceeds to the stage. Billy is watching for his mark and trying not to hyperventilate. *Boom-diddy boom-diddy diddy-diddy BOOM.* Disco strobes, hump dancing, lum rounds and flares, marching bands marking time in regal high step, and here is Billy soldiering through the vast mindfuck of it, coiled into himself and determined to deal.

"Lay-dees A N D gennelmunnn," booms the PA announcer in the fawning, basso profundo lilt of the pitchman who doesn't know he's a fool,

Puh-leeeeeze wel-cum

Kelly

Michelle

A N D

BEEE-YON-SAY

the hit singing sen-say-shuns

DESTINY'S CHILD

Such an unholy barrage of noise pours forth that Billy thinks he might be lifted off his feet. It is a dam bursting, bridges collapsing at rush hour, tsunamis of killer froth and boulder-sized debris revising the contours of the known world. *Just assume you're going to die,* so they were instructed the week before deploying to Iraq. Affirmative! Roger that! Sir yes sir! Carnage awaits us, we are the ones who will not be saved, the poor sad doomed honorably fucked front line who will fight them over there so as not to fight them here! A harsh thing for any young man to hear, but this is part of every youth's educa-tion in the world, learning the risks are never fully revealed until you commit. Destiny's Child is really laying into the strut, they could be wading through a storm surge up to their waists, *goddamn,* Billy thinks, watching them sling it, *goddamn,* so how is he supposed to redeploy with such sights in his head? Within days, no, *hours,* Bravo is back in the shit and he's waiting for them to say it again, he dreads it but the harsh words need to be said, *you're going to die,* just get that part of it over with please, but no, no one will do it, they get Beyoncé and her mouthwatering ass instead!

Maybe it's not supposed to make sense. Or maybe not for you, Billy reasons, because you are a duh-umb shit. Then they turn, he's missed the hash mark by half a beat, the Drill grunts razor-sharp on the mark while Bravo flops around like loose shoelaces. "Change step *march,*" Day woofs sotto voce; as team leader he's responsible for getting them through halftime with some semblance of their dignity intact, and now he counts time with the Drill grunts, trying to shoe-horn the Bravos into lockstep. "Left, left," the mantra settles Billy's mind and his feet start to follow, though it would help if he had a weapon in his hands. Just ahead are the Rots, a herd of shambling, big-assed kids, many of them no doubt older than Billy and yet they look so young from the back, their soft, fleshy, baby-fat necks practi-cally screaming for the sacrificial ax to come down.

"Left *face,*" Day softly woofs. They've reached the sideline. Bravo steps off seven strides, left face again, *halt.* For the moment their job

is to stand next to the Drill grunts and look pretty. High school girls in fringed leotards go skipping past, waving long twirly streamers from six-foot poles. The Prairie View drum line has reconvened at midfield, glide-stepping to the beat of crunchy snare rolls, and everybody except Bravo is moving it seems, the field has become a huge jam-up of hip-hop choreographics and rigid blocks of synchronized marching-band mass. The stage apparatus belches gouts of flame and fireworks as Destiny's Child ascends with their prancing diva strut. The stage dancers go right on humping like the nastiest video on MTV as Beyoncé and her girls bring the microphones to their lips.

You say you gonna take me there

they sing in kittenish, pouty trills,

> *Say you know what I need*
> *Show devotion to the notion of our mutual creed*

    The Drill grunts are doing their thing, snapping their Springfields around in the rock-star version of close order drill. *Chack, chack, chack,* the strike of palm to rifle stock a high-fiber sound, perhaps a skilled listener could follow the stunts just by cadence alone. Out here on the end Billy has only a peripheral view, the rifles flitting in the corner of his eye like cards shuffled and stacked.

> *You think it all in the moves*
> *Like some robot lover do?*
> *That ain't the way you get*
> *A grown woman into her groove*

    Beyoncé slinks one hand down the inside of her thigh, then drags it toward her snatch, not quite cupping herself at the critical point; this is the PG-rated crotch grab, suitable for family viewing.

The streamer girls go skipping by, their pale skinny legs like pogo sticks. Those strobes are doing a number on Billy's head. He narrows his eyes to slits and everything blurs, it is a rat-bite fever dream of soldiers, marching bands, blizzards of bodies bumping and grinding, whoofs of fireworks, multiple drum lines cranking go-team-go. Destiny's Child! Drill grunts! Toy soldiers and sexytime all mashed together into one big inspirational stew. How many dozens of times has Bravo watched Crack's Conan DVDs, many dozens, they know every line by heart, and out of all the streamings and veerings of his over-amped brain Billy flashes on the palace orgy scene, James Earl Jones as the snake king sitting on his throne while his stoned minions sprawl about the floor, slurping and licking and humping in glassy-eyed bliss. It creeps him, the overlay of that sludgy sex scene on what he sees before him now, the complete and utter weirdness of the half-time show and the fact that everybody seems okay with it. The stands are packed, the fans are on their feet and everyone is cheering, everything makes them happy today. Fine, be happy, is Billy's attitude. They can cheer and scream and holler all they want, but it's nothing, their show, just fluff, filler, it's got nothing to do with Billy or going back to the war.

> *I ain't scared, I'm comin' through,*
> *I ain't scared, I ain't scared,*

> *Big man can't you handle this good thing I'm offerin' you?*

In the stands behind the stage a huge American flag appears, a card stunt, each one of a mass of twenty thousand fans comprising a pixel in this antique special effect. The cards spin, and now the flag is presented as if rippling in the wind, though on second look it's more like the thing's been badly pressed, the pattern gashed through with wrinkles and kinks. For several moments Billy's eyes play tricks with it, tweaking the perspective back and forth, then his inner ear jolts

and the ground seems to tilt, a lurch that sets him down in a different place. It occurs to him that maybe he's wrong. Maybe the halftime show is as real as anything; what if some power or potent agency lives in it? Not a show but a means to something, something conferred or invoked. A ceremony. Something religious, so long as "religious" extends to such cold-blooded concepts as mayhem, chance, nature out of control. He feels the pull of a superseding reality that trumps even the experiential truths of a grunt on the ground—the blood on your hands, the burn in your lungs, the stink of your unwashed feet. Merely thinking about it sets off a pounding in his skull, not his headache but a heavier sonar throb deep in the lower brain stem. And very clearly the thought comes to him, *that's where it lives*. The god in your head, all the gods—is that what's happening here? He's too self-conscious and church-averse to accept a completely straight notion of god, so how about this—chemicals, hormones, needs and drives, whatever is in us that's so supreme and terrifying that we have to call it divine.

> *Lemme break it down for you again,*
> *Stop actin' like a boy, stand up and be a man,*
> *What's sad is all your talkin' 'bout love and affection,*
> *You get yours and leave me hangin' like a prepubescent*

Billy is cold where the warmest part of him should be, as if meaning naturally registers first in the most delicate instrument he has, his balls. He's scared. He knows this is a bad place to be. They love to talk up God and country but it's the devil they propose, all those busy little biochemical devils of sex and death and war that simmer at the base of the skull, punch up the heat a few degrees and they rise to a boil, spill over the sides. Do they even know? he wonders. Maybe they don't know what they know, given that what he sees before him is so random, so perfect, porn-lite out of its mind on martial dope. Short of blood sacrifice or actual sex on the field, you couldn't devise a better spectacle for turning up the heat.

Left face, Day softly woofs, and they step off, *right face* and they're crossing the field toward the belly of the beast, Lodis following Billy, Billy following Crack, Crack following Day, who tails the Prairie View drum corps through a blur of fancy uniforms and bared flesh. Individual sounds spire out of the din like guitar drones, the squeanings of whales. Time gears down to a lower speed. The strobes pulse in stretchy Day-Glo smears. Billy knows where they're supposed to end up though he's vague on the mechanics of getting there. As each Bravo crosses the sideline they face left, then they're hustled along a gauntlet of stressed-out handlers to a chaotic holding pen behind the stage. A tall slender woman in a knee-length parka pulls the Bravos out of line. She's pretty, at least the part of her that shows between the flaps of her Russian officer's cap. "All right," she says, gathering the Bravos into a huddle, yelling like a sailor in a gale, "we're gonna get you guys in position backstage, then when we give you the go you step out and take the stairs down to the middle level. You'll be marching, right? Like this?" She mimes a military strut. "You turn left on the middle tier and march out along there. Look for the purple X's, one for each of you, that's your mark. Then just turn and face the field and stand at attention."

The Bravos nod. No one speaks. They're all quietly freaking.

"There's gonna be a lot going on out there but you guys don't move. That's your job, just stand there. No-brainer, right?" She smiles, gives Day a light cuff on the shoulder. "You guys okay?"

The Bravos nod. Even Day seems rattled, his neck bulging like he's swallowed too much air. Crack is looking at the ground and mumbling to himself.

"Guys, come on, chill, you've got the easy part." The woman laughs, exasperated by how tight they are. "Once you're on your mark just stay there till the show's over, I'll come up and give you the all-clear."

"This about to be *stoopih,*" Lodis grumbles, but the handler lady pretends not to hear. Bravos can deal, you bet, though none of them

is looking particularly good at the moment. There's too many people running around, too much bug-eyed panic, all the freak-out flavors of an ambush situation without any of the compensating murderous release. Fireworks crews to their left and right keep shooting off nasty little rockets that hiss and sizzle like RPGs. Portable sets of metal stairs lead up to the highest stage level, and the Bravos are placed at the tops of these stairways, one Bravo per. A narrow catwalk is all that separates them from the stage backdrop, and Billy is standing there, a step below catwalk level, when a magnificent female creature bombs through the backdrop, it is a louvered sort of opening she steps around as several handlers swarm in. One takes her microphone, another offers Evian, a third presents some sort of small, furry garment that the woman proceeds to pull over her head. Beyoncé. If Billy chooses he could reach out and touch her thigh. Her hair springs free of the pullover like a solar flare, and from Billy's vantage point a foot below the catwalk she towers with a Rocky Mountain majesty. Up close her skin is the honeyed brown of apple butter, limned with a film of perspiration that holds the light. Michelle and Kelly have their own handlers farther down the catwalk. No one speaks. They are all business, these show people, as quiet and lethal as sniper teams. Beyoncé shoots her arms through the sleeves of the jacket, a cropped, off-shoulder sateen number with a fur-trimmed collar, and as she arranges herself inside the garment her eyes meet Billy's. Excuse me, he wants to say, go on, go on, she's so focused and fierce in the moment that he's sorry to impinge even to this small extent. Carrying the show in front of forty million people makes her one of the top human beings on the planet, and what strength of nerve that must take, what freakish concentrations of soul and energy. She's not even winded! A yogic mastery of the mind-body balance. She inhabits some far distant astral plane, yet her eyes do something when they meet his, for an instant he seems to register there. In that split second Billy searches for something in her look—not mercy, exactly, nothing so grand as compassion, maybe just a bare acknowledgment of their

shared humanity, but she's already turning, she takes the mike and one of the handlers is saying *kick butt* as she steps through the slot and disappears.

Someone pushes Billy onto the catwalk, then pulls him up short of the opening. The noise out there is just tremendous. He looks to his right and sees more Bravos similarly positioned, and at this instant he wishes he was back at the war. At least there he basically knew what he was doing, he had his training for guidance and the entire god-damn country wasn't watching to see if he'd fuck up, but this, this is all wing-and-a-prayer shit. *Middle level* a voice is yelling in his ear, *turn left and look for the purple X*. Abruptly the music gears down to a meat-grinding crawl, *kah-thunka, kah-thunka,* it is a trash compactor mulling over more than it can chew. On the lowest tier of the stage Destiny's Child is standing in front of three Prairie View drummers, the girls have taken the sticks and are pounding out the beat with the flailing elbows and lunging stance of fashionable women trying to jack up a car. By the time Billy gets stiff-armed onto the stage he's barely breathing. It's like stepping into a sun-filled cumulus cloud, a dazzling, cottony glow all about your person and nothing but air beneath your feet. He moves right-oblique toward the center stairs and arrives, small miracle, in sequence with the other three Bravos and everyone is marching more or less in step. He hears a rushing in his head and not much else. Directly in front of the stage the Drill grunts are doing the overhead rifle toss *with fixed bayonets,* the fuck, they could kill themselves and wouldn't that be the shit, stabbed through the eye on live TV with your own bayonet!

Need me a soldjah, soldjah boy
Where dey at, where dey at

Billy is last in file, thus he ends up on the purple X closest to center stage. Right face, halt. The rest of the Bravos have somehow appeared on the bottom tier, Dime-Sykes-Mango-A-bort all in a row.

Soldjah gonna be real fah me, Beyoncé sings against Michelle's and Kelly's bass-line chant,

> *Soldjah gonna be real fah me*
> *Yeah dey will, yeah dey will*
> *Soldjah gonna get chill fah me*
> *Yeah dey will, yeah dey will*

They are serenading the bottom-tier Bravos, slinking and spooning about on dainty cat feet, mewling minor-key trills of do-me angst. The entire stage has become a blowup of foreplay aerobics, rocket thrusting, shadow humping, knurling hips and ass, here on the second tier the dancers are twurking Bravo and not a damn thing you can do except stand at attention and get pole-danced in front of forty million people. It's not right. Nobody said anything about this. What might be merely embarrassing in real life is made obscene and hostile by TV. Billy hates to think of his mother and sisters watching this, then one of the guys starts dancing a little too close, punking Billy with glide-by swivels and squats. Like I really wanna see your junk, fool! Billy gives him a look; the guy smirks and spins away. Then he comes back around, and Billy speaks with all the feeling he can jam through his teeth:

Fuck off.

The guy laughs and he's gone again. The beat quickens as a line of Prairie View drummers comes marching down the stairs, *boom-Lacka-Lacka-Lacka boom-Lacka-Lacka-Lacka.* The Drill grunts are doing the Queen Anne Salute while troupes of smiling dancers decorate the flanks with jazzy kung fu moves. Down on the bottom tier Sykes is weeping. For some reason Billy is not surprised, he only hopes it will be over before all the Bravos lose their minds. Destiny's Child regroups at center stage as a gathering storm of lights and fireworks signals crescendo time. Sykes's back is a heaving pantomime of sobs, yet he maintains strict attention, chin up, chest out, and he has never seemed so brave or dear to Billy as at this moment.

I ain't scared, I'm comin' through,
I ain't scared, I ain't scared,
Big man can't you handle this good love I'm offerin' you?

Far across the field the Cowboys cheerleaders have formed a kick
line, and even at this distance, through the haze of sleet and fireworks
smoke, Billy's eyes go straight to Faison, his groan a mere drop in the
ocean of sound. Destiny's Child is mounting the stairs, pausing every
few steps to throw sassy looks over their shoulders, T&A bait for the
TV cameras. Billy doesn't so much as twitch when they pause on his
tier, a fulmination of animal heat roaring at his side. For as long as
they pose he doesn't move, but once they're gone he raises his eyes to
the sky, then lifts his face a few degrees to get the weather's full effect.

The sleet stings, but he doesn't blink. He lets it come, the spray
of ice like a billion needles showering down on him, then it's like the
sleet is dangling and Billy's flying through it, zooming toward some
unnamed but promising place. Everything else falls away and he's
happy, free, the sting in his eyes is all speed and upward motion. It
feels like escape velocity. It feels like the future. He's still standing
there, rocketing toward the world to come, when Day taps him on
the shoulder and says halftime is over.

IF IN THE FUTURE

YOU TELL ME THIS IS LOVE,

I WILL NOT DISAPPOINT YOU

NO ONE COMES FOR them. They gather around Sykes and wait as instructed for the woman in the Russian officer's cap, but Bravo has fallen through a crack in the collective mind and so they stand there marooned while a roadie crew swarms over the stage and ash from the fireworks settles on their heads. They have been through the wringer of a world-class spectacle and need some time for their nerves to recover. Like, about six years might do it? Bravo is roasted, toasted, and ready to pop, or maybe already popping in the case of Sykes, who sits himself down on the bottom step and weeps sparklers of racy little hopeless tears. "I don't know why I'm fuckin' cryin'!" he squawks when Lodis asks. "I just am, dammit! I just am!"

"You guys have to leave," the roadie foreman barks at Bravo.

"Well fuck you too," Mango mumbles as the guy stalks off, and the Bravos stay put. Day and A-bort sit down on either side of Sykes

while the rest of them mill around feeling torn and frayed, fluttery hands shoved deep in their pockets.

"Dudes, we finally saw Beyoncé," Crack points out.

"Woo, ain't we special."

"Yeah, but we saw her up close."

"Uh-huh, she's hot and everything. But I've had better."

They manage a few yuks at that. Billy finds himself standing next to Dime, and confides:

"Sergeant, I feel sick."

Dime gives him a once-over. "You look okay to me."

"Not like sick sick. More like bent. Baked." He taps his head. "Halftime sort of skitzed me out."

Dime laughs, *at-at-at,* a machine-gun rattle high in his throat. "Son, try to look at it this way. It's just another normal day in America."

Billy's heart melts a little at that *son*. The stage is disappearing around them like a mortally wounded ship beneath the waves.

"I don't think I even know what normal is anymore."

"You're fine, Billy, you're fine. I'm fine, you're fine, everybody's fine. He's fine." Dime nods at Sykes. "Everything is fine."

Billy looks at Sykes and starts to ask, Yeah, what are we going to do about him? but the foreman is coming at them again, snapping at Bravo to get the hell off his stage.

"So where we supposed to go?" Crack snaps back. "Nobody told us where to go."

The foreman stops, spares them a harried moment's regard. He's well over six feet, bearded, broad shouldered, with a face slack and frowzy as a blown-out air bag, but there's a shot of chemical voltage in his eyes, the crazed-lumberjack look of the veteran roadie. His gaze lingers for a second on the hot mess that is Sykes.

"Look, I have no fucking idea where you're supposed to go, but you can't stay here."

"All right, Rufus, tell you what," Crack answers. "We'll go right after you're done sucking my dick, how about that?"

Later, thinking back on it, Billy will be struck by the fact that he never saw an actual punch being thrown. It doesn't last long—ten, fifteen seconds at most? Though in the way of such things it seems to go on for hours. At first the foreman tries to *lift* Crack like he thinks he's going to bodily throw him off the stage, so he's bigger than Crack but not *that* much bigger, and what a bummer it must be for the guy when he finds himself locked in a young-buck clench. For an instant the two men hardly move. Only their bulging eyes and necks betray the tons of thrust at work, then they're twisting, spinning, they are the hub of a free-radical swirl of bodies that slides off the stage onto the field. People are pushing, chesting up, there's much half-assed shoving and garbled smack talk about who dissed who and who crossed whose line and of course everybody's gotta have their boy's back. A melee, you'd call it. A fracas. Not quite a throw-down brawl right here on the sacred turf of Texas Stadium. Billy is skying on a full-bore adrenaline rip as arms, hands, faces go crashing by, then there's Dime stroking past like a man swimming rapids, push-ing through bodies to pry Crack clear. A roadie swipes at Dime's back and Billy grabs his collar and there's the guy's wild look as he twists around, and Billy thinks: Whoa shit, don't let go now. The guy reels as Billy rides him from behind, riding, riding, he wishes it didn't look so much like he's humping the guy but he hangs on until the cops wade in, and all it takes is a word from Dime for Bravo to disengage, "like a bunch of excellent hunting dogs" as he likes to say of his squad.

Casualties, minor. Crack has taken an elbow in the eye; Lodis's lip is split and bloody; Mango's ear tenderized by a roadie headlock. The cops herd Bravo down the sideline and hear out their story, then send them packing across the field toward the home sideline. "Somebody over there can tell you where to go," the cops say, so like the remnants of some long-lost jungle patrol Bravo makes its straggling way across the field. They've passed the first hash mark when Billy looks up and sees, oh mother of mercy, Faison coming

out to meet them, her head cocked at a questioning skew, face full of concern. She's pumped, Billy can tell. This is a girl who likes her drama.

"What happened?" She peers up at him, touches his arm as they meet. The rest of the Bravos lapse into reverential silence.

"It was stupid, just this stupid little thing. We kind of got into it with the roadies over there."

"Were yall fighting? We couldn't tell if yall were fighting or goofing around."

"I guess we were fighting. Though you couldn't call it much of a fight."

"All we did was ask if we could help!" A-bort says, and everybody yuks except Sykes, who breaks down all over again.

"Are you hurt?" Faison asks Billy, then she's speaking to all the Bravos. "Is anybody hurt? Oh my God, look at your *lip*!" she cries at Lodis. "Who's supposed to be taking care of you guys?"

She's incensed to learn that Bravo has been left on its own. "All right," she says, turning, motioning Bravo to follow, "yall come with me, we'll get this figured out. I can't believe they just left yall stranded out here, that is *so* NOT the way we treat our guests."

The Bravos clump about her in a loose bundle, murmuring their thanks. "Listen," she tells them, "that stage crew? We've had problems with those guys before, it's like they think they own the place. They almost beat up Lyle Lovett a couple of weeks ago, they were like, *Get off the stage! Get off the stage right NOW!* And Lyle and his guys had all their equipment up there, it's not like they were gonna just walk off and leave it. Lucky security was right there or we mighta had a situation."

"I think they're tweekin'," says Mango.

"They sure act like it, don't they, they act like they're on something. Somebody ought to speak to management about those guys."

More cheerleaders are coming out to meet them, and it dawns on Bravo that this might turn out all right. A kind of mixer develops

there along the home sideline, Bravos and cheerleaders chatting it up while calls are made upstairs on the soldiers' behalf. The fracas gives them something to talk about; the cheerleaders are shocked at first, then indignant as the story gets around, the flip side of which is a bonus serving of sympathy for Bravo. Ice is fetched for Crack's eye and Lodis's lip. A couple of cheerleaders tenderly probe Mango's rug-burned ear.

"What's wrong with him?" Faison asks, nodding at Sykes. She and Billy are standing somewhat apart from the others.

"Oh, that's Sykes."

"Is he hurt?"

Billy considers Sykes, who's squatting in the lee of a portable equipment locker, quietly weeping.

"He misses his wife."

"Wow." Faison seems impressed. "Really?"

"He's kind of an emotional guy."

She keeps glancing over at Sykes. She's fascinated, or perhaps just troubled that nothing's being done about him.

"Does he have kids?"

"One on the ground, one on the way."

"Oh my God, I can't imagine. Do you think I should go over and talk to him?"

"I think he just wants to be alone right now."

"You're probably right. Sheesh, the *sacrifices* you guys make! How long did you say you're gonna be over there?"

"Through next October, unless we get stop-lossed again."

"Oh Lord." It comes out as a kind of rattling moan, *oh Lord,* like she's rollerblading on a gravel road. "And you've been there how long already?"

"We infilled August twelfth."

"Oh me. Oh my God. You must dread going back."

"I guess. In a way." Somehow their faces have ended up mere inches apart, and this seems like the most natural thing in the world,

as basic as wind, tides, the magnetic north. "It is what it is, I guess. But we'll all be together, that's something. That counts for a lot, actually."

"I think I know what you mean. There's that whole bonding thing when you're challenged as a group." While she talks Billy is trying to memorize her face, the supreme excellence, for example, of the delicate butterfly clasp of the bridge of her nose, or the smattering of freckles high on her forehead, the way their gingery carotene tint matches her hair exactly. The desire comes over him to stretch his mouth wide open, as wide as a lion's, say, and tenderly hold her perfect face between his lips for a while.

"Sometimes I wonder if the whole thing might be a mistake. I mean, I think we ought to be fighting terrorism and everything, but it's like, okay, we got rid of Saddam, maybe we should just bring our guys home and let the Iraqis work it out for themselves."

"Sometimes we think that too," Billy says, remembering something Shroom once said: *Maybe the light's at the other end of the tunnel.*

"Ha ha, no doubt." She peers past his shoulder. "The second half's gonna start in a minute," she says, then pulls back and looks Billy in the eye. "Listen, can I ask you something personal?"

"Sure."

"Are you seeing anybody?"

"Not me," he allows bravely, with breezy resignation. He doesn't care if she knows he's not a player.

"Me either. So how about if we stay in touch."

"Ye-uh," he says, half choking on it, then "*yes*. Yes, I think we should."

"Good." She's suddenly very brisk and businesslike. "You've got your phone? Get out your phone and I'll give you my information, then call me and leave a message so I'll have yours. Because, frankly, I don't wanna lose you."

She says it just like that, a casually earthshaking statement of stupendous fact. Him, Billy, a person not to be wanted lost! His life has

become miraculous to him. Maybe he should just go ahead and ask her to marry him.

"What's your last name?" He's got his phone out.

"Zorn."

Billy clears his throat.

"I know, everybody thinks it's funny."

Billy says nothing.

"It means 'anger' in German."

"Roger that," he deadpans.

"Stop it! You're so funny."

She's at his side, their heads practically touching as she watches him key in her information. The phone gives them socially acceptable cover for standing so close, good thing because it's happening in front of thousands of people. Billy breathes deep, pulling in her clean outdoors smell, the sharp vanilla tang of snow and winter wind. It's as if she's absorbed the sweetest essence that the season has to offer.

"Who's Kathryn?"

Billy is scrolling through his contact list. "My sister."

"You've got a call from her."

"I know." He highlights the next name. "That's my other sister."

"They older, younger?"

"I'm the youngest. There's ol' Mom."

"Denise? Not 'Mom'?"

"Well, that's her name."

Faison laughs. "Where's your Dad?"

"My Dad's disabled. He doesn't have his own phone."

"Oh!"

"He had a double stroke a couple of years ago, impaired his speech."

"I'm so sorry."

"It's all right. It's life."

She's holding his arm just above the elbow, her grip concealed by the bush of her pom-poms. "Are you going to see them before you leave?"

Billy gets a sudden clutch in his throat. "Ah, no." He swallows. It's fine. "We all said our good-byes yesterday."

"That sucks." She snugs a few millimeters closer.

"There's you." He's scrolled all the way to the end.

"Zorn. I'm always last on everybody's list."

"I'll change you to Anger, that way you'll be first."

She laughs, looks over her shoulder. The cheerleaders are moving toward the tunnel to welcome the players onto the field. "Sweetie, I gotta go," she says, and gives his arm a squeeze. Her hand recoils as if electrically shocked, then she's squeezing again, then palpating his entire upper arm.

"*My God,* what a great body you've got. Do you have even an *ounce* of fat on you?"

"Not so much, I guess."

"Not so much I guess," she echoes in a gruff voice, and laughs. She's still feeling up his arm. "You don't even know how good you are, do you? That makes it even better!" she declares with lip-smacking enthusiasm, then gives him a fierce fast hug, as if grasping a buoy before the storm tears her away. Billy practically keels over in a delirium of bliss. How wonderful, how absolutely holy to be appreciated for yourself, to be handled, petted, groped, pawed, and generally hungered over. "Okay, I gotta scoot," she says, releasing him. "Come see me at the twenty, same place."

Billy says he will, and she goes trotting down the sideline after the rest of the cheerleaders. Bravo turns as she jogs past, their eyes helplessly drawn to the bounce of her bottom inside those teeny tiny cup holders that pass for shorts. Billy punches up her number and waits through six rings while watching her take position at the mouth of the tunnel. The first players come jogging onto the field like rhinos on the plod. The Jumbotron cranks up a Guns N' Roses riff, the cheerleaders rise on their toes and wave their pom-poms high, and a swell of applause rolls through the stands like thunder rumbling down the mountainside.

"Hi, you've reached Faison! I'm not able to take your call right now . . ."

It makes for an odd sensation, watching her real-time person in the middle distance while holding her disembodied voice to his ear. It puts a frame around the situation, gives it focus, perspective. It makes him aware of himself being aware of himself, and here is a mystery that seems worth thinking about, why this stacking of awareness should even matter. At the moment all he knows is that there's structure in it, a pleasing sense of poise or mental ordering. A kind of knowledge, or maybe a bridge thereto—as if existence didn't necessarily have to be a moron's progress of lurching from one damn thing to another? As if you might aspire to some sort of context in your life, a condition he associates with adultness. Then comes the *beep,* and he has to talk. The funny little message he leaves for her—two seconds after clicking off, he can't remember what he said.

TEMPORARY SANITY

THE LAST FEW PLAYERS are straggling out of the tunnel and here comes Josh trotting with them, looking like he just stepped out of a Polo ad. How does he do it? Every hair, every thread, every crease and pleat in place, as if he's sheathed in a varnish of pussy-boy perfection. *"My bad, my bad, my bad,"* he chants in a furious monotone, "I am so so sorry guys, we blew it, *blew it,* no way you should've dropped off the radar like that," and he launches into a detailed explication of post-halftime logistics, the gist of which is he's been waiting at prearranged point X for the past twenty minutes.

"So you're saying one of the clipboard chicks was supposed to bring us up," Dime clarifies.

"Essentially, yes."

"So how does that make it your bad?"

Josh opens his mouth, he's going to try to try, but Bravo saves

him the trouble with a group razz. Jaaaaaasssssshhhhhh! Dah Josh-
ster. *Jash*. He is too damn nice for his own good, which is why Bravo
loves the big lunk.

"Yo Josh, you hear about our fight?"

"Wait, what. What fight?"

"The one we just had." Crack grins and holds up his ice pack.

"Yeah, Josh, that your bad too," Day says.

"Wait, wait a second. You're kidding me. Oh shit, guys, what—"

"Jash, chill. It's cool."

"Yeah, Josh, we like to fight. It's like our main thing to do."

"You gotta remember, man, we're basically just a bunch of apes."

Day asks about the after-party, which he defines as wherever
Beyoncé and her girls are, which is where he'd like to be. Bravo offers
this a unanimous second but Josh thinks Destiny's Child has already
left the stadium. Billy is tired of asking about the Advil, so doesn't
even. They take a freight elevator up to the first-level concourse.
Crack, Mango, and Lodis head for the men's room to primp their
injuries. The rest of the Bravos hang out on the concourse and phone
home. *Didja see me? How'd I look?* Billy decides this is the grunt ver-
sion of the after-party, calling up the fam. He pulls out his cell and
dials Kathryn, but his sister Patty answers.

"Helloooo little brother," she trills from deep in her cups, her
voice all woozy and sickly sweet. "You looked so handsome on TV!
We're all really proud of you, baby bro."

"Thanks."

"Soooo"—she pauses for a sip of her drink—"what's she like?"

"What's who like?"

"Beyoncé, fool!" Billy hears his mother wail in the background,
Please don't call your brother a fool.

"Oh, her." Billy affects a yawn. "Yeah, she's okay. She's a little
thick through the hips."

Patty knocks that down with a braying *Hah!* "Did you meet her?"

"Never got the chance."

"But you were right up there onstage!"

"Yeah, but that's as close as I got. And it didn't seem like the best time . . ."

She wants to know if he's met any other celebrities. Billy doesn't mind, but it sort of brings him down, talking about those people. There was the actress from *Walker, Texas Ranger,* the blonde who played the spunky district attorney role. Senator Cornish, who has the largest head of any human Billy has ever seen. Jimmer Lee Flatley, medium-heavy country music star, and Lex, the Fort Worth hunk who made it all the way to the final round of *Survivor*. He throws out a few more names like change from a dollar bill.

"Listen, that thing you were doing at the end, what was that? We were all wondering."

What thing?

"Well, right there at the end, when you were looking up at the sky. Like you were praying or something."

"They showed that?"

"Well, yeah." She laughs at the rise in his voice.

"Like a close-up?"

"Not *real* close, but they showed it. For a second it was pretty much just you on the screen."

This freaks him, though he doesn't know why. "Well, I sure wasn't praying." He frets in silence a moment. "Did it look weird?"

"No," she laughs, "it looked *sweet*. You were *cute*. We're really proud of you."

"I don't remember that at all," Billy says, though he remembers perfectly well. "It was hot up there with all the lights and everything. Maybe I was just trying to get some air."

She starts to tell him again how handsome and brave he looked, but Kathryn takes the phone from her.

"Hey."

"Hey."

"So no Beyoncé, huh."

" 'Fraid not."

"Just as well, she's probably a total bitch. Hang on a sec . . ." Doors open and close; the house noises fall away, replaced by an airy, bottomless quiet. Kathryn has stepped outside.

"Jesus Christ!"

"What?"

"Cold as dammit out here. I would *not* want to be wildlife today. You staying warm over there?"

"Warm enough."

She tells him she and Brian spent several hours playing in the snow this afternoon, scraping enough together to make a runt snowman. "He's crashed in your room right now, I think I wore his little hiney out. We recorded halftime so he can watch you later. But, um, listen." She lowers her voice. "Patty told me what you said, about Brian. About telling him never to join the Army."

Billy closes his eyes, silently curses.

"And I don't think you should go back."

"Kathryn."

"Just listen, just please hear me out, okay? I got in touch with some people, those people I told you about. The group in Austin."

"I'm really not interested in talking about this."

"Just listen, please, Billy, just listen for a minute. I talked to them twice, they're good people, they know what they're doing. They've got lawyers, resources, they aren't a bunch of flakes. And they really want to help you. They've been hoping somebody like you would reach out."

"Somebody like me."

"A war hero. Somebody the movement could really rally around."

"Oh Jesus."

"Just listen! One of these guys, one of their group, he's got like a ten-thousand-acre ranch where you can stay. I'm telling you, man, these people have some serious stroke. They can have some people meet you at the stadium and drive you to the airport, they'll fly you

out to the ranch on a private plane tonight. You'd just disappear for a couple of weeks while the lawyers get everything set up."

"That's AWOL, Kathryn. They shoot people for that."

"Not you, not after everything you've been through. These lawyers know what they're doing, Billy, they have all kinds of strategies for cases like yours. And they'll have a PR firm on it too, these guys are pros. Can you imagine how shitty they could make the government look, prosecuting you? After the whole freakin' country saw what you did on TV?"

"I'm not psyche, if that's what the lawyers are thinking. So they can forget about that."

"Of *course* you're not psyche, only a nut would want to go back to the war. We'll have the lawyers plead temporary sanity for you, how about that? You're too *sane* to go back to the war, Billy Lynn has come to his senses. It's the rest of the country that's nuts for wanting to send him back."

"But, Kathryn."

"But, Billy."

"I sort of do want to go back."

She screams. He thinks he can hear it echoing off the trees in the backyard.

"No, no way, I don't accept that. You *cannot* want to go back to that place."

"But I do. I can't stay here if the rest of the squad's going back. If they're over there getting shot at, I want to be there too."

"Then maybe all the Bravos should stay, how about that. Bush pinned medals on all you guys, nobody's going to think you're cowards for not going back."

"That's not the point."

"Okay, enlighten me here. What's the point?"

"Well, I signed up."

"Under duress! Thanks to *me*! Me and my shit!"

"No, it was my choice. It's what I wanted to do. And I knew they'd probably send me to Iraq. It's not like anybody lied to me."

She groans. "Billy, all those mofos ever do is lie. You think if they halfway told the truth we'd even be in a fucking war? You know what I think, I think we don't *deserve* to have you guys die for us. No country that lets its leaders lie like that deserves a single soldier to die for it." ·

She breaks down crying, an awful sound like the scraping of a shovel hitting bedrock. "Kathryn," Billy says, and waits a minute. "Kathryn," he tries again. "Kat. It's okay. I'm gonna be fine."

"I'm sorry," she says, her voice gone swampy and blear. "Shit. I told myself I wasn't going to cry on you. It's just that everything's so, whatever. Everything about it sucks."

"Yeah, pretty much."

"Listen, don't be mad at me. But I gave those people your number."

Billy grits his teeth, says nothing. The main thing is not to get her started crying again.

"Just talk to them, Billy, please? Just hear what they have to say. They're good people, they can make it all right for you."

He doesn't say yes and he doesn't say no. She goes inside to hand the phone off to Denise, and as he waits he tries to imagine how it will be for them if he doesn't come back. He knows Kathryn would survive, a triumph of rage over guilt. Patty also; she has Brian. But his mother? All ego aside, it would be awful for her, possibly fatal, though not right away. He envisions a long slow process of interior numbing-out that takes form in his mind as weather, a plague of bitter-cold days with wind, freezing rain, a pall of daylong dusk fading to black. Days like today, in fact.

But at the moment she's doing okay; halftime got her pumped. "It was disgraceful," she tells Billy. "All those lewd gyrations, they're like something you'd see at the hoochie-coochie show at a county fair. How that mess even gets on TV is beyond me."

"Not arguing, Mom. It wasn't my idea."

"Like that woman revealing herself at the Super Bowl, remember? If it keeps going like this people will just stop watching. A lot of folks are fed up. Did you see it? You couldn't even call it dancing . . ."

"Mom, I was there." She's had a glass or three of wine, apparently. More power to you, Mom, have another. God knows the woman could use a party.

" . . . I remember when Tom Landry was coach you never saw anything like that. They had standards. He kept that team on a tight rein. I don't know if it's since Norman Oglesby bought the team, or that coach he's got or some of those other people he's hired . . ."

The longer she talks, the whinier and more righteous she gets, and the less attention she pays to herself. Billy offers small hums of agreement and waits for the momma-logue to wind down.

"I hear you're fixing an awesome feast over there."

"Well. It's no different from every year."

"Then it'll be great. Don't wear yourself out."

"No, I'm fine, the girls are helping out. Did you have Thanksgiving?"

"Sure did, they fed us really well. They took us to a club here in the stadium."

"Well, that's nice."

It strikes him again how pitiful her life will be if he gets smoked, all ego aside. Stove-in husband, dead son, piles and piles of medical bills . . . He thinks maybe he should up his GI insurance, then wonders if the hospitals would take it all.

"How's Dad?"

"He's fine. He's in the den watching the game with Pete."

"Hey, there's a fun couple."

"Well, they seem to get along."

Poor Mom, she can't help being the straight man of her own life.

"Where are you now?"

"The concourse. I think they're taking us back to our seats."

"Are you warm enough?"

"I'm great, mom."

"Because I saw you weren't wearing any kind of coat."

"I'm fine. It's pretty warm here inside the stadium."

"Well, I'm sure you're busy, so I'll let you go."

"Not really," he says, exasperated. Maybe the last time they'll ever talk—*not to be dramatic about it!*—and she's giving him the bum's rush, her own son. Not that she means anything by it, he knows. This is simply her lifelong habit of moderation at work, her need to tamp everything down to the routine, the modest, the tepid everyday. He understands the whole concept of boundaries, but there's a point where this mania for normalizing turns toxic.

Perhaps this is why he tries something new. "Okay, Mom, give everybody my love. And I love you too."

"Yes bye thanks have a nice day," she says in a rush, and he can't help the small laugh that gets loose from him. Let her be, he tells himself. Just let her be. Pressing her for something real seems almost cruel at this point. He clicks off and has a spasm of grief so intense that his knees buckle slightly. His hand finds the wall, and he has to remind himself that it's not absolutely certain he will die in Iraq. Just looking at the odds, he even stands a reasonably good chance of coming through without the proverbial scratch, aside from the laceration and shrapnel wounds he already received from being blown up on Dead Girl Road, and he knows if he makes it back he will *be so good*. Good for Mom, good for the family. And transcendently good for Faison. He can feel it rising in him, this powerful if not quite choate sense of how to live a strong and decent life. Not that you'll actually know except by doing it, by putting in the years—as if there's a salvation specific to combat soldiers, one that comes of learning passion for daily things? So he suspects, at least. That's his sense of it. He would like the chance to find out, anyway.

WILL SLAY VAMPIRES FOR FOOD

BRAVO IS ON THE move again. The concourse is thick with fans taking a break from the weather, and more than a few are already heading for the exits. People call out to Bravo, veer over to shake hands, but not as many as before. Major Mac has been holding the fort on row 7, the lone sentinel in their block of ice-spackled seats. Billy ends up on the aisle *per* normal with Mango on his left, and as their post-fight cheerleader buzz wears off Bravo starts to realize how shitty their situation is. Here they sit fully exposed to the sleet and freezing drizzle watching a dull-as-hell 7–7 third-quarter tie two days before they fly back to the war. Sucks! Mango groans and hunches over.

"Dawg," he says to Billy, "I just wanna go to sleep."

"Uh huh. How's your ear?"

"Hurts like a motherfucker." After a second they both find this extremely funny.

"What'd he do, try to rip it off?"

"He won't doing nothing except weighing about three hundred pounds. I woulda flipped him 'cept his leg was so fat, couldn't get my arm around it. I was like, dude, you never heard of diabetes? You might wanna shed a few, lay off the supersize for a while."

They try to watch the game, but it's so slow, what's the point. The fans around them are sheltering under blankets, umbrellas, here and there a plastic trash bag; only the Bravos sit there like stock in a pasture, wide open to the weather. Billy pulls out his cell and stares at Faison's number. He is tempted to call just to hear her voice message, which sounds more southern than her real-life voice, the vowels rounder, the hard palate hollowed out, the vox equivalent of a Hill Country feather mattress.

"Dawg, I think I'm in love."

Mango laughs. "It'd be gay if you weren't. I saw the way you guys were moshing back there on the field. It means something when they do that shit, you know? They don't touch you unless they dig you."

Billy stares at his phone.

"You get her digits?"

Billy solemnly nods.

"Well, fuck, she definitely likes you. Kind of sucks it's coming on the back end of the trip."

Billy moans with the pleasure and pain of it, these violent oppositional forces that are physically molding him into something new. The Jumbotron plays the American Heroes graphic again, then grinds through the deafening commercial cycle, the same ads always playing in the same maddening order. FORD TRUCKS BUILT TOUGH! TOYOTA! nissan! TOYOTA! nissan! FOR ALL YOUR BANKING NEEEEEEDS DUM-DEE-DEE-DUMMMMM! Then Sykes sings out in his gruesome falsetto, *If you can't make me say ooo!,* then he pauses to tell the fans fore and aft how much he loves them, how much he loves all Americans everywhere, then he's singing again—

WhaaaAAAtttt's love got to do with it, got to do with it,
WhaaaAAAtttt's love but a secondhand emooooo-shun

Word comes down the row that Dime slipped him a big fat
Valium about twenty minutes ago, and now he's the happiest girl in
the whole USA.

Billy startles, nearly drops the cell when it rings. He checks the
screen.

"Her?" Mango asks.

Billy shakes his head. He doesn't recognize the number. The call
rings out, followed a minute later by the chirp of a waiting voice
message. Billy stares at the phone. He wishes it would tell him what
he wants. He dials up the message and listens, then sits back and
closes his eyes. What would Shroom do? Shroom would return to
the war, definitely, but that was his destiny in this life cycle, he was
fulfilling his warrior incarnation and only by seeing it through would
he move on to the next stage. "So what stage am I?" Billy asked,
joking, sort of, but Shroom didn't laugh. You won't know until you
work at it, he said. Study, meditate, contemplate, focus. You won't
find out just by drifting through your time. So with his eyes still shut
Billy tries to envision himself at the ranch. *Very secure and remote,* the
voice in the phone message said. *It's a good place. We'll make sure you
won't lack for anything.* In the vision Billy is walking down a path.
He's wearing jeans, Timbs, a flannel shirt, and a corduroy jacket.
The path leads through some woods, and there's a river nearby. He
can hear the *shoosh* of rapids, sometimes glimpse the flash of water
through the trees, but the vision yaws and stutters until Faison mate-
rializes at his side, and then it all unfolds in gorgeous HD, he and
Faison living quiet in their secure location, loving each other, screwing eight or nine times a day, cooking meals and watching movies,
going for walks with the dogs. There would be dogs. And lots of
books, books piled everywhere. He would apply himself to study in
the best Shroom tradition, so he'd know that much more when the

shit-hammer came down. And when it did—when the time came to make his stand? He'd have Faison, the lawyers, his Silver Star on his side. He could do it. He'd make statements. Ain't gonna study war no more.

Rrrrraaaahhhhhxxxx-annnnnn, Sykes is screeching at the top of his lungs, *you don't have to,* then he turns and starts chattering to the fans in row 8 about how much he loves the Bravos, hell yes he loves his boys like brothers, he's just a poor white dumbass from Coon Cove, Florida, but at least he's got the Army, hooah! Down on this end Lodis is slumped in his seat, fast asleep. Dustings of sleet have accumulated on his shoulders and arms as in a comic advertisement for an antidandruff shampoo. A squirt of subcutaneous tissue spills from the cut in his lip. The nice boojee lady in front of them happens to notice the sleeping soldier, such a compelling sight that she turns all the way around for a closer look.

"Ain't he sweet?" Mango says.

"How can he *sleep* in this weather?" she cries.

"Technically he's not asleep, ma'am," Crack informs her. "He's passed out."

The lady laughs. She's a cool boojee lady. Her husband and friends are chuckling too.

"But it's just *miserable* out here," she protests. "Shouldn't he at least have a blanket or something? Doesn't the Army give you *coats*?"

"Oh, ma'am, don't worry about him," Crack assures her. "We're infantry, that's kind of like being a dog or a mule, we're too dumb to mind the weather. He's fine, believe me, he don't feel a thing."

"But he could freeze!"

"No ma'am," Mango chimes in. "We punch him every once in a while to keep his blood moving. See, like this." He delivers a sharp whack to Lodis's bicep. Lodis snarls and throws out his arms, but his eyes never open.

"See?" Mango beams. "He's fine. He's happy. He's like a cockroach, you can't kill him!"

The lady rustles around in her pack, then kneels backward on her seat and drapes a Snuggie over Lodis, one of those personal lounging blankets with built-in sleeves as advertised on late-night dumb-dumb TV. Before long the Bravos have tucked a homemade sign under Lodis's chin. HOMELESS VET—WILL SLAY VAMPIRES FOR FOOD. Below that, HAVE A BLESSED DAY. Then a smiley face. The crowd perks up when a Cowboys lineman boosts an enemy fumble and staggers, slips, and slides all the way to the Bears' three, but then the refs get into it, they convene at the sideline replay machine and discuss, peer, point, and discuss some more, they are a team of Nobel scientists tweaking the breakthrough cure for cancer. At last, a decision is decided. *Upon further review* . . . The fumble is revised to an incomplete pass and that does it for the boojees, they start packing up. Mango reminds the nice lady to take her Snuggie. "Oh, I can't do that," she says, smiling down at Lodis, so soundly racked with his eyelashes flocked with sleet, that lip chunk dangling like a squashed bug. "He looks so cozy. I want him to keep it. You tell him it's my gift to him."

Bravo erupts: Noooo!

"You're gonna spoil him!"

"He grew up in a ditch, he don't know from being cold!"

"It's like giving a pig a Rolex, ma'am, he's got no appreciation for the finer things in life."

The lady laughs and waves them off. "Thank you!" the Bravos cry as she and her group file out of the row. "Thank you for supporting the troops!"

"Nice lady," Mango says, settling back in his seat. Billy agrees. They look at Lodis and laugh, then Mango shivers. He hunches over and clasps his hands between his thighs.

"You look like you gotta piss."

"I sorta do gotta piss." Mango winces and shivers but stays put. "You gonna see Faison before we go?"

"Hoping."

"Dude, gotta be some way you can get with her."

"I don't think so. I don't know. I don't wanna push it."

Mango laughs.

"No, I'm serious. I mean, if this was a normal situation all I'd be thinking about right now is where to take her on a date. Trying to nail her, I mean, come on. I've only known her about four hours."

"Billy, our situation ain't normal, in case you hadn't noticed. You think she's gonna keep on liking you a whole year, and you a million miles away sending her dipshit emails? *Dear Faison how are you I am fine today we busted down a house and killed many bad fuckers as much as we could.* That shit gets old, dawg, shit gets old real quick. Even our moms don't wanna hear it after a while."

"You are one depressing fuck, you know that?"

"I'm just sayin'! This is your best shot, dawg. This is as close as you're gonna get, so go for it. If she's a nice girl and she wants to support the troops . . ."

"You're an idiot."

Mango laughs. Billy's cell is ringing again.

"That her?"

"No," Billy says, checking the screen. "My sister."

"You ain't picking up?"

Billy shrugs. The call rings out. A minute later he gets a text.

> *Dont go pls.*
> *B hero x2.*
> *CALL HIM BACK.*
> *Pls.*
> *Yr sis loves u.*

Billy punches up the phone message again, this time listening not so much to what the man says as to the sound of his voice, whatever information might be coded in timbre and pitch. The voice is white, male, educated, middle-aged; Texan, but with a big-city crispness

to his words. Strong. Assertive. Sympathetic. *Son, if you're thinking about taking a new direction in your life, we can sure help with that.* It is a good voice. Billy is tempted to listen again, but here comes Dime barreling down the row, blasting through the obstacle course of Bravo knees and feet. He reaches the aisle and pulls out his cell, crouches by Billy's seat. "Sykes is driving me fuckin' nuts," he says, studying his messages.

"Better living through chemistry, eh, Sergeant," says Mango.

"Yeah, well, it was either meds or ball-gagging the little shit. He'll be fine," Dime says, though no one has asked. "He'll be fine once we get him back on post. It's all this other . . ." He falls silent. Billy clears his throat.

"Sergeant, if you had a choice, would you go back? To Iraq, I mean."

Dime lifts his head; he is not pleased. "But I don't have a choice, do I? So your question lacks relevance."

"But if you did have a choice."

"But I don't."

"But if you did."

"But I don't!"

"But if you did!"

"Shut up!"

"I'm just—"

"SHUT!"

Billy shuts. Mango is giving him a WTF? stare. Dime snorts and shakes his head.

"Do you wish we had a choice, is that what you're saying?"

"Well." Billy understands he's gone too far. "But we don't."

"That is correct, Billy, we don't. We're going back, and we all know what we're going back to, and that's why we're gonna have our shit high and tight and look out for each other twenty-four/seven. But I will say this." He pauses; his cell is ringing. "If I'm never in another firefight as long as I live, that'll be okay by me. *Hey.*" He's

got the cell to his ear. "Uh huh. Uh huh. Interesting. How about this, how about if Swank sits on his face, would he do it then?"

Billy and Mango look at each other. The damn movie.

"So it's either that or . . ." Dime looks up at the scoreboard. "Albert, we're running out of time."

Mango turns away, hissing something low and hot in Spanish. Down the row Sykes has launched into the old boot camp chant, *Pick up your wounded, pick up your dead . . .*

"He's right here," Dime says, glancing at Billy. He listens for a moment, then asks Billy: "Are you available for a meeting?"

Billy laughs. "Am I *what*? Sure, yeah. When?"

"Now. With Norm. Josh is coming for us."

Billy's throat knots up. "Okay."

"Yes he is available," Dime says to the cell. "Anybody else?" Dime listens, then grunts and clicks off. For several moments he just crouches there, staring at the field.

"Sergeant, are you okay?"

Dime snaps out of it. "I was just thinking, rich people are crazy." He turns to Billy and adds, with feeling: "Don't ever forget that."

"Roger, Sergeant."

MONEY MAKES US REAL

THEY COME UPON ALBERT in the corridor outside of Norm's suite, head down, back propped against the wall, tapping on his BlackBerry with his silver tapping stick. He beams when they turn the corner.

"Guys! What up?"

"Up, down, all around," Dime answers.

"Let's hang here a minute, I'll bring you up to speed." He turns to Josh with a pleasant, pointed look.

"I'll go tell Mr. Oglesby we're here," Josh says.

"Excellent idea." Albert herds Dime and Billy down the corridor some distance from the suite. "Looking good at halftime, guys, you did yourselves proud. You meet Beyoncé and the girls?"

"Hell no," Dime grumps.

"What? No? That's lousy. So what was that about down on the

field, after? Looked like a flash mob or something, Black Friday at a Wal-Mart out in North Jersey. We couldn't figure out what was going on."

"It was nothing," Dime says. "Just boys being boys."

"Somebody giving you a hard time?"

Dime looks to Billy. "Was somebody giving us a hard time?"

"No, relatively speaking," Billy answers.

"He'll go far," Albert says to Dime. "All right fellas, here's the deal." He pauses to smile at a passing couple, waits for the swish of their fur and cashmere to recede down the hall. "Norm's in. He wants to put together an investor group to make our picture, but that's not all. He's *inspired,* shall we say, you guys have inspired him to think big thoughts today. He's decided to form his own production company and start making films."

"Might as well. His football team sure sucks," says Dime.

Albert sniggers, glances up and down the hall. "Apparently he's been mulling it over for quite some time, then we show up and he figures that's God's way of telling him to make his move. And frankly why not, the studios are looking to slough off risk any way they can. A guy who comes in with his own product, his own money, this is a very desirable commodity in Hollywood these days."

He pauses while several more couples pass. One of the men snaps his fingers at Dime.

"Hey, great job at halftime!"

Dime snaps his fingers back. "Hey, you too!"

Albert waits until they're gone. "It helps that he's going all in, we'll have that much more credibility shopping our picture around. With a one-off deal you're sort of a lame duck, but if they know you're sticking around? All the more reason for him to make a statement with this picture. Anyway, as far as our deal goes, as soon as he gets the company formed I'll assign my option over to it, then when we've got the package together the company exercises the option, you guys get some money, and we go into production."

"Cool," says Dime.

"I'll need you guys' consent to transfer the option over."

Dime hesitates. "But you'll still be our producer."

"You better believe it."

"What about the Swank situation?"

"He's still got a blunt up his ass about Hilary, but we can deal with that. All kinds of ways to deal with that. Believe me, having her in the mix is nothing but good for us. But listen." Albert coughs into his fist. "You need to know going in, Norm's got somewhat of a problem with the option price."

"What kind of problem."

"A size problem. A hundred thousand per Bravo, ten Bravos, that's a tough nut to crack right out of the gate. We're already looking at plunking half a million for the script, then getting a lead on the level of a Hilary, a Clooney, we're talking multiple millions here."

Dime turns to Billy. "Here's where we get fucked."

"No!" Albert cries. "No, no, no, no, Dave, have some faith! We've come this far together, you think I'm gonna toss you over the side *now*? Dave, Dave, you guys are *my* guys, either we make it together or we go down together. That's what I told them in there, but I'm not gonna bullshit you, Norm's not Santa Claus, he's not spending one more dime than he has to. He, they, one of his guys—look, these are businessmen, okay? Understand they're very crude in their thinking, just by definition. They floated the idea of dealing with just you two, they see your stories as the principal elements in this and the rest of the guys as, well, ancillary. I said I'd run it by you, but—"

"*No.*"

"—uh huh, total nonstarter, that's what I told them. Bravo lives by the warrior code, I said. They won't ever leave one of their own behind."

"For them to even—"

"I know! But you have to understand that's the mentality we're

dealing with here. Streamlining, return on capital, all that MBA shit, but I think they got the message. It's gotta be all Bravos or no Bravos, nothing in between."

"Damn straight," Dime woofs, with volume enough to raise giggles from the busboys down the hall.

"David, relax."

"I'm totally relaxed. Billy's relaxed too, aren't you Billy?"

"Totally, Sergeant."

"Hang with me, guys, I'm gonna get you there. Right now what they're offering is, well, what you'd be doing is deferring moneys up front for a net-profits percentage in the movie. You get an advance when the option is exercised, then you get another pop when we go into production—"

"How much?"

"—David, let me finish, please. Look, just ballparking this thing, if it has even decent success on the scale I'm thinking of, you guys will come out considerably better than a hundred thousand, but you'll have to hang in there and be patient. When I set our up-front number two weeks ago I was thinking we'd be playing with studio money, but it's a whole different game when you go independent. The numbers scale back across the board, people usually end up taking a profits percentage in lieu of cash. Even stars take percentage if it's a project near and dear to their hearts."

"Fine, I hear you. How much."

"Well, initially it's pretty minimal. Fifty-five hundred against profits when the option's exercised—"

A gurgling commences in Dime's throat.

"—but you'll get that second advance when production starts—"

"Fifty-five fucking *hundred*?"

"I know it's not what you were hoping for—"

"No shit!"

"—but then you'll get that second advance—"

"How much?"

"Well, we're still working on that, but usually it's tied to production budget. The bigger the budget, the bigger your advance—"

"Not our deal, Albert. You said a hundred thousand up front."

"I did, because I believe in your story so much, and I still think we're gonna home-run this thing. Look, two weeks ago I thought we had a real chance of taking studio bids, you guys had such outrageous buzz coming in. But we get a couple of no's, and Russell Crowe taking a pass, that really hurt us. It doesn't take much for the buzz to fade, and I admit, maybe I got a little ahead of myself, I jacked up everybody's expectations and now we're all going to have to adjust. Plus the fact that the war's put up some spotty box-office numbers, didn't I say that might be a problem? So we're bucking that too. I know fifty-five hundred sounds pretty lame after the numbers we've been talking about, but for young men like yourselves, young soldiers on Army pay, it's not nothing, right?"

"Albert, don't even talk to me like that."

"Dave, I'm just trying to get you to think long-term here. This is equity, think of it as stock, stock options, you're deferring a chunk of money up front for a shot at real money down the road. And you guys would be helping to build something, that's what equity's all about. If the company makes money, you make money, you'll be fully vested partners with Legends on this deal—"

"Wait, *who?*"

"Legends. That's the name Norm wants for his company."

"Jesus Christ, he's already got the fucking *name?*"

"You better believe he's got the name and that's great, I got no interest being partners with a ball scratcher, and neither should you. He's ready to *go,* Norm'll pull a damn trigger—do you not realize the value of that? How freaking *rare* that is in my world? You die by the slow no in this business, *lemme get back to you, lemme get back to you, lemme get back to you,* everybody's so scared of screwing up they'd rather lose a kidney than make an actual business decision. So

here we are in Dallas, we meet this guy, he sizes up the situation and wham, he's good to go. I'm not saying you have to love the guy, but you've got to respect the power of that."

Respect this, Billy can practically hear the Bravos woof. As if in pain Dime swags his head side to side.

"But Albert."

"What?"

"You said they love us."

"I did, David, but that was two weeks ago. People move on, they start to focus on other things."

"So you're saying this is the best offer we're going to get?"

"Dave, I'm saying this is the only offer we've got."

"Does Norm know?"

Albert shrugs. "He knows we've been talking to people."

"So what he's offering is, basically, fifty-five hundred bucks apiece. And that's all he's on the hook for. No guarantees we'll get anything else."

"Dave, you want a guarantee, go buy a microwave. No guarantees in my world unless your name is Tom Cruise."

Dime sighs, and to Billy's profound alarm he turns and asks, "What do you think?" but before Billy can answer an unmarked door pops open between them and the suite, and Mr. Jones leans out.

"Mr. Ratner, the third quarter's about to end."

"Thanks. We'll be right there."

Mr. Jones withdraws but leaves the door ajar. Albert turns to Dime and Billy, lowers his voice. "Guys, tell me what you want. You wanna go in there and talk, or should I just yell through the door no thanks."

"No," Dime says.

"No what?"

"This sucks," Dime says to Billy.

Albert gives them a big smile. "Always, guys, always, it's just a question of degree. Be thankful it's not rectal bleeding."

"What happens to the rest of it if we say no? His big production company, all the movies he wants to make."

Albert drops the smile. "I think he's planning to go forward with that. He seems committed."

"Are you going to be involved?"

Albert's mouth forms a tidy little purse. "Well, I'd be foolish not to consider every opportunity."

"Albert, you're an asshole."

The producer doesn't bat an eye. "Dave, I got you an offer. If you think you can do better, let's go in there and talk to the man."

"Okay, fuck it. Let's go in there and talk."

Billy says he'll be fine waiting in the hall, but Dime gives him such a blistering look that he's shamed into coming. Mr. Jones is standing just inside the door, which he shuts and locks behind them. They descend a couple of steps into a dim, cramped, low-ceilinged space furnished along the ad hoc lines of a waiting room at a car wash. It's a super-private adjunct to the official owner's suite next door, a man place, ripe with the muzzy smells of sweat, burnt coffee, vestigial cigarette smoke, plus a percolating flatulence that might be stale lunch meat. Everyone turns and smiles for the Bravos. "Gentlemen! Welcome to the war room!" someone cries, and they are urged forward, offered chairs and refreshments. TVs mounted on wall brackets are tuned to the game, the announcers nattering like parrots in a cage. A bare wet bar occupies one corner of the room. Norm and his sons are seated at a counter that runs the length of the plate-glass front. Scattered about the countertop are laptops, spreadsheets, loose-leaf notebooks, bottles of water and sports drinks; as his eyes adjust to the bad light Billy sees not a drop of alcohol in sight. Two Cowboys executives are moving about, big, burly guys with the trouser-hitching swagger of management who started out on the loading dock. Mr. Jones perches on a stool by the wet bar, still with his suit coat buttoned. Everyone else is down to loose ties and rolled sleeves, except for Josh, who's doing his mannequin thing at the back of the room.

Dime asks for coffee. Billy says he'll have the same. Norm has swung his Aeron chair around to face them, and now he rubs his eyes and tips the chair back, giving the scoreboard a last glance as the quarter expires.

"Sorry about the lights," he says, nodding at the ceiling. "We keep them off during games, otherwise it's like a fishbowl in here. Damn irritating to look over at the TV and see yourself staring at yourself on the tube."

"Or dropping the f-bomb," says one of the execs. "Not that *that's* ever happened here."

Norm shakes his head as the others laugh. "We try to keep at least an R rating up here."

"Not many people ever see the inside of this room," says the second executive, who has introduced himself as Jim. "This is the inner sanctum, boys. A lot of folks would give their left arm to be sitting where you are."

"You should charge admission," Dime says, and everyone laughs but him.

"I'm not sure we could get it today," says Norm. "Not our most stellar effort, I'm sorry to say. I was really hoping we'd put on a show for you fellas. But maybe we'll turn it around in the fourth."

"Some pass blocking from Stennhauser would be nice," says f-bomb, to sour laughs. Norm turns to one of his sons.

"Skip, how many carries does Riddick have?"

Skip consults his laptop. "Nineteen. For thirty-four yards."

Groans rise from several sectors of the room. "He's done, coach," says Jim. "Let's give Buckner a go, at least he's got fresh legs."

"He don't have any holes to hit, what does it matter," says f-bomb. "We need to be pushing some bodies around up front."

Norm frowns and takes a sip of Fiji water. Skip hands him a sheet of paper he's just printed out, from which Norm proceeds to read aloud third-quarter statistics. A waiter enters through a side door, showing a momentary slice of the main suite. Over there it's a pretty

good party; over here, a long day at the office. Billy accepts his coffee and takes some sips. He likes it here. The close quarters evoke
a sense of primal security, a kind of hunkered-down campfire inti-
macy that seems specifically masculine. It's that long-sought place of
ultimate safety, all the better for its cave-like feel, its air of chummy
exclusivity. He would love to wipe the war from his brain, if only for
a moment, and indulge in the luxury of pretending that he's permanent here.

"This defense is as tough as any we've faced all year," Norm says,
perhaps rehearsing for the post-game press conference. He sets the
printout aside and speaks past the Bravos to Albert, who's chosen to
sit where the soldiers can't see his face.

"Albert, did you tell our young friends about our plans for their
film?"

"Sure did!" Albert answers, spreading the pep a bit thick.

"Congratulations on your movie company, sir," says Dime.
"Sounds epic."

"Thank you, Sergeant, thank you very much. It's something we've
been kicking around for a while, and we're excited to get it going,
incredibly excited. It's definitely going to be a challenge, but with
Albert on the team I like our chances. And I'm especially excited
about bringing *your* story to the screen, and let me pledge to you right
now, and I can't emphasize this enough, we're going all-out on this.
Anyone here will tell you, when I decide to do something, I don't go
halfway."

"Norm loves his work," says f-bomb.

Everyone laughs, and Norm joins in with a boyish chuckle, he
doesn't mind this sly poke at his workaholic rep. Billy is struck by the
depths he finds in Norm's watery blue eyes, the sincerity, the evident
eagerness to concur and connect. Watching him at close range, it's
hard to believe he's as mean as people say.

"I believe in your story," Norm tells the Bravos, with only the
briefest glance at the field, "and I believe in the good it can do for

our country. It's a story of courage, hope, optimism, love of freedom, all the convictions that motivated you young men to do what you did, and I think this film will go a long way toward reinvigorating our commitment to the war. Let's face it, a lot of people are discouraged. The insurgency gets some traction, casualties mount, the price tag keeps going up, it's only natural some people are going to lose their nerve. They forget why we went there in the first place—why are we fighting? They forget some things are actually worth fighting for, and that's where your story comes in, the Bravo story. And if the Hollywood crowd won't step up to the plate, well, I'm happy to pinch-hit, more than happy. This is an obligation I willingly assume."

Son Skip is absorbed in his computer screen. Norm's other son—Todd? Trey?—has swung his chair around to listen to his father, though at the moment he's tapping out a text on his cell. Jim is pouring himself a soda at the bar. F-bomb executive is leaning against the wall, munching a sandwich and nodding his head to the beat of his boss's speech.

"I have my doubts about Hollywood anyway," Norm is saying, "their politics, the whole cultural attitude out there. And some of the concepts they've been throwing around? This whole thing with Hilary Swank—look, I know she's a great actress, I'm sure she'd do a great job. But having a woman in the lead just sends the wrong message, in my view. This is a story about *men,* men defending their *country,* and I'm sorry, that's just what it is."

"But Hilary's still a prospect," Albert pipes up, and everybody laughs.

"She is, she is," Norm concedes, grinning, "I didn't say she isn't. And if casting her turns out to be the best thing for our movie, that's what we'll do. I'm not interested in making a *good* movie, I want something *great,* something people will be watching a hundred years from now. I want a movie that's going to rank right up there with the best American films of all time."

And with that everything seems settled and fine, until Dime speaks up and spoils it.

"What makes you think you can?" he asks, taunting, jeering, lifting his chin as if dismissing some object of contempt. Someone gasps, or so it seems when Billy later recalls these moments. Skip turns from his computer, slowly folding down the screen. Todd stares, fingers poised over the keypad of his phone. F-bomb executive has paused in midchew.

"Pardon?" Norm's dazed smile makes a pudding of his face.

"Can you do it, can you deliver. You want to buy our story for fifty-five hundred bucks, that sure sounds like chump change to me. We could sell it to pretty much anybody for that, hell, my granny could swing that deal with a trip to the ATM. With all due respect, Mr. Oglesby, sir, show us you're serious. Show us you're a player."

Still with that knocked-wonky smile, Norm sits back and carefully crosses his arms. He turns to his sons, then to the two executives, and as if cued by some mysterious signal, they all bust up laughing.

"Look around you, son," Norm says, regarding Dime with a warm, pitying cast to his eyes. "Look around and think for a moment about everything you see. Then you tell me, am I a *player*?"

Billy knows if it was up to him, he would fold right now. It's too strong, the dark mojo of these rich, powerful men operating in the comfort of their home turf, and Norm above all with his kindly blue eyes, his fatherly patience, the paralytic force field of his mesmerizing narcissism. Billy wishes Albert would speak up and pull them back from the brink, but Dime presses on.

"Sir, may I speak frankly?"

Norm smiles, shows his palms. "Why stop now?"

More yuks from the cheering section. The small of Billy's back is a peat bog of sweat. Does Dime plan these things or just wing it? *Wings it,* he decides with a fierce burst of pride. He'd follow his sergeant through forty hells.

"I've been told it'll take a budget of around eighty million dollars to get our movie made—am I correct on that, Albert?"

"Ideally," Albert intones from somewhere south of the Bravos. "Sixty to eighty million to make a first-class war picture."

"That's a lot of scratch," Dime says, turning back to Norm.

"It is," Norm agrees.

"So where's it coming from?"

"Ah." Norm chuckles, looks to his son. "Skip, remind me again, where does the money come from?"

"Capital markets," Skip says briskly, only slightly condescending as he turns to Dime. "Banks, insurance companies, hedge funds, pension plans, there's always plenty of money out there looking for deals. Assuming the economy cooperates, we think we can get Legends fully funded in the three-, three-hundred-fifty-million range with a series of private offerings, roll them out over a period of, say, eighteen months. Then with additional funding to come as needed, maybe on a per-project basis."

"GE Capital's been begging to put some money with us," says Todd.

"That's right. And that's not counting individual investors. Just with our friends next door"—Skip nods toward the main suite—"I bet Dad could step over there and have commitments for twenty, thirty million by the end of the game."

"We have access," Norm says patiently to Dime. "We have ample experience raising capital. I think you could even call us"—he pauses and smiles—*"players."*

"Yes sir, I sure hear you on that, sir. Those are some stout numbers you're talking about, but with all due respect, sir, fifty-five hundred for each of my Bravos just seems kind of . . . small."

"Albert, they understand how we need to structure this deal?"

"I explained," Albert answers in a studiously neutral voice.

"So you know"—Norm turns back to the Bravos—"your fifty-five hundred is just an advance, correct? We could buy you out with a

big lump sum, sure, but that makes it harder for us to get your movie made. We need maximum flexibility to put this package together, and what we're asking from you, what we need from you, is in the nature of an in-kind equity contribution. In exchange for the rights to your story you'll have a vested interest in the project, which means you share with us in the upside—"

"And the downside," says Dime.

"Sure, sure, and the downside. There's going to be risk, just like with any investment. But it won't be any greater for you than it is for any other investor, myself included."

"Mr. Oglesby sir, with all due respect, sir. We're soldiers. We feel like we've already got enough risk in our lives."

"And I'm certainly sensitive to that, but we're talking about an entirely separate arena here. If we're going to sell this project to potential investors, we've got to show them a solid package. We can't afford to be cutting sweetheart deals here."

Norm swivels his chair for a look at the field, and Billy realizes that their host was hoping to close the deal before the fourth quarter began. Too late; the players are taking the field. "You do understand, I trust," Norm says, turning back to the Bravos, "this is about a lot more than just money. Our country *needs* this movie, needs it badly. I really don't think you want to be the guys who keep this movie from being made, not with so much at stake. I sure wouldn't want to be that guy."

"We understand, sir. And I can assure you sir, if anything terrible happens, Bravo is ready to take full responsibility."

Norm cuts a glance at his execs. He's almost smiling, Billy sees. He's enjoying this. There is a vast asymmetry in the dynamic here that Billy can't quite put his finger on, even though it's the elephant shitting all over the room.

"Sergeant," Norm says, "that's our offer. Based on what I'm hearing, it's the only offer you've got, and now, well, you're going back to Iraq. Wouldn't you like to have something before you go? Some-

thing to show for all your hard work and sacrifice, the magnificent service you've given the country? Maybe it's not as much as you were hoping for, but I think most people would agree, something is better than nothing."

"Something would be nice," Dime says. "Something would be great. But it's"—he breaks off with a choking gasp—"it's just, I don't know, it's just so *sad,* sir. We thought you kind of liked us."

"But I do!" Norm cries, lurching upright in his chair. "I *do* like you! I think the world of you fine young men!"

Dime clasps his hands to his heart. "See?" he gushes to Billy. "He *does* like us! He likes us so much he's going to fuck us in the face!"

In a second Albert is on his feet, chousing the Bravos out of their chairs with a bright furious smile and asking Norm for a place where he can talk to his "boys," and though the Oglesby team takes it all more or less in stride, Dime has offended, clearly. He has crossed the bounds of couth. A very curt Mr. Jones leads them down the hall to a small, windowless room with a half bath attached, a kind of massage and decompression chamber, Billy gathers, furnished with a heavily pillowed daybed he would describe as "French," a couple of leather and steel-tube chairs, a massage table, and a deep-pile Persian rug. The ubiquitous TV is mounted high in a corner, the first they've seen today that's not switched on. Mr. Jones ducks into the bathroom and has a look, then walks a circle around the massage table. He seems to be doing some sort of security sweep.

"Hey, Mr. Jones, is this place bugged?" Dime asks. "It's okay if it is, I'm just asking. Do you think it's bugged?" he continues, turning to Billy and Albert as Mr. Jones leaves without saying a word. "I bet it is, hell, I bet it's wired for video. I bet this is where Norm does his day-shift hookers—"

"David, chill."

"—um *umph,* check this action out." He's feeling up the daybed, then testing its bounce with his rump. "I could definitely jam some high-dollar ass on this. I betcha anything he's got it fixed for video—"

"Settle down, Dave, please—"

"—it's always the billionaires who're the biggest pervs—"

"—would you shut up, Dave, please, please just shut the fuck up? Please? Can you? Yes? Thank you!"

Dime sits on the edge of the daybed and primly crosses his legs, looks over at Billy, and laughs. Albert looks to Billy and rolls his eyes. Billy has taken the leather chair by the bathroom door, as far out of the line of fire as possible.

"You're on his *team*?" Dime snarls.

Albert seems to rear, grizzly-like. "Hell yes, if that's what it takes to get your picture made."

"He's an asshole."

"And that's supposed to mean anything? This is business, there's an asshole every time you pick up the phone. Stop thinking like a twerp and get your head in the game."

"Oh gee Albert, I'm sorry. I'm really sorry if we're messing up your brand-new partnership."

"Tell me this, David, do you think *you're* a player? You wanna be a player, you better learn to keep a civil tongue in your head. What you said in there—look, you cannot let emotion escalate into drama, not if you want a deal. You can whine and bitch and argue and everything else, but you *cannot* blow it up just because you're pissed off."

"Like we haven't heard some rank stuff out of your mouth."

"That's different, I know how far I can push. And some of these studio guys, they like the abuse, but you're punching way above your weight here. Norm doesn't have to take that kind of shit from you."

"Norm can lick every pimple on my pretty pink ass."

"Oh, lovely. Wonderful. I can see how well you're listening. You know what, maybe Billy should represent the squad in there. How about if you stay here, David, stay here and grow some brains. Billy and I'll go represent the squad in there."

"I'm not going back in there," Billy says, not that anyone's listening. Dime holds up his hand.

"All right, all right, okay, truce. Okay." He takes a breath. "Albert, just tell me this—is Norm just fucking with us? Does he really need to bust us down like this, or is he being a corporate dick just because he can?"

Albert leans against the massage table and sucks his lip, considering. "Both, probably. I think he could do a lot better by you guys, no question. Fifty-five hundred is pretty thin. But you'll have equity."

"He'll wanna screw us on that too, that's the vibe I get from this guy. If he's doing us on the front end he'll do us on the back, it's a matter of principle with this guy."

"He's a pretty tough nut, I'll grant you that. You get in a fight with Norm, you better be wearing a cup, but listen, bottom line? He wants this deal as much as we do. So we just keep him at the table for as long as it takes, when he gets tired enough he'll come around."

"Not if he runs out the clock on us. You heard him, he knows what we're up against. We don't have unlimited time here."

"Well, I've always viewed your departure as a somewhat artificial deadline anyway. Signatures can be faxed. They can be e-mailed."

"Not if we're dead."

Albert folds his arms and stares glumly at his shoes. A brief, startling vision comes to Billy of big old Albert standing in a rainy field somewhere, head down, shoulders hunched, hands in his pockets, weeping. It has never occurred to him that their producer might be capable of actual tears.

"How about this," Dime offers, "how about if we hold a gun to his head?"

"Oh David, don't even talk like that."

"Hell yeah, vets on the edge, baby! Everybody's got their breaking point."

"He's just kidding," Billy tells Albert, looking to Dime to make sure.

"Everybody *supports the troops,*" Dime woofs, "*support the troops, support the troops,* hell yeah we're *so fucking **PROUD** of our troops,* but when it comes to actual money? Like somebody might have to come

out of pocket *for the troops?* Then all the sudden we're on everybody's tight-ass budget. Talk is cheap, I got that, but gimme a break. Talk is cheap but money screams, this is our country, guys. And I fear for it. I think we should all fear for it."

Albert blinks, unsure how seriously he should take that last part. "Dave, all I can tell you is the only way we're going to get a deal is to keep talking to this guy. He made his offer, if you don't like it we'll make a counter and see what comes back, that's how it works. But you keep your emotions out of it and focus on the deal, okay? That's the only way you're going to get some money for your guys."

"I need to call them," Dime says, pulling out his cell.

"So call. I gotta take a leak."

As soon as Albert's in the bathroom Billy moves to the other chair, so that he doesn't have to listen to the movie producer pee. Dime calls Day, and at certain points in the conversation Billy can hear Day's side as plainly as Dime's. *What the fuck?* comes through quite clearly, in addition to *fuck that, fuck that shit,* and *fuck that motherfucking shit.* Dime asks Day to poll the rest of the squad, and their answers boom through like the bellowing of cows in a slaughter chute. Billy pulls out his own cell and clicks on. He's missed calls from Kathryn and the unknown number, and there's a text from Kathryn as well—

> *Sending car 4 u tx stadium*
> *CALL HIM 4 meet.*
> *JUST GET IN THE CAR.*

Dime clicks off. "They said no."

"I heard."

Dime pockets the cell. "Your thoughts, Billy. What do you think we should do."

Billy shuts his eyes and tries to have coherent thoughts about everything that has happened today. Into the still of his concentration sails the crash of a flushing toilet.

"He's wrong."

"Who's wrong?"

Billy opens his eyes. "Norm. Remember what he said in there, he was like, you guys oughta take the deal because it's all you've got, and something's better than nothing? But I don't think so. I think sometimes nothing is better than something. I mean, I'd rather have nothing than let this guy use me like his bitch. Plus"—Billy glances around and lowers his voice, as though the room in fact is bugged—"I just sort of hate the son of a bitch."

For some reason this is suddenly hilarious to them. Albert emerges from the bathroom to find the two Bravos laughing like baboons.

"Sorry, guy," Dime tells him, "but fitty-five hundred don't cut it. And Bravo speaks as one on this."

Albert pulls a poker face. "Okay, so what cuts it?"

"Hundred thousand up front, then we're out of Norm's hair. And he can keep all that wonderful equity for himself."

"Guys, I think you're going to have to bend a little bit. What if we—hang on." His cell is buzzing. "Speak of the devil. Lemme just . . . Yes, Norm."

Billy remains in the chair, Dime on the daybed. They listen.

"You're kidding me."

"You can't be serious."

"Can you even do that? On what grounds . . ." Albert laughs, but he's not happy. "National *what*? Are you serious? I've never heard of . . . Jesus, Norm, at least give us a chance. The least you could do is wait to hear what we come back with."

"Five minutes?" He turns to the Bravos. "You guys know of a General Ruthven?" But before the soldiers can answer, he's back to the phone.

"Norm, I really don't think you have to do this. If you'd just . . ."

"Of course I know it's not just about the money. Tell me about it, tell my guys. They put their lives on the line every . . ."

"All right. I guess so. I guess we'll see."

Albert clicks off and slips the cell into his blazer side pocket. He turns to the Bravos, and the way he looks down at them, it's as if they're in their coffins and he's having a last look before the lid comes down.

"Whut," Dime says.

Albert squints; he seems surprised to hear Dime speak. "It's pretty incredible," he says. "They've gotten your chain of command involved. Apparently Norm's good buddies with the deputy-deputy secretary of defense or some such crap, he had that guy call your superiors at Fort Hood. He says he talked to a General Ruthven? And the general's supposed to call here in a couple of minutes, to talk to you." Albert shakes his head; his voice wavers. "I think they're going to make you do the deal." He looks at them. "Can they even do that?"

The Bravos know full well the Army does whatever it wants, and any rights they claim will be shunted into the catch-all category known as "collateral," i.e., things to be administered after it's too late. Mr. Jones comes to lead them back to the bunker, where the Bravos are greeted civilly, almost warmly. They're offered refreshments. They're shown to the same two seats. "The wheels came off," Todd says, indicating the scoreboard, which shows 17–7 in favor of the Bears. "Interception and fumble, ten points in two minutes."

F-bomb executive snorts. "We're gonna send out a search party after the game, help Vinny find his ass."

This raises a bitter laugh.

"Why the hell does George keep sticking Brandt in the slot? Like he thinks he's gonna block?"

"I haven't seen him throw a block since spring training."

"Of '01."

More yuks. Norm sets his headset to the side and swings around to the Bravos. "Not our day," he says with a weary smile.

"No sir," Dime says stiffly.

"I hate to lose, hate it about as much as anything. My wife says I'm

addicted to winning, and I guess it's true, thirty-eight years she's been trying to calm me down. But I can't, I need that rush. I'd rather cut off my little finger than lose."

"We figured back in June it was going to be a tough season," Jim says. "With Emmit gone, Moose, Jay, they left some mighty big shoes to fill. When you lose your core like that . . ." He trails off when he realizes no one is listening.

"I expect you fellas are kind of cross with me right now," Norm says, and by way of response Dime and Billy say nothing. Norm regards them a long moment; nods. He seems impressed by their wall of silence.

"I don't blame you," he goes on. "I know I'm being kind of heavy-handed here, but my instinct tells me to get it done. This is a movie that needs to be made, *now,* for all the reasons we talked about. And if it works out the way I think it's going to, you fellas are set to do very well. Someday before too long I think you'll be thanking me—"

Somewhere in the room a phone rings. Mr. Jones answers, speaks briefly, and brings the phone over to Norm. It is the general. Dime stares straight ahead, into the far distance, it seems. Billy can hear him pulling in deep, measured breaths that he holds for several moments, then releases in finely calibrated jets through his nose. Meanwhile Norm is doing big-guy banter with the general, thanking him for his time, wishing him happy Thanksgiving, inviting him to some future unspecified game. You bet, ha ha, we'll do our best to arrange a win for you. Dime rises, as if the general has actually entered the room. Norm looks up, registering the weirdness of the move, and indeed Billy fears that his sergeant is contemplating something extreme, but Dime just stands there exuding waves of soldierly discipline until Norm extends the phone his way.

"Sergeant Dime." Norm's smile is jacked a couple of clicks beyond mere courtesy. It is triumphant, one might say. Imperial. Magnanimous. "General Ruthven will speak to you now."

Dime takes the phone and makes his way to the shadowy back of the room. Josh sidles away to give Dime some space. After a moment Billy leaves his seat and also moves to the back of the room, simply to be near his sergeant and for no other reason. He takes up position near Josh, who shoots him looks of feverish sympathy. The entire room can't help but listen.

"Yes sir," Dime says crisply.

"Yes sir."

"No sir."

"I understand, sir."

For a full minute Dime says nothing, during which time the Bears score again. Skip and Todd toss their pens, but in deference to the general no one says a word.

"Yes sir," Dime says presently. "I didn't know that, sir."

"Yes sir."

"I think I do sir, yes sir."

"Thank you sir. I will, sir. Out."

Dime pivots and lofts the phone in a high, soft arc toward Mr. Jones. "Come on Billy," he says, and without another word he's exited the room and goes booming down the corridor at a brisk pace. Billy has to jog to catch up.

"Sergeant, where we going?"

"Back to our seats."

"What happened? I mean, shouldn't we . . ."

"It's okay, Billy. It's cool."

"It is?"

Dime nods.

"He said we didn't . . . ?"

"Not in so many words." For several paces Dime is silent. "Billy, did you know General Ruthven is from Youngstown, Ohio?"

"Uh, no, actually."

"I didn't either, till just now." For a moment Dime seems lost in thought. "It's just over the state line from Pennsylvania."

Billy begins to think maybe his sergeant has lost it. "Near Pitts-burgh," Dime continues. "He's a big Steelers fan. The *Steelers,* Billy, yo? Which just by definition means he hates the Cowboys' guts."

"Hey guys!" someone calls, and they turn. It's Josh, trotting after them. "Where're you going?"

"Back to our seats," Billy answers.

Josh slows for a moment, glances over his shoulder, then gath-ers speed. "Wait up, I'll come with you." He has a sheaf of manila packets under one arm, and with the other he's reaching into his coat pocket. Something white flashes in his palm.

"Billy," he calls, holding out a small plastic bottle. "I got your Advil."

THE PROUD GOOD-BYE

WHY MAKE A MOVIE anyway? It seems pointless to go to all
that trouble when the original is floating out there for all to see, easily available online by searching "Al-Ansakar Canal," "Bravo snuff
movie," "America's throbbing cock of justice," or any one of a couple
of dozen similar phrases that summon forth the Fox News footage,
three minutes and forty-three seconds of high-intensity warfare as
seen through a stumbling you-are-there point of view, the battle
sounds backgrounded by a slur of heavy breathing and the bleeped
expletives of the daring camera crew. It's so real it looks fake—too
showy, too hyped up and cinematic, a B-movie's defiant or defensive
flirtation with the referential limits of kitsch. Would a more polished
product serve better, one wonders—throw in some story arc, a good
dose of character development, artful lighting, and multiple camera

angles, plus a soundtrack to tee up the emotive cues. Nothing looks so real as a fake, apparently, though ever since seeing the footage for himself Billy has puzzled over the fact that it doesn't look like any battle he was ever in. Therefore you have the real that looks fake twice over, the real that looks so real it looks fake and the real that looks nothing like the real and thus fake, so maybe you do need all of Hollywood's craft and guile to bring it back to the real.

Then again, everybody always says how much like a movie the Fox footage is. Like *Rambo,* they say. *First Blood.* Like *Independence Day.* Or, as one of their new neighbors in row 6 says, a perky, chatty, twentysomething blonde who's shown up with her husband and another young couple, "It was just like nina leven all over again. I sat down and cut on the news and got the weirdest feeling I was watching a movie on cable."

"You guys rock," says her husband, a handsome, strapping fellow in a Patagonia parka and heirloom-quality cowboy boots. "It felt damn good to see us finally getting some payback."

The other young husband and wife echo the sentiment. They aren't much older than Billy, these two young couples who've migrated down from the upper deck for a sampling of the money seats at garbage time. They remind Billy of certain kids he went to high school with, the sons and daughters of the small-town country-club elite who were firmly embedded in the college track, and now here they are in their midtwenties, duly credentialed and married, starting out their grown-up lives on schedule. The young couples are eager to meet the Texas Bravo, but for a moment they don't know what to make of him in the flesh. "You're just a kid!" one of the wives cries, breaking the ice, then they're introducing themselves and thanking him for his service, the two young wives breathy and fond, the husbands racking his arm with welcome-to-the-frat handshakes.

"Awesome," they say, "outstanding," "an honor to meet you" and so forth, their words sloshing around Billy's brain like soft ice cubes

currj

honor

sacrifice

bravery

proud

and

Kicking Ass!

Billy resumes the aisle seat. Sleet pounds down around them like a spray of fine-grained fertilizer pellets. "No deal?" Mango asks, and Billy shakes his head.

"So what's that about?"

Lodis and A-bort are leaning in, they want the story too.

"Norm's just a cheap bastard, I guess. What can I say."

"We thought Day was shitting us when he told us the deal. Fifty-five hundred—"

"—shit's *cold*," A-bort breaks in, "all the coin he's got running

through his pockets, and that's the best he can do for us? Dude's got millions."

"Maybe that's why he's got millions," Mango points out. "He's careful with his money."

"I be careful with my money, I had some," says Lodis, his splotch of lip quivering like a big juicy booger, or a nib of entrails dangling from a gut wound. Josh comes down the row calling their names and handing out manila packets. Inside his packet each soldier finds an assortment of Dallas Cowboys swag: headbands, wristbands, a combination key chain/bottle opener, a set of decals, the cheerleader calendar for the upcoming year, a glossy eight-by-ten photo of the Bravo shaking hands with Norm, signed and personalized by the great man himself, along with several eight-by-tens of the Bravo posing with his trio of cheerleaders in the post-press-conference scrum, signed and personalized by each of the girls. The Bravos sort of shrug once they've gone through their packets. Outright derision is beneath them. Billy's cell buzzes and it's a text from Faison.

Meet after game?

Yes, he answers, love blanketing his heart like a slab of melting cheddar. *Where u be?* he adds, then waits, phone in hand, while the ranch fantasy does a number on his head. Maybe, he thinks, pondering the possibilities. She was into him. She *got off* on him. He and Faison shacked up at the ranch doesn't seem much more extreme than anything else that's happened lately. He scrolls through his call list to the unknown number, intending to see what kind of vibe might come of staring at it, but an incoming call beats him to it. He clicks on.

"Billy."

"Hey, Albert."

"Where are you guys?"

"Back at our seats."

"Is Dime there?"

"Yeah, he's here."

"He won't pick up. Tell him to pick up for me."

Billy yells down the row and says Albert wants to talk. Dime shakes his head.

"He says not right now." For a moment they're silent. "So did the general . . ."

"You're good, Billy. He's not going to make you guys do anything."

"What'd Norm say?"

Albert hesitates. "Well, it's kind of tough on him. Like he said, he's *addicted* to winning." Albert allows himself the softest of snarky laughs. "It's okay. He's one of those people who could probably use some humility in his life."

"He's pissed," Billy concludes.

"Just a little."

"Are you?"

"Pissed? No, Billy, I can honestly say I'm not. I love you guys way too much for that."

"Oh. Well. Thanks."

Albert chuckles. "Oh, well, you're welcome."

"So what happens now?"

"Well, I'm in the main suite right now, Norm's back there in his hideaway. Maybe he'll come out with another offer at some point. We'll just have to see."

"Okay. Uh, Albert, can I ask you something?"

"Of course, Billy."

"When you ducked out of Vietnam, I mean, you know, when you got your deferment and everything, how did it feel?"

Albert gives a little yip, the way a coyote might as it dodges a sprung trap. "How did it *feel*?"

"I mean, like, was it hard. Did it feel like you were doing the right thing. How do you feel about it now, I guess is what I'm asking."

"Well, it's not something I spend a lot of time thinking about, Billy. I won't say I'm hugely proud of it, but I'm not ashamed of it either. It was a very fucked-up time. A lot of us really struggled about what we had to do."

"You think it was more fucked up then than it is now?"

"Huh. Well. Good question." Albert ponders. "You could probably make a pretty good argument that for the past forty years it never stopped being fucked up. Why do you ask?"

"I don't know. I was just thinking, I guess. About why people do the things they do."

"Billy, you are a philosopher."

"Hell no, I'm just a grunt."

Albert laughs. "How about both. All right, guy, hang loose. And tell Dime to call me."

Billy says he will and clicks off. He dry-swallows two more Advil; the first three made no appreciable dent in his armor-plated headache. Mango asks for some, and Billy ends up passing the bottle down the row, never to return. A steady flow of fans is heading up the stairs for the exits, while a smaller contingent makes its way down, looking to squat in the premium seats for as long as the game lasts. A group of five or six guys piles into row 6, friends of the young marrieds it seems; they arrive with much laughing and razzing and immediately pull out pint bottles of Wild Turkey. "Bro!" one of them caws at Lodis. "Get some stitches in them dizzles!" They have the clean-cut, mainstream, Anglo looks that Billy imagines must be soothing to bosses and clients, suitable for careers in banking, business, law, wherever it is the money lives. The guy sitting in front of Crack turns all the way around.

"Dude, what happened to your *eye*?"

"It's always like this," Crack answers. "But, dude, what happened to your *face*?"

Brrraaaaahhhh, even the guy's own friends send up a howl. "Hey, these are the Bravos," one of the young husbands says. "Don't mess with these guys."

"The *whos?*" cries Crack's new friend. "The *what-hoes?* Oh yeah yeah yeah I heard of you guys, yeah, goddamn, you're famous. Hey, tell me something, what do you think about that whole don't-ask-don't-tell deal?"

"Stop it, Travis!" one of the young wives scolds. "You're being a jerk."

"I am not either being a jerk, I really wanna know! This guy's a soldier, I'm just curious what he thinks about gays in the military."

"I think more of them than gays not in the military," Crack says. "At least they've got the balls to join."

The rowdies send up another howl. "I hear you, dude, hear you," Travis says, laughing. "Serving your country and all that, very cool and everything. But I don't know, it just seems kind of wack to me, say you're in your foxhole at night and some queer comes on to you, what're you supposed to do? Guys blowing each other in foxholes, that just doesn't sound right to me. Like maybe it's got something to do with why we're getting our butts kicked over there, you know?"

"Tell you what," Crack says, "why don't you join up and find out. You can get in a foxhole with me and see what happens."

Travis smiles. "You'd like that, dude?"

Billy wishes Crack would just smack the fool and be done with it, but his fellow Bravo merely stares the guy down. Perhaps one melee is enough for this Thanksgiving Day. Billy checks his cell. Nothing from Faison. Yet. He indulges in another episode of the ranch fantasy, but now while he and Faison are having sex ten times a day he's also thinking about Bravo back at FOB Viper, getting slammed every time they go outside the wire. So he puts that inside the fantasy, how much he'd miss his fellow Bravos, he would *mourn* them even as they live and breathe. They are his boys, his brothers. Bravos would die for one another. They are the truest friends he will ever have, and he'd expire from grief and guilt at not being there with them.

So it seems the war is fucked and his fantasy no less so. He sends another text to Faison. *Wd like to see u and say g-by after game.* She responds almost immediately, *Yes!,* but when he asks where and when, nothing. Dime makes his way down the row and kneels in the aisle by Billy's seat.

"What'd Albert say?"

"Well, he's not mad at us."

"No, Billy, what'd he say about Ruthven."

"Oh. He said it's cool. Ruthven did just what you said he'd do." Dime smiles. "We need to send that man some flowers!"

"Albert said Norm might come back with a better offer—"

"Fuck that, we're not doing a deal with that guy, not for any amount of money. Not for a million bucks apiece."

Billy and Mango look at each other. "A million bucks—" Mango attempts, but Dime cuts him off.

"Look at it this way, say we do the deal and Norm makes his big-shit Bravo movie, gets everybody all pumped for the war again. What happens then? I think what happens is they'll keep stop-lossing our ass until we're dead or too damn old to carry a pack. Well, fuck that. I got no use for a deal like that."

Dime turns and bounds up the aisle. The Bears score to make it 31–7, and the game has officially become a rout. One of the rowdies in row 6 drops his bottle, and the sound of shattering glass sends his buddies into hysterics. "Assholes," Mango mutters, and Billy agrees. They're too drunk, too loud, too pleased with themselves—-more people who could use some humility in their lives?

Billy's cell chirps, signaling a new text. He checks the screen.

"Faison?" Mango asks hopefully.

"Sister." Billy waits for Mango to turn away before he opens it.

> *CALL HIM.*
> *They r ready.*
> *They r waiting 4 u.*

Oh Jesus. Oh Shroom. What would Shroom do? What would he
do if he was Billy, that is the better question, one that turns on the
most intimate, pressing issues of soul, self-definition, one's ultimate
purpose in life. The two-minute-warning gun fires, which means,
great, he has about 120 seconds to figure out what he's doing here
on planet Earth. Oh Shroom, Shroom, the Mighty Shroom of Doom
who foretold his own death on the battlefield, how would he coun-
sel Billy here at the *Victory Tour*'s end? He needs Shroom to make
sense of the situation, to calm the neural scramble of Billy's brain, but
now the Jumbotron is playing the American Heroes graphic and the
rowdies in row 6 send up a big whoop and holler, clapping, stomping
their feet, the young marrieds try to shush their friends but there is
just no stopping the fun.

"Brav-ohhhh!"

"Hay-yull yeah!"

"Woooo-hooooo!"

"Army of one, dudes!"

"See?" says Travis, twisting around to grin at Crack. "We're all
kick-ass patriots here, we totally support the troops."

"Hell yeah," yells one of his buddies.

"Hell yeah," Travis woofs. "Listen, don't-ask-don't-tell, I'm
totally down with that. I don't give a shit if you guys are gay or bi
or tranny or screw lesbian monkeys for all I care, you're studs in my
book. You guys are real American heroes."

He raises his arm for a high-five, but Crack just stares, lets him
dangle. "No?" Travis flashes a smile. "No? Whatever, it's cool. I still
support the troops." He laughs and turns away, reaching under his
seat for his bottle. When he sits up, Crack leans forward and method-
ically, almost tenderly it seems, locks his arms around Travis's neck
and proceeds to choke him out. All soldiers learn this in basic training, how a forearm applied to the carotid artery cuts off blood flow
to the brain, rendering your victim unconscious in seconds. Travis
flops a bit, but it's not much of a struggle. He grabs at Crack's arms,

kicks at the seat in front of him, then Crack squeezes a little harder and Travis goes limp. Several of the rowdies start to rise, but Crack warns them off with a grunt.

"What's he doing?" hisses one of the young wives. "Tell him to stop it. Somebody please tell him to stop."

But Crack just smiles. "I could break this asshole's neck," he announces, and shifts his hold, applies some experimental torque. Travis gives a spastic kick; his friends can only watch. They seem to understand he's beyond their help.

"Crack," says Day, "enough. Turn the motherfucker loose."

Crack giggles. "I'm just having a little fun." There's a masturbatory aspect in the way he twists Travis one way and then the other, squeezing, relenting, squeezing, relenting, probing the physiological point of no return. Travis's face is dark red, shading to purple. A full-on carotid choke results in death in a matter of minutes.

"Damn, Crack," Mango murmurs. "Don't kill the son of a bitch."

"Stop him," pleads one of the wives. "Say something to him."

Billy thinks he might be sick to his stomach, but part of him wants Crack to go ahead and do it, just to show the entire world how fucked the situation is. But finally Crack relents; it's as if he loses interest, the way he turns Travis loose with a casual slap to the head, and Travis sags into his seat like a broken crash dummy. In short order the rowdies decide it's time to leave. They brace up their woozy friend and file out of the row, careful to avoid eye contact with the Bravos. "You guys are crazy," one of them mutters as he sidles past, and Sykes shouts Hell yes we're out of our motherfucking *minds!*, and adds a burbling Valium laugh that in fact sounds pretty batty.

Dime returns in time to watch the rowdies hurry up the aisle. He rubs his chin and regards his suspiciously silent squad.

"Something I need to know about?"

The Bravos manage a weak *brah*. "Mofo kept mouthing off," Day says. "So Crack give him some, uh, training guidance."

Crack shrugs, forces up a smile. He seems chastened and at the

same time deeply satisfied. "I didn't hurt him, Sergeant," he says in all modesty. "Just messed with his head a little."

Down on the field, the final two minutes of play have resumed. Dime looks at his watch, looks at the scoreboard, then has a moment's communion with the storming sky. "Gentlemen," he says, turning back to Bravo, "I think our work here is done. Let's blow."

The squad sends up a lazy or possibly sarcastic cheer. Josh says they're supposed to meet their limo at the west-side limo lane, and he will show them the way. For the final time Bravo trudges up the aisle steps, Billy fighting the tug of all that horrible stadium space. As soon as they reach the concourse he pulls out his cell and texts Faison—

Can u meet west side limo lane? Look for white hummer limo

Bravo falls into line and follows Josh through the concourse. Sykes and Lodis have managed to hang on to their autographed footballs all this time, while the rest of the Bravos have only their swag packets, precious mainly for the cheerleader calendar and those trophy-cleavage photos. It's going to be a long, lonesome eleven months in Iraq, long and lonesome being best-case scenario. On this final walk through the stadium no one stops to thank the Bravos for their service, to harry them for autographs or cell phone snaps. Cowboys nation is in full retreat; cold, wet, tired, whipped, they are bent on getting home as fast as possible, the hell with geostrategy and defending freedoms.

Oh my people. When they come in sight of the gate Josh leads them over to the side of the concourse, out of the traffic flow. "We're supposed to wait here," he tells Bravo. "Some people are coming down to see you off."

Who?

Josh laughs. "I don't know!"

The Bravos look at one another. Whatever. Presently there's a surge of bodies into the already packed concourse, and from this

Bravo infers that the game has ended. The fans move in a toil-some mass toward the exit, and in their numbers and necessarily shambling step they seem to take on allegorical weight, as if their gloom, their air of bedraggled wretchedness, is meant to conjure up the ghost of every tribe that ever bestirred itself to leave one place and journey toward another in hopes of a life of lesser evil. Billy thinks, in other words, that they look like refugees. His cell buzzes, and he turns to the wall before daring to look. It is a two-word text from Faison.

Coming. Wait.

His eyes close, and his head tips forward and clunks the wall, his silent thank-you released as a pent-up breath. Then he's nervous. He doesn't know what he's going to do. He's got no training for this, no drill, nothing to fall back on. He can visualize himself and Faison at the ranch, but the transition, the getting there, his mind won't grant him that. Maybe if he actually *rams* his head against the wall? Suddenly Albert and Mr. Jones appear, popping out of the crowd in a cartoon sort of spurt.

"Hah," Dime screeches in his Will Ferrell voice. "Like a *dog* returning to his *vomit,* here he is!"

Albert grins, he seems perfectly cool with the greeting, though he's careful to keep some distance between himself and Dime. *Albert, Albert, Albert,* the Bravos woof, making a kind of song.

"What about our deal?" Sykes cries.

"Guys, I tried. Believe me, I tried like hell, and I'm going to keep on trying, you can count on that. If there was ever a story that's made for the movies, it's you guys', and I'm fully committed to making that happen."

"But dude—"

"I know, I know, it's a huge disappointment, I really wanted to nail this thing while you were here. What can I say? We gave it our

best shot, but it's not over, hell no. I'm gonna keep working this deal till it happens, I promise you that."

Monklike murmurings rise from the Bravos, *thankyouthank-youthankyou*. A car is waiting to take Albert to the airport; he's flying back to L.A. tonight. Even though his option extends for an entire two years, this feels like the end of something, with all the nostalgia and melancholy natural to endings. Albert says he'll walk out to their limo with them; evidently Mr. Jones is coming too, perhaps to ensure Bravo departs without further insult to the Cowboys brand. They join the weary masses moving toward the exit. A kind of drone, a bottom-register vibraphonic hum emanates from somewhere up ahead, from the threshold, Billy realizes as they draw near. It is the ongoing moan of successions of fans as they step onto the plaza, a windswept barrens of icy concrete with nothing between here and the Arctic Circle but thousands of miles of recumbent plains. The Bravos curse, lower their heads, jam hands in pockets. The sleet gouges micro-divots in their faces and necks. Josh calls the soldiers to him and does a head count, then leads them across the plaza toward the limo lane, limos lined into the murk as far as the eye can see, and, oh Lord, just among these dozen in plain sight Billy counts four in the snow-white Hummer style.

"Billy." Albert has fallen into step beside him. "I think your sergeant is mad at me."

"Well, he's kind of a moody guy." Billy wishes Albert was on his other side, to block the wind.

"Listen, you've got my e-mail, right? And I've got yours. Let's stay in touch."

"Sure." Billy is scanning the line of limos. How Faison is ever going to find him out here . . .

"I admire Dave a lot, but sometimes I wonder how reliable he is. So how about this, whenever I can't get up with him, I'm going to contact you. You'll be my point man for the rest of the squad."

"Fine." Billy raises his windward shoulder, digs his chin into his chest. The wind cuts across the plaza like an unmoored guillotine.

"Listen," Albert says, lowering his voice, "you've got the most sense of all these guys, you and Dime. I trust you. You're developing into a real leader. I know I can count on you to keep the communication flowing in a positive way."

"Sure." Billy is thinking if Faison hasn't showed by the time Bravo is ready to leave, he'll just bail, go AWOL right then and there. He'll say he's got to take a whiz or something, duck out of the limo; he'll be as good as committed then, more so once he locates Faison and spills his guts at her feet.

"I meant what I said about the deal," Albert is saying. "I'm going to keep working it. Sooner or later it has to happen, it's just too good not to."

Billy looks at him. "Really?"

"Well, sure. With Hilary basically attached, it's only a matter of time."

The plaza is lit like a prison exercise yard, all glaring white lights and jabby shadows. Billy turns to scan the area for Faison and almost at once registers a pattern within the crowd, a kind of rippling or cross-current aimed this way. There's a blank moment, then Billy is opening his mouth, he knows what's coming an instant before his mind forms the thought. He's actually shouting as the roadies step from the crowd, then all he knows is that he's down in a fetal curl as a ball-peen sort of thumping pummels his back. He realizes that's himself he hears grunting with every whack, not that it hurts, it's pressure weirdly stripped of pain, and about the time he figures out someone is kicking him here comes Mr. Jones stepping into the light. At this point time doesn't slow down so much as congeal into a series of overlapping blocks. Here is Mr. Jones standing upright, pulling his gun from his suit jacket, then the massive body slam from behind that sends him flying, and the gun—a Beretta Px4, in the freeze-framed

moment Billy sees it quite clearly—launched with great force from Mr. Jones's hand. It takes off like a skate across the ice, skittering, spinning just beyond Billy's reach, away it goes and he twists around despite the foot in his ribs because he has to see where it's going—

Straight for Major Mac, as it turns out. With a veteran goalie's timing and economy of effort, the major lifts his toe a couple of inches and traps the weapon under his shoe. He scoops up the Beretta, checks the safety, and chambers a round while holding the weapon down and away from his body, then with the elegance that comes of many hours of practice, he raises his arm and fires straight overhead,

BAM.

In all of tomorrow's exhaustive media coverage of the game—the straight news stories, the human-interest piffle, the brain-draining chatter of the TV and radio jocks—there will be not a word about gunfire after the game. The Bravos will agree this is very strange. Surely thousands heard the roar of the gun; certainly those many hundreds on the plaza who ducked at the report, screamed, cowered, threw themselves on their children, or took off running, and whoever was kicking the shit out of Billy abruptly stopped. For some moments Billy simply lies there, enjoying the profound inner peace that comes of not being kicked. He tips his head to keep the blood from running into his eyes and watches Major Mac, who sets the safety on the Beretta and carefully places it on the ground. Then the major stands tall with his arms T-squared, not crooked at the elbows, not with his hands on his head, postures too suggestive of surrender. No, he stands with his arms straight out to the sides, simply to show the charging cops he is no longer armed.

"Major Mac dah man," Billy mutters. He says this mainly to hear himself, to see if he's basically all right.

It takes the police some while to sort things out. That there are so many different kinds of police seems to complicate things. Eventually the Bravo limo is located and brought forward, and the soldiers are herded into it while discussion continues on the plaza nearby.

Albert and Dime are out there, and Josh, and Mr. Jones, all conferring with a cadre of the higher-ranking cops. Major Mac stands slightly apart, not in custody per se but with an officer meaningfully placed on either side. The handful of roadies thus far apprehended stand in a miserable clump, handcuffed, heads down, their backs to the wind.

An officer leans into the limo's open rear door. "Anybody here need to go to a hospital?"

The soldiers shake their heads. Noooooo.

The officer hesitates. Almost every Bravo is bleeding from the face or head. The roadies came at them with wrenches, pipes, crowbars, God knows what else.

"Just checking," the officer says, and withdraws.

They find two cold packs in the limo's first-aid kit and pass them around. Mango has a gash over his left eye. Crack lost two teeth. A goose egg of a contusion is rising on Day's forehead. Sykes and Lodis are bleeding from the nose and scalp, respectively. Billy's cheek has been laid open, a two-inch tear along the ridge of the bone—that's the shot that took him down, he guesses. His torso throbs with a muffled, tumbled sort of ache, nothing major, but he's not fooled. He knows tomorrow it's going to hurt like hell.

Dime climbs in and takes a seat. "Cops want everybody's name and contact info," he says, passing a clipboard and pen to Day.

"Sergeant, are we going to jail?" Mango asks.

"Nah, we're victims, dawg."

"How 'bout Major Mac?" Lodis wants to know.

"Major Mac's a goddamn national treasure. Nobody's putting Major Mac in jail."

"Sergeant," says A-bort, "we're thinking conspiracy here. Norm put the roadies on us 'cause we wouldn't take his deal."

"I'll mention it to the cops," Dime says, not smiling. This is a joke. Billy's cell buzzes and it's a text from Faison, *Which white hummer,* and he bolts from the limo even as he's punching in her number. One of the cops huffs, "Where do you think you're going?" but Billy's

focus is such, all his being attuned to the one true thing, that a kind of godly aura repels the officer's challenge.

Her cell barely rings and she's clicking on. "Hey!"

"See where the cop lights are, all the cops standing around?"

"Uh, yeah?"

"That's ours. I'm standing outside."

"Stay there," she says, "I'm walking that way." Then, "I see you! Don't move, I see you, I see you . . ."

He sees her cutting through the crowd, white boots flashing underneath a dark overcoat, and her hair, a muted silver under the horrible prison lights, spilling everywhere, over her shoulders, down her back, across her breasts. She looks so good that he feels himself empty out, no breath, no pain, no thought, no past, his whole life distilled to the sight of Faison striding toward him in all her sleet-spangled glory.

He must have started walking toward her, because they meet with a satisfying crunch. For several moments they can do no more than clutch each other. The crowd parts around them, so many people moving past that a kind of privacy is conjured from the sheer multitudes.

"What happened to your *face?*" she cries, pulling back, touching his cheek. "Omigod, you're bleeding." She glances past him at the cops and emergency lights.

"Those guys from halftime, the stage crew. They jumped us." He laughs. "I guess they were still pissed off?"

"Oh God. Oh my God, you're hurt." She's studying his cheek, fingers brushing the edge of his cut. "Trouble sure seems to follow you guys around."

They kiss, hard. It is impossible for them not to be all over each other. "This sucks," she soon murmurs, and pulls away just enough to unbutton her coat, a swift downward sweep of her hand and the coat is opening, wrapping around him. She pulls him close and moans as her chest meets his. She's still in her cheerleader uniform. He moves his hands inside the coat and grasps her hips. She shudders, then

rises on her toes, her pelvis striving for purchase on that hump in his pants, her mouth clamped so hard that his lips turn numb. "Go for it," someone says, brushing past them. Another passerby advises them to "get a room." After minutes or possibly hours Faison drops back on her heels and slumps against him.

"Oh God. Why do you have to go?"

"I'll be back on furlough. Probably in the spring."

She lifts her head. "Seriously?"

"Seriously." If I'm still vertical, he thinks.

"Then you better make time for me."

"Count on it."

"Seriously, I mean it. How about if you come stay with me?"

He can't speak. He can barely breathe. She's looking from his left eye to his right, back and forth, back and forth, always her two double-teaming his one.

"I know it's crazy, but we're in a war, right? All I know is that it's right, it just feels right. I want every second I can get with you." She shivers, shakes her head. "I'm not the type to get bowled over, not like this. I've never felt this way about anybody."

Billy pulls her close; her head falls against his chest. "Me either," he murmurs, the sound of his voice vibrating through their bodies. "Girl, I'd just about run away with you."

She lifts her head, and with that one look he knows it's not to be. Her confusion decides it, that flicker of worry in her eyes. *What is he talking about?* Fear of losing her binds him firmly to the hero he has to be.

She touches his cheek. "Baby, we don't have to run anywhere. You just get yourself home and we'll be fine right here."

He doesn't resist, because there's just so much to lose. He will forgo the greater risk in favor of the lesser, even though the lesser— and isn't this funny, *funny!*—is the one that might get him killed. He plants his face in her hair and breathes deep, trying to store enough of her smell to last for all time.

YO BRAAAAVOOOOOO booms across the plaza, Sergeant Dime's parade-ground bellow. MOO-HOOOOVING OUT! LET'S GOOOO!

"That's me," Billy whispers. Faison moans, and they fall into another bruising kiss. There's a violent moment when they try to pull apart—they grab at each other, pick and jab at clothes, body parts, a weird rage burning through them that they can't quite control. Faison's face suddenly crumples and she mashes into him.

BRAAAVOOOOO! **NOW!**

Billy kisses her lips and pulls away, and it feels like the last thing he'll ever do. "Be careful!" she calls after him, and he raises his fist in acknowledgment. "I'll pray for you!" she calls louder, and that just makes him feel hopeless. He's dying out here, dying, and that thing in his pants makes it difficult to walk, the rock-hard prong of his virgin member like a flag that refuses to fly at half-mast. He knocks at it with his wrist, the back of his hand, trying to force the creature down without the whole world seeing, and then, oh shit, they're on him, a group of seven or eight fans who want him to sign their game programs. *So grateful,* they say. *So proud. Awesome. Amazing.* This only takes a couple of moments, but while he's scribbling his name it dawns on Billy that these smiling, clueless citizens are the ones who came correct. For the past two weeks he's been feeling so superior and smart because of all the things he knows from the war, but forget it, they are the ones in charge, these saps, these innocents, their homeland dream is the dominant force. His reality is their reality's bitch; what they don't know is more powerful than all the things he knows, and yet he's lived what he's lived and knows what he knows, which means what, something terrible and possibly fatal, he suspects. To learn what you have to learn at the war, to do what you have to do, does this make you the enemy of all that sent you to the war?

Their reality dominates, except for this: It can't save you. It won't stop any bombs or bullets. He wonders if there's a saturation point, a body count that will finally blow the homeland dream to smithereens.

How much reality can unreality take? He's in somewhat of a daze as he passes off the last program and starts walking toward the curb, hands fisted in his pockets to hopefully hide his crazed erection. *Thank you!* the nice people call after him. *Thank you for your service!* Sleet pecks at his eyes, but he hardly feels it anymore. The cops step aside as he approaches, revealing Josh and Albert standing by the limo's rear door, and Albert is grinning, waving him on. "Hurry!" he cries playfully. "Come on! They're leaving!" As if this was the ride you couldn't miss, the one that would save your life? Albert gives him a quick hug as he slides past. Josh says good luck and squeezes his arm, then Billy is stepping off the curb, half-falling onto the limo's rear banquette.

Albert slams the door behind him and throws out a final wave. "We're good," Dime calls to the driver. "Let's go."

"Hell yeah, get us the fuck out of here," says Sykes.

"Before they kill us," Crack seconds. "Take us someplace safe. Take us back to the war."

"Seat belts, everyone," Dime tells the squad, and Bravo paws around the seats, sorting out their belts. Dime notices the steeple in Billy's lap.

"Looking proud there, soldier," he murmurs, just between the two of them.

"Some things can't be helped, Sergeant."

Dime chuckles. "You say good-bye to your girl?"

Billy nods and turns to the window. He knows he will never see Faison again, but how can he know? How does anyone ever know anything—the past is a fog that breathes out ghost after ghost, the present a freeway thunder run at 90 mph, which makes the future the ultimate black hole of futile speculation. And yet he knows, at least he thinks he knows, he feels it seeded in the purest certainty of his grief as he finds his seat belt and snaps it shut, that *snick* like the final lock of a vast and complex system. He's in. Bound for the war. Good-bye, good-bye, good night, I love you all. He sits back, closes his eyes, and tries to think about nothing as the limo takes them away.

Acknowledgments

Thanks are owed and cheerfully given to the Ucross Foundation and the Whiting Foundation, both of which supported the writing of this book. Many thanks to Gary Downey, Evan Mayer, Bethany Niebauer, and Eric Reed for guidance on military life. Very special thanks to Heather Schroder and Lee Boudreaux, for keeping faith. And, finally, profound thanks to my wife, Sharie, without whom I would be, quite simply, lost.

B.F.